THE TERRAWORKS TRILOGY

EXCLUSIVE TOME EDITION
TERRAWORKS
HELIOS
ANATHEMA
RICHELLE MANTEUFEL

Man Devil Press

BOOK INFO

This publication's content is recommended for 17+ for fantasy violence, drug/alcohol use, mild swearing, and brief scenes of sexual intimacy. Reader discretion is advised.

To obtain the trilogy set or the ebooks, search author Richelle Manteufel on Amazon.

Visit manteufelbooks.com for latest publications.

TERRAWORKS
BOOK ONE OF THE TERRAWORKS TRILOGY
RICHELLE MANTEUFEL

Man Devil Press

CONTENTS

1

CALL ME ELI

"*E*hyrbight!*"

A tumultuous wreath of blue lightening answered her call. Ean ducked, partially blinded by her ambitious attack, and knowing all too well that Ophidious would not take kindly to it. Sure enough, her foe's snapping, static-infused reply rang through the forest clearing. "*Techarin-sleigh!*"

Shit. He knows fire magic, too. Cursing herself for not studying the Compendium of Spellwork more thoroughly, Ean tucked and rolled to avoid the fireball cascading toward her. It sailed over her head. Ean chuckled as she leapt to her feet and brandished her weapon, Necrowave, for its vengeance.

Ophidious emitted a low hiss. He lifted his long, pale hands into the position of prayer to Kanthesis the Damned.

OK, double shit.

Ean knew she had no effective defense against necromantic attacks. *What else does he know? He's making the fight against Isis look like a tea party.* Scowling, Ean wheeled 'round and took to her heels, stomping through the thick foliage in the direction of her concealed skyboard.

With every step she took, Ean expected to hear the crunch of her foe's pursuit through the leaves. Much to her surprise, Darkling Forest was soundless minus her own footfall and heavy breathing. Finally, she spotted a silvery flash beneath the bushes. She wrenched her rental skyboard free. "Enter the launch code, Hex!"

Hexadecimal shimmered into view on her left shoulder, looking (as she thought) irresponsibly placid, considering the situation. "Certainly, Ean-san." A pleasant chime from Ean's earpiece signaled the power-up. Her skyboard shuddered to life. Ean groaned as the SkyRate program initiated the redundant voice of protocol. *"Thank you for choosing SkyRate Rentals. Your skyboard charge is at twenty-nine percent. To commence your flight, please mount your skyboard and disengage the safety brake–"*

Ean muted the remainder of the message. She leapt onto the board, snapped off the brake with practiced ease, and launched with vicious acceleration. "Well, that went fabulously," she snapped. "Are you *certain* you checked everything on TerraWiki for battling Ophidious?"

"Yes, Ean-san. May I remind you that there is precious little information, as Ophidious is not often seen nor engaged in battle?"

"Well, you'd think *somebody* would know that he can throw basically anything at you, including necromancy!" She huffed her displeasure, tossing her windblown hair out of her eyes. "At any rate, I am not ready to battle him on my own. And you're also certain that no guilds have defeated him yet, either?"

"That is correct, Ean-san."

The half-elf sighed. Glancing at the vast countryside beneath her, she noticed she'd lost altitude during her hissy fit. She directed her board upward, then – in vague protest against all fay rogues – broke one of the main rules of skycraft by powering down and free-falling. Ean crossed her arms against her chest. Laughing rebelliously, she hurtled toward the earth, twirling until her hair twisted into hopeless tangles.

Hex's tranquil voice informed Ean of her delinquency. "You are aware, Ean-san, that I must report you as disobedient to the TerraWorks code of skycraft. Upon strike two–"

The insubordinate one re-engaged the engine and righted herself. "Save your lecture for later, would ya, Hexy? It's been a rough day. I deserve to have some fun."

Ean's Holopal continued undeterred: "You are likewise aware that the consequences of such a fall would render your HP to zero. You would be transported to the nearest hospital, and would be responsible for paying the transport fee, plus the cost of any healing apparatus your recovery would require."

The half-elf growled her impatience. "You know, Hexy, it's times like these when I understand why some players don't use a Holopal."

"My condolences to them."

Ean giggled, pleased with the unpredictable sauciness her Holopal sometimes displayed. "I had to get one because I'm directionally challenged. Not everybody likes the Holopal's involvement, though. Some players argue that they enjoy a more authentic experience without one."

"I have yet to meet such players as you describe."

"So do I." Ean grinned at the pastel-blue hologram on her shoulder, six inches of iridescent equability and support. Hexadecimal floated among the miniscule petals of cherry blossoms, the length of his sable hair rivalling her own ruddy locks. "Well, Hexy, it's still early. What should we do for the rest of the night?"

"The Spectral Tyrants are performing at the TerraDome."

"Sweet. Why didn't you tell me earlier?"

"You did not ask me to."

"Like Hades I didn't! You know they're my new favorite band. Well, from what I've heard of them so far, anyway." Ean adjusted her course for the TerraDome, licking her dry lips. "I'll have to stop by the Pulse first, though. I'm craving an equinox sunset. Book me a spot at the Dome, please."

"Very well, Ean-san."

Shifting Necrowave across her shoulders, Ean Lightcross whistled her way through the radiant passerby. Everyone was decked out in lustrous gothic gear, and Ean followed suit. She delighted in her new ruby-amethyst glasses. Her long jacket billowed behind her, and her platform boots granted her authoritative satisfaction as she stomped through the crowd.

A service Holopal sped past her, balancing a tray of assorted Whisker smokes. "Hey, you!" Ean hailed, stooping after it and snatching a pack of magenta Whiskers. "Slow yer wheels, matey; there's a good 'un." Straightening up, the half-elf removed one curved cigarette and lit up. She tossed her rosy hair, merrily observing the puff of pinkish smoke as it tinged the air with cinnamon sugar and spice.

Ean resumed her graceful navigation of the Dome audience, packed with Spectral Tyrants enthusiasts. The TerraDome programs could propel even the most inexperienced singers into stardom, so the musical industry in TerraWorks was outrageously competitive. There were far more eager performers than time slots to book them into. However, a select few of these countless bands managed to pack 'em in every night they played, and the Spectral Tyrants held this enviable position with ease. Ean tapped her foot against the floor, giddy with anticipation.

"Hey, Lightcross!"

Ean turned toward the sound of a familiar voice. Mallie was waving to her by the glass doors of the balcony. She gestured for Ean to join her. Ean consented, offering her friend a magenta smoke. The two indulged in sugar-saffron seclusion while awaiting the concert.

"So, how was your day? What have you been up to?" Mallie exhaled with satisfaction, trying without success to shape the pink smoke into a flawless bubble.

Ean shrugged. "Tolerable. Didn't do much. How about you?"

The woodland pixie leaned against the railing, observing the darkening skyline. The tiny silver crowns of buildings gleamed beneath TerraWorks City. Lean shadows of skycraft junkies zipped across the horizon. "I hunted, mostly. I didn't plan on becoming one of the primary hunter/gatherers of my guild, but here I am."

"That's good, though." Ean joined her against the railings. "You can level up consistently that way. How is your guild doing? Did you breach the fort near Helios City?"

"Yeah, we did. Got some GP for our troubles," she added, laughing. "As if we needed more! I don't know how Cyrus gets anywhere... His wallet must weigh him down."

"Cyrus the cyborg?"

"That's him." Mallie's short blond hair tumbled across her pointed ears as she leaned forward, trying to shape the smoke again (using magic this time). "He and Byron get into tiffs now and then, but he's an excellent leader. I'm proud of his progress."

"Who's Byron? You've got a new member?"

Mallie nodded. "Yeah. People are logging into TerraWorks at an insane rate these days." Her peach-tinted lips curved into a smile. "Those who laughed at the concept of virtual reality roleplay are looking like proper idiots now. I've watched a lot of debates lately about how the developers are pushing to increase the real-world currency value per TerraWorks GP. Consistent gamers could quit their jobs and make a living as TerraWorks avatars."

"No way," Ean said, slanted eyebrows raised. "Honestly, that sounds too good to be true. Besides, there's staff and shortage problems already. Wouldn't that just cause more?"

"Well, sure, at least initially. But it will force a lot of obsolete positions to be revamped, or obliterated completely, and that would be a good thing. Sometimes modernization needs one big, fell hit to make the necessary changes."

"I don't know, Malone. That sounds kind of dangerous to me."

"New ideas usually do, Lightcross." Unruffled, Mallie tossed her spent Whisker over the balcony. "I think I hear the band. Let's rock and roll!"

Upon re-entry into the Dome, the crowd was even more dense. Mallie and Ean joined hands to keep from being separated. "You've been to one of their concerts before, right?" Mallie shouted. "Their lead singer is *incredible.*"

Ean winced, motioning toward her elven ears. *No need to shout.* "No, but I've listened to their instrumentals. Sorry, but why don't you go ahead toward the front? I'll stay back here. My hearing is rather sensitive."

Mallie shrugged. "OK, suit yourself. I'll come find you later." She scurried toward the stage, joining the clutch of fans stamping their feet and chanting *"Elias Mage! Elias Mage! Elias Mage!"*

A minute later, the chant tapered off into a rousing roar of delight.

Ean focused her finely-tuned vision on the tall, leather-bound figure moving above the audience, saluting to his fans. At first, the half-elf mistook his lustrous pallor for a fair complexion. She realized her mistake when she noted the pale skulls printed on the band's t-shirts. Elias Jacoby Mage, lead singer of the Spectral Tyrants, was a rare avatar type: a cyberpunk skeleton.

Elias Mage straightened the collar of his ebony jacket and bowed. His piercing black eyes were aglow with joy. Ean watched him with intense curiosity. Skeletons were not a popular pick among the choices for avatars. They didn't have very good defense (at least initially), so they weren't favored for combat. Skeletons did make exceptional mages or sorcerers, though, and they were immune to necromancy and zombification. Nevertheless, it took a lot of grinding to get them where they needed to be… particularly to the insanely high power emulation of Elias Mage. Most players didn't have the patience.

Intrigued, Ean wanted a closer look. She wedged herself deeper into the crowd, praying that her new glasses wouldn't get knocked off and smashed to kingdom come. Having wiggled and elbowed her way to a more favorable position, she resumed her private calculations of the famed skeleman. The band was warming up, hurting her ears with their proximity, but she refused to move back again.

Elias stepped up to the microphone. His icy hand gripped it firmly. The drums and guitars gradually rose to a crescendo, sending a rippling effect of exhilaration through the onlookers. Ean could feel the beat resounding in her chest. Entranced, she jumped with the audience, inviting the frustrations of her day to go screw themselves as the intoxicating rhythm pushed them aside.

Eyes closed, eyelids painted black, Elias parted his ivory jaws to utter the first verse.

"YOU COULDN'T KNOW ME, EVEN IF YOU TRIED.
STILL, IT IS AMUSING TO EXPOSE THE SINS YOU HIDE.
DON'T YOU THINK WE'RE SORRY FOR THIS PSYCHO–FANTILE GAME?
DO YOU THINK IT CREDITS YOU TO CITE MY HOLY NAME?"

The dusky savor of his voice was preternatural and chilling. Ean closed her eyes, also, relishing it with every thrilling breath. The atmosphere of the stadium was a hypnotic, chaotic mixture of magenta, indigo, and ebony smokes all writhing together, staining and provoking one's senses. *Now, THIS is music.*

Laughter boiled in Ean's veins. The sensation sang through her heart, leaping into her wide ice-blue eyes as they reopened. Elias stretched his deathly hand toward the audience.

"CONFESS YOUR SHAME!
YOU NEVER KNEW THE GRACE OF DRACO'S SON;
I TELL YOU NOW, IN CONSEQUENCE,
YOUR DEATH HAS JUST BEGUN!
THE GODS WILL NEVER COUNTENANCE
A MAN WHO PRAYS IN VAIN;
YOUR STUTTERED WORSHIP THREATENS YOU,
MY GIFT TO YOU: YOUR PAIN.
YOUR SWEET PAIN!"

Approving screams echoed through the Dome. Elias Mage swayed to the beat, bare skull glimmering in the spotlight, deep-sunk eyes slanted with dire passion. Multicolored smoke whispered around his frame, curling through the crevices of his body. The sign for Draco's Son started to be offered here and there. Soon the whole Dome joined in, Ean included.

The Spectral Tyrants knocked out one majestic song after another. It was a night Ean never forgot. Elias closed with a devilish ballad that settled the audience into a lethargy of contentment. The avatars nodded and slouched in a stupor. In sharp contrast, Ean was standing bolt upright, knuckles white as she clenched her fists in a passion. Her gaze remained earnest and voracious, magnetically fixed on the lead singer.

The skeleman glanced across the crowd. As he sang "The Ballad of Helios," his attention was arrested by the enthralled half-elf. His demeanor betrayed a slight surprise. Elias quickly resumed his poise, and finished just as masterfully as he had begun. He waved once more to the cheering audience before vanishing behind the curtains.

Ean Lightcross, energized from the roots of her hair to the ends of her toes, tried to plough through and find Mallie. The sprite had vanished more thoroughly than Elias Mage, however, so Ean gave up the search. Recalling that she was low on magenta smokes at her apartment, Ean stopped at a Whisker vending machine and scanned the chip in her wrist for a pack.

While waiting, she aimlessly combed her fingers through her hair. She was about to ask Hex when the Spectral Tyrants were due to perform next, when a certain decadent, compelling voice startled her. "I wouldn't smoke too many of those, if I were you."

An impromptu leap broke the rhythm of Ean's heart. The half-elf was exceedingly glad to cover her flushed face with her hair as she retrieved the cigarettes. She could feel the tips of her ears burning. "Elias Jacoby Mage, I presume?" She turned to face the singer, rapidly pocketing her Whiskers and offering her hand.

Shaking hands was a dated practice, but Elias didn't seem to mind. The skeleman's glacial grip was smooth and firm. He tucked his ivory hand back into his jacket pocket. His gaze inspected her mirrored lenses, striving to catch a glimpse of the eyes behind them. "I didn't intend to be rude. Whisker smokes are addictive, you see. I wouldn't smoke more than one per day."

Ean tried to laugh, averting her fascinated eyes from his surprisingly buff physique. His bones – excluding his skull and hands – were embedded partially in his skin, or glowing softly as tattooed inscriptions. "Um, they're not real, though… it's VR. What's the harm?"

Elias lifted his shoulder blades in a shrug. "True, but the habitual effects will foster a real dependency. You'll find yourself craving them even while you're logged off."

"Oh. I see your point." Ean resolutely banished the second blush that strove to color her face. "Anyway," she indicated the double cross – half scarlet, and half violet – swinging from her necklace. "I'm Ean Lightcross."

"Ah, yes. The retro double cross. I've seen your avatar symbol in the entries for SkyRate. You fly competitively?"

"Yes. I've won a few races. I'm hoping one day I might…" Shyness cut her confession short. "Lately, I've been grinding so I can join my friend's guild. I mean, I'm thinking about joining… maybe." Ean knocked her glowing platforms against the trim of the wall. "I'm not all that interesting, I'm afraid. But you… you're *amazing*. How did you learn to sing like that?"

Elias shrugged again and chuckled. The skeleman's low, velvety rumble sent shivers – not unpleasant ones – trickling down Ean's spine. "I know the TerraDome's programs extremely well. That, plus attending to my performa level, puts me at a significant advantage."

"Damn straight!"

Elias looked amused by her archaic expletive. Ean's persistent flush came crawling back. A pause intervened, and Ean noticed that Elias was still trying to see past her mirrored glasses. "Sorry, they're new, and I'm a bit of a show-off. I guess they aren't great for making new acquaintances." Ean removed them, and something in the skeleman's demeanor brightened. "How interesting."

"What's interesting? Before you admire my eye color too much, I have to admit that they're nowhere near this pretty in reality."

"Oh, they're remarkably beautiful, of course. You chose a flattering contrast shade for the color of your hair. But I meant their particular import." His skull tilted to one side. "The limbal ring, with its peculiar electric streaking, is most significant. Deft, but distinguishable... but then, the unbroken smoothness of the iris presents a substantial disparity. Those designations are typically vice-versa, you know."

This bizarre monologue halted as he continued to study her eyes. He resumed, "The pupils are sensitive and tremulous; they swell and contract with the slightest passing of emotion. Their delicacy is profound, indeed. And yet, their capacity for reception is..." Elias noticed her bafflement and stopped. His voice dropped quite low, almost to a whisper. "Forgive my madness. I've never seen such eyes before."

Ean Lightcross didn't comprehend him in the slightest, but his final sentence implied a fixed attraction. She struggled to keep from smiling too widely. "Thanks, Elias. That's a very... detailed compliment."

"Call me Eli."

"OK, Eli."

A silent moment passed while Eli concluded his inspection of her optics. Keeping any further discoveries to himself, he extended his skeletal hand in farewell. "Goodnight, Ean Lightcross. I'm very glad to have met you."

Their handshake lingered. "You'll see me around," Ean smiled.

"Sans the mirrored specs?"

"If you insist."

"I do."

Ean couldn't tell if his rock-solid countenance was in jest or in earnest. At length, she marked the subtle crinkling of the dark creases beneath his eyes. They both broke into laughter. "In all seriousness," Eli persisted. "The eyes are the window to the soul. Why hide them?"

"Goodnight, Eli."

Ean casually slipped past him, but could not resist glancing back as she walked away. Hands in his pockets, skull bowed, Eli was engaged in deep contemplation. On the back of his leather jacket, a pair of gray angel's wings faded into curved talons. They embraced a skull carrying a rose between its teeth. The avatar symbol of Elias Mage.

As Ean faced forward, she felt a tickle meandering down her earlobe. Her fingers instinctively grazed it, and came away wet. Her ear was bleeding.

2

SCINTILLATING SKYCRAFT AND LAZY LARKING

Breathless, Ean urged her skyboard higher, straining against the wind that tore at her body. Extending her arms, she drew them to her chest, guiding her momentum into a tight spiral. Ean maintained her control, cut the power, then leaned back to drop headfirst.

"Yeah!" the half-elf yelled in pure elation. Killing a hundred zombies in the Undead Campaign never thrilled her like skyboarding did. The radiant tints of sunset marbled the skyline as she descended. Hex, adapted to her recreant ways, just counted down the seconds until she must restart the engine and regain altitude. "Seven… six… five… four…three…"

Ean righted herself and powered up. The skyboard resurrected beneath her with a reassuring shudder, and she directed it into a sharp upward curve. "Hex?"

The Holobox that retained Hexadecimal glowed blue. "Yes, Ean-san?"

"Has anyone defeated Ophidious yet?"

"I will review TerraWiki for you." A slight pause. "Not yet, Ean-san."

Lightcross asked this out of habit. She wanted to be the first to master Ophidious the Tormented, which was far from an uncommon goal among TerraWorks players. However, she was determined to do so *alone...* a vaguely idiotic notion that wasn't quite so common.

"Just a reminder, Ean-san. The Firestone Guild awaits your response to their invitation."

Ean sighed. "Oh, yeah. Mallie's guild." She set course for her TerraWorks City apartment, slowing down so she could contemplate the option. "I'm no combat prodigy, you know, so I don't want to disappoint them. Besides, I don't have the patience for joining guilds. I'd have to fulfill all those obligatory assignments, waste time on boring errands..."

"And have to take orders."

"Right." She chuckled. "Which sucks. I didn't sign up with TerraWorks to be ordered around, same as in real life. If I can't play the game in my own way, I'd rather not play at all."

"As you wish." The Holobox gleamed intermittently, awaiting a reply. The device went back to sleep when Ean remained quiet.

She reviewed the first time she had ever run into Ophidious, which had been a total accident. He didn't attack her. When she consulted TerraWiki later, it seemed normal for his *MO* to include rarely striking first. He was an ancient wood-elf that had committed some fierce crime in the lands of the fay. As a result, he had been cursed by them to obtain unsightly, ophidian features and a serpent's soulless eyes. Despite frightening Ean with his petrifying design, he didn't move. He just looked at her, as if sizing up whether or not she was a threat to him.

Lightcross just stood there like a gods-forsaken moron, awed. Her mind cast wide for a plan of attack, but its fishing hook came up empty. Neither of them moved. At length, his slender, delicate forefinger reached for her face and grazed her forehead. Ean flinched. His gaze was quite calm and steady, as if he were merely studying her identity and memorizing it. "Greetings!" Ean stupidly chirruped.

Ophidious disappeared.

Nobody on TerraWiki could settle exactly what he was. His design was more extraterrestrial than that of other TerraWorks villains. His reputation as a sorcerer was reverenced, but vague and unspecific. And, unlike the other rogues in the TerraWorks universe, he never spoke at all unless he was casting a spell. Some players speculated that he was the rival of the Fell Sorcerer to Kanthesis, a powerful position in the Kanthesis Temple.

Since running into him, Ean was fascinated with his character. However, she was even more interested in the thought of defeating him.

While Ean Lightcross openly declared her intention of winning the SkyRate Grand Championship, she kept her intention to defeat Ophidious close to her chest. She was aware that her prized custom weapon, Necrowave, would not be adequate – an oversized, glowing ruby-amethyst hammer, with a handle nearly as long as she was tall, and a head and face infused with electric orbs. She adored it, and she couldn't bring herself to trade it in for something more suitable. And she didn't have enough money to buy another weapon.

Considering all this, Ean breathed a low sigh and descended to the SkyRate landing decks. Descent protocol babbled from her earpiece. She scowled in annoyance. Automatically, the skyboard searched for and selected an empty parking locker and lowered into it, safety locks clapping shut around its base. After making sure they were closed, Ean powered down and removed her boarding shoes. "I guess I'll head over to the Pulse before calling it a night. I don't really have the energy to train today."

"Very well, Ean-san. They're hosting a drink special for two more hours."

She stifled a tired yawn. "Yay."

As the half-elf donned her platform boots, swinging the rented boarding boots over her shoulder, Ean wondered why she'd felt so deflated today. Skycraft had revived her, of course (it always did), but the exuberance was already melting out of her as swiftly as butter on a hot sidewalk. As she entered the SkyRate rental building and handed her shoes to the clerk, a sudden picture of Elias Mage forced itself from her subconscious.

The skeleman's alabaster visage enhanced the shadows of his eyes, his stare, and his voice; he was the epitome of a fallen angel. Ean tried to imagine the creative genius who had customized such a unique avatar, but failed to satisfy her own attempt. She fell to considering the archetypal avatars in TerraWorks. The elves, the dwarves, and the fay creatures of Helios City... the shield maidens and the swordsmen... the knights and the princesses in the Kingdom of Klad... the witches and wizards of Stellos... and the orcs, ghouls, and goblins of the Darkling Forest. Occasionally, Ean would see something more unique and memorable among the avatars. But on the whole, the characters were trite representations of a collective, generational understanding of high fantasy, and what they should and shouldn't emulate.

So, why would anyone spend substantial time and effort on a skeletal avatar? When someone mentioned "skeleton," most players thought of the generic, unimpressive NPCs that guarded tombs and treasure chests.

It was a curious question.

Ean roamed through the tight, neon-embellished streets of central TerraWorks City. Passing a large window, she was surprised to notice a curling Whisker smoke between her lips. *When did I light that?* Shrugging, she walked a little faster to her apartment in High Rise 158.

A happy grin illuminated her face as she scanned her wrist. The door slid open. Although it was true that guild members could pool their money and split the rental of large, luxurious suites, Ean adored her modest downtown getaway. Everything in it was either red, purple, or black: the tenacious indicators of Ean's energy, vitality, and mystery. A crimson Japanese tea set reposed on the matching *kotatsu*. A wide, low chest of drawers stood in one corner, facing thick purple drapes that concealed some quaint Asian bedding. A kitchenette and half-bath completed her apartment. Blazing across the western wall was an extravagant painting of a sakura tree in full bloom, with ebony bark, and glittering gems for blossoms.

Ean fixed herself a cup of brown sugar milk tea. She tucked herself into the kotatsu with a sigh of contentment. Taking a sip, she suddenly lowered her cup and hurried over to the Holobox's charging station. "Sorry, Hex. I forgot to put you on the charger."

"No worries, Ean-san. I'm at thirty-three percent."

"Oh. Not as bad as I thought. Anyway, I like to keep in the habit." Ean detached the slender Holobox from her shoulder, docked it, and waited for the indicator light to turn yellow. "OK, you're charging now. Could you look up Elias Jacoby Mage for me?"

"It will be my pleasure."

The indicator light pulsed green as Hexadecimal searched TerraWiki for the latest information. "Elias Jacoby Mage, lead singer for the metal band 'Spectral Tyrants.' Avatar: Undead category, a skeleton. Talents: Recreational performer and artificer mage. Weapons preference, restricted-"

Ean sat upright. "Say that again, Hexy? Artificer mage?"

"Yes. He rents a duplex in Helios City, and has stationed his workshop there. His main abilities include infusing weapons with fire, lightning, or poison. He can also work protective spells into clothing, jewelry, and armor, or healing spells into food. His work is quite well-known in Helios."

"Hmm. Lightning, eh?" Ean flicked her wrist to open her inventory. She selected Necrowave and thoughtfully perused it. "It would be really nice if Necro was permanently imbued with electricity. I hate having to stock up on electric orbs all the time. That gets expensive."

"I agree. His fee would be significant, however. Perhaps a few friendly neighborhood quests are in order?"

Ean groaned dramatically and collapsed on the floor. "*Noooo*, Hexy. I don't want to!"

"I am aware of your aversion to errands and quests, Ean-san. But unless you are willing to consider selling some of your possessions, that is the only solution."

"Or… maybe I could sing."

"Pardon me?"

"I could sing. I could sign up at the TerraDome, too. You know I've had some lessons, though I'm a bit rusty at present. Are there any slots still open for this weekend?"

"I shall evaluate your options." The green light spun around a few times. "The first opening is a slot for ten P.M. on Saturday, in two weeks. I suggest we book it now."

"Yeah, book it. Thanks, dude."

"You are very welcome, my friend."

Ean rose from the floor and paced around the living room, absently tugging her hair. "Two weeks. I should pick something I already know. Vocal covers aren't too popular anymore, since composing your own song is so easy now… still, I don't want to rely on the program too heavily. Not at first."

"That is logical."

"Hey, this could be really cool." Anticipation fired through her nerves. "What should I wear? I should probably get a whole new outfit. Even if the stadium isn't full at first (and I have no reason to expect *that*), looking good often draws more players in."

"Might I supply a cautionary reminder, Ean-san? Novice performers in the Dome are paid in voluntary donations *only*. If you are not successful, you will not earn any capital to purchase the upgrade to your weapon. It seems to me that accepting a side quest remains the better option."

She flapped her hand dismissively. "You know me, Hex. I'm here to have fun, not run around doing the same grunt work I've been plagued by in a thousand other games. Besides, I've got all the time in the world. I want to try my way first."

"Understood." The yellow light changed back to blue, indicating a full charge. "Shall we review some options for your wardrobe?"

The half-elf rubbed her hands together. "We certainly shall."

Two weeks later, Ean Lightcross was standing backstage, petrified.

Ten minutes remained until she would be announced onstage. Despite her vocal training and practice, she felt she couldn't take a proper, deep breath. A breath her restricted lungs desperately needed.

"I don't know if I can do this, Hex. My gods, look at all the people out there! I didn't expect half so many. What in Hades was I thinking?"

Hexadecimal sensed her agitation and appeared on her shoulder. "There aren't as many avatars out there as it seems," he consoled her. He extended a tiny blue hand, resting it soothingly against Ean's face. "Whether or not the count dwindles depends on your performance."

"Gee, thanks. That's helpful." She struggled to draw a sufficient breath of air. "Just channel Elias Mage. Channel Elias. Emulate his energy. *You can do this.*"

"Incoming message for you, Ean-san."

"Is it short? I don't have the time to spare right now."

"It is succinct. It is from Elias. He says 'Good luck tonight.'"

"From… from Eli?"

"Yes, from your inspiration himself. Do you feel better?"

At last, she was able to inhale more to purpose. "Actually… yes. Is that all? Does he say he's going to be here?"

"That is all. Regardless of his attendance or lack thereof, you should do your very best. Pretend he is listening."

"OK… OK. I can do that."

The TerraDome's MC announced her name. Ean stretched, relaxed her shoulders, and stepped into the spotlight.

From Ean's perspective, the entire song passed in one long blur. Faces bobbed up and down, with either smiling or critical demeanors. Applause scattered through the crowd between verses, echoing in the void of her nervous mind. And despite how much she wanted to, she *couldn't* look for Elias. Whether his stoic countenance would give her peace or anxiety was anybody's guess, and she felt she couldn't risk the latter result.

As the symphonic metal track came to an end, Ean bowed and hurried backstage. She leaned her hands against the wall and panted, long hair draping in silky ribbons, heart bounding in her chest. She jumped when Hex's voice interrupted her muddled thoughts. "Incoming message. Elias Mage congratulates you, and asks if you'd be willing to join him at the Pulse in half an hour."

Before she could answer, the *clink-clink-clink* notification of received donations chimed from her Holobox. Stunned, Ean peered at the amount. Her lips broke into a shaky grin. "Not much, but it's a start. I guess I wasn't terrible."

"What shall I tell Elias, Ean-san?"

"Tell him I'll be there."

"It is done."

Ean peeled her trembling hands off the wall and walked into a changing room. Hesitating, she glanced into a mirror. She was shaking and a little sweaty, but her ice-blue eyes were regaining their tranquil steadiness. "I suppose I'm presentable. But… should I change into something more casual?"

"That is up to you, Ean-san. Would you be more comfortable?"

"Absolutely." She tapped the makeup icon on the mirror and removed her bronze lipstick. "We're going for an old classic. Ripped jeans and a hoodie, coming right up."

3

AT THE PULSE

The Pulse was a popular establishment of navy-blue bricks, cement flooring, and industrial décor. There was an immense bar on both floors, and long stripes of neon lighting slanting over the modern booths. TerraWorks City residents practically owned the place, and could rent and customize booths, as well as conjure a minibar to practice making their own drinks. Helios City and the Kingdom of Klad offered traditional taphouses, but the Pulse was the TerraWorks go-to.

Ean, infinitely comfortable in torn jeans and a retro *Metallica* hoodie, entered the bar and inquired for Elias Mage. At the welcoming podium, the Pulse's signature Holopal directed her to a large corner booth. Eli was waiting, also dressed down in ebony jeans, t-shirt, and the same devil-wing jacket. He stood politely as the half-elf approached. "You did very well tonight."

Ean laughed as they seated themselves across from each other. "Humbug. I was scared stiff. I haven't a clue whether I sounded good, bad, or indifferent."

"Oh, you were good." Elias tapped the silver button on the end of the table. A holographic screen popped up, offering countless snacks and beverages. He rested his gleaming mandible in one hand while he scrolled through the options. "A tad breathless from nerves, no doubt, so your

notes were cut short at times… but that's probably something I alone
noticed."

"Do you ever coach other singers?" Ean couldn't help asking.

"No, but I've been asked to before. I never saw it as worth my while,
but for you… I think *you* would be." He spoke in the same peculiar, low
tone that he had used when first examining her eyes. Ean blushed at the
memory. "Well, I happen to be somewhat broke at the moment. But if
I ever gather a promising cache, I'll ask you about some voice training
then."

"Looking forward." The skeleman shrugged out of his jacket. Something about the plain t-shirt beneath it helped to humanize him. "So,
what's your drink, Lightcross?"

"Equinox sunset on the rocks."

"Ah, a very colorful beverage. Sounds about right." His gaze smiled
warmly at Ean as he ordered one, then selected the Oktoberfest Schwarz-
bier for himself. "Mind if I smoke?" he added, digging in his back pocket
until he seized a pack of ebony Whiskers.

"Thought you warned me against the use of those identical objects,"
Ean teased him. Eli shrugged. "As I said, it's not going to hardwire your
brain as long as you stick to once in a while."

"I don't mind."

Eli lit up, exhaling a dark aroma of spice. "So, you're a singer, too.
You're a woman of many talents. May I ask what else you're into?"

"That's pretty much it. I'm into skycraft, music, and smoking too
much." They both chuckled at her last admission. "There *is* one other
mission on my bucket list, but I'd rather not get into it. It's a bit daft."

"Mmm. 'A bit daft,' she says. I would very much like to hear it." Elias
leaned back and crossed his arms, observing Ean with amusement. "No,
no," his companion laughed, tossing her hair over her shoulder. "I've
sworn myself to secrecy… and Hex has been suitably threatened, should
he ever wax communicative."

"Hex? A friend of yours?"

"Oh, I forgot that I didn't introduce him yet. He's my Holopal."

Ean tapped the curved Holobox on her shoulder. Hexadecimal hovered into view. Hands folded in his sleeves, he executed a charming little bow. "Good evening, Ean-san. Good evening, Elias Mage. I am Hexadecimal."

Their drinks arrived. Elias drained the bottle in a few swigs, while Ean sipped from the dome-shaped crystal glass, frothing with orange, pink, and purple liquid. "I see your Holopal has already matched my face to my name," Eli remarked. "Snooping, were we?" He tried to sound gruff, but Ean could divine a beam of pleasure in his eyes. "Well, at least this miniature profligacy can entertain us. Tell me what you learned, and I can tell you what the Wiki editors have right, or wrong." His empty bottle vanished and was replaced by a new one.

"I didn't get through the whole article. I got distracted when I heard you were an artificer mage. I'd love to take a peek in your workshop sometime, by the way."

"My weapon infusions are my pride and joy. Speaking of which, I've been meaning to ask what weapon you carry. But first, let me guess." Eli tapped a fingerbone against his mandible. "You're an archer?"

"*Bzzzzzt.* Wrong!"

"Hmm. I see your Holopal's style is customized for the Edo period. A katana, then?"

Ean's smile broadened. "Wrong again."

"That's odd; I'm never wrong twice. Then, deduced from your unique and often gothic sense of fashion: a black mace. There! That has to be it."

The half-elf laughed. "Strike three." Eli collapsed against the back of his booth while Ean cackled. "You'll never guess. I forked over a hefty chunk of GP to design it from scratch. It'll be easier just to show it to you."

"Weapons aren't allowed in here. We'll have to go out on the sidewalk. Do you mind?"

"Not at all."

Elias waited while Ean finished her drink, then scanned his wrist at the doorway to pay for both of them. Ean's protestations were in vain. "Be rational, my friend. I have two excellent sources of income."

Ean rolled her eyes. "Implying that I *don't*. Are you aware of your abruptness, sir?"

"I am. But I wouldn't choose to be otherwise. Elusive language is inconvenient."

As they ambled down the street, Elias stopped to gesture toward a lean, aerodynamic motorcycle. A chrome skull leered at them from between the handlebars. "That's Simulacra. Isn't she a beauty?"

"Yours?"

Elias nodded. Ean reached out to touch the shining handlebars reverently. "I've never gotten to ride a motorcycle in my life, and I've always wanted to."

"Is that so?" The skeleman's eyelids crinkled to indicate a smile. "I don't suppose you'd want to take her for a spin?"

She squealed with delight. "Can I drive?"

"Absolutely not."

"Aww, why not?"

"I doubt that I need to explain why not."

"I swear by the Terran Pantheon that I'll drive thirty miles per hour."

Eli crossed his arms. "Nice try."

"Twenty miles per hour. Just call me Grandma."

The skeleton chuckled, chatting his teeth together and shaking his skull. "Nope."

"I'll obey the stop signs so thoroughly that the mediators will flag me down for stalling traffic."

That one earned her a boisterous laugh. Eli's ribcage flexed with mirth. "Delightful! Still, my answer is no."

Ean clasped her hands, standing close to him to gaze into his ivory face. "But I'll be *ever* so careful, Eli. We shall be invisible. *Please?*"

"Mmm." Catching his breath, Eli extended his forefinger to brush against her chin. "That look nearly does it for you, Lightcross."

His midnight eyes shone beneath the misty yellow lamplight. A few skyboard junkies flew past them on the levitation tracks, casting the beams from their board lights across his mirror-like visage. Ean could smell the footprint of ebony smoke clinging to his jaws and clothing, combining with the enticing scent of leather.

Abruptly aware of how *very* close they were, Ean's pointed ears turned scarlet. She took a step backward. "I guess you'll have to win this one. Take me for a ride!"

Elias consented with a deep chuckle. "Put on my helmet, then. And be sure to hold onto me."

The engine throbbed and snarled beneath them like a wild beast. Ean whooped as Elias careened around the corner. It was quite easy to maintain one's grip on a skeletal avatar, and she felt fearless as he performed several low, sweeping turns for her gratification. TerraWorks City smeared past them in a pleasing chaos of neon flashes, silvery buildings, and the landing lights of the levitation tracks.

After a lengthy ride, they stopped outside of High Rise 158 (which Ean had mentioned as her building). She removed Eli's helmet and handed it back to him. "Gods, that was epic! If you ever want to drive Simulacra while I swing at our opponents from behind, let me know. We'd stun all of TerraWorks with our sheer awesomeness."

Elias seemed pleased with her enthusiasm. "Duly noted." To Ean's surprise, Eli turned off the engine, dismounted, and walked her to the main entrance. "We never did demonstrate our weapons," he reminded her. "Want to meet at the training grounds outside of Helios? I have a few orders to fill tomorrow, but I should be finished by around nine o'clock."

"Oh, yeah. I completely forgot about that. It's a date."

If Elias had an eyebrow to raise, he'd have raised it. "A date?"

Ean flushed, dropping her gaze to search for a rock to kick. "Um... well... yes?"

The skeleman broke into another hearty laugh. "You may rival my own directness, given a little more time. It's a date." He hesitated, then tucked her hair behind her pointed ear. "I'm honored, Lightcross."

"See you tomorrow, Eli."

When Ean donned her TerraWorks helmet and logged in the next evening, she tried to convince herself that she hadn't been chomping at the bit the entire day. Work had seemed to drag on indefinitely, and the customers asked far more questions than usual... but, no. She *wasn't* experiencing palm sweat and palpitations due to committing herself to what, only a week prior, she would have considered a capital exercise in stupidity: a VR date.

Elias Mage could be anybody… anyone at all. Heck, maybe he was a *she!*

Why does he have to be so damned real?

Ean fretted around her apartment, killing time by straightening random objects and changing clothes half a dozen times. She finally chose a pair of faux-leather leggings and a long, sleeveless dress with high slits on either side. After adding the hunting boots she'd purchased in Klad, she announced to Hexadecimal that she was ready for inspection.

"It is feminine, but practical. I believe it is appropriate for your destination."

"Thank you, Hexy." Ean shot one last look into the mirror. Seizing the hairbrush, she gave her lengthy tresses another hurried brush until the ends snapped with static. "I hope Elias doesn't propose that we fight anybody. I'll need my hair up for that."

"Should that be the case, I will aid you in selecting the proper hairstyle."

"OK." She tapped the makeup icon on her mirror to choose slanted eyeliner, which highlighted the brilliant, icy glow of her eyes. "All right. I really need to get going. If I have too much time to fuss with my looks, I'll render myself ridiculous."

"Incoming message from Elias Mage."

Half afraid that he was canceling, she swallowed hard. "Let's hear it."

It was a voice recording this time. Eli's majestic baritone floated into the room. "Evening, Lightcross. I was wondering if it would be convenient for you to meet me at my workshop in Helios, instead of the training grounds? I haven't finished my final order yet… the requested spell has been giving me some trouble. I'm sending the directions to Hexadecimal. There's no rush, so please take your time."

Hex appeared beside a holographic map. Ean studied it. "He's pretty much in the center of Helios, so even a dunce like me shouldn't get lost. Truthfully, I'm glad. I'm curious to know his combat style, of course, but

I'm much more interested in seeing his workshop. Well, Hexy, shall we travel by skyboard?"

"What a silly question."

Ean giggled, remembering to snatch her hairbrush and stow it in her inventory before dashing out the door. She jogged to the SkyRate launching towers.

The first star or two of TerraWork's vast legion were appearing overhead. Ean drifted mechanically through the system checks and admonishments, fingers flying over the locks, tightening the buckles on her boarding shoes, and ensuring that her Holobox was properly fastened to the shoulder strap. *Destination coordinates verified. You are ready for takeoff. Please enjoy your flight, Ean Lightcross.*

All skyboard fliers had two options. First, they could elect to fly along the levitation tracks, which were mounted track lines secured by a powerful magnetized field. These tracks connected all the major cities and kingdoms. They took full control of your acceleration, cruising speed, descent, and parking. While traveling, you could chat with your Holopal, message your friends, or sort through your inventory; you didn't have to pay any attention. Second, skyboarders could fly manually. There were no tracks, and minimizing distractions was highly recommended.

Ean preferred manual flight. She tapped the default preference and signaled to Hex to keep the map screen open on her lower right-hand side. "Just in case, you know."

"Of course, Ean-san."

The half-elf chose drifting speed so she could enjoy the scenery. The City of Helios was embedded in the heart of Verdant Valley, smocked with colossal trees and peppered with gemlike flora. All the traditional festivals were held there. Helios was especially famous for its immense maypole for May Day, which was plated with white gold and studded with emeralds. When the wood-elves and Darkling Forest sprites danced around it, expertly weaving and braiding its silken ribbons, it inspired many an avatar to declare that May Day in Helios was the most magical of all the year.

Initializing descent. Welcome to Helios City, Blessed of the Elder Goddess, Nymphoria.

SkyRate's landing decks in Helios were picturesque. Ean was too nervous and excited to notice particulars, but she did recall climbing vines, potted plants, and the sturdy scent of oak. A small fountain bubbled cheerfully in the lobby as she turned in her boarding shoes to the clerk. "Please enjoy your time in Helios!" the dwarf piped. Ean nodded to him and walked into the courtyard.

Though a threat of clouds loomed on the horizon, it was a lovely evening. Cool breezes carried the aroma of budding foliage and honey. Woodland sprites laughed while dwarves chatted and told jokes. An elven choir sang, and human couples roamed, conversing in low, romantic tones. A bard plucked his guitar and praised Nymphoria, goddess of springtime and spiritual dance. As a half-elf, Ean felt quite at home in Helios, and many fellow half-bloods greeted her with their race's elegant gesture of kinship. *"Vhelcomet,"* Ean replied with a smile. When she had chosen her residence in TerraWorks City, she had been sorely tempted to choose Helios instead… but, all things considered, Ean Lightcross preferred to live in modernity and visit tradition, rather than vice versa.

Elias Mage's pale-yellow duplex emerged into view. He rented the right side out, which was currently a bookshop; Ean could smell the antique leather-bound leaves as she passed the doorway. On the left, above an iron-studded door, a painted sign read "Elias Jacoby Mage, Master Artificer."

Ean drew in a quick breath and pushed open the door.

4

A REVELATION VIA TERRAFORMA

A soft bell clinked as Ean entered. Her face brightened as she absorbed the workshop's soothing atmosphere. The wheat-colored walls were speckled with silver grain. Several high bookshelves, cluttered with artificer tools, manuals, herbs, and volumes of spellcraft, impressed Ean with their consistent indications of frequent use. A few scarlet chairs for clientele (currently empty) faced an enormous oak desk. Elias stood before it, hands braced against the tabletop, pouring diligently over the Compendium of Spellwork.

"I see you're still hard at work," Ean remarked, as Elias was too absorbed to notice her. As he glanced up, his sharp eyes looked vaguely annoyed at first. They softened when they recognized his visitor. "Gods, Ean! I apologize. I'd almost forgotten about our date."

"That must be some spell you're working on," she replied, sitting in one of the red chairs. "There aren't many circumstances in which one would forget about a first date. However, I must humbly admit that my personal experiences are few and far between." Eli's inkstand was molded into the shape of a glaring skull. Amused, Ean picked it up to scrutinize it.

The skeleman's eyes depicted remorse. He snapped the Compendium shut with a bang, circling to the front of the desk to take Ean's hand. "I'm sorry. This isn't the best first impression, is it? Although, if I insisted that I'm not a workaholic, that would be a strike against my soul for fibbing."

"That's all right." Ean's hand faltered in his skeletal grasp, conscious of its chilly but tender pressure. "Can I see what you're working on?"

"Of course. I'd be happy to have your opinion."

Gesturing for her to follow, Elias led back around his desk and picked up a silver ring. He held it gingerly between forefinger and thumb-bone, squinting with derision. "My client ordered a regenerative healing spell conditioned to 15% – simple enough – but she insisted on this ring as the vessel. As you can see, its sole ornament is a pink pearl. Pearls aren't quite so… impressionable as gemstones, but especially these rarer shades. I explained that to her, but *noooo*, she just has to use *this* ring."

Ean inspected it also, casually leaning her arm against his shoulder. A brief, warm tint tickled Eli's cheekbones. She pretended not to notice. "So, you're saying pearls have some sort of natural resistance to spell infusions?"

"Yes. Exactly." He tossed the ring back into its case and huffed. "I'm exasperated. I didn't anticipate there would be quite this level of resistance." He paused, then pointed ruefully at his leather chair, which lay on the carpet face-down. "I fear I have something of a temper."

"Hmm. So, do you *have* to finish this tonight?"

"I would prefer to. She's coming for it tomorrow evening."

"You could always cheat."

"Cheat?"

"Yeah. Just look up the answer on TerraWiki. Bound to be there somewhere."

Elias grunted. "I hate doing that."

"Somehow, I'm not surprised." Grinning, Ean reached down to raise the fallen chair. "I noticed you don't seem to own a Holopal." She sat down in it and stretched luxuriously.

"Correct."

"You think the gaming experience is more authentic without one?"

"I *know* it's more authentic without one."

"Harsh," Hex interjected. Eli glanced at Ean and laughed. "My apologies, Hexadecimal. At any rate," pushing the pearl ring as far away from him as his arm could reach, "I'm sick of this ridiculous nonsense, and I don't intend to keep you trapped in here for the evening. I'll cheat after our date is over."

"*Terraforma* is performing tonight."

Eli's eyes widened in mock disbelief. "You mean you *don't* want to spend our first date getting all sweaty on the training grounds? I'm shocked."

"Oh, come on. Grunge may not be your thing, but it beats just getting drunk at the Pulse."

"Sound logic, Lightcross. Just a minute." Elias swept into a back room. He emerged a minute later in dark leather pants and a hooded jacket with a spiked lapel. He lifted the hood over his skull and posed. "Acceptable?"

"That'll do."

Elias waved Ean into the back room. She ducked inside and, with Hex's aid, reappeared in a cold-shoulder minidress and strappy heels. "You look nice," Eli nodded. "Oh, I also got this for you. It's nothing fancy, just something to commemorate our first date." Reaching for the bookshelf, the artificer mage lifted a small gilt bag secreted in the corner. "I think it'll suit your style."

"Elias! You didn't have to get me anything." Embarrassed, Ean reached inside and lifted out a white gold bracelet. A tiny double cross – her avatar symbol – swung from the clasp. "It's so delicate. How did you figure out my taste in jewelry already?" Delighted, she immediately slipped it onto her wrist.

The skeleman shrugged. "Oh, I have eyes. And I use them."

Ean burst into laughter at his coolness. "There's not a single sentimental bone in your body, is there?"

His sable eyes glittered impishly. "I guess we'll have to find out."

Terraforma's grunge riffs pulsed through the Dome. Ean was already dancing her way through the crowd. Elias, towering above the majority of the audience, mildly bobbed his skull to the beat. "Come on, Elias!" Ean cried, seizing his cold fingers in her warm hands. "Dance with me."

"I'm a cyber skeleton. I don't dance."

"You will if you're with me, buddy."

Eli parted his jaws to object, but Ean raised their hands, slipped her fingers between his, and swayed. Her momentum tugged him to and fro until he swayed with her. "Like this. That's all I want," she murmured. Her dilated pupils took on a curiously wide, electric sparkle.

"How interesting," Elias breathed.

The half-elf's aura of pure but controlled exhilaration was captivating. Waves of rhythm surrounded them, drenching them in contentment. Ean risked moving closer, resting her hands near his lapel. After a long, gaze-locked hesitancy, Eli's hands trailed around her waist to rest at the small of her back.

Ean didn't move away.

The next song commenced with an energetic beat, flooding the stadium with cheerful whoops and hollers. Elias snapped out of it. "Thirsty?" he asked, a second rare blush staining his pale cheekbones.

"Yes."

They held hands as they walked into the immense TerraDome lobby. Elias ordered the usual – equinox sunset for Ean and a dark draft for himself – and they sat on a couple of lounge chairs to consume them. The skeleman cleared his invisible throat. "I hope I wasn't... I don't mean to be too forward." His finger traced the rim of his bottle as he eyed her quizzically.

Ean waved her hand. "No, no! You're fine."

"I've never dated anyone in VR before. It seemed like such an idiotic idea."

"Same." Ean giggled and sipped her equinox. "I feel safe with you, though."

Eli gave a sarcastic snort. "With a skeleman. You're somewhat eccentric, aren't you?"

"Hey, takes one to know one." Ean smiled and finished the rest of her glass. "Let's go back. The night's still young!"

"Sure." Elias stood up and drew Ean to her feet. "I think I might like dancing now."

"I'll pretend I don't know what you mean."

During the rest of the night, Eli gradually misplaced his inhibitions. He leapt with the audience, punching his fist in the air; he twirled Ean and even dipped her once; and for the finale, everyone stood together in a series of infinite chains, arms around their neighbors' shoulders, swaying and singing along at the top of their lungs.

"I didn't expect to enjoy Terraforma that much," Ean exclaimed as they left. "I mean, I've always heard that they're a great VR show. But I'm more of the hard rock, heavy-metal purist persuasion."

"I appreciate every genre, barring country music." Elias took her hand. "Ready to go home?"

Ean shot him a saucy look. "Never."

"Unfortunately, I've got work tomorrow. I need to log off."

"Yeah, I do, too. Will you message me tomorrow evening?"

"If you want me to."

Smiling, she held up their entwined hands. "Do you really need to ask?"

"Mmm. I suppose not."

Succumbing to an impulse, Ean balanced on tiptoe to kiss his cheekbone. "Goodnight, Elias," she whispered. "And thank you."

Dazed, he merely stared after Ean as she walked away, humming to herself. Shaking his skull hard, he jogged to catch up with her, swept her off her feet, and cradled her, touching his forehead to hers. "You don't know what you just did," he murmured, his dark eyes flashing. "You *really* have no idea what you just did, Ean Lightcross."

She blushed to the points of her ears. "What did I do?"

Elias replied with that low, deep chuckle that thrilled her nerves. He lowered her back onto the ground, his hand slipping from the side of her face to comb through her hair. "You'll see."

Dammit, dammit... Dammit!

Lurid was flying way too close, forcing Ean to glide against the rails. She knelt into a ball, whipping into a backward tumble to escape him. She flipped him off as he – of course! – took advantage of the opening she left, soaring ahead on the SkyRate track. "Hey, eat rocks, man!" she yelled. *I'm sick and tired of him cornering me like that!*

"That was not an illegal maneuver, Ean-san."

"Hex, I don't want to hear from you right now." Gritting her teeth, the ginger-haired elf accelerated until she was riding Lurid's heels. Sensing her irritated presence, he swayed in front of her tauntingly. "There's only one lap left," Ean muttered. "Time to flip the script!"

Ean waited until a looping curve offered her an opportunity. It wasn't a particularly *safe* opportunity, but Lurid's predatory skycraft left her no other choice. The SkyRate competitors entered the turn. Snapping the nose of her board toward the inside line, she struggled to maintain control while risking a perilously tight arc, accelerating instead of braking.

Ean's skyboard missed Knightmoor's by a mere inch. "Watch it!" Knightmoor shouted. Ean ignored her. Continuing to gather speed, she shot ahead of the pack until only one person remained for her to pass: Piragor.

His telltale shock of choppy blond hair stuck out in all directions. Ean strained every muscle in her body as her board reached full speed. In a moment, the contenders were side-by-side; but Piragor, with his customary coolness, didn't seem concerned about it. He tossed Ean a hurried but friendly nod. "Nice evening for a race, Lightcross!" he called over the wind.

She held up her hand to block her view of his face. "Don't talk to me."

"Who else can I talk to?" He jerked his thumb backward to indicate the rest of the competitors, who were behind, but steadily gaining on them.

"Talk to yourself!"

The SkyRate MC's voice blared in Ean's ear. "It's Piragor and Lightcross, folks! Piragor and Lightcross! Who will take the lead?"

Their skyboards remained nose-to-nose. They tackled the final lap in faultless harmony, leaning, braking, and accelerating in synch. The

crowds roared their appreciation. "What a fine pair we make!" Piragor
yelled. Ean grinned and retorted, "Sorry. Spoken for now."

"Oh, really? Who?"

"Elias Mage."

Piragor pantomimed a slight deafness. "Sorry, who?"

"ELIAS MAGE."

"Who's he?"

"Gods, Piragor! What rock are you living under?"

He shrugged, emitting a roguish smile. Ean realized he was only
teasing her. She tossed her head dismissively and focused on the finish
line.

They reached the final stretch. Ean knelt, gripping the nose and back
of her skyboard in aerodynamic position. Piragor did likewise. With drag
reduced, but mobility compromised, their skyboards reached their peak
speed. A rippling, pulsing thrill – constricting her chest until Ean felt
half-choked – dulled everything around her, including the screaming
audience. Even Piragor was a mere blur of inconsequential color at
her side. *I'm going to beat you today, Piragor. I'm going to qualify for the
championship race.*

Lightcross blinked in the brilliant flash of the finish line. Setting her
teeth, she closed her eyes as their boards shot over it. The levitation
track's safety magnets locked onto them, gradually reducing their speed.
"Aaaand, it's a photo finish! A photo finish, everyone! My Gods, what a
race tonight!" the SkyRate MC cried.

Red, blue, and purple fireworks exploded overhead. Cheers and applause echoed through the neon-red bleachers. Ean's skyboard came to a
stop, and she dismounted, an excited grin stretched from ear to ear. She
waved to the crowd. Her fans waved back, shouting their support and
holding up signs bearing her avatar symbol. "Thank you!" she called out,
saluting them.

Piragor dismounted beside her. "That was a smooth race, Lightcross. Regardless of who won, you're a great SkyRate competitor." He smiled and held out his hand to her.

"Thanks, man." They shook hands. The applause and cheers redoubled, and Piragor lifted their clasped hands before the masses. He spoke aside to her, "I know you'll be busier now that you're dating… but we'll always be friends, right?"

"Right."

Ean's good-natured rival released her hand, still grinning. "I'd like to hear more about your Elias. He must be quite a guy for Ean Lightcross to break her own vow *never* to date in VR."

Ean flushed and tugged at her hair. "I'll tell you about him later. I don't want to jinx myself by speaking too soon, or with too much enthusiasm. We'll see how it goes."

Winking, Piragor borrowed one of Ean's exclamations. "Sweet."

The MC's vibrant voice interrupted their conversation. "The results are in! The powers that be have spoken. The winner is… Ean Lightcross! Just by a hair, ladies and gentleman! It's Lightcross! Give it up for our city's contestant in the SkyRate Tournament of Champions!"

Roaring applause flooded the stadium. Ean breathed a deep sigh of relief, her tense shoulders relaxing. It had required plenty of practicing to place for the tournament in TerraWorks City. Now that she'd beaten Piragor, she would be invited to the SkyRate Tournament of Champions. If she won *that*, her avatar's name and symbol would be everywhere. She'd have a free pass to all the best races – including the opulent Metro Cross Track in Gravesend – and fly anywhere in TerraWorks that she fancied. She'd get a new skyboard, official SkyRate sponsorship, and *one million* GP.

Although the idea of fantastic wealth and honor was enough to make anybody giddy, Ean was busy imagining how impressed Elias would be.

5

ELI'S RECKONING

W hile Ean was shaking hands and posing for holographic images, Elias was stalking around his workshop like a maddened fiend.

Nothing had gone according to plan. First, his illustrious client of the pearl ring had returned. Was the regenerative spell working to satisfaction? Yes, it was. Was she experiencing any problems with it at all? No, she wasn't. She then presented an entire jewelry box to Elias, full of pearl-set pieces, all staring up at him like so many wide, innocent eyes. Well aware of the time it would take to infuse them with the spells she was requesting, Elias quoted her an appropriate ETA, at which she balked. Wouldn't he *please* get started right away?

"'Crucial accessories for my mermaid imagery,' indeed. Hmph." Still sulking, Elias snatched up his notebook and thumbed through his notes on pearl infusions. He had a few other clients to attend to, including some scheduled pickups; the Spectral Tyrants were asking to meet up and start practicing for their October concert; he had a secret project in the works, which he was impatient to optimize; and to top off this sticky sundae of commitments with one giant cherry, he was missing the TerraWorks City skyboard race. Ean's performance would determine whether or not she qualified for the Tournament of Champions next month, so... that was *kind of* important.

Ean had accepted his explanations without complaint, but that hadn't eased his mind much. Heaving a dejected sigh, the skeleman flicked through a few more pages. He stole a look at a holographic image of Ean that hovered above his work tablet. "I'll make it all worth the wait. I promise."

That got him thinking about his secret project again. Uttering a snort of impatience, Elias thrust his notebook aside and picked up a volume about the magical properties of gold instead. His narrowed eyes flew across the leaves. Settling on the paragraph in question, he tapped the page thoughtfully, then set the book aside and began sketching a golden staff.

Just then, Eli's workshop bell interrupted his musings. One of his most frequent clients, Cyrus Agillus, thumped his way inside in full armor and massive boots. "Evening, Elias! I've come to pick up my order." He took a gander 'round the room, noting the strewn papers and paraphernalia. "Still working at this hour?"

"I suppose so." Eli surreptitiously pushed his notebook over the sketch. "Have a seat, Cyrus, and I'll get it for you."

"Appreciate it." Cyrus settled his bulky frame into one of the lounge chairs. Glancing at a nearby footstool, he hooked one of its legs with his sword, and dragged it beneath his feet. "Gods, it feels nice to put my feet up." Yawning, the cyborg's yellow eyes blinked with drowsiness. "You've got a nice vibe in here, Elias. It's so homey. You should add a fireplace just about there." He pointed to the empty wall in front of him, embossed with creeping vines.

"No doubt you're right." The artificer mage reappeared with a tan parcel, secured with yellow twine and stamped with Eli's avatar symbol. "I've added the same light modifications as your last order. I trust that's to your liking?"

"Yeah, that's awesome, man. Hey, thanks a lot!"

"My pleasure." Elias handed the parcel to Cyrus. The cyborg relayed instructions to his Holopal. A moment later, a soft chime notification sang from Eli's work tablet, signifying a received payment. "Thank you, Cyrus. I hope you have a pleasant evening."

"Mind if I stay and chat for a bit? If you're too busy, just tell me to hop along. It won't hurt my feelings. But your wisdom is a sight for sore minds, if you get my meaning."

"How kind of you to say so." Eli's voice was grave, but his eyes sparkled with sarcastic amusement. He crossed his arms. "What's on your mind, Cyrus?"

"Remember what we talked about a few months ago? We were complaining about the moronic stupidity of VR dating, and how neither of us would ever partake in that silly, but admittedly fascinating, little game. Right?"

A minute twitch in the corner of Eli's eye betrayed his humiliation. "I remember."

"Well, *I* think (and this is just my personal opinion) – I think we should add an exemption. A diminutive addendum to our declaration, aye?"

"Oh? Your feelings on the matter have changed?"

"Not yet, sir, not yet. But it's only fair to reserve a bit of wiggle room for matters of the heart. Yes?" The cyborg cast him a cunning sideways glance. Elias refused to cave. "At least," Cyrus recommenced after a long pause, "I think it's only logical to agree that, as slim as the chances are, it's not *impossible* to find one's other half amid the masses of online personas."

"It's improbable, but not impossible."

"Agreed. Well, then. To finding true love!" Cyrus toasted Eli with an imaginary glass. Elias repeated the pantomime stiffly. "To true love."

"That will do. I must be off!"

Cyrus Agillus winked as he strode from the workshop. Puzzled, the artificer mage shrugged and began the onerous task of sorting his books and notes. As he cleared his desk, he noticed that his tablet was still projecting the glistening image of Ean Lightcross, as broad and brazen as daylight.

The skeleman froze in place, glaring at nobody in particular. *Shit.*

Cyrus hopped on his chrome skyboard, chuckling to himself. It wasn't easy to read a skeleman's moods, but Eli's touch of petulant naïveté was quite entertaining. "Hey, Vash," the cyborg called, tapping his Holobox out of sleep mode, "Wake up and text Mallie. Ask her if her friend Ean is Ean Lightcross from the SkyRate tournament."

"Sure thing, Cyrus."

A soft *beep* indicated a text response. "Sir, Mallie confirms your surmise and adds that she'd like to invite Lightcross to the next Undead Campaign battle. Would that be an acceptable notion?"

Cyrus shrugged, bracing himself as the levitation tracks launched him to cruising speed. "Ask Mallie what Ean's combat level is (if she knows), and what weapons she uses. Not much good in inviting someone I know nothing about. Our Firestone Guild is new, and we can't afford to have a weak link right now."

"Yes, sir."

As the countryside of Helios tore past beneath him, the cyborg wondered what sort of a woman had managed to infatuate the stoic Elias Mage. Propelled by curiosity, Cyrus added "And, Vash? Ask Mallie if she knows anything about Ean and Elias, you know, as a couple. That would be big TerraWiki forum news, eh?"

Back at the workshop, Elias flipped his sign to "Closed." He kicked off his shoes and sank into his chair with a groan. Multiple enigmatic sketches fluttered from beneath various paperweights. A crystal skull decanter of whisky indicated his current presence of mind. He drained a second glass, toying morosely with the clod of ice left in its wake. "*Eclipsis* will be my testimony. But... how to strike the balance...?"

Removing a paperweight, Elias glanced over his staff sketch. The design was quite elaborate by now, and he threw it into the trash with a deprecatory grunt. "That's too much. As vain as it may sound, I need to be the focus, not what I'm carrying in my hands." He grabbed another blank sheet of paper and commenced further scribbling.

"That's better." Satisfied, Elias leaned back in his chair and absently gnawed the end of his pen. "Now for the centerpiece." He applied pen to paper with confident, broad strokes, then paused mid-stroke to grab his tablet. "It's late, but she might still be up."

I'm sorry I've been so busy tonight, Ean. How did the race go? Although TerraWiki's news forums would have been more than adequate to answer his question, he'd waited to hear the news from Ean herself. The skeleman resumed his drawings.

A gentle chime signified her reply. The text of her message was projected above the tablet in glittering white font. *Hey, Elias! I thought you would be logged off by now. I WON!!!*

Eli's dark eyes beamed as he relayed his response. *I had my suspicions. If you'd lost, you'd have contacted me to complain by now.* He chuckled, expecting an indignant reply.

Screw that, I'm complaining anyway. I don't know if you've ever streamed one of my races, but Lurid always cuts me off, and he did it again! That bastard deserved to be knocked down a peg or two. I guess Piragor is my true rival, technically speaking, but at least he's a gentleman about it.

Elias set his pen aside, resting his mandible in his hands. *I must confess that I miss you dreadfully. Where are you right now?*

The afterparty at SkyRate Tower. It's still going pretty strong. Want to swing by?

He glanced at the time. *Sure, I'll stop by for an hour.*

OK! I'm so glad you're coming. It doesn't seem like a true victory without you here.

Elias hesitated, then shared the concern that had been tugging at his mind. *It's not a big deal, Ean, but you should probably know that my friend Cyrus caught me with your SkyRate application image. He's a great guy, but he's chatty, you know? Don't be too shocked if you see our names plastered all over the TerraWiki gossip threads soon.HH*

No worries, Eli. I figured that would happen. I'm dating a seriously hot lead singer in one of TerraDome's top bands! Comes with the territory.

He cocked his skull and tapped a fingerbone against the edge of his desk. *Do you really think I'm attractive, Ean?*

A silent minute or two elapsed. Eli's growing embarrassment dotted his frontal bone with a glossy drop of sweat. At last, her reply shimmered into view. *If I told you I'm insanely attracted to you, would that make me a skelephile?*

Eli's laugh of relief rattled his chest. *I guess so! But we're all skeletons, aren't we? Memento mori.*

Ah, now I'm envisioning us rotting together in the same grave. You've got that classic romantic touch. What's a girl to do?

The skeleman fumbled about in his wardrobe app. He added a sweeping steampunk coat. *I'm almost out the door. Will I be forced to dance tonight?*

You know the rules.

Well, I've got to keep up appearances. I'll protest for just under two minutes, then give in. Agreed?

Agreed.

Elias selected his black boots. He checked his pale countenance in the hallway mirror, and headed out the door, transport gem in hand.

SkyRate Tower was massive. Levitation tracks and trick ramps looped around (and occasionally through) it, gleaming red and blue with the oft-repeated SkyRate logo. The first floor was dedicated to admissions desks, skyboard rentals, and SkyRate employees, along with a few lounge areas and cafeterias for skycraft enthusiasts. The rest of the tower staggered its floors between launch and descent platforms, skyboard design studios, commercial spaces, and party arenas for the tournaments.

Hefty speakers boomed from various corners with hard rock, grunge, or metal. The entire building, Elias privately concluded, reminded him of a colossal world-class roller coaster. That impression was heightened by the laughing, whooping figures of skyboard junkies, who utilized the tower's tracks and ramps for hours on end.

Eli stopped at a Whisker machine for a few packs, making sure to grab magenta smokes for Ean. He approached the main desk to obtain directions. "Sixteenth floor and on your left," the clerk replied. "It's pretty loud, so I doubt you'll be able to miss it. The elevators are that way." He pointed out the appropriate direction. "Thanks," Elias replied.

As the elevator rose, increasing anticipation caused him to shift his weight from one foot to the other. *Insanely attracted to you* kept echoing in his cranium. By the time the elevator doors slid open on the sixteenth floor – revealing Ean Lightcross, alone, waiting there to greet him – the skeleman's cheekbones were aflame. "How's the party?" he asked, trying to seem nonchalant.

"Who cares?" Ean took his hand, grinning shamelessly. "We could walk around the tower instead, if you want. There's a 24/7 mall in the basement, and it's freaking awesome!"

"Let's dance first. Then we'll go take a look at it."

Ean darted him a coy glance. "Thought skeletons didn't dance, Eli."

"I like dancing with you."

She hooked her arm through his. "What if someone takes a video of us and posts it on TerraWiki?"

"Oh! Didn't think of that. In that case…" Eli whipped around 180 degrees and headed back to the elevator. Ean snagged him by the humerus, laughing. "Just be cool, man. Be cool."

He chuckled, regarding her curiously. "Why do you use such archaic expressions?"

She smiled, motioning toward her outfit (which, as usual, included several retro accessories). "Because I'm nostalgic."

They entered the party arena. "Speaking of which," she added, raising her arms above her head and snapping her fingers, "this is a *great* song to dance to." She took his hands and pulled him onto the dance floor. As they danced, Elias basked in her energy, reveling in the graceful bliss of her movements. Their mutual glances and tones waxed warmer; her touch sent a thrill down his spine.

Although startled by the rapidity with which Ean Lightcross had stolen his heart, Eli didn't intend to waste time questioning it.

As the night advanced, avatars started logging off. "Let's go see that mall," Elias suggested. "You said it's open, right?"

"Right." Ean leaned against him and wiped away imaginary sweat. "I thought you needed to log off after an hour, though. It's been about an hour and a half."

"Trying to get rid of me?"

The half-elf rolled her eyes. "I don't want to be blamed when you collapse from exhaustion, that's all."

"Being with you is worth it."

Ean's bronze-tinted lips curved into a smile. Hesitating for an instant, she began to lean closer to him, as if for a kiss. Elias trembled, drawing her in…

A pack of rowdy all-nighters interrupted them, loudly demanding for the music to be turned back on. Ean backed away. "I'm… I'm sorry," she spluttered, face scarlet with mortification. "I forgot where we were."

The skeleman's eyes glittered with a diabolical mixture of affection and amusement. "Let's go." Emitting that low, rumbling chuckle she didn't quite understand, Elias grasped her hand and led her into the elevator. "First floor," he instructed it.

She glanced up at him. "No mall tonight?"

Elias shrugged. "You weren't wrong when you admitted concern for my state of fatigue. I shouldn't stick around much longer. I'll fly home with you, though. Got your skyboard?"

"Oh, yeah! I finally have one of my own, thanks to my win." With a flick of her wrist, she opened her inventory and pointed to the miniature ruby and amethyst-tinted skyboard, ready to magnify on command. "You'll have to rent one, though."

"That's not a problem."

"Seriously, you don't have to. My apartment is a short flight from here, maybe two minutes tops. You should log off and go to sleep."

"I'll enjoy it. I don't fly half so often as I'd like to; I don't have the time."

The elevator doors opened, and they stepped out together. "In that case, want to make a bet who can get there first?" Ean queried mischievously.

Elias adopted one of her favored expressions: "Damn straight."

6

IN THE FLAMING PENTACLE

In the weeks that followed, Ean and Eli's communication apps were bombarded with innumerable messages between them. However, they saw little of one another. Elias was incredibly busy. Ean, being less so, had abundant time to pause and reflect on their accelerating relationship. A certain TerraWiki gossip column (sprinkled with images of the two of them dancing) doubled her doubts, as it included the accusation that Ean Lightcross was trying to bolster her own fame by dating someone famous.

As Ean's will battled against her inclination, her messages to Elias were sporadically warm or distant. Elias, rather to her surprise, had been all-forgiving. He never offered a word of remonstrance or complaint. A few weeks later, Hexadecimal relayed the following message from him:

"If you could spare an hour or two this evening, meet me in the TerraDome studios at ten. I've been working on something special. Studio 13."

Ean nodded to Hex. "Tell him I'll be there. Ask if I need a room key or something to get in."

"Understood." A few minutes elapsed as Ean got dressed and fixed her hair. The Holopal added, "Elias says he won't lock it. You can just walk in when you arrive."

"OK. You don't mind if I leave you here, do you? The studios aren't far, and I'll be with Elias. I can't possibly get lost."

"I'll be content, Ean-san. Shall I review the latest information on TerraWiki regarding Ophidious the Tormented? I will send you a summary."

"Oh, yeah. Thanks. That would be helpful." *As if I'll ever get around to defeating him. I've forgotten about him completely.* Ean scowled at herself in the mirror. "Get a grip, Lightcross. Don't let romantic nonsense crowd out everything else. You still have *goals,* you know!"

"Have a nice evening, Ean-san."

"You too, Hexy."

An array of turbulent red and navy planets circulated overhead, framed by blinking stars. A blue shooting star traced the horizon. The half-elf traveled at a leisurely pace, trying to convince herself that her heart wasn't pounding. Elias must be working on a song – most likely for his *Eclipsis* concert – and he wanted her opinion about it.

That's all, right?

Unbidden, the memory of their first date intruded upon her thoughts: his strange, deep laughter, and the way he'd touched his forehead to hers while he held her. *"You don't know what you just did."*

What had he meant by that? She could still feel the force of his stare, his eyes holding her gaze captive with devilish intensity.

As Ean passed the Dome studios, music pulsed from one room after another. She recognized the authoritative riffs of "March of Mephisto" increasing from Studio 13. Ean's heart skipped a beat. She extended her hand and turned the doorknob.

The insulated room was dimmed by thick, black drapes. Elias Mage towered behind a metallic black-and-gold pentacle on the microphone stand. He lifted his skeletal hand to trace it, murmuring the Latin phrases of the song's introduction. Ean's focus drifted to his outfit: pure black, with the sole exception of a floor-length, flowing scarlet coat. A gold ring glinted from his right forefinger, set with rubies in the shape of a double cross.

The skeleman's ghostlike aspect glowed in the light of numberless candles. Some flickered from tall silver stands, and some were gathered in golden-red clusters on the ebony floor. The flames' trembling smoke framed Elias, touching his deathly face, curling over his shoulders, and trickling over his shoes in a scented fog of crushed roses and vanilla.

His black eyelids were closed as the track leapt into a surge of guitar and drums. The artificer mage raised his hands to drop the red hood that covered his skull. His midnight eyes opened, shining masterfully into Ean's.

He sang.

The elegant, meticulous power of his voice engulfed Ean in a rush of sensations. Eli's fingers brushed her cheek. Enchanted, she hid a gentle smile behind her guarding hand. Delving into the chorus, Elias seized the stand with both hands, leaning over it, vested confidence flowing from every melodious word. The studio's mirrors depicted a white phantom on the verge of possessing his enraptured prey.

Elias detached the microphone, circling Ean throughout the second verse. Glancing downward to catch her breath, Ean noticed that the candles immediately framing them were arranged in a large, sweeping pentacle. Intrigue sparkled in her ice-blue eyes. *How interesting.*

Her haunted face thrilled Elias. Breaking his commanding stare, the skeleman returned to the stand with powerful strides, the red folds of his coat billowing like a cape. He reached for her as he sang. The bones of his hand reflected consuming firelight. As his voice embraced the bridge in melting tones, the skeleton returned to her. He stood inches from Ean, holding very still… waiting for her answer to the question brimming in his eyes.

She closed the distance.

Elias breathed a low sigh of pleasure from her impassioned kiss. His hand caressed her hair, then braced her lower back. Ean grasped his lapel to pull him closer. She felt his empty chest heave as he leaned over her, then lifted her into his arms. Their embrace, far more ardent than Eli had dared to hope, continued throughout the instrumental solo.

Brought back to earth by the mounting score, Elias broke away, lowering her to the ground. Breathing hard – struggling to regain control – he walked steadily backward, beckoning her to follow him to the center of the pentacle.

He extended the microphone toward her. Ean's hand touched his as they both held it. They chanted the final chorus as one, with neither their voices nor their locked gazes once faltering. Eli's countenance shone ablaze as they paced one another in a slow, steady circle, each raising a hand to the ceiling. The fire of the candlelit pentacle fluttered and magnified, its golden flames darkening until they were blood-red.

THE MICROPHONE FELL WITH A RINGING THUD.

"So, are you going to tell me what book of black magic *that* came from?"

"Hmm?" Elias ceased trailing his fingers along Ean's back. "I don't know what you mean."

The half-elf smiled and kissed him. "That spell you cast on me. You didn't mention you happen to be a sorcerer, too."

The skeleman chuckled, fingering a lock of her tussled hair. "I merely studied you, as any intelligent suitor would. Music resonates with you like nothing else does... besides skycraft. And one can do almost anything with the TerraDome programs, so *voila.*"

Ean snuggled up to him. "You know, it's odd. I didn't think twice about this. Even now, it doesn't seem weird at all." She explored his deep bone-plated chest inquisitively, grinning as her touch drew a shudder of pleasure from him.

"Yes, it appears we'll have to officially coin the term 'skelephile.'"

Ean frowned, pretending to be insulted. "You're not nervous that I'm just after you for your good looks, are you?"

"Nervous? Me?" He laughed again. "Perfect love casts out fear. Know what I mean?" Elias tilted her chin upward for another kiss.

It was well past midnight. The couple relaxed in Eli's bedroom, which was a pleasant surprise for Ean in deference to cleanliness and detail. Most of the furniture was black. The walls of the Gothic-styled house were of sober silver-gray stone. Plentiful accents of red creeping vines, a long ebony water fountain, and scattered volumes on various technical subjects invoked an aura of masculine mystery.

"I'm glad you liked that song," mentioned Elias. "Took me days to decide which one to perform. I couldn't wait any longer, though it could have done with some tweaking and more visual enhancements. Unfortunately," stroking his finger along her clavicle, "I seem to be in short supply of patience where Ean Lightcross is concerned."

"Can't say I'm likely to complain." Ean toyed with his ruby ring, putting on her own finger, then returning it to his.

"Well, you did almost throw me off." Eli's tone was accusatory. "You weren't supposed to kiss me like that. Where were your manners?"

Ean scuffed his skull with the palm of her hand, laughing. "You scoundrel! You were just standing there, staring down at me, and singing like a male siren. You know *exactly* what you were doing, sir."

"Maybe." Eli reached over to his nightstand and lit an ebony smoke. The scent of dusky spices and crisp autumnal bonfires wafted into the room. "You'll never be able to prove it, Sherlock Holmes. At any rate, I deserve an award for getting through the whole song."

"Ha! As if. Shyness certainly wasn't your problem."

Chuckling, Elias leaned in close to cradle the side of her face. His voice dropped to a whisper. "I almost had you on the floor the second you stepped inside. Have I mentioned how beautiful you are?"

Ean's ears glowed. "Not in words, perhaps... Pity that I'm not really this good-looking."

Elias chatted his gleaming teeth, lifting his thick shoulders in a shrug. "Pity that I'm not, either." Ean giggled and stole his smoke for a minute, relishing the flawless relaxation that settled over her. "Well, I don't imagine I'll be able to go back to my standoffish ways," she remarked teasingly. "You wouldn't let me."

"That is correct."

"We shall shock the world of VR with the passion of our love."

Eli propped up his skull with his hand. "Tell on, dear."

"We will probably get carded for PDA..."

"Looking forward."

"And we might get flagged as the most cringey cyber couple ever to be endured."

"I shall wear my disgrace as a badge of honor."

Ean glared at him. "You have to promise me one thing."

"I'm all ears."

"You *cannot* sing to me like that in public. I can't answer for the consequences; I'll be put right out of my head."

"How *very* interesting." His mien sparkled dangerously, and he positioned himself to graze her neck with his teeth. Ean restrained him at arm's length. "Promise me, now! I'm not joking."

"Very well." Elias held her hand. "But you need to promise me something in return."

"Ah! Pray tell."

"While we're in public, don't *ever* do that thing you did to my chest."

Ean tilted her head, falsifying ignorance. "What thing?'

"You know what thing!"

"*Ooooooh*, this thing?" Ean deliberately stroked her fingertips along his ribs, utilizing a particularly subtle, featherlike touch. A tremor of pleasure vibrated through his body. "Yes, that thing," he remarked. His cheekbones burned, and suddenly he was on top of her, holding her down by her wrists. He leaned in close to murmur in her ear, "Phantom pleasure is no joke, Ean."

7

THE FIRESTONE GUILD

Elias growled and snapped his teeth. The conglomeration of zombies before him slowed their pace, confused. The skeleman's eyes gleamed diabolically as he leveled his flaming sword at them.

"Ricobyurn."

A circle of the grasping, writhing undead burst into flames. Laughing, Cyrus leapt into the mob. "Nice going, man!" he shouted, caving a zombie's face in with the swing of his mechanical fist. Mallie kept close at his heels, healing spells at the ready, while Byron fought nearby.

"No problem." Elias sliced through the frantic mass with graceful ease. Byron trailed after him, hacking apart any undead creature that yet moved; there wasn't much for him to target. "Come on, Eli, I'm getting bored back here. Let me take over for a while, yeah?"

"Certainly." The artificer mage stepped aside, allowing Byron to take the lead. *It is pretty boring back here,* he realized as he half-heartedly picked off the stragglers. Left with ample room for imagination, his thoughts floated back to Ean, as they did all too often these days.

"Whoa, Eli! Look out!"

Elias hadn't noticed the zombie lurking behind him. He snapped around to face it, but he was too late. The monster seized onto his arm and bit down. "Damn it!" the skeleman bellowed, hacking at the zombie with his sword. Byron ran to his rescue, beating it aside with his mace, and examining the bitemark closely. "Mallie!"

"I'm coming!" The woodland pixie flittered over the motionless piles of their enemies. Fetching a cupped blossom from her inventory, she tipped its curled petals over the bitemark and watched the aqueous drop fall. "You may not be yourself for a while, so we'll need to keep an eye on you. But the effects should be reduced."

"I'll be fine." In truth, Elias could already feel a mindless lassitude seeping into his marrow. "Are we done here?"

Cyrus nodded, knocking Eli on the shoulder blade. "Yeah. Thanks, buddy. If you ever want to join us officially, just say the word!" The cyborg paused to admire Eli's sword, Sacrimony. "How do you find the time to train, anyway? I had no idea your combat level was so high."

Elias chuckled, swaying a bit. "Optimization is key, my good sir. I don't pussyfoot with TerraWorks; I'd never be able to leave Helios unguarded."

"*Pussyfoot?*" Cyrus and his friends laughed. "You sure you're all right, Elias?"

The skeleman blinked, eyes glazing over with a grayish film. "Never better," he drawled, tossing Sacrimony into the air (and almost dropping it). Mallie seized his arm and drew him aside while Cyrus snickered. "You need to rest, Elias. The venom is kicking in."

"I'm *fine*, Mallie."

"No, you're not. Cyrus, we should make sure he gets home."

"OK, let's go." Cyrus stood alongside Eli and propped him up. "Now, just one foot in front of the other, there's a good lad. Hey, Byron?"

Byron glanced up from sorting his gem case. "Yeah?"

"Think you could beam us to Helios City from here?"

Byron winced, glancing at the map his Holopal projected. "We can make it, but it's going to be a major drain on my transport gems."

"Byron, we didn't bring a gem mage on board so he could hoard them. They're meant to be *used*, remember?"

"You wouldn't be so flippant if *you* had to restore them," Byron muttered beneath his breath. "What was that, now?" Cyrus asked, raising an eyebrow.

"Nothing." Byron fished through his jewels until he pulled out a few emeralds. He evaluated every shining facet with a jealous eye, sighing, then submitted to the cyborg's glare. "OK, everybody stand still. It'll drain them twice as fast if anybody's wiggling around."

"Well, fuck. I was just seized with the burning desire to dance a jig." Elias crossed his arms and kicked his feet. Cyrus, spent with laughter, nearly collapsed too, and Byron rushed to seize and subdue them both with a hearty shake. "Gods! Would you two quit messing around? Do you know how long it takes to restore transport gems?"

Cyrus nudged him aside. "Calm the heck down, would ya? We'll be good, won't we, Elias?"

Eli's jaws parted in a wide yawn. "Good as gold."

Byron longed to add further admonishment, but the atmosphere around them glowed green. "Now *keep still,*" the gem mage hissed. The Firestone Guild was frozen into obedience. For a moment or two, everything around them solidified into a deep forest green. Eventually, the verdant tinge lifted, and the scent of roses and honey revealed the blossoming countryside of Helios.

"Somewhat off the mark, but close enough." Pleased, Byron consulted his jewel box, and uttered an exclamation of delight when he saw his precious emeralds retaining a little sparkle. "Everybody here?" he asked, turning to face the rest of the guild.

Thump.

Elias lay motionless in the clovered grass, jaws agape, and snoring hard.

"Elias?"

The skeleman was vaguely aware of a soft fabric being applied to his arm. "Ean?" he muttered, struggling to force his heavy eyelids open.

Instead of Ean's warm, lyrical mirth, Mallie's childlike giggle accosted him. "I think that just about confirms the TerraWiki gossip. You're dating Ean Lightcross, aren't you?"

"Of course not. Who says so?" Grunting, Elias rubbed his bleary eyes and sat up. "What happened? Why am I back at my workshop?" He was stretched across the couch in the back of the room.

"You were bitten. There's no mortal danger – since skeletons can't be zombified – but you acted a mite drunk, and then you passed out."

"… Oh."

"Actually, it was pretty funny. Could you do it again?"

Eli fired a derisive glare, causing her to giggle some more. "Where's everybody else?" he added, realizing that she sat alone at his elbow.

Mallie shrugged her petite shoulders. "They're restocking in the city. I didn't really need anything, so I said I'd wait here with you until you woke up."

"No need. I can take care of myself." Elias wobbled off the couch and strode across the room for his tablet, stumbling once or twice. Mallie huffed and crossed her arms. "Gee, a 'thank you' would have been nice."

"Thank you, Mallie, but you can rejoin your comrades. I'm all right now."

"We're supposed to look after each other. That's what joining a guild is for, you know?"

"I'm not part of your guild." Eli removed the cloth over his arm and studied the toothmarks curiously. "How interesting."

"Well, you could be. I happen to know that Cyrus is practically ready to get down on his knees and beg. Skeletal avatars aren't always ideal (no offense!), but you're indispensable against the undead."

"Oh? Much obliged."

"Seriously, I'm a little jealous. I've got a great position as the company healer, of course, but I just *adore* watching you and Cyrus fight! If only I could absorb a smidgen of your powers." Mallie gleefully swooped an imaginary sword through the air, then threw a punch *à la* Cyrus the Cyborg. "Anyway, you should keep your eyes peeled for an official invite in a couple of days. I have good reason to think you'll be getting one."

"As I said, I'm much obliged to you and Cyrus. But I won't be joining any guilds. I have far too much on my plate already." Elias swapped his tablet for a handful of sketches and proceeded to sift through them. Mallie gasped and posed dramatically. "You'll break the poor cyborg's heart, Elias! What's keeping you so busy? Your artificer work?" She stood up and tried to peep around him to see his drawings, but Eli swept them out of sight. "Partially. But I'm also finishing the plans for *Eclipsis,* and I'll need to practice for it as well."

"*Eclipsis?*" Mallie looked temporarily confused, then she snapped her fingers. "Oh, yeah! That's the title of your October concert. Oh my gods, I can't wait!"

"I'm afraid you'll have to." Elias coolly tilted his skull in the direction of the front door. "If you don't mind, Mallie, I really do have to catch up on some work here. I'll see you later, OK?"

Mallie's pink lips melted into a pout, but she meekly skipped to the door. "OK. I hope you're back to your energetic, sober old self. Good luck with *Eclipsis!*"

"Thank you."

Elias locked the door behind her with a relieved sigh. Snatching up his tablet, he eagerly scanned his missed messages. "An order… another order… special thanks for last week's shield infusion. Hmm, it appears even an orc can have manners. I appreciate that." He scrolled further down. "A fan letter. Another fan letter. I should try to answer some of these. Ah-ha!" Ean's avatar symbol popped into view. Elias tapped it to read her message.

Hey, Eli! Despite my dread of sounding clingy, I just wanted to say that I miss you. I know you'll have your hands full in the Undead Campaign with the Firestone Guild, so I'll try not to distract you. Tell Mallie I said hi!

The skeleman's eyes smiled as he touched the microphone icon to speak his reply. *It's been an interesting day. Mallie will have a very amusing tale to tell, next time you guys meet.*

Settling into his oversized chair, Elias swiped through his apps to find his music folder for *Eclipsis.* He studied a few song sheets before switching to the TerraDome app. His finger rapidly selected *Design, Options, Stage Level 1,* then *Front and Center.* A facsimile of the Dome's stage appeared above the screen. From the middle of its reflective ebony flooring rose an immense gold-and-black throne.

Eli began to fiddle with various designs and shades, adding and removing several details. Happily absorbed, he jumped when the tablet surprised him with Ean's answer. *I'm a sucker for amusing tales. Why don't you tell me yourself?*

Trust me. This one has to be delivered by somebody with a sense of humor.

You have a sense of humor, Eli! It's just very… subtle.

Elias cackled at her rejoinder. *That's adorable. What are you up to now?*

I'm training at SkyRate Tower. I still can't believe my name is in the list for the Tournament of Champions! My arms are sore from pinching them. How many zombies did you decimate today?

I didn't keep count. One of them got me, though. I'm not completely back to normal yet.

Gods, Elias! Mallie was there, right? Did she heal you?

Yes, I'm fine. I'm just a little groggy right now.

Oh, right. I forgot that skeletons are immune to zombification. You scared me for a minute there!

Elias stared at the white font floating in the air, fighting an increasing need to have her in his arms. *I've been stricken by a venom far more potent, Lightcross. I don't think there's an antidote.*

Ean took a few minutes to reply, but it wracked Elias with mirth. *Bite me!*

Ean powered down and dismounted with a tired sigh. She flicked her wrist to open her inventory and deposit her skyboard into it. Her feet dragged as she walked down the hallways, indifferently lighting a magenta smoke with the vague hope that it would revive her. "Well, I'm beyond exhausted. I wanted to fly out and visit Elias, but I don't have the strength. I'd crash and wake up with 1 HP." Sighing again, she stopped at a viewing balcony and flicked her cigarette into a tray. "Of course, I'd start dating somebody before the Grand Championship tournament. Why wouldn't I make my life as difficult as possible?"

Her skeleman's calm baritone stole into her monologue. "Life is more interesting when it's a challenge, isn't it?"

She turned in the voice's direction, her face brightening. "Eli?"

Elias Mage leaned in the corner behind her, arms crossed. Flushed with delight, Ean wrapped her arms around him. "I'm *so* glad you're here! How did you sneak up on me like that?"

"I've got more than a few tricks up my proverbial sleeve." Elias emitted her favorite warm, diabolical chuckle. As his arms embraced her in return, she noticed the fresh toothmarks on his humerus. "Poor Elias! Will it go away?" She kissed it tenderly, causing him to blush.

"I doubt it. I could probably buff them out, but I think I like them. It's like having a wicked scar after a shark attack. Know what I mean?" Elias flexed, provoking her laughter. "Well, maybe it does add to your general vibes of badassery. TerraWiki will eat that up faster than a dog at breakfast."

"Badassery?" Eli cocked his skull.

"Oh, sorry. It's old slang. Calling someone a badass means they're super cool."

"Ah." Elias leaned his arm across her shoulders, and the couple headed for the elevator. "Mind if I crash at your apartment before we log off?"

"Will you sing me to sleep?"

"Yes, my dear."

"Will you… pet my back?"

"Yes."

"Will you brush my hair?"

"Now, *that's* pushing it. You have a lot of hair."

"Will you brew me some tea?"

"Hex can do that. Since when did you become so high-maintenance?"

"Oh, I can be quite pathetic. You've no idea."

"I've got some idea now, it seems." The elevator light illuminated, and the two stepped inside.

"I'll make it worth your while." Ean touched his chest with a seductive smile. "Not here!" Elias protested, grasping her hand and guiding it away from him.

"Why not here?"

Elias laughingly tussled with her for a minute, at length submitting as her lips met his jaws. "Gods, I adore you," he whispered.

8

EAN'S RECKONING

"*Our readers would be sorely out of touch not to be familiar with the TerraDome's heavy metal band, Spectral Tyrants, and their lead singer Elias Jacoby Mage. Furthermore, they've likely been logged out altogether for the past month if they haven't heard the rumors surrounding that lyrical phantom and the TerraWorks City Tournament winner, Ean Lightcross.*"

"*The progressively famous couple has been spotted at multiple social occasions, allegedly dancing or conversing in a manner denoting intimacy. Nevertheless, they've proven successful at giving our HI crew the slip. Until now, we had nothing to go on but the TerraWiki gossip columnists, which we must agree is not reassuring. Therefore, we call upon you to rejoice, fair readers! At long last, we can give our romantic fans tidings of great joy. We present attached the first bona fide holographic image of Elias and Ean. An anonymous member of our crew captured the tender image of the couple sharing a private, star-struck kiss, as the elevator doors in SkyRate Tower opened to reveal their love. It's official, ladies: Elias Mage is spoken for. But how long will it last? And what are Ean's true motives? Alas, these questions can only be answered with time.*"

Ean wrinkled her nose, further venting her feelings with a derisive growl. "OK, first of all, who writes like that anymore? Their phraseology is positively archaic. It's growing mold."

Hex's voice answered soothingly. "I agree with you."

"Second of all," she paced angrily around her apartment, "what did I ever *do* to all these gods-forsaken journalists, anyway? 'What are Ean's true motives?' Do people just not know how to fall in love anymore? It happens! Some of us don't have motives!"

"There, I must beg to differ, Ean-san. The current statistics of dating and marriage in TerraWorks clearly indicate that most couples unite in order to realize a common goal, or to share inventory and/or property."

Ean raised her hand to cut him off. "I know all about that, Hexy. I'm not trying to say we're so madly in love that VR marriage has occurred to either of us."

Has it? Ean froze. *He's been kind of cagey lately, always telling me he's busy with this or that project. What if he's planning to...?*

When TerraWorks avatars got married (usually for the unromantic benefits Hex so aptly described), it was typically done in a quick, pre-packaged ceremony, complete with a standard one-week "honeymoon." The process of divorcing was just as rapid and simple. Precious few players took VR marriages seriously. Conversely, some of the more high-profile avatars made quite a show out of their proposals. Others would order or even design customized, elaborate ceremony stages and honeymoons.

Is it possible that Elias is... going to propose?

Ean ceased pacing to glower at her reflection. Her burning face, icy eyes, and slanted brows reminded her that she was nothing more than a common half-elf, who had beaten her rival Piragor by the merest stroke of luck. She had knelt into the aerodynamic position a few seconds before he did. Lightcross would have thrown herself over the finish line if that would have done it, but dismounting before crossing the finish line would have disqualified her. She'd have returned to her apartment with 1 HP and the disgrace of shame to crown her.

Well, at least you don't have to think about that anymore. "Hexy," Ean pleaded, tugging at a lock of her hair, "can you calculate the probability that Elias Mage might… maybe… propose?"

"To whom?"

Ean gave a short, sarcastic laugh. "Gee, thanks, buddy. Nevermind."

"As you wish."

Ashamed and a little shocked by her own forwardness, Ean distracted herself by sorting through her wardrobe app and trying on different outfits. That irritating article still lingered next to Hex's image. True enough, attached at the bottom of the pulsing white text was the damning evidence itself: The covert HI of Ean and Elias in SkyRate Tower. She suffered from an undeniable need to download it and keep it forever. "Save that image for me, Hex."

"Yes, Ean-san."

She emerged refreshed in a long burgundy robe, prepared to relax before she logged off for the night. "Fix me some milk tea, please. Oh, and could you project that HI above my kotatsu?"

"With pleasure."

Powered on by Hex, her garnet teapot automatically refilled and heated. Ean poured herself a cup and sipped with luxuriant enjoyment. "Wow, I really needed this. Want to join me, Hexy?"

"I thought you'd never ask, my lady." A full-scale projection of Hexadecimal sat across from her, holding his own cup of steaming tea. "And here is the holographic image you requested." The Holopal had already enlarged and enhanced it. Ean sat forward eagerly, committing every possible detail to memory.

A blueish light tinted the scene. The chrome doors of the elevator were slightly blurred, obviously in the act of retracting when the HI was taken. Behind the doors, Elias grasped the safety rail with one pearl-white hand, resting his other hand on her waist. Ean was leaning against him, hands curled against his chest, red lips brushing his ivory jaws. Their eyes were closed, oblivious that the elevator doors were open. Indeed, they were the sublime picture of blissful lovers. "You're blushing again," Hexadecimal remarked. "I take it things are proceeding well for you and Elias?"

Ean looked into her Holopal's peaceful Asian eyes. Although artificially rendered, they held a remarkable power to bestow tranquility. "Yes. Things are going extremely well. I'm so happy that I feel ridiculous, like the whole universe of TerraWorks must be laughing into their sleeves at me. What sort of feeling would you call that?"

"According to my vast programming in human history, I'd call it love."

Meanwhile, Elias nodded over a pile of crumpled sketches. "Brilliant. Inspirational. Perfection itself, that's what it is." He congratulated himself with a dark, ruthless chuckle, and… proceeded to inject zombie venom into the site of the deepest toothmark.

He'd found the effects of the venom to be fascinatingly *liberating*. Normally – both within TerraWorks and in real life – he felt caged and isolated by the constructs of society, whether imaginary or otherwise. He struggled to balance reality with VR life, day in and day out, maintaining and optimizing his reputation in two worlds… but for *what*, exactly? What was the point?

Memento mori.

Well, his fame would live on long after he was dead. At least that was something. To that end, *Eclipsis* would be his treasured epitome, his immortal statement to all the world that Elias J. Mage would not be outdone. His voice was good enough, but that alone wouldn't take him far. His showmanship, his artistry, and his sheer ingenuity would be the tools to grant him a legendary position in TerraWorks.

That strange, giddy lethargy settled into his bones once more. He felt light and comfortable, but not to the point of outright fatigue. Elias felt certain that he'd administered the correct amount. He stumbled across his workshop to the couch and threw himself onto it. "Yes, I think this will do very nicely." He hummed a quiet little tune, carelessly flexing his boney hand and admiring his golden ring as it caught the light.

A page he'd studied from the *Magical Properties of Gold* floated through his skull. "Gold is remarkably susceptible to infusions, but never more so than in plated or foil form. In both states, the daintiness of this precious metal can absorb powerful incantations, while retaining the flexibility to administer them with the utmost delicacy and direct refinement…"

"Hmm." It was an extravagant idea, but no other avatar had done it before. "Perfect!" Elias shouted to no one. The skeleman tumbled off the couch in his enthusiasm. "Jot this one down, Eli. *Eclipsis* rises before you!"

Crawling to his desk, he reached up to snatch one of his drawings, turned it face-down, and started sketching furiously on the back. "You don't know what you've done, Ean. But I'll make you see it! You'll understand! I *know* you will."

Elias panted with eagerness as he completed one design after another, slapping them down triumphantly into one disconcerted heap. Once this task was completed, he scrambled to his knees and unsheathed his sword. With it, he gave his designs a solemn salute. "I dub thee the Testament of Eli, the righteous forest of my love, the tree of my confidence, and the seed of my deepest fear. Amen!" Having uttered these inscrutable ravings, Elias collapsed on the floor, laughing loudly.

The following evening, Elias snapped his fingers to get the band's attention. "All right, boys, settle down. We've got a long night ahead of us."

Oleon groaned, looking up from snaring Travis into a brotherly head-lock. "It's our first meeting since *Ghostfire.* Can't we at least stop at the Pulse first? Order some liquid courage, you know?"

Eli shook his skull. "We can't be drunk for this, Ollie. Travis! Put them down."

Sindaya took her drumsticks from Travis, sat on the stool, and effort-lessly wacked out a rousing beat. "I'm ready, Elias. These thugs will fall into line once we get started."

"Where's Kaspar?"

"On his way," Sindaya's Holopal piped up. "He mentioned that he would bring a case of beer and some Whiskers as consolation for his tardiness."

Ollie and Travis cheered. The skeleman rolled his eyes. "So be it. Desmond! I need you to take a look at the TerraDome app. Did you bring your tablet?"

"Yes, sir." Desmond tapped on the shared stage file. His eyes widened. "Damn. How long did it take you to plan this?"

"One night."

"There's literally no way in Hades you did this in one night."

"I did."

Oleon and Travis started wrestling each other again. Elias crossed his arms and darted them his best demonic glare. Desmond frowned as well.

"Kindly get your bees out o' your bonnets now, lads. Our fans will be expecting an even higher standard after *Ghostfire*."

"Sorry. You're right." Ollie rumpled Travis' hair in his final ploy for conquest. "What's the big plan, Elias?'

The skeleman projected the stage file before them. "My gods," Sindaya breathed. "That's brilliant, Eli!"

"Thank you. Now, I suggest we start warming up."

"I still don't understand why you use a tablet, though. Why not trade it in for a Holopal?"

The studio door burst open. Kaspar scurried inside. "Sorry, Elias. I'm here!" He opened his inventory, proudly depositing a small ice chest. "And I've brought some goodies."

"Thanks. Let's go!"

Sindaya and Travis led off. Oleon joined in on the bass, then Kaspar on the keyboard. Elias rolled his shoulders, then swayed to the rhythm, a fiendish enjoyment igniting his countenance. Raising his hands, he began the symphonic metal lyrics of "Poetic Justice."

"A VIBRANT PERSECUTION,
TRITE DEBT I CANNOT PAY.
'NEVERMORE,' THE RAVEN'S CRY;
SIGNIFY THE END OF DAYS.
ICY STILLNESS, SEIZING FAST,
PRESERVE ME SO I'LL SMILE!
THE REAPER'S FOOTFALL ECHOES PAST,
MY CAPTURED SOUL BEGUILED."

Midway through, Sindaya waxed a mite too enthusiastic. One of her drumsticks flew straight out of her hand. "Sorry!" she yelled over the music, ducking down in shame as Elias levelled another scowl. Thankfully, the rest of the song was successful, and the skeleman nodded. "We're a little stiff, but not as bad as I feared we'd be. Shall we continue?"

"I vote for a beer break first!" Travis insisted, shaking his long black hair out of his face. "Honest to the gods, I play better when I'm relaxed."

Elias surprised them by shrugging, walking to the ice chest, and cracking open a beer. He crushed the empty can against his skull as the Spectral Tyrants cheered and executed mock bows before him. "You're as moody as a cat this evening," Sindaya smiled. "Don't suppose your new girlfriend has anything to do with it?"

"Have no idea who you're talking about."

"Emmy Lightcross?"

Eli's tone was a touch miffed. "*Ean.* Ean Lightcross."

Sindaya winked at Travis, and the five of them leaned in close to sing "*Eeeeaaaannn!*" before commencing an old love ballad, snapping to the beat. Incensed, Elias rushed them like a bull in a ring. They scattered laughingly. "So, you've all been gearing up to tease me, eh?"

"Hey, man, you asked for it." Oleon snorted. "You've mocked VR dating countless times. Now that you've proven your god-like sensibility to be every bit as human as ours, you'll have to stand for a little ribbing. No pun intended," he added, elbowing Eli in the ribcage.

"We're getting distracted here," Elias answered, planting a skeletal hand on Oleon's scalp to push him aside. "We're not here to discuss my love life, which I may or may *not* have. Let's run through 'Illusory' next."

Sindaya pouted. "Won't you at least tell us how you two met? This could be the greatest love story in TerraWorks since Xander and Syren."

"I'll leave that to your superior imagination."

Eli's tablet chose that auspicious moment to ring with a message receipt notification. The Lightcross avatar symbol was projected into the atmosphere. "Let's get to work," Elias firmly stated, picking up the tablet and shutting it off. "In fact, all of you need to silence your devices. No Holopals, either. Put them in sleep mode."

Desmond shook his forefinger in warning. "Never keep a woman waiting, Elias. Tale as old as time itself."

"I'm the lead singer of the Spectral Tyrants, and we have a concert to finalize. She's going to wait."

"*Ooooh,* touchy!"

"Just felt a chill go down my spine."

"Anybody got a pickaxe to break that ice?"

Elias growled. "*Shut it.*"

9

EAN'S RECKONING, PART TWO

Ean opened her eyes to the familiar scent of milk tea. She had programmed Hexadecimal to brew it for her as soon as she logged in, and the comforting aroma wrapped around her like a warm embrace. "Any messages for me?" she asked, approaching Hex at the charging station.

"Good evening, Ean-san. No messages."

"None at all? That's odd." Ean frowned. Her gaze instinctively skimmed the projection of herself and Elias in the SkyRate elevator, which still floated above her kotatsu. Hex seemed to read her thoughts. "Elias Jacoby Mage is a high-profile avatar. The daily volume of orders and correspondence alone conflicts with his practical work as an artificer mage. In addition, his upcoming performance in October is-"

"Yeah, I get the picture." Sighing, the half-elf finished her tea and stared morosely at the lifelike details in the bottom of her teacup. "I guess I have two options tonight," she added. "I could train at SkyRate Tower again (which is what I should be doing), or I could take out some of my frustration and impatience on Ophidious." Ean laughed at the thought.

"In all seriousness, though, I could train with Necrowave instead. He's been so neglected lately that I fancy he's lost some of his color."

"If that is the route you choose, I would recommend a focus session. You are badly out of practice, and you may be injured if you enter battle right away."

Ean chuckled at her Holopal's cynicism. "You never were one to spare my feelings, Hexy. Can you start a session now?"

"Yes, Ean-san."

The scarlet focus session alert hovered in the center of Ean's apartment. Her rooms faded to black, and a crimson grid showed her the dimensions of the arena. Ean's ornate silver earpiece relayed the system's session prompts. *Welcome to Focus Session Five. We will begin by testing your defensive maneuvers before proceeding to assess your attack. Please assume a defensive position.*

Ean braced herself and held Necrowave to one side. *The system will monitor your HP and adjust the session according to your aptitude. If you need a break, say "Pause." If you wish to terminate the session, say "Exit." Do you have any questions?*

"Nope."

Then we will begin. Good luck, Ean Lightcross.

Without warning, a blinding ball of fire magic erupted from the eastern wall. Ean dove out of its path, leaping back onto her feet to face the next attack. A second conflagration exploded from the corner. Ean whipped Necrowave backward, targeting the flaming orb, and used the hammer to knock it aside. The flames were turned red and purple from Necrowave's mysterious tincture. The orb blazed and snapped like fireworks, then harmlessly petered out on the floor. "I forgot how fun this is!" she cried exultantly, continuing to utilize Necrowave as a deflective shield.

Difficulty level set to increase. Please confirm.

"Yeah, genius, hurry up!"

Ean dashed across the arena, lobbing fire, electric, and poison orbs left and right. Her half-elf speed and lightness played in her favor, as did her human confidence. Defense had never been much of an issue; her Achilles heel rested in offense, which she wasn't quite so confident about... especially since her first encounter with Ophidious.

Remembering that disgraceful loss got her thinking. *Elias and I still haven't demonstrated our weapons. I wonder what his fighting style is? I see him with an enormous mace! But what would he say about Necrowave? Would he criticize it? Would he say I'm a fool for not prioritizing a long-range weapon? Loners need a long-range weapon. I know that, but...*

Distracted by her ponderings, Ean missed an electric orb launching from the lefthand corner. Her body was seized in its ruthless grip. Ean yelled – more in sheer surprise than in pain, although it did hurt – and spluttered an assortment of choice curses as she watched her HP drop thirty percent. Hex's voice admonished her from afar. "Get it together, Ean."

"Right, right. Got it." Ean pushed herself upright, glowering at the new challenge that was morphing into view. Ophidious the Tormented towered before her, staring hellishly with his snakish eyes, as if Ean had just found and destroyed all his offspring.

"Damn, you're scary. Even during a focus session." Ean resumed her defensive pose.

Ophidious, true to form, said nothing. He raised his hands and spoke the words of some gods-forsaken spell. Ean gritted her teeth, mimicking his own hiss back to him, and rushed toward him with all the speed she could muster.

"And that's when I got my ass handed to me. *Again*."

Elias just laughed at her, which earned him a not-so-subtle pinch on the funny bone. The skeleman jerked away. "Gods, that felt weird! Don't do that."

"Serves you right." Ean sighed and extended her feet toward the crackling fireplace. "I should just stick to skyboarding. I have a natural gift for that. It'll take me quite some time to be good enough to defeat Ophidious… and after all, somebody else will most likely beat me to it."

Eli gazed at her, eyes brimming with midnight mischief. "If I didn't know any better, I'd ask if you have a crush on this Ophidious fellow. Your sole references to any combat whatsoever are exclusively invested in *him*."

Ean positioned her finger and thumb for a second pinching. Undaunted, Elias pinned her hands to her sides and affected to bite her ear. "It's very ambitious to face a fay sorcerer single-handed, so I admire you for that. But I have to agree that it's unlikely you will succeed before another player does."

"Yeah? Why's that?"

Elias nuzzled her ear. "Because I plan to kidnap you and keep you here with me."

"Ha! You'd never get anything done. You might as well close up this workshop right now."

The artificer mage shrugged. "I could take on an apprentice to run it for me, and only contact me with questions or advanced orders. I've thought about doing that for a while now, but… You know how I am."

"Yes, I know. You're something of a control freak."

"So are you."

"Not really; I'm too lazy. How do you figure?"

Eli's face dropped lower to graze her collarbone. His cool, smooth hand cradled the back of her head. "You won't join any guilds because you want to play the game in your own way. Above every other goal, your greatest determination is to control the experience. You will claim every victory you achieve beneath your own flag, and yours alone." He turned to speak directly into her ear. "Am I right, Lightcross?"

He felt her catch her breath, frozen by his nearness. "Come again? I only heard about half of that." She caressed his cheekbone in the palm of her hand, her ice-blue eyes glittering with affection.

"'Come again,' she says." Elias chuckled. "How quaint."

"It's part of my charm."

Elias leaned in for a kiss, lacing their fingers together. After they parted, Ean laughingly wiped her lipstick off his face. "Guess I'll have to lay off the lipstick as long as we're together."

The skeleman heaved a blissful sigh, encaging her in his long arms. "Then you'll be lipstick-free for a long, long time. Hope you don't mind."

"Is that right?"

For his answer, Elias slipped his ruby ring off his fingerbone and transferred it to her thumb. Ean stared at the tiny, cross-shaped gems, shining like the sacred blood of the moon elves. "It's beautiful, Eli, but you know this will only ramp up the gossip around us. You really want me to wear this?"

"I think it's time we made our relationship official. Don't you?"

"But you hate intrusions into your personal life. And with your concert coming up..."

"Let me worry about that, Ean. Just wear it for me, please?"

"All right. But remember, when the day comes that we can't find a single solitary place to kiss in peace – and the TerraWiki gossip fandom is swarming your workshop – and you awaken to a million messages from avatars demanding to know when the wedding shall take place – remember through all of that nonsense that *I warned you*, Elias Mage."

"Bite me, Ean."

She started to laugh, but his gaze took on a solemn intensity. "No, seriously. Bite me."

"Um… Can I ask why?"

"Just try it. Right here." He tapped his clavicle. "I want to know what it feels like."

Ean hesitated. "What if I hurt you?"

"You won't."

"How can you be sure?"

"You won't!"

"OK, then." Flushing, Ean leaned into his lap and softly bit his clavicle.

"Harder," Elias commanded, inhaling deeply. She increased the pressure until a shudder trembled through his frame. *"Ah,"* the skeleman breathed, his dark eyelids closed in ecstasy. "Even better than I thought."

Ean tilted her head, witnessing his reaction with bafflement. "I suppose it makes sense that physical pleasure can get a bit… weird… with cyber-skeleton avatars. But where did you get the idea from?"

Eli's eyes opened. "Oh, it's much more than a mere physical pleasure, and it certainly didn't *hurt* me. In fact, it helped me in a practical sense."

"What do you mean?"

"Well, I'll explain it to you sometime. It's a bit technical. TerraWiki lacks comprehensive information on high-level skeletal avatars, so a little experimentation is in order… paired with some desultory reading that would bore you to tears, Miss Lightcross." His mien sparkled with contentment and cheer, but he spoke in that same inscrutable manner he'd used before.

"I'm sorry, but you're speaking Greek again. Could you translate what you just said?"

"Put simply, then. I am the first of my kind: a customized skeletal avatar that has attained a high combat level *and* a high performa level. I've gained certain traits and subtle abilities that remain unknown to most players in TerraWorks. I'm exploring them at my own pace."

Ean nodded. "I see. You make me feel ashamed of myself for only having *two* main goals in TerraWorks. Just how in the name of the Terran Pantheon do you have the time for everything you do?"

"I make the time." He drew Ean into his lap. "Just like I'm doing now. I'm sorry you had to wait up for me."

Ean rested her forehead against his. "You're worth it."

10

ENTER ECLIPSIS

"**B**y the gods, Ean! You're finally here!"

Mallie squeezed herself past several fans, grabbed her friend by the arm, and pulled her toward the front of the audience. "I was starting to freak out. Did you just log in?"

"Yeah. Take it easy, girl." Ean looked intense in a gothic outfit and makeup. "You're even more excited than I am."

Mallie shrugged. "Well, I'm sure you were invited to all his rehearsals. I guess you wouldn't be as thrilled in that case."

Lightcross started to explain that no, she'd never been invited – in fact, now that Mallie mentioned it, *why* hadn't she been invited? – but a rising orchestra interrupted her. "*Oh my gods!*" Mallie squealed above the roar of the crowd. Ean caught her breath, nervously twisting Eli's ring around her thumb.

The virtual curtains lifted.

A daunting black-and-gold throne rose from center stage, reflecting against the smooth ebony flooring. Elias Mage lounged in it with an informal air, brandishing a tall staff in one hand. The sole cause of the audience's collective gasp, however, was the elaborate change to his body. His entire skeletal frame, from skull to phalanges, was shining with gold.

Rubies and diamonds alternated across his cranium like an embedded crown. Even his clear, dark eyes mirrored a gilt shimmer. The skeleman wore studded pants, boots, and a sweeping hooded vest, but no shirt. His golden chest gleamed as if it was on fire.

As everyone stared in fascination, Elias rose to his feet and soberly pointed the head of his staff toward the audience. The drums of the orchestration increased exponentially, and the crowd responded as if by enchantment. Their screams rebounded across the stadium; Ean realized that Eli's staff was also his microphone. "How interesting," she murmured, crossing her arms and smiling. Eli bowed his head, the bright gems in his skull glittering, patiently waiting as the crowd worked itself into a frenzy.

Gradually, the rest of the Spectral Tyrants joined Elias on stage, dressed in embellished jeans and leather jackets. A lengthy guitar instrumental ensued. As it progressed, a second set of curtains opened behind the band to reveal an animated mechanism – an enormous golden skull – that opened its mouth to expel smoke and yellow flames.

Elias waited, posing with his staff, while his dark gaze searched for Ean. Locating her at last, he felt disappointed to see her standing so calmly, arms crossed, with the struggle of admiration versus resentful longing radiating from her stiff body language. He knew she felt so far away from him… and as he shone like the king of the dead, countless avatars screamed his name.

Elias couldn't allow this evening – *their* evening – to continue like that. He handed his staff to Desmond. Striding powerfully to the beat, he walked to the edge of the stage, holding Ean Lightcross captive with his eyes.

He bent, shifted his weight, and jumped off the stage.

His fans burst with exhilaration. Hands brushed against him and tugged at his vest from every direction. The skeleman continued walking as if he felt nothing at all. Ean knew damn well that he was heading straight for her. She couldn't resist the tug of a smile lifting her lips.

Once he stood directly before her, his gilded aspect was nearly blinding. He examined her searchingly. Marking her subtle but irresistible smile, he grasped both her hands in his and initiated a kiss, right there, in front of a thousand hyperactive souls.

Ean's elusive resistance came crashing down. She sensed an unbridled passion and vigor infusing her senses, as if Elias was pouring it into her veins. As he pulled her closer, a mock lightning storm thundered above the arena, showering them in a simulated golden rain. The half-elf felt her hair crackle with static. In that moment, she honestly thought that she (along with the entire audience) would burst with overwhelming stimuli and dark energy. *Hot damn. He really thought of everything.*

The heavy metal score was reaching its pinnacle, Eli's cue. He broke away and brushed her chin with his forefinger. "Mmm. You look really nice tonight, Lightcross." With that casual remark, he readjusted his rumpled vest and stalked back to the stage, regaining it with ease and receiving his staff back from Desmond.

"I TELL YOU MY TALE FROM A THOUSAND YEARS AGO,
CASTING 'ROUND FOR THE GEM OF GREAT PRICE.
BLOOD OF GOLD, BOUGHT IN PINTS, TO REVEAL THE PLACE,
COUNTLESS SONS OF THEIR RACE,
ALL BUT LOST IN WAR;
DID YOU KNOW?
OH, DID THEY KNOW?"

Deepening an octave for the chorus, Elias raised his golden fist to the lightening-infused ceiling.

"NO GEM, NO INHERITANCE,

No precious stone was found.
Search on in restless agony,
Fell treachery abound!
Oh, listen well, my blessed son,
And heed now what I say.
This rumored gem of boundless price
Awaits you on her wedding day."

Elias, himself affected by the Dome's surging energy, fell to his knees and raised his hands to the ceiling. His long vest billowed across the floor. The skeleman's god-like figure reflected in Ean's wide, entranced eyes. The crowd's answering rumble crashed against her ears like the distant roar of the sea. The half-elf stood unmoving, utterly unconscious of Mallie's persistent yanks on her long black sleeve. "Did you hear me, Ean? Ean!" she shouted. Ean returned to Terra with a short gasp. "What, Mallie?"

"I said, *he's going to propose to you!*"

Mallie gaped as Ean just glanced at her and vacantly replied, "How do you know?"

"What in Hades do you mean, 'how do I know?' Didn't you hear the lyrics?"

"Oh. Come to think of it, yes, I suppose they're rather suggestive."

"You *suppose?* They're *rather suggestive?* By the Pantheon, you're chilly! Did you get bitten by a zombie today? This isn't like you."

"No. But I do feel a little bit... odd." Ean's stare remained chained to Elias.

"Need to sit down somewhere? Take a break?"

"I'm not leaving."

Ean's hands clenched into fists, and she bit her lower lip until a drop of blood spilled from it. Her body was hot and rigid. Mallie continued to tug on her sleeve, frowning with concern. She yelled over the music, "Do you need to log off? What's going on?"

Ean wisely kept the answer to herself. Her grasp tightened until her knuckles were white and her nails pierced her palms. *Ha, log off? No, Mallie. I need Elias. I need him NOW.* The force of that thought resounded with such clarity that for a minute, Ean was afraid she'd screamed it. Her chest felt tight, as if an entourage of writhing snakes were steadily constricting it. Just as she began to think she was literally losing her sanity, the song ended.

The tightness in her chest lessened. Drawing a grateful breath, Ean clutched Mallie's shoulder to avoid collapsing on the ground. She panted, wiping away the sweat that beaded the roots of her hair. "Spectral Tyrants, indeed. What in Hades did he just *do?*"

"Here, this might help." Mallie opened her inventory and scrolled through it until she withdrew a violet smoke. "I know it's not a magenta, but it should calm you down."

"Thanks, Mallie. You're a good friend." Ean lit up and exhaled in relief. "Gods, I can breathe again. You don't suppose…?"

"Suppose what?"

The next song began. The mournful tones of a funeral bell struck twelve as Eli's attire morphed into the clothing of the Reaper. The golden atmosphere dimmed to dark gray. "Hmm… from glistening life to the dusk of death. Great transition. He *has* thought of everything."

"Yeah, you didn't tell me your boyfriend was a literal *genius.* Feeling better?"

"I'm myself again, thanks." Too lazy to pinpoint an ashtray, Ean covertly dropped and crushed the Whisker beneath the thick sole of her boot. "I wonder, though… Can singers imbue their songs with spellcraft?"

"I wouldn't know. But wouldn't that be, I don't know, cheating?"

"Maybe. And he does hate to cheat."

Still, Elias was a master artificer. If he didn't infuse his songs themselves, then what could have been the cause of...

Ean's gaze landed on the gilded staff he continued to wield for the rest of the concert. It was a unique idea to combine a majestic prop with a cordless microphone. He'd even taken especial care to thicken its base, so he could stand it up on its own if he wanted to. "His staff," she murmured. "He's infused his *staff* to enhance his voice's effect on the audience. And it's made of pure gold..." She twirled the golden ring he'd given to her.

Elias Mage, you magnificent, damnable beast. What exactly are you up to?

He performed as one possessed, at one point standing in the thick of the flames that rampaged from his mechanical replica's jaws. At the height of the finale, Elias beckoned Ean to the stage. Piercing shrieks and cheers surrounded her as the audience escorted her to the front, some patting her on the back or indicating a tacky thumbs-up. Eyes ablaze, Elias stretched out his hand for hers and pulled her up beside him. "Just like we rehearsed it," he said, holding the staff toward her.

Eli nodded to Kaspar, indicating the change to "March of Mephisto." The skeleman and the half-elf held the staff together, treading in a measured circle as their voices combined. A flaming pentacle blossomed at their feet.

Elias saw and heard no one but Ean. His stare said as much, betraying a despotic concentration that caused her hand to quake against the staff. At the song's conclusion, scarlet rose petals fluttered down on the couple, and the crowd screamed itself hoarse as Elias set his staff aside and got down on one knee.

"Ean Lightcross."

She caught her breath. Her ice-blue eyes sharpened with trembling intensity.

"I pledge myself to you, and to you alone, before these witnesses and the Terran Pantheon. Will you accept my devotion, my protection, and my love?"

"I will."

Ean flushed with pride and exhilaration. Elias rose as Sindaya approached Ean, carrying a diadem of white gold and rare ice gems wrought in elfish design. "Really, Elias! This is too much," Ean panted, trying to decline it at first. "Isn't a ring sufficient?"

"You're already wearing it," Elias laughingly pointed out, arms akimbo for the benefit of their audience. The crowd echoed his mirth. "Be a good girl and accept, my dear. I've spent many a sleepless night on this."

"Gods, you're full of it! If you insist."

The skeleman chuckled. "Oh, I insist." Elias lifted the delicate circlet from Sindaya and placed it on Ean's head. "Wear it often, my dear. It will keep you safe." Seizing her hand in his, he raised them triumphantly before the audience. "Well, how was *Eclipsis?*" he yelled, relishing the legendary response he received.

That night, he merged with his fans far more than he'd ever done before: posing for holographic images and recordings, signing band posters and t-shirts, and thoroughly embarrassing his fiancé by proclaiming her virtues to anyone who would listen. Despite her experience as a SkyRate competitor, Ean was bewildered by the volume of attention she received. Fortunately, Elias sensed her growing fatigue. He made his excuses. "Let's get out of here," he commented, taking her hand and leading them out of the TerraDome.

They left on Simulacra. Innumerable avatars who had streamed the concert waved at them or shouted their congratulations. Ean was relieved when they reached her apartment. "I feel like we just got back from the wedding itself," she giggled as they dismounted. "Will you promise me that we'll have a quick, quiet wedding instead? I don't think my brain could handle a second overload."

Elias gathered her weary form into his arms. "We'll plan it however you want." He carried Ean up to her apartment. For once, she was far too exhausted to assert herself.

11

SHIORI ISLANDS

*P*lease scan your wrist to enter your room code.

Ean took a deep breath and scanned. *Welcome, Ean Lightcross.* The door to her room slid open. She entered slowly, savoring the luscious smell of island produce and florals, and grinning at the twinkle of the sea beyond her private balcony. "Yes!" she yelled, running across the room and leaping onto the enormous bed. "We're here, Hexy. I made it! Can you believe this?"

"Congratulations, Ean-san. You're in the Tournament of Champions."

"And I get to practice on the Shiori Track itself, starting tomorrow." An elegant painting of the famous SkyRate course was hanging over her hotel suite's desk. Ean scampered across the room to have a look. "Awesome! Just look at all those corkscrews and tight turns. I'm going to have the time of my life, even if I don't win."

Hexadecimal hovered over her shoulder. He nodded sagely, hands tucked into his flowing blue sleeves. "Some of the races will take place at nighttime. According to TerraWiki, the tracks will be well-lit."

"That reminds me…" An immense HoloTablet was built into the desk. Ean's fingers raced across it as she composed a brief message for Piragor.

"I'm going to ask Piragor if he'd be my training partner. We're allowed to select one at our own discretion, right?"

"That is correct. However, most of your competitors will be engaging a flight coach instead. That is what I would recommend."

Ean snorted as she hit *send*. "I won the TerraWorks City tournament without a coach, didn't I? I'd look like a wuss if I suddenly booked one now. No, thanks."

"You are taking a substantial risk by this refusal, Ean-san."

"So what? I take risks. That's what I do, Hexy." She scrolled through the HoloTablet for the pairing app, then scanned her wrist when prompted to synch her current data and communications. "Could you fire up Livewire for me?"

"A holographic video for Elias, I presume?"

"You presume correctly, sir. Wait a moment." Ean took a few steps backward, so the video capture would show more of her private suite. "OK, action!"

"Here is your order, sir. I bid you a pleasant evening."

Elias handed the wrapped parcel to his client. "Thanks again, Elias!" the dwarf rumbled, cheerfully saluting the artificer mage and stomping out the door. Eli's workshop bell chimed pleasantly as the door closed. Sighing, Elias rubbed his skull with a weary expression in his eyes. "Cyrus mentioned he'd swing by later… but for him, 'later' could mean any time from now until midnight. I don't know if I'll last that long."

Since *Eclipsis,* Elias Mage's personal inbox, interview requests, and professional orders had barely given him a moment's rest. He was logging in less often because he felt he was reaching a breaking point. Having chatted with Cyrus about it over a couple of beers, the sociable cyborg had stressed the wisdom of Elias taking on an apprentice. "Your musical career has exploded, so now's the time to focus on it," Cyrus had commented. "You've also got a VR wedding to plan now, too. While we both know you're quite capable of handling several projects at once, this is one too many, my good man."

Elias nodded. "I guess you're right. I'll need to write up an advertisement."

"Say, did you know the Pulse has hired an artist to add your album cover to its eastern wall? Can't get away from your avatar symbol these days."

The skeleman stretched and walked outside, standing on his workshop steps to admire the sunset. The soft orange radiance tinted his golden frame. The leaves of the climbing vines trembled in a whispering breeze. Eli closed his eyes, relishing a rare moment of peace.

"Elias!"

Her voice – the one voice in the TerraWorks universe that did not result in a demonic grumble – gave him a start. He turned and re-entered his workshop. His tablet was on his desk, and above its screen hovered the live holographic video of Lightcross, prancing proudly around her hotel suite on Shiori Islands. "How about this, eh? What do you think?" Miniature Ean spread out her arms to indicate her glamorous surroundings.

Eli sat in his leather chair, affecting indifference. "Nice place to visit. Wouldn't want to live there." He rested his fingerbones together, eyeing her roguishly.

"Like Hades you wouldn't. Your tastes are significantly more extravagant than mine." Ean sat on the edge of the oversized bed, quilted with delicate silver fabric. "Sorry I didn't message you before now, but I was so excited to get here, I figured it would be better if I settled in first. My brain's like a wild stallion on the run. What are you up to?"

"Just finishing up with some clients. I owed them for making them wait until after *Eclipsis.*"

"Why don't you take on an apprentice artificer? Let him run the shop for you."

"Yes, that suggestion has been made. I started planning the advertisement right before you streamed."

Ean nodded, merrily brushing her bare feet against the carpet. "Good, good. The training itself won't be a picnic, I guess, but you'll be much better off once that part is over."

"How's the crown holding up, my lady?" he questioned, gesturing toward the gleaming circlet settled above Ean's brows. She colored slightly, reaching up to adjust it. "It's so light that I forget I'm wearing it, so I love that. But… I have to admit, I wish it was just a good old-fashioned engagement ring. Maybe I wouldn't get stared at so often."

Elias chuckled and shook his skull. "Trust me, it wouldn't help. Your face and avatar symbol are both all over TerraWiki. Look at this; somebody even merged our symbols together." Elias hit a few buttons on his tablet screen, dragging and dropping a small HI into Ean's background. The skull and rose symbol for Elias Mage now had Ean's double cross engraved on the frontal bone. Tiny, thorny stems curled around the cross, bursting with rosebuds. "Hey, that's really cool," Ean exclaimed. "You know what we should do?"

"What's that, my dear?"

"When we get married, we should keep it short and sweet. No long speeches. Let's just change both our avatar symbols to this one. 'The twain shall become one,' etc. etc."

Elias stroked his mandible. "Are we permitted to do that?"

"Well, you have to pay a fee, but you can change your avatar symbol as many times as you want. And there's no way accidental duplicates between avatars aren't already out there. We'll just be doing it on purpose, to… you know, reflect on our oneness."

Eli's gaze smiled warmly. "I think that's an excellent idea. Just wish I'd thought of it first."

"Hey, I can't let you have *all* the good ideas, Eli."

"I guess not."

They shared a brief, pleasant silence. Ean continued to brush her feet against the carpet. "Have you seen the Shiori Track yet?" Elias added.

She tossed her long, rosy hair and smiled broadly. "Only by proxy. I *cannot* wait for the night races! It's the greatest dark coaster in all of Terra, so they say. Also, rumor has it that they're going to be playing one of your songs at the opening. Don't suppose that has anything to do with me at all," she added, patting her diadem.

Elias yawned. "What a vain idea. Are you training with a flight coach?"

"Not going to. I've gotten this far without one, and I expect Piragor will jump at the chance to be my training partner."

Elias stiffened. "He's not the hapless bastard who's always trying to corner you, is he?"

Ean laughed at the skeleman's acidity. "No, that would be Lurid. He'd have to kiss my pale elven feet to be invited here, and even after that, I'd expect him to fetch my meals and clean my hotel rooms for nothing."

"What about Knightmoor? She'd make a decent training partner."

"Yes, she's very good, too. I just have a solid bond with Piragor. We're friends as well as competitors, so I don't have to be afraid that he might sabotage me out of spite, or something. I can trust him."

Elias hesitated. "You're certain Knightmoor wouldn't be a better choice?"

Ean looked confused at first, then burst into giggles. "Elias Jacoby Mage, you're *jealous!*"

"Am not!" The skeleman's cheekbones gleamed. "I've studied all the finalists' flight patterns. Knightmoor is solid. Piragor tends to react on impulse, just like you do. I think you should train with a steady partner to minimize your weaknesses."

"I love it when you blush," Ean breathed (causing him to blush all the more). "Thanks for the advice, Elias, but I think I've been racing long enough to know whom I should train with. Knightmoor is steady, as you've aptly noticed. But if you want to win, you need to trust your instincts. It was risky for me to kneel into aerodynamic position before that turn was completed, but that's how I beat Piragor. I wouldn't be here today if I wasn't a little impulsive, you know?"

Eli shrugged. "Understood. It's your race, Ean. Anyway, I wanted to say that I'm really proud of you. It's flattering to see my name linked with one of SkyRate's best racers."

"Are you kidding?" Ean laughed. "Gods, I wish I could snatch up a transport gem and kiss you! You're the most popular avatar in Terra-Works. Seriously, look it up if you don't believe me. Your name and the Spectral Tyrants are everywhere. I'm just a teeny drop in the bucket compared to you."

"Stop making me blush!" Elias grabbed a book from his desk and hid his face behind it. "By the gods, Lightcross. It's those eyes of yours. I've still never seen anything remotely close to them, all my gem infusions included."

"And I still don't understand your monomania for them… but I'll count it as a blessing in my case."

Elias peeked from his impromptu safeguard. He faltered an instant, then declared, "Ocumancy."

"Sorry, ocu-whatmancy?"

"Ocumancy. You're familiar with ancient palmistry, I assume? When a witch examines the palm of your hand, and can tell you things about yourself from the depth and arrangement of its lines?"

"Yeah, I think I've seen that in some old books or movies. So, ocumancy is…"

"Reading and interpreting the limbal ring, the iris, and the pupil. One might call this ability the secret weapon of the skeletal avatars. I can read a character's skills. I can also determine whether or not they can be affected by magic, or are currently under enchantment."

"Oh." Ean pondered this notion. "Naturally, you know what I have to ask you now. What did you notice when you first saw me?"

Elias put down the book, inhaling a quick breath. "Honestly, that's difficult to explain, but I'll do my best. As I said, I've never seen eyes like yours. Most avatars (including me) have a smooth, unbroken limbal ring, and what I refer to as a torpid iris. There are two uniform levels of pigmentation throughout it, neatly melded, and the pupils' dilation or contraction is quite subtle. Are you with me so far?"

"Yes, I think so. Go on." Ean propped her chin in her hands.

"In your case, these regularities are reversed. Your limbal ring is electric. Erratic streaks of deeper blue contrast against the ice-blue base. Your iris – far from being torpid – takes on a white, reflective quality in certain lights or moods, and a sparkling caerulean in others. What I found most fascinating, however, was the extreme sensitivity (or reactiveness) of your pupils. They shift with every change of the light, no matter how elusive the change is."

Ean's smile increased with Eli's enthusiasm. "Well, I try not to admit this to a lot of people… I don't wish to be called out for my vanity… but I commissioned my avatar's design from a freelance designer. I asked her to pay special attention to the eyes. I wanted my avatar to stand out, but not so much that the other players would notice it right away."

"Dare I ask how much you paid for that?"

"Can't risk telling you. You'd probably faint."

"At any rate, it paid off. You caught my attention. I remember glancing across the audience, and feeling two sparks of ice-blue energy devouring me from the gloom. When I used the term *electric* to describe your eyes, I meant it in the fullest sense of the word. Your whole countenance seemed to snap with electricity."

Ean nodded. "I've always been fond of music, but I'd never been quite so deeply affected before. That brings me to another question I've been dying to ask you, Eli." She paused, nervously biting her lip. "You'll be honest with me, right?"

"Of course. Ask me anything."

"Do you infuse your microphones with enchantments?"

Elias cleared his unseen throat, then nodded slowly. "I do."

"What kind of spellcraft do you use?"

He tapped his fingerbones together, indicating his philosophical mode. "I use one of two recipes. The first, which you are extremely susceptible to, transfers my own energy, enthusiasm, and passion to the audience. It works them up, so to speak. The second is reserved for quieter songs, like the 'Ballad of Helios.' It generates a placid, comforting state of mind. To put it simply, Ean, I'm gathering my own intimate feelings and sensations when I sing, and passing them onto the audience. No more, and no less."

"And there's no TerraDome rules against doing that?"

"None at all. Casting spells directly is against the rules, of course, but artificer craft is much more subtle, and is permitted in the form of prop enhancements. I used it to design the skull mechanism in *Eclipsis,* as well."

"Thanks for telling me, Eli. But why do you keep it a secret?"

"Because that's an essential part of the concert experience. If you went to see a famous magician, but you knew all of his tricks, would his show even be worth seeing?"

"No, I guess it wouldn't." Ean lifted her head from her hands and smiled. "Well, that's certainly fascinating. But why didn't I react to the second 'recipe' you used? I recall staring at the lethargic audience around me, wondering what in Terra was going on. I was still so fired-up from your opening song, I could barely stand still."

"Ah, that's where ocumancy comes into play. Once you removed your glasses, I could read what magic you were (or weren't) susceptible to. You're highly sensitive to any spellcraft which heightens your energy, or raises your performa level. In a word, you're passionate. Conversely, you're hardly affected at all by magic that would subdue you or lull you into a slumber. Again, in one word: you're tenacious." He chuckled, leaning back in his chair. "A passionate and tenacious woman appears to be my weakness."

It was Ean's turn to blush. Elias admired the pink bloom creeping up her pointed ears. "I miss you, my dear."

"I miss you, too."

A knock resounded against Eli's workshop door. "Anybody in?" Cyrus cried. Elias groaned in childish dismay. "Cyrus asked if he could stop by and indulge in a fireside beer or two. I guess this is goodnight?"

"I may log back in if I feel my ears burning," Ean warned him.

"You'd better wrap them in ice, then."

"Mage!"

"Lightcross!"

She smiled. "I love you, Eli. Goodnight!"

12

ENIGMATIC ANDROGYNOUS NEUROPSYCHOSIS

SkyRate's Shiori Track was a colossal assembly of purple, black, and silver levitation tracks. They all gradually curved upward, stacking on top of one another, or at times entwining into an enormous knot like octopus legs. Once the competitors reached the highest point, the track careened back down, guiding them into a dizzying one-hundred-seventy-degree freefall. This section of the track rendered the "Shiori dive" the most perilous endeavor in TerraWorks skyboarding. Collisions were inevitable.

Ean Lightcross was training with Piragor, hollering with elation through the corkscrews and double loops. As she approached the Shiori dive, she heeled the brakes to stop and look over the side. "Damn, Piragor! It's even scarier in person than it was on the holomap." Her maniacal chuckle implied that she was far more delighted than intimidated. "Watch me tackle this monstrosity." She kicked the reverse lever and whizzed backward, her lengthy ponytail flying amuck.

Piragor also shifted into reverse, speeding up to coast alongside her. "You're on! Loser orders dine-in at the hotel?"

"Done."

"Dessert included!"

Ean spluttered. "Goes without saying. Are you ready?"

"Are you?" Piragor revved his skyboard engine. The two miscreants shot forward like bullets from a gun. Whooping, they lifted their hands in the air as they soared downward, wind watering their eyes and tearing at their skycraft uniforms. The end of the dive shot into a tunnel, glowing with neon-purple arrows. Their gleeful shrieks rebounded through the underpass.

Impeccably synchronized, the two knelt into aerodynamic position and zipped over the finish line. "My gods, what a rush!" Piragor yelled, pumping the brakes. "Let's do that again!"

Lightcross decelerated, eyeing Piragor impishly. "I guess we'll have to, since that race was a draw. I do *love* a shrimp cocktail."

They resumed starting position. "Wait a moment," Piragor requested, dismounting. Ean followed suit and rose a questioning brow. "What is it?"

"I never properly thanked you for inviting me." Piragor extended his hand. "Experiencing the Shiori Track is once-in-a-lifetime stuff. Seriously, thank you."

Ean smiled and gestured for a fist bump instead. "Dude, we're friends. Who else would I have invited to train with me?"

Piragor settled his tangled blond hair with a laugh. "Lurid, of course. You two would have gotten along *so* well!" He ducked Ean's mock punch. "I'm just glad to be here. I hope you know that I'm rooting for you with all my heart."

Something in his tone denoted a faint but undeniable tenderness. Ean flushed and jumped back onto her skyboard. "It's getting late, and I'm hungry. Let's go!"

They raced a few more times before retiring to the hotel. Piragor – having lost one more race than Ean did – ordered them dinner, and the two chatted and joked over shrimp cocktails and seafood baskets. Afterward, they sauntered onto the balcony with drinks and dessert, admiring the starlight mirrored in the ocean waves.

Lightcross heaved a deep sigh of contentment, kicking off her boarding boots and lighting a magenta smoke. "This has been a day for the books," she commented. "If only Elias was here, I'd be perfectly happy."

"Speak of the devil," Piragor mentioned, lighting an ebony smoke himself, "when is the wedding?" Ean shrugged and exhaled a bright pink cloud. "We haven't settled on a date yet. I'd rather enjoy being engaged for a while, you know? It still seems like a dream to me."

"It's kind of odd for me, too," Piragor admitted, stealing a low glance. "You've always been so adamant that you'd never date (much less marry) in TerraWorks. What made you change your mind?"

Ean indulged in a few more thoughtful puffs before answering. "Well, I'd love to look all philosophical and shit with a profound, insightful answer. But it's the same as any other romantic affair. He fascinates me. I've never met anybody else like him. I'd venture he'd say the same about me, since he never wanted to date in VR, either."

"Pardon the old expression, but you *are* quite a catch," Piragor averred. "I'm sure half the population of TerraWorks would date you if they could."

Ean shrugged off the compliment. "That's just because I'm linked to a famous name now. Most avatars crave to be in the spotlight, even if it's just for a little while before some other couple is trending. I don't read too much into my fans' love letters."

Piragor forced a laugh. "You're still getting them?"

"Oh, yes. Marriage isn't taken very seriously in TerraWorks, though. It stands to reason that engagements wouldn't be, either."

"But *you're* serious about it, right?"

Ean leaned her head back, smiling, gazing earnestly at the stars. "Damn straight."

After Piragor had logged off for the night, Ean brushed her hair and rummaged around the suite, reorganizing some of her things. *I guess Eli's instincts about Piragor were right.* She colored with embarrassment as she recalled Piragor's pointed remarks. *Well, as long as I make sure we eat in public from now on, there shouldn't be a problem.* He was a good-looking avatar with plenty of people asking him out; it wasn't as if his dating pool was in short supply. No, this was a temporary bump in their friendship that would smooth over. She felt certain of it.

Ean changed into her burgundy robe and pinged Elias for a Livewire chat. The notification chimed repeatedly with no response. "Strange," Ean muttered. "I told him I'd be calling about now. I wonder what he's up to?"

"I'm sure there's no need to worry," Hex interjected. "If his post for a new apprentice was answered, he may be conducting interviews."

"That's true." Still, the timing was oddly coincidental, and Ean couldn't ease her sense of discomfort. "I shouldn't have had dinner with Piragor in my own suite. Nothing happened, but it still wasn't smart for me to do. Damn, why didn't I think of that before?"

"You do tend to be impulsive, Ean-san."

"Yeah, no shit." Grumbling, Ean flung herself onto the bed. "Guess I might as well log off. Tell Elias goodnight for me, Hexy."

"Will do. Goodnight, Ean-san."

"Later, Hex."

Ean's frustration multiplied as several days went by with only casual, fleeting contact from Elias. His apparent nonchalance annoyed her. However, the resulting aggravation fueled her energy, propelling her through the Shiori Track with a speed and precision that astounded even Piragor.

"How the track is *not* consumed with flames after that run-through, I have no idea," he proclaimed, gaping at the holographic stop watch. Lightcross snapped her board into an abrupt halt, banking sharply to avoid sailing into Piragor.

He stared at Ean while she panted hard. "Sorry to mention it, Ean, but you seem to be fuming a little today. Everything OK?"

The half-elf paused, debating whether or not to confide in him. His keen, sympathetic green eyes shattered her resistance. "It's Elias. We haven't spoken much since I arrived here. I can't help but wonder if he's upset with me for some reason."

"Why would he be upset with you?"

"I have no idea."

She did, however, have *some* idea – the prospective issue was standing right in front of her. "I'm sure he's just busy, Ean," Piragor reassured her. "He gets fan mail, campaign invites, and artificer orders. Every columnist for TerraWiki is scrambling to book an interview with him. On top of all that, he's got your wedding to think about. Personally, I'd hold off on worrying unless he stopped initiating any communication at all."

Ean exhaled a quick breath of relief. "You're right. It's silly for me to be worried. Want to swing through the track with me this time?"

"Sure. Want to do yourself a favor?"

"Huh?"

"Pretend that you're still upset. You race much better that way. Your turns are tighter, and you brake with… I don't know… *determination.*" He distributed a mock scowl and threw his arms akimbo in comic imitation. Ean laughed. "So, you're saying I have a better chance of winning if I road-rage?"

"Call me crazy, but I think you do."

Nevertheless, Piragor beat her that time around. She shook hands with him before they dismounted and walked out through the SkyRate lockers. "Your new board is wicked, by the way," Piragor enthused. He surveyed its deep red and purple coloration, alternating in gradual flashes, with the black double cross shimmering in the center. "Did you customize the matching boots, too?"

"Yeah. My days of skyboarding rentals are finally over." Ean stomped across the sidewalk with heady satisfaction. "Want to have lunch in the hotel restaurant? Reportedly, their handmade pizzas are a Terran delight."

"Gladly. But, do my eyes deceive me? Is that Elias over there?" He pointed.

"What? Where?" Ean eagerly followed the direction of Piragor's forefinger. Sure enough, a broad skeleman in a leather jacket and embellished jeans stood below the bleachers, leaning against the supports. His midnight eyes were watching them with a faintly amused expression. "Eli!" she shouted, sprinting into his outstretched arms. "How did you get here? And when?"

"A few minutes ago. I borrowed a transport gem from Byron, though it cost me a hefty bribe." Ean's prior frustration melted away as Elias nuzzled her affectionately. "I couldn't wait any longer to see you."

Ean rested her head against his ribcage. "Did you see us race just now?"

"I did. Gods, you were nothing but a blur! I teased you about your board's rave vibes, but now I'm glad it's so bright. It'll be easier to keep track of you."

Piragor cleared his throat and extended a hand to Elias. "Awesome to meet you in person, Elias. You're a verified TerraWorks legend."

"Thank you." Elias shook hands cordially. "And thank you for looking after Ean. She sang your praises as her only true friend among the SkyRate competitors."

"I fear that's no exaggeration," Piragor chuckled. "SkyRate rivalry tends to be pretty stiff. Well," beginning to shuffle away, "I'll let you two catch up. See you in the restaurant, Ean. You want pepperoni, right?"

"Right. Thanks."

Piragor departed. The second his form vanished behind the restaurant doors, Elias pulled Ean deeper beneath the bleachers until they were masked by shadows. "I thought he'd stay the whole time," the skeleman murmured, playfully nipping her earlobe. "Would you have kissed me anyway, Lightcross?"

"Most likely, yes." She tucked her hands into his jacket pockets as she kissed him. "Mmm," he breathed, slipping his hands around her waist. "Gods, I've missed you."

Ean pulled away to pout. "Then why have you been so distant this week? Why didn't you answer my Livewire calls?"

"My apologies, my dear. I've had a lot to do at the shop. On the upside, next time you visit, I can introduce you to my new apprentice."

"Oh, great! You've put him (or her) to work already?"

"He's called Tirion. He's completing a flame infusion to a quiver of arrows as we speak. Elementary, but helpful. I won't have to spend so much time on rudimentary orders."

"Thank the Terran Pantheon for that."

"Indeed." Eli's gilt fingers drifted through her red hair. "Actually, I planned to take you to lunch today. Do you think Piragor would expire from loneliness if we ditched him?"

"I'm sure he'd understand. He knows I've been missing you." She relayed a brief message to Hex, explaining the change of plans to Piragor. "Message sent," Hexadecimal relayed.

Ean slid her hand into Eli's as they returned to the sunlight. "Where should we go?"

"How about my house? Byron's emerald still has some juice left in it."

Ean nudged Elias with her elbow. "Yeah, we'll definitely be eating if we go *there*, right?"

Her fiancé widened his dark eyes. "Whatever do you mean? What else would we be doing, pray tell?" He started to tickle her. Ean squirmed away, laughing, and the couple chased each other down the street.

At the restaurant window, Piragor lifted the curtain to watch them. A short, barely-audible sigh escaped his lips. "At least she's happy with him. It's still weird, though. I mean… he's a *skeleton.*"

13

THE INITIATION RACE

"Humans, half-bloods, and creatures all, welcome to the Tournament of Champions Initiation Race!"

The Shiori Track bleachers were packed. The audience rose to their feet, cheering wildly as fireworks exploded over the open-air stadium. The levitation tracks flashed red and blue as they were set for the first nighttime race. A loud, consistent whirring signaled the competitors' approach, and the crowds leapt with excitement as the racers sped into view above them. "Right up front in blue, we give you Gale Emodicus, two-time winner of the Helios City Tournament!"

Gale's fans chanted his name, pounding their radiant azure staffs against the floor. "In green, we present Phyline Silverthorne from this year's Klad Kingdom Tournament!"

Several bright green banners glowed in response. One after another, the racers were announced as they tore across the sky. Rockets exploded above them in the shape of their avatar symbol. Many of them showed off for their fans with elaborate tricks and corkscrew turns. Elias waited patiently for his half-elf beauty, gilt-bone arms crossed, eyes keenly scanning each throbbing skyboard.

"And now, please welcome Ean Lightcross, our latest victor from the TerraWorks City Tournament!"

United by their rousing cries, Ean's fans held up flashing double crosses in red or purple. "Marry me, Ean!" somebody shouted. Elias expressed his feelings with a snort. The Tournament MC laughed. "No doubt about it, folks! Lightcross has the crowds tonight. Officially affianced to the lead singer of the Spectral Tyrants, Elias Mage, there's been more than a few articles extolling Ean's honors lately. Say, when's the wedding, Lightcross?"

Ean's lithe, dark figure held her arms aside in a wide shrug, provoking laughter from the audience. The MC continued, "Well, looking forward to hearing the news soon! Our racers are positioned for the opening ceremony. Let the Tournament Initiation begin!"

A dizzying plethora of fireworks embellished the sky. The stadium's speakers burst with heavy metal – a hit from the Spectral Tyrants – and the skyboard racers arranged themselves into an intricate design. They took turns soaring across it in rigid patterns. Ean broke formation once to fly over Elias and blow him a kiss. Elias saluted her, his eyes smiling in response, while the crowds shouted their approval.

Piragor appeared at Eli's side. "Hey, man. Mind if I join you?"

Elias shrugged. "Don't see why not."

"Thanks. You got this, Ean!" her training partner cheered, raising a fist in the air. Ean held up her fist in response, then directed her board back into formation.

"So, does winning (or losing) this race contribute to their scores?" Elias asked Piragor.

Piragor shook his head. "The Initiation just pumps up the audience, and it gives the racers their first taste of the Shiori Track as competitors.

It's not going to count. However, it'll give everyone a good indication of who has their act together, and who's not looking so good."

"Mmm."

Piragor glanced at the intimidating avatar beside him. Elias fingered his mandible, lost in contemplation. His solemn eyes reflected the fireworks. The blue-white gleam of the stadium lights danced across the gems embedded in his golden skull. *I guess he's handsome in his own way. If you like monsters.*

"How do you think she'll do?" the skeleman asked next.

"I'm guessing she'll place third. Her biggest problems are going to be Emodicus and Silverthorne. Emodicus has the most experience on the Shiori Track, since he's placed in the Tournament of Champions before. He's going to be especially determined to win. And Silverthorne is pretty much the last word in textbook skycraft form. Ean is going to have a hard time keeping up with her."

"Understood." Elias swept through his inventory and extracted his tablet. Opening the tournament streaming app, he spoke "Lightcross" into the entrant search bar. A holographic projection of Ean sparkled above the tablet screen. She was settling into launch position, eyes narrow and focused, lips firmly set. Silverthorne coasted into place beside her. "Best of luck, Lightcross," the elf said, nodding.

"Best of luck." Ean returned her rival's nod and drew in a deep breath. *"This is for you, Elias."*

The holographic starting gate vanished with a bang. A colossal rush ensued as the competitors slammed into full throttle. "Yeah! Let's go, girl!" Piragor screamed, accidentally punching Elias in his excitement. "Keep it steady! Stay in the middle!"

Ean held her position at fifth, a wide smile of enjoyment plastered across her face. She cut the first turn with grace, hugging the inside line and watching her back. "Good, good!" Piragor cried. "You're starting strong! Keep it going!"

Elias glimpsed at him with slight annoyance. Piragor continued to shout encouragement and cheer loudly, regardless of the fact that Ean couldn't possibly hear him. "OK, start picking it up! You need to secure third position. Aim for third and hold it until you can cut Silverthorne!"

Just then, as if she *could* hear him, Ean began to pick up speed. A wicked corkscrew series dubbed the Devil's Gate loomed ahead. Fearless, Lightcross continued to accelerate, despite the fact that everyone else was braking. Piragor broke into a sweat. "Careful, careful! Don't be rash! Keep your heel on the brake!"

Ean braked at the last possible second, the nose of her board wobbling uncertainly for a few seconds. She grabbed fourth place. "Excellent! Hold it steady!" Piragor yelled. Elias, glued to the tablet's projection, ground his teeth with repressed suspense. The racers soared over the flashing red and blue tracks, their figures blurred into a confusing mob of color.

The skeleman's breathing accelerated. Two miniature suns burned on his cheekbones. "By the gods. You're incredible, Lightcross." He couldn't imagine traveling at such a deadly speed himself… yet his fiancé handled it like it was nothing.

"Darn right, she is." Piragor crowed with delight. He slapped Elias on the shoulder. "As long as nobody cuts her, she's definitely finishing in the top three. And that's what she needs to do."

"Right." Elias drew his sleeve across his cheekbones, trying to mask their flush. "It's really something, seeing a skyboard race in person. I can't believe I've been streaming all this time."

"Well, we get it. You're a busy man." Piragor shrugged, eagerly returning his attention to Ean's progress. "OK, this is the wide sailor's loop. She should be able to cut into third place here."

As Piragor had predicted, Emodicus was first, with Silverthorne riding on his heels. Vanderbuilt was in third, but Lightcross was gaining on him, eyeing him like an eagle preparing to dive-bomb its prey. "She's going to move in. And there… she… is!" Piragor punched the air victoriously as Ean banked ahead of Vanderbuilt. "Just as I thought. She's got a chance at winning the SkyRate Grand Championship! All right!"

The competitors were about to reach the infamous Shiori dive. Elias could practically feel Ean's anticipation throbbing through the holographic projection. She broke into a delirious ripple of laughter as she shot over the edge, careening downhill at a velocity that sent Eli's heartbeat into his neck. They entered the tunnel. "Keep steady here, Ean. Don't get crazy on us now!" Piragor begged, wringing his damp hands. "This is where things usually go wrong."

Ean Lightcross did *not* want to settle for third. While the other racers braked coming out of the tunnel, she carried her momentum forward, edging steadily toward Silverthorne. "Gods, no! You're way too close at that velocity. Brake, Ean! Brake!" Piragor groaned. "You've got to brake *now!* Oh, shit-"

It happened so quickly that no one was entirely sure how. The nose of Ean's board either brushed or caught on the back of her rival's. Silverthorne's board tipped upward, sending her spiraling out of control, and Ean crashed to the side. Her skyboard exploded in a wave of red and purple sparks.

"My Gods!" Shocked, Elias stared in horror at the projection of Ean's feeble, crushed form. Her body was lying motionless against the siderails. *"Ean!"*

"Dude, it's OK!" Piragor seized his arm, trying to slow his own panicked breathing. "It's VR, man. It's VR. She's going to vanish in a minute, then wake up at the Shiori main hospital."

Elias braced himself against the bleachers. "Thank the gods. I'd forgotten." His ribcage expanded with a deep, thankful breath, and every bone in his frame trembled. "I'd forgotten. My dear, insane Ean Lightcross, what were you *thinking?"*

"That's what I'd like to know." Piragor grunted and crossed his arms. "Third place is perfectly acceptable for the Initiation. She should have known better than to push herself. She'll still be considered viable for the win; but she can't afford to pull a stunt like that twice."

As they watched, Ean's body shimmered and dissolved. "What hospital did you say she'd be at?" Elias demanded, standing up.

"The Shiori main hospital. I've got a couple of transport gems with me, if you need to borrow one."

"Yes, I do. I appreciate it."

"No problem, Eli."

Lightcross woke to the mumble of low, critical voices. She stared at the white ceiling in confusion. Her HP status floated into view, indicating a measly 1 HP. "Oh, shit."

"An appropriate phrase for the occasion."

Blinking, she turned her head to face Elias, who was glaring down at her with his bone-plated arms folded. "I'd like to thank you for giving me the biggest scare in my whole gods-forsaken life. You're really something, aren't you?"

"Or something." Ean smiled sweetly into her fiancé's irritable demeanor. "I just need a healing gem or a potion, and I'll be all fixed up." As she spoke, a hospital android approached her with the aforementioned objects. She accepted the potion, paid the nominal fee, and absorbed it in one enormous gulp. "See? I'm good as new!" she chirruped, leaping off the bed and stretching her limbs. "No need to glare at me anymore, Eli."

Elias sighed, gathering her into his arms and sitting on the edge of the hospital mattress. "I've never been so terrified in my life," he confessed, cradling her on his knees. "*Please,* don't ever try that again. I'll wring your neck."

"But I wanted to win!" Ean kissed his cheekbone. "I appreciate your concern, but you know my policy about taking risks. If I don't try, I'll spend the rest of my skycraft career wondering if I should have tried. And the Initiation race doesn't count, you know."

Piragor entered the room with a few bottles of mineral water. "Ah, the scoundrel is awake. Did you give her a scolding, Elias?"

"I tried to. But I can't seem to keep up my rage." Elias cuddled her shamelessly, emitting a low growl. "She's very cute, especially when she's at my mercy."

Piragor distributed the bottles among them. "I guess all's well that ends well," he muttered. "Just don't try that again, OK? Crashing is *not* an option from here on out."

"Yes, yes, I know!" Ean waved her hand impatiently. "It was fun. Besides, it's exciting for the crowd when there's a crash. The HV viewings will go up. I'll be known as 'the daring one,' and I'll probably have even more fans now."

Elias resumed his glare. "You planned this beforehand, didn't you?"

"Maybe." Ean wrapped her arms around his neck and batted her lashes. "You'll never be able to prove it, though."

The skeleman's frame rumbled with his dark laughter. He touched his forehead to hers. "At any rate, I demand recompense for the shock I've endured. I'll have to take you back to the hotel and oversee your full recovery."

"Dammit. How inconvenient."

Piragor made a discreet exodus as Ean gave Elias a passionate kiss. Elias leaned over her, running his golden hand along the thigh of her skin-tight SkyRate uniform. "We should probably... go... now."

"I'm busy." Ean pushed his jacket off. She traced her fingers along the outline of his chest. Elias sighed with pleasure. "Yep... we need to leave."

14

OF CERTAIN SHORTCOMINGS

"Elias, sir? I'm sorry to bother you, but I can't seem to get this transport gem right."

The skeleman looked up from his desk. "I'll check it in a minute."

"Thank you, sir."

"And you needn't call me *sir*. Just Eli will do."

"OK, Eli. Thanks." Tirion grinned and began to dust and sort the shelves. Elias heaved an inaudible sigh of fatigue. Ean's next race was tomorrow morning, but the Spectral Tyrants were shooting him message after message, wanting to know when their next practice session would be. They were booked to play at the Klad Castle courtyard next month. Time was closing in like a rampaging beast.

Elias logged into his messaging app to compose instructions for the Spectral Tyrants. *Jam session tomorrow night at eight P.M. TerraDome Studio 12. Travis, you'd better show up on time, or I'm going to eat you.*

Message sent, Eli furtively unlocked and drew open his desk drawer. Inside lay a slender green needle next to a half-full vial of zombie venom. The skeleman gave his implements a long, hard look, then slowly closed the drawer again. "OK, Tirion. Let's take a look at that transport gem. Are you having trouble balancing the infusion itself?"

"Yes, that's it. It doesn't seem to be taking."

"You need to watch your timing. If you combine the recipe too quickly, the ingredients will be merged before you've finished speaking the incantation for them. Patience is the key." Elias deftly mixed the potion, and poured it over the dull, lifeless jewel while murmuring the phrases of the transport spell. The gem flashed with color, taking on the verdant facets of an emerald. "There. That's what it should look like when it's done."

"Thanks, Eli!"

"Don't mention it."

The notification chime sang from Eli's tablet. He crossed back over to his desk and snatched it up, leaning back in his chair. *All's fair in jam sessions and Travis for dinner. Congrats to your girlfriend, by the way. She's all over TerraWiki thanks to that little stunt she pulled. – Ollie*

"Fiancé, not girlfriend," Elias muttered. "Not that you miscreants would know the difference."

"Sorry, did you say something?" Tirion hollered from the work table.

"Just talking to myself," Eli replied with a shrug. "You'll have to get used to hearing the occasional incoherent mutterings."

Tirion laughed. "No problem."

Hesitating for a moment, Elias commanded his tablet to open a new document and labeled it *Wedding*. He stared at the blinking cursor for a long time, an abnormally blank expression reflecting in his eyes. *Come on, Elias, think. You've got to start getting some ideas down, at least.*

Nothing. His skull echoed with meaningless images and gibberish. The skeleman groaned and touched his temporal bones. "I've got to get out of here. Tirion, can you close up shop for me before you log off?"

"Sure thing, Eli. Have a good evening."

"You too." Checking to be certain Tirion was occupied, Elias thrust his hand into the drawer and pulled out the needle and vial. "See you tomorrow."

He knew precisely where he'd go. While striding down several quiet streets, Elias opened his inventory to don a large, loose-fitting cloak. He extracted the vial's contents into his needle, carefully tapping it to remove any air bubbles, and injected the venom into the marrow behind his bite mark.

As Elias traveled the back street, cobblestone became dirt pathway. The pathway dissolved into a dim, wooded clearing, burbling with the soothing sounds of a fledgling waterfall. Elias sat cross-legged in the grass, breathing deeply with exhilaration and relief as the venom began to take effect. *I should get plenty of ideas now.*

Stretching his hands behind his skull, Elias lay on the ground and watched the starlight and planets wobbling overhead. He closed his black eyelids.

Visions of screaming audiences, skyboard crashes, and whispered songs crashed through his mind. He could feel Ean leaning over him, nestling against him, warming his cold frame with her body. *"Elias,"* she breathed, bending her head down to his clavicle...

"Elias?"

Wait... did somebody say his name?

Elias dragged his heavy eyelids open. "Cyrus? That you?"

The battle cyborg towered above him. "Yeah, man. What in Hades are you doing out here?"

Elias tried to prop himself up, but – submitting to the full grip of the venom – found it quite impossible to achieve. He fell back onto the grass with a resounding laugh. "I'm surfing. What does it look like?"

"Thought skeleton avatars couldn't get drunk." Cyrus knelt to extend an arm around Eli's ribcage. "Let me help you up."

"No, no. I'm very comfortable here. I needed an ideas session."

Cyrus rose a silver eyebrow. "So, I take it you *can* get drunk, after all?"

"I'm not drunk. Haven't had a drop all day. Hey, a smoke would just hit the spot, though. Got any ebony Whiskers, buddy?"

Cyrus shrugged and extracted one from his inventory. "Why not. You look like you're settling in for a grand old time. Why are you out here by yourself?"

"I told you; I'm here for the harvest. Those golden apples grow too damned high."

Cyrus shook with laughter and lit an ebony smoke for himself. "Well, if it doesn't bother you, I'll just sit here with you until you emerge from whatever-the-Hades state of mind you're in. If I didn't know any better, I'd say you've been visited by your zombie pals again. But I see you still just have the one bite mark." The cyborg examined it with interest, exhaling wreathes of black smoke. "Can't you buff it out, or something?"

"I like it. It's like a tattoo, but cooler." Elias gripped his cigarette between his golden teeth. "Ean likes it, too."

A crafty sparkle entered the cyborg's yellow eyes. "Thinking of the lady love, are we? Is that why you're out here alone? Trouble in paradise, mayhap?"

"Shows how much *you* know." Elias managed to sit up, huffing his derision. "We're getting along very well, Cyrus Agillus."

"Mighty glad to hear it." Cyrus slapped the skeleman on his shoulder blade, inadvertently knocking him back down. "Sorry. You two are madly in love, then?"

Elias didn't respond. "Did you pass out, Eli?" Cyrus queried, leaning over him. The gilt skeleton shook his skull. "It's just an odd phrase, you know. 'Madly in love.' *Madly.* Is true love only madness? Is it monomania? An unrealistic, dramatic fixation that will shatter when the veil of virtual reality is torn in two? What will happen when we enter the holiest of holies? Will the Terran gods strike us down for our presumption?"

"You're talking like a sphinx, Eli. Are you sure you're all right? Maybe you need to log off. Get some rest."

Another long pause supervened. Elias sighed and sat up again. "Shame it doesn't last longer. I'll have to increase the dosage next time."

Cyrus blinked. "What are you talking about?"

Elias faced him with a placid expression. "Oh, it's just a little experiment I'm conducting. It's best if I remain the sole test subject. Care to return to town with me?"

Cyrus stood up and helped Elias stand, also. "I'm going to log off. We've been training for the next phase of the Undead Campaign, and I'm beat. I'll see you around, OK?"

"Goodnight, Cyrus."

The cyborg stalked away, whistling a cheerful tune. Elias stared into the glistening waterfall. His dark eyes narrowed. "It's getting to be too much again. I'll have to ask Ean to..." Tapering off, Elias dissolved his spent Whisker and invoked the home screen to log off.

"On my count."

Elias snapped his fingers four times. The Spectral Tyrants launched into their warm-up instrumental, rattling the studio walls with raw intensity. Eli nodded to the beat, pulling up a metal chair and relaxing while the band practiced. He stole a glance at the time posted above the door, his aspect brimming with impatience. *She's usually early. What's taking so long?*

A firm knock calmed his nerves. "I'm here!" Ean's clear voice reported. "Lightcross is in the house!" The half-elf entered the studio, trailing the scent of warm Shiori winds and confidence in her wake. "Thanks for inviting me, Eli."

The skeleman stood up as she came in. Gesturing for the band to continue, Eli took her hand and marched her right back out the door into the hallway. "What gives?" She started to say, then smiled when she noticed the despotic spark in his pupils. "Oh."

Elias pinned her against the wall, holding her by the wrists. "You smell amazing." He buried his skull into her neck, breathing deeply, making her giggle. "Elias, that tickles!"

"You like it."

"Maybe." Her fingers brushed the gems on his cranium. "Just out of curiosity, are you ever going to go back to your original design?"

"Would you prefer it if I did?"

Ean shrugged. "Honestly, can't make up my mind. I love them both."

The skeleman leaned in for a kiss, but Ean ducked out of the way. "Just a minute, sir. I must know if you streamed my race this morning like I told you to!"

"Oh, yes. I was a good boy."

"Did you see I came in first against Vanderbuilt and Lois? And I didn't kill anybody, not even myself!"

"Delightful news, indeed."

"That means I'll be racing against Fenrah and Silverthorne next. I suspect that Silverthorne might try to massacre me, since I clipped her board at the Initiation... but otherwise, I'm feeling pretty good about it."

"Marvelous."

"Elias, are you listening?" Ean tapped his frontal bone. "You've got that far-off look right now. What are you thinking about?"

Elias stared into her eyes until she blushed. He released her wrists and stepped back to take off his shirt. The golden array of death's framework reflected the hall lights. "I need you to bite me again. Same place."

"Um… it's not that I mind, since you like it so much, but… what if somebody walks by?"

"So what? The entire Terran universe knows we're engaged."

"It's not that. It's just the whole biting thing. You have to admit it's a little weird."

"Nobody else is around right now. And it won't take long." Elias leaned in close, getting into her clothes to caress her in ways that made her dizzy. "Just once, Ean. Please?"

Ean complied, gradually increasing the pressure until Elias relaxed. "Thank you," he murmured, affectionately nipping her ear. "Guess I'd better put my shirt back on, eh?"

Ean tilted her glossy head. "You look wicked without one. I mean, you perform shirtless anyway. I doubt any of us are going to care."

"How true." Swinging his shirt over his shoulder blade, Elias re-entered the studio with Ean in tow. He snapped his fingers to get the band's attention. "Look alive, miscreants. I'm in the mood for 'Neuropsychosis.'"

"Yeah, baby!" Travis shouted, his were-cat eyes insanely dilated. "We're riding the same vibes, my man. Let's get Ean something to play!"

"Who, me?" Ean flushed and hid behind Elias. "I don't know how to play any instruments."

"You can play anything you want," Sindaya called out from behind her drum set. "Elias just needs to tweak our Dome Studio program. The point of TerraWorks performa is fluidity and charisma-building skills for every player, and that includes concerts."

"Which makes it much more challenging to stand out," Oleon added, devotedly stroking his bass guitar. "Gotta love that lowest common denominator. But, thanks to Elias, we don't have much of a problem making a dent in the musical world."

"And thanks to all of you," Elias added. "My particular thanks to Desmond, my backup singer." The auburn-haired elf bowed to Ean in introduction. "And the keyboard master is Kaspar. Sindaya commands the drums, Travis is on the guitar. That's Oleon on bass; he usually goes by Ollie."

"Hey." Ean grinned as they each hailed her with enthusiasm. "Well, if I get to pick what I play, I'd like to play the electric guitar, too. Is that OK, Travis?"

"Phantasmic. Just watch me and learn!" Travis posed dramatically with his guitar, earning an eyeroll from Ollie. "Don't be nervous, Lightcross. This will be a sinch."

A few minutes passed as Elias tweaked the program. Travis helped Ean choose a guitar. As the music began, Ean could sense her apprehensions dissolving. They stood in stage formation, and across from them, a holographic projection reflected their images like a mirror. Elias winked at her before growling the introduction into his microphone/staff.

"Oh, I almost forgot to tell you!" Travis yelled to Ean. "We all sing the bridge and the chorus, and we try to sound as drunk as possible. Got it?"

Ean burst into laughter. "Why?"

The were-cat smiled. "It's an old joke. Welcome to the Spectral Tyrants!"

15

THE LIGHTCROSS MANEUVER

E an tossed her hair as she evaluated the distance between herself and Silverthorne. Her rival had taken care not to give her any chances to steal the foremost position. The Shiori dive was approaching, and Lightcross knew it was now or never.

But first, the track's largest 360 loop would have to be conquered.

As the racers began their ascent, a scene from an archaic sci-fi movie popped into Ean's head. *Hmm. Far as I know, that wouldn't be against the rules.* As usual, her idea was risky, but it would be a much safer option than attempting to overtake Silverthorne on the Shiori dive. *Nothing ventured, nothing gained.*

Nodding firmly, Ean waited until she'd just passed the 180-degree point, then switched her board's magnetic adherence setting to *OFF.*

Freed from constraint, her skyboard lurched straight down. Ean struggled to regain control as it bounded beneath her feet. Winded, she aimed the skyboard's nose at the point where the loop levelled off. She kicked the magnetic adherence setting back *ON,* and exhaled in relief as she felt the pull of the levitation tracks righting her course. Hazarding a backward glance, she punched the air as she realized her trick had worked. "Yes!" she cried.

Her skyboard zipped past the bounding audience. Triumphant, Ean made the sign of a cross with her forefingers. Her fans thundered their support. Elias himself passed in a golden blur; the half-elf just barely caught a glimpse of his approving nod. Laughing, Ean knelt into aerodynamic position and tore down the Shiori dive, crossing the finish line that glowed red and purple to indicate her victory. The SkyRate MC also saluted her. "Thanks to another daring maneuver, Lightcross takes the win! She's won herself a place in the final!"

Ean coasted to a stop, waving to the onlookers. Piragor was the first of her friends to elbow his way through the stands. He pumped his fists in the air, yelling an incoherent something, his face fairly splitting apart with his elated smile. Ean chuckled and shot him a cheery salute.

The SkyRate MC noticed a tall, golden skeleman also making his way toward Lightcross. "Step aside, folks! Make way for the lovebirds!" Ean rolled her eyes, but Elias laughed, joyfully lifting her into his arms and twirling her 'round. "I'm *so* proud of you, Ean!" He placed her back on the ground, holding both of her hands in his.

"Don't get too excited, Eli. There's a 99.9% chance I'll be racing against Emodicus, and his skycraft skills are no joke."

"He's also a dark elf," Piragor shouted above the chanting audience. "They're a lethal combination of intrepid and agile. You'll need to spend every spare minute in training if you want to have a chance against him."

Ean grinned. "Sounds like fun." She slipped her arm around Eli's ribcage as they walked back to the track entryway. "I'm starving."

Her fiancé chuckled. "Didn't you eat before the race?"

"Nope. I learned pretty early into my SkyRate career that it's a terrible idea to do that."

Elias rested his arm around her shoulders. "What are you hungry for?"

Ean, jovial with success, darted Elias an evil smile. "Your soul."

"Afraid I haven't got one."

"A steak!"

"Too expensive. What do you think I am, made of gold or something?"

Ean prodded his gilt jaw, about to deliver a witty reply. She was interrupted by none other than Emodicus. The dark elf approached the pair with a suave, feline tread that earned admiring or intimidated glances from the avatars in his circumference. "Congratulations, Light-cross. You're a rival worthy of my steel." He faced Elias next. A faint shimmer of cool approbation lit his slanted, indigo eyes. "Elias Mage."

Elias grunted. "Emodicus."

Neither of them made a motion to shake hands. Ean's slanted brows lifted in amusement as she felt Eli's grip tighten on her shoulder, his protective instincts on override. "When's your semifinal?" Elias asked the dark elf.

"At the end of this week. I trust you'll both be there?"

"Certainly," Ean smiled, "We wouldn't miss it for love or money. Right, Eli?" She covertly distributed a pinch to one of his ribs: *Be nice!*

Elias flinched. "Looking forward. See you then, Emodicus."

The dark elf bowed and murmured his race's traditional farewell, *"Namyonet."*

Elias emitted a low growl as Emodicus strolled away. "I don't like him."

"What's the matter, Eli? Jealous?"

"In a way. He's a top-notch sorcerer."

"Emodicus?" Ean stared after his muscular form in surprise. "I had no idea. Then again, I've only read about him in the context of a SkyRate competitor."

"There's no doubt about it. He's also maxed out his combat level *and* charisma gauge."

"Maxed out? As in, level *one hundred?*"

"Yes."

"How can you tell?"

"Ocumancy."

"Wow. I don't personally know any avatars that have maxed out. It's crazy to be face-to-face with one." Ean's stare shifted from surprise to deep respect.

Her fiancé's eyelids crinkled in a skeleman's smile. He tilted his skull to one side. "Actually, Ean…"

"Yeah?"

Elias shrugged. "Nevermind. It's not important."

"Oh… OK. Well, you know what *is* important, right?"

"And what's that, my dear?"

"Lunch!"

Elias climbed the sharp crags to study the battlefield. Arms folded, the skeleman released a low whistle between his teeth. "Now, *that's* interesting. Cyrus?"

The cyborg's head popped out from behind a set of boulders. "What's up, man?"

"Might want to see this for yourself."

Clambering up next to him, Cyrus' mechanical jaw dropped open. "Woah, that's a lot of zombies."

"Feeling lucky today?" Elias snapped his teeth together with an eager *clack.* Cyrus shot a glance at Mallie. "We've got plenty of healing potions, right? What about transport gems?"

Byron looked up from sorting his jewel box (again). "We're good."

"Well, Elias, I'll leave the attack in your capable hands. Where to?"

"Straight into the fray." Eli unsheathed Sacrimony with a hellish chuckle.

"So be it. May the Terran Pantheon have mercy on our souls."

"So mote it be!" Elias cried, charging into the scrambling mass. The Firestone Guild followed his glinting aspect closely. Their undead foes mauled them with heightening ferocity, ravenous for flesh to sink their teeth into.

The artificer mage shone like pirate's treasure among circling sharks. Beneath his shining guidance, the group kept together with ease, felling the undead right and left until they lost count. Cyrus switched his blade attachment for his mace, relishing the satisfying crunch of his weapon crushing muscle and bone. At length, they cleared a path into the overrun fort, and eventually rid it of enemies.

"Well," panted Elias, sheathing his blade, "is everybody unscathed?"

"Almost." Cyrus indicated Byron, who sat on a rock clutching his bleeding knee. "He's at risk of zombification. Mallie?"

"Already on it." The company healer flew to Byron's side. "He'll have to be out for a while for the antidote to take effect. Let's carry him to one of the cots."

"I've got him." Elias swung the groaning gem mage over his shoulder. "Lead the way."

While Byron slept, Cyrus, Elias, and Mallie started a fire and cooked some food. "It's been a long time since you've been able to hang with us like this," Cyrus grinned, knocking Eli a friendly punch. "Wouldn't you like to do this more often?"

"As in, officially join your guild?" Elias shrugged and leaned back against a wooden chest. "Sure, but it's not practical to think of just now. Especially with the *Eclipsis* tour and my new apprentice."

"And the SkyRate Grand Championship," sang Mallie. "Ean's been on fire lately. Do you think she'll win?"

Eli chatted his jaws together, lighting an ebony Whisker. "At the risk of sounding cold-hearted, I'll be surprised – though *overwhelmingly* proud, of course – if she is able to beat Emodicus. He's obtained superior training; he's experienced on the Shiori Track; and his skycraft abilities and signature flight pattern are universally marked. He's well known for his grace and adaptability." The skeleman's face darkened in a puff of sable smoke. "Also, he's maxed out."

"In combat or charisma?"

"Both."

"Both?" Cyrus and Mallie gawked at each other. "I'm guessing the player behind Emodicus is a game master, then," Mallie added. "Possibly a beta tester."

"Wouldn't that disqualify him from the races, if he tested the SkyRate tracks themselves? At least, the ones included in the tournaments."

"Haven't looked into that," Eli admitted. "It wouldn't make sense to allow a beta tester to compete. However, I imagine that would depend on what elements of the game he tested. If he spent the entire test period in combat, for example, it wouldn't matter if he decided to compete in skyboarding afterward."

"I guess Lightcross will have to depend on luck for her win," Cyrus stated. "That's a real shame. She's won the popularity vote, for sure. Every time I consult TerraWiki, her name pops up somewhere."

"Along with somebody else's," Mallie teased, prodding Elias with her chopstick. "I saw the announcement for *Eclipsis* at the Kingdom of Klad. I can't wait!"

A satisfied glint winked in Eli's eye. "Neither can I. Music empowers me like nothing else can, fist-fighting the zombies included."

"Or getting bitten?" Cyrus chortled. "Pardon me for saying so, but you seemed to enjoy that. Did the venom give you some kind of a rush?"

"That's for me to know, and you never to find out," Elias replied coolly. "I'm going to take a walk. Be back in a bit." The skeleman rose to his feet and strode away, leaving Mallie and Cyrus to keep watch over the snoring Byron.

"Has he said anything about the wedding yet?" Mallie asked in a longing voice. "I keep messaging Ean about it, but she's too busy training to answer. I *love* VR weddings!"

"No, he hasn't said anything. Not to me, at least."

"Maybe we'll hear something definite after the Grand Championship race."

"That's what I think. However, it's also possible that they'll end up calling it off."

"Noooooo!" cried the woodland pixie. "They wouldn't do that to me! Why would you say such a thing, Cyrus?"

"VR marriages between avatars are downright silly," the cyborg insisted. "Elias and I had a long chat about it before he fell for Lightcross. There's like a seventy-percent divorce rate, or something. Such alliances are strictly practical for gameplay, like sharing inventory or merging and maintaining property."

"They could meet up in person, though," Mallie persisted. "Then it would be a real love story. So, there!"

The cyborg shook with mirth despite Mallie's glare. "Oh, I can just see it now! Eli's player is a forty-year-old married man, and Ean's player is a teenage lesbian. Mark my words, it would end in disaster."

"Hmph!" Mallie crossed her arms and tossed her head. "You're just a heartless conglomeration of flesh and mechanisms, Cyrus. You have no faith in the goddess of love!"

Cyrus produced a good-humored shrug. "You never know who the player is behind the avatar, Mallie. You were my first friend in Terra-Works, and I *still* don't know who you are."

16

EMODICUS

A steady cheer arose as the dark elf stepped forward. He carried his cerulean skyboard with ease, walking gracefully through the masses that parted for his advancement. His dusky complexion shone with an indigo gleam, and many a female avatar directed flattering glances toward him. Focused on the Shiori Track, Emodicus ignored them and powered up his board, mounting it with one dignified leap.

His semifinal competitors, Hyrule and Undine, started their engines on either side of him. According to informed spectators, Undine's flight pattern had been erratic during her practice runs, and therefore she presented but little risk to Emodicus. Kristenia Hyrule, on the other hand, had completed each of her run-throughs with precision. The dark elf stole a wary glimpse of her, scrutinizing her thick strawberry-blond hair and pale face. Hyrule was a human-fairy hybrid, petite and agile; when it came down to sheer speed, she gave even the almighty Lightcross a run for her money.

The SkyRate MC proceeded with his inane babbling about the racers and their various qualifications. Emodicus tuned him out. Hyrule didn't seem to be paying attention, either. Instead of ignoring the dark elf or acting shy, she faced him and boldly returned the full force of his scrutiny.

"Will the darkness or the light prevail, I wonder?" she lisped, her voice quite soft and musical.

A haunting smile flickered across her foe's lips. "Only the gods know."

"Best of luck, Gale Emodicus."

"Best of luck, Kristenia Hyrule."

Releasing Hyrule from the tyranny of his gaze, Emodicus braced himself for launching speed. The countdown began. *3... 2... 1... Accelerate.* His semifinal race was under way.

Elias and Ean watched from the stadium bleachers. Ean's hands were clenched with anticipation, her fingernails cutting thin red lines into her palms. Elias took notice and uncurled her hand, lacing his fingers between hers. "Here. Dig in as much as you like."

"It won't hurt?" she asked in a vague, offhanded tone. "Not at all," Eli answered, shifting himself closer to her. "Any pain you inflict unfailingly brings me pleasure."

Ean inclined her head toward his, but still couldn't tear her optics away from the azure smudge of her dark-elf rival. "Any pain does what now?"

"I'll explain later." Elias unclasped his fingers to tuck his hand around her waist. "Looks like Emodicus is determined to keep first position throughout." The sorcerer deftly shifted his weight to and fro, keeping his slight movements unpredictable. He was ensuring that his competitors couldn't cut past him.

"That's how he races." Ean indulged in a few choice Terran obscenities. "TerraWiki speculation says he's going to win the grand championship. He lost to the last season's champion by *one* board length, and he's been training tooth and nail ever since." She toyed with her necklace anxiously. "*Why* didn't I listen to Hex and get a flight coach?"

"Because you're stubborn."

Lightcross groaned. "Don't remind me."

"Hey," Eli murmured, cupping her chin, "No matter what happens, you're one of two Tournament of Champions finalists. That's no small achievement. Don't ever forget that, all right?"

"All right. Thanks, Eli." Ean stretched her limbs in an effort to relax. "Could you give me a shoulder rub?"

Elias blinked serenely. "What will I get out of it?"

"My undying gratitude."

"That's all?"

"That's all, Mage."

"I do not find these conditions sufficient, Lightcross."

"You need to be bribed?"

"Affirmative."

"Well, I'm not paying you; that's certainty itself."

"Are you willing to discuss the type of currency I request?"

"No."

"You don't even know what it is!"

"You're looking as fiendish as Hades in the apocalypse. I'm not stupid."

"Then how could you possibly object, Aphrodite?"

"Three very good reasons, Mephisto! I need to watch this race; I'm wearing lipstick today; and we're in full view of thousands of avatars."

"Nonsense. You can stream it later; wipe it off; and our relationship is old news by now."

The half-elf sighed dramatically. "OK, but just once." She gave him a quick peck on the cheekbone. "There, I paid you."

"Not there." Elias touched his jaws. "Here."

"Spoiled thing, aren't you?" Ean obeyed. She attempted to break away much sooner, but the skeleman held her tight against him. She laughingly wiggled out of his grasp. "My turn!"

Chuckling, Eli massaged her tense shoulders. "Nearly forgot about the race. Who's winning?"

Ean rolled her ice-blue eyes. "As if you have to ask."

"Still Emodicus, huh?"

"Naturally. I'm no saint for saying so, gods forbid, but it would be in my best interest if he slipped up enough for Hyrule to win. She's an enchanting little speed demon, but I've got more experience. I could probably win against her."

Elias removed his tablet and opened the race's streaming app. "Looks like she's angling to cut him now, Ean."

"No way!" Lightcross snatched the device from his protesting hands. "They're almost at the Shiori dive. She's going to wreck them both."

"Remind me what happens in that case?"

"With minor collisions, the race is reset at the halfway point. If you're in a devastating crash (like I was… *whoops*), then you're sent to the hospital with a fee, and a rematch is scheduled."

Emodicus and Hyrule were approaching the 360 loop. Ean was hypnotized by the tablet's projection, eyes wide with disbelief. "She wouldn't!"

"Wouldn't what? What's she doing?"

"She's going to do it!"

"Do what, Ean?"

Lightcross spluttered with indignation. "She's going to try the-"

The SkyRate MC answered for her. "Looks like Hyrule is trying the Lightcross maneuver! She's disengaged magnetic adherence! She's in free-fall!"

As had been the case for Ean, Hyrule struggled to keep her skyboard's nose fixed on the levitation tracks ahead of Emodicus. She re-engaged magnetic adherence, taking advantage of the track's intense pull to propel her forward. "Will she make it, folks?" cried the MC. The audience went mad, extracting their tablets or Holopals simultaneously to get a closer view of the outcome.

Her skyboard levelled off just ahead of the dark elf.

Hyrule's fans screamed. Elias laughed at his fiancé's offended expression. She cleared her face with a shrug, smoothing her hair. "If my move

helps her win against Emodicus, I guess I should be cheering, too."
Lightcross climbed to her feet and cupped her hands around her mouth.
"Serve him his shiny blue ass, Hyrule!"

The audience around her chuckled. Ean blushed slightly and sat down
again. "Got a bit carried away there. After all, she doesn't have a very
strong lead. He could still win."

Elias played with her hair as they watched the end of the semifinal.
Emodicus was slowly but surely gaining on Hyrule, cautiously evaluating
the distance between the nose of his skyboard and the back of hers. "It was
a good race," Eli predicted, "much closer than I would have anticipated.
But Emodicus is going to win."

"You think so?"

"Yep. They're getting into aerodynamic position now. Here comes the
dive."

The competitors melted into two colorful shadows as they shot into
the dive, leaving poor Undine far behind them. A few seconds later, the
indigo flash of Emodicus' avatar symbol illuminated the finish line. "By
the gods! A triumphant win for Gale Emodicus!"

Cobalt fireworks and dark-elf symbols erupted from all directions. Ean
scowled. "I guess I'm finished, then. Even the Lightcross maneuver won't
save me from that bastard."

Elias winked at her. "Never say never."

Before logging off for the night, Ean and Elias met up with the Spectral Tyrants at the Pulse. Travis lit up when he saw Ean approaching, scurrying ahead to meet her first. "That's one Hades of a rival you've got there, Lightcross. What's the master plan?"

"I've hired an assassin," Ean replied.

The were-cat's wide eyes sparkled with amusement. "I won't ask, and you won't tell me. Want a drink?"

"Are you kidding? I *need* a drink." Ean slid into the large purple booth with a groan. "About ten of them, I believe. What's your drink, Sindaya?"

"Equinox sunset." The attractive drummer tossed her braids and smiled.

"Really? That's my favorite, too."

Multiple conversations ensued. Elias, Oleon, and Kaspar talked *Eclipsis,* while Travis and Desmond settled their private bets on Emodicus versus Hyrule. Sindaya and Ean engaged in some light girl talk, swinging their feet beneath the curve of the veined tabletop. "Forgive me, but I have some friends who would kill me if I didn't take the opportunity to ask you this," Sindaya confessed. "When's the wedding, and where's the venue?"

"Haven't got a clue," Lightcross admitted. "We've both had too much going on to sit down and plan anything. Anyway, we're not in any particular rush. We like being engaged."

"Any idea what your dress is going to look like?"

"Probably a simple design in red. That's my favorite color."

Sindaya grinned. "Ah, I like it. White wedding gowns are so archaic."

Ean nodded. "Tell me about it."

"Is Elias going to keep his golden avatar design?"

"I'm assuming so. He doesn't seem to be interested in changing back."

"Do you like it?"

"To be honest, I thought it was too much at first. Outside of the concert, I mean. But I've grown fond of it. It's really easy to pick him out of a crowd."

The two girls shared a giggle. "That's enough about me," Ean asserted. "So, tell me about yourself, Sinnie. How long have you been part of the Spectral Tyrants?"

"Three years. It started out with just me, Travis, and Ollie. We advertised for a keyboardist, so that's when we got Kaspar. Our band was originally called Metaphysical."

"Wow, I had no idea. When did Elias come on board?"

"We discovered him by accident. We'd booked studio seven for a jam session, and Elias was tweaking vocal programs in studio six. Travis heard him first. He forced all of us into the hallway to listen. We were unanimous in the opinion that he was extremely good, so we…" Sindaya laughed. "We basically stalked him until we got a chance to corner him and beg him to be our vocalist."

"Who was singing before he joined?"

"Kaspar. He has a fair voice, but he'd admit himself that he can't hold a candle to Elias Mage. That creature has sacrificed his soul to the demon of song."

Elias caught the tail end of her comment. "My invisible ears are burning," he called. Lightcross chuckled. "Mind your own business. So," turning back to Sindaya, "did Elias change the band name?"

"Yes. As I'm sure you noticed, his preferred genre is heavy metal. He insisted that Metaphysical just didn't have the proper energy for the band. We fought him on it, labeled him a dictator, etc. But he just marched in one day and announced that he'd hit on the perfect name. He presented a holographic album cover he'd knocked together with Spectral Tyrants written on it. We couldn't resist."

"And Desmond joined after that?"

"Yes, he's the newest member. Mostly the backup singer, but he takes Travis' place on the guitar for the times Travis is late, or misses practice completely." She directed a glare at the were-cat's shaggy black head. He was busy persuading Desmond to take shots with him. "He's a fun guy, but he doesn't practice as much as he should."

"Well, I didn't sound half bad, if you ever decide you need a replacement," Ean joked. Sindaya rose an eyebrow. "That's not a bad idea. Would you consider joining?"

Ean's heart fluttered as she considered all those long, music-filled, ecstasy-inducing hours with Elias Mage. "I'd say yes, but I need to improve my performa level before I play at any concerts. I tried to sing for filthy lucre once, and it didn't go as well as I'd hoped for."

"Is that so?" Sindaya crossed her arms, sizing Ean up with a knowledgeable eye. "I know I've only seen you once or twice so far, but I have streamed your SkyRate races as well. You're practically dripping with charisma, which is closely linked to performa, as I'm sure you know."

"I am?" Ean's tone betrayed earnest confusion.

"What's your current performa level?"

"I don't even remember. My SkyRate career has taken full control of my brain these days."

"Take a look."

Ean opened her profile screen and looked at the performa gauge. "Oh... my... gods."

Sindaya leaned across the table. "So, what level are you?"

Ean gulped. "Forty-seven."

"I knew it had to be high! Nice going." Sindaya knocked her a fist-bump. "You practiced a lot for your first song, huh? Did you accelerate your training with magic?"

"Never thought of that. I was in a rush."

Sindaya tilted her head. "Then, how...?"

Perplexed, Ean bit the end of her thumbnail. "I don't know."

17

OF CONFESSIONS

Ean wandered around the workshop while Elias gave closing instructions to his apprentice. They bid Tirion goodnight, and the couple departed hand-in-hand through the streets of Helios.

The half-elf turned her head to face him. "Eli?"

"Mmm?"

"How is it possible for me to suddenly achieve mid-level performa?"

Elias sighed and rubbed his temporal bone. "You don't beat around the bush, do you?"

"I'd very much like to know."

"Let's get to my house first. The answer is somewhat involved."

Ean shrugged. "OK."

The skeleman stole an anxious glance or two. Ean hummed a low, cheerful tune as she walked, occasionally breaking into a few skipping steps. He relaxed. "You're not angry with me?"

"I'm a *little* miffed that you would keep something from me, whatever that thing is. But I'd be lying if I said I was all-out angry."

Elias nodded. He scanned his wrist at the front door, unlocking it, and they entered together. "Now," Eli proceeded, sitting next to her on the couch and tapping his fingerbones together, "I think the first thing I should explain is that I'm maxed out."

"I had my suspicions."

"You did?" His midnight optics widened.

"Well, yeah. At least in charisma. What about your combat level?"

"Maxed out."

"Cool." Ean stretched out across the couch, laying her head in his lap. "When did you find the time to do that?"

"The beta testers for TerraWorks were encouraged to focus on combat. I was a beta tester. Having maxed out my combat level, I focused on charisma and became an artificer mage once the game was officially released."

"Guess that explains why you don't want to join any battle guilds. Been there and done that, right?"

"Pretty much." He gave a modest shrug. "Once the Spectral Tyrants started making a name for themselves, I realized that my band was the project I wanted to concentrate on. Throughout my life, I've always found music to be strangely – I could say preternaturally – empowering. Performa also strengthens my skills as an artificer mage. And then, reaching a high level of performa in TerraWorks can have an almost drug-like effect on the mind, it seems. Like ecstasy."

"I've experienced that effect as well," Ean murmured. "But how did *my* performa level increase so much, and so quickly? Did I siphon it off you somehow?"

"Hmm. Well, I suppose that would be a very loose understanding of the process. Since I'm maxed out, my avatar wields expert-level dark performa. However, I'm constantly saturated in dark performa/charisma thanks to the band's popularity (and the need for us to practice). Over time, excess dark performa builds up in my vicinity but has nowhere to go. The effect is like sipping on an energy drink. I'm happy and animated, but I can't rest, and sometimes I can't think straight. It gets overwhelming."

Ean laughed. "Is that what's happening when you launch into an unsolicited soliloquy about nothing in particular?"

Elias rubbed his skull. "I guess so. Sorry about that. In my own defense, I'm not always aware that I'm doing it."

"It's OK. It's kind of cute." The half-elf smiled as he mussed her hair. "Anyway, does simply being around you expose me to this pool of surplus charisma?"

"It does, although the effects are gradual. You absorbed a good deal more at once when you bit me."

"*Ooooh!*" Ean breathed. "I always thought that was a weird request. You knew what would happen?"

"Had no idea. The first time I asked you to do that, I was merely curious."

She chuckled. "Yes, you do like to experiment."

"I had the vague inclination... a plain old urge, I guess... that such a sensation would bring me some level of pressure-induced satisfaction." He fingered his jaw thoughtfully. "I would explain further, but I doubt I could state it more precisely than that."

Ean nodded. "I think it makes sense. When I absorbed the excess energy, it gave you some kind of a release."

"Speaking of which..." Elias took her hands and pulled her up, then laid beneath her so she straddled him. "I could use a dose of your medicine right now, Doctor Lightcross." He parted his shirt to expose the clavicle.

"Coming right up." Ean graced him with a spirited kiss. "But first, I have one more question."

"Yes?"

"Why me?"

"Why you?" Elias gazed questioningly into her earnest face.

"That first time you saw me, you were singing 'The Ballad of Helios.' Remember?"

"How could I forget?" Elias smoothed his hands along her arms, affection bright in his eyes.

"There was an entire TerraDome full of avatars. Plenty of gorgeous women, elves, and fairy hybrids. All of them were shouting your name. Any one of them, picked at random, would have been beside themselves to date you. What made you approach *me?*"

"Mmm." Elias hesitated for a long time, tracing his fingertip against her cheek. "It's rather difficult to summarize, but... I think it was your energy."

"My energy?"

"Yes. You're so mysterious, but at the same time, so exuberant and open. The exhilaration in your eyes (once I could see them), your stance, and even your outfit, drew me to you. And I adore the way you walk through a crowd; you hold your head up with such confidence. And (as you know) I'm fascinated by your eyes and hair. By the way, did you know that in certain moods, the ends of your hair sparkle purple and scarlet?"

"Another vain customization of mine," she admitted. "But I'm flattered that you even noticed it. Most avatars don't."

"That's another trait I admire about you... your attention to artistic detail. Which leads me to ask *you* something else, before I get my medicine."

She snapped a salute. "Fire away, commander."

"Would you consider joining the Spectral Tyrants?"

Her ice-blue eyes jolted with electric glee. *"Would* I?" she practically shouted. "That's just what I've been longing for you to ask me." Delighted, she kissed her way to his clavicle, brushing it softly with her lips. "Phantom pleasure is no joke, Elias," she warned him.

Back at the Shiori Hotel, Piragor slipped from his room and headed for the bar. He had hoped that Ean would be free, so he wouldn't end up drinking alone. But, as usual, she was spending every spare minute with Elias.

"She's not training half so much as she needs to be, either," he mumbled, very much in the mood to sulk. "If anyone asked *me,* I'd assure them that combining engagements and the SkyRate Grand Championship is a universally bad idea. But nobody ever asked *me.*" Sighing, he ran a hand through his blond hair until it stood on edge. "At any rate, I'll keep trying to look on the bright side. She's a finalist; she invited me here; and the Shiori Hotel has a splendid selection of beverages."

He slipped onto a stool and motioned for the barkeeper. As he waited, his fingers aimlessly traced the wood grain of the tabletop. Another avatar took the stool beside him, but he ignored the newcomer and continued to draw imaginary pictures.

"You're the training partner who works with Lightcross, correct?"

Piragor flinched with surprise. "Uh, yeah." Turning to face the speaker, Piragor's startled eyes absorbed the image of Gale Emodicus. The dark elf, clad in a long navy vest, leggings, and elven boots, returned his stare with an amused smile. A piece of cobalt twine held Gale's blue-black hair in a glossy ponytail. "My apologies. I did not mean to startle you."

"No problem. I didn't expect to see you here."

"Oh?" Emodicus raised one finely-sculpted eyebrow. "You think I consider myself too good to mingle with my fellow avatars?"

"That's not what I meant. You just don't strike me as the bar type."

"Ah." The barkeeper served Piragor, then slid Gale's order across to him. As the elf caught it, Piragor noticed that even his fingernails shimmered with a dim indigo light. "If it is not too impertinent for me to ask," Emodicus resumed, "how are the run-throughs proceeding? They are going well, I trust?"

Piragor shrugged and took a swig from his glass. "Her flight pattern is consistent, if that's what you're angling to know."

Emodicus chuckled, his thin dark mouth barely lifting into a smile. "There has been a massive amount of publicity regarding her engagement to Elias Mage. (My congratulations to them.) I hope it does not become too *distracting* for her."

"I'll bet," Piragor muttered beneath his breath. He took another draught of liquid solace. Gale's fine pair of pointed ears heard his comment, but his complacent expression remained unaltered. "You do not seem pleased," Emodicus said. "Do you not approve of Elias Mage?"

"If you're looking for an informant, Emodicus, you'll have to look elsewhere."

The dark elf lowered his empty glass. He cornered Piragor with a slanted stare, appearing to read every subtlety as clearly as textbook print. "Ah. Classic jealousy."

Piragor slammed down his glass with a bang. "I'm *not* jealous!"

"It's either that, or you disapprove of Elias Mage for subconscious reasons. Which is it?"

"Why should I disapprove of him?" snapped Piragor, eager to steer the topic away from himself. Emodicus chuckled again with a light, silvery cadence. "Nevermind. I do not expect the general public to know certain… *intricacies* about skeletal avatars in general, nor Elias Jacoby Mage in particular. Still, even I cannot deny a certain gentlemanly charm about his person. He is truly unique, and that is something I can always appreciate, even in a rival."

"A rival?" Piragor shot the elf a confused look. "Elias is your rival?" The tone of his query implied "*And not Ean Lightcross?*"

A long, awkward pause intervened as Emodicus casually ordered and consumed a second drink. "They are a formidable pair," Gale assented. "However, I am far less concerned with Lightcross on a skyboard, than I am with Elias Mage before a golden staff."

Piragor's forehead wrinkled in confusion. "What do you mean," he started to say, but was cut off as the dark elf rose from his seat, left exact change, and departed from the hotel.

Puzzle as he might (and did), Piragor could not make sense of what Emodicus had implied. All he could deduce was that Emodicus knew something about skeleton avatars that few people knew... and he had some reason to either dislike or distrust Elias Mage in particular.

18

SKYRATE GRAND CHAMPION

Elias lounged in the empty bleachers as Ean and Piragor tore through the Shiori Track. He was keeping an eye on the stopwatch for them, as well as glancing over some new music for the Spectral Tyrants. As he hummed the tune, he heard his fiancé's ecstatic *"Whoo-hoo!"* accompanied by the crackle of her electric laughter. "That's the Shiori dive," he murmured, not needing to look up and confirm.

The familiar ruby-amethyst flash - signifying Ean's victory - caught the corner of his vision. Eli stopped the timer. A sardonic grin crinkled his eyelids as he overheard her banter. "*Haaaaaa!* In your face, man! That's three times in a row."

Piragor's distinct voice echoed across the stadium. "Look, I think it's obvious by now that you need to book a few sessions with a flight coach. You're not going to learn anything more by just racing against me."

Eli's eyes smiled again, this time at Ean's answering groan. "You know I don't like flight coaches, Piragor. They're so stiff and... and *programmy*. Know what I mean?"

Piragor's reply was firm. "They can teach you techniques that I don't know. Sorry for being so blunt here, but you'd be a fool at this point not to spend at least a couple of hours with one. You're precise and alert, your turns are tight, and your A-position has improved. But, having said all that, you're becoming too settled, too predictable. You need a trick or two up your sleeve."

"I've got the Lightcross maneuver!"

"Which Emodicus has studied inside, outside, and backwards."

"How do you know?"

"Because he's not stupid."

As Ean continued to protest, the skeleman chuckled at the unmistakable ring of Piragor's mounting frustration. Elias closed his sheet music app. Pocketing his hands in his leather jacket, he strolled down the stairs and, following their voices, wandered into the track's parking deck.

Ean slipped her arm through Eli's, gazing up at him pleadingly. "*You* wouldn't subject me to the droning instructions of a flight coach, would you, Eli? You believe in my inherent skycraft skills, don't you?"

Elias bent and graced her earlobe with a brief, playful nip. "I agree with Piragor on this one, my dear. Emodicus is the best there is – in many ways, I might add – and if you want to beat him, you're going to have to utilize every tool at your disposal. Come now, be a good girl and book a few sessions."

Ean pouted. "What are you going to do, then?"

Elias un-pocketed his hands and extracted his tablet. "I've got some new songs to review for the Spectral Tyrants. And I perceive that you've wearied Piragor half to death with your nonsense, so he needs a break."

"All right, all right. You needn't rub it in. I'm going!" Ean stood on tiptoe to kiss him. Elias dodged her attempt, forcing her to chase him. He jokingly wiped her kiss away once she'd finally landed it. "Get out of here, Lightcross. We're expecting you to *win,* gods-dammit!"

"Love you, Eli." She skipped away, singing a winsome elvish tune. Eli's dark eyes shone with affection. "Love you, too."

Piragor couldn't resist a smile. "The chemistry between you two is unreal. Have you guys…" He shook his head. "Nevermind. That's not any of my business."

Elias tore his attention away from Ean's dancing form. "Ah, what the Hades, man. Go ahead and ask. Have we what?"

"Have you guys met up in person? You know, outside of Terra-Works?"

"Not yet. But I've been considering it."

"Before or after the wedding?"

Elias grunted, brushing his fingerbones against his mandible. "By the gods, that's a very good question. I'll have to prioritize the answer."

"Do that *after* the grand championship race," Piragor insisted. Elias laughed. "Yes, of course, *after!* She's scatter-brained enough as it is."

"I'm glad you agree."

Suddenly, Eli looked past Piragor's shoulder. His eyes narrowed. "Hey, I'll talk to you later, OK?" Patting him on the shoulder, Elias walked back toward the bleachers. Piragor shrugged and extracted a transport gem from his inventory. "I'm craving some sushi." He vanished in a bright green flash.

Elias glanced over his shoulder to ensure that Piragor was gone. Quickening his pace, he confronted the avatar standing in the shadows. "You wanted to speak with me?"

Emodicus nodded. "I won't take up much of your time."

The skeleman leaned against the bleacher supports, arms crossed. "And how the devil have *you* been, Emodicus? You seem to be even more… *blue…* lately. If that's possible."

"I prefer the term cobalt." The dark elf's lobes glittered with sapphire-studded ear chains. "As gratifying as your observations are, however, I came here to discuss Ean Lightcross."

"How interesting." Elias drew out his words with significance, eyeing the elven sorcerer up and down. "You're afraid she's going to beat you."

"*If* she does," Gale Emodicus said, arms likewise crossing, "it will be because you helped her."

"Define 'helped.' I'm not exactly trained in skycraft, Emodicus."

"No. But you are versed in ocumancy. Am I right?"

A slight twitch creased the corner of Eli's eye. "You're familiar with the term?"

"Oh, yes. Quite familiar. In fact, I myself find ocumancy useful from time to time."

"Is that right?"

"Just like you, I can see something that most other avatars cannot: the other players' skills and state of enchantment."

"Right, then." Elias shrugged and tilted his skull. "Just spit it out."

Emodicus lowered his voice. "Is your fiancé aware that you're using her to get to me?"

Eli's chest rattled with his low, diabolical chuckle. "I haven't the faintest idea what you're alluding to."

"I think you do. *Ophidious.*"

The skeleman's eyes narrowed. His teeth snapped together with a sharp, intimidating *clack.* "You think I am the cursed fay sorcerer?"

"Now, listen to yourself, Elias. Does it really matter to you what I think? No, my old friend." The elf's dark blue eyes twinkled deviously. "The only thing that matters is what I *know.*"

Elias resumed his former indifference. "You don't know anything. You've always tried to bluff your way into business that doesn't concern you." He shifted through his inventory for a Whisker smoke, lighting it with cool nonchalance.

Emodicus assumed a cold smile. "I understand. Consider this your first and last warning. If you intend to subvert my position as the Fell Sorcerer, you'll live to rue the day."

"Well, the joke's on you, buddy." Elias exhaled scented wreathes of jetty smoke. "Skeletons are nocturnal."

Gale Emodicus bowed and walked away. "Ophidious isn't."

"Beloved citizens of TerraWorks!"

The SkyRate MC's call blared across the packed stadium. Casting his gaze across it, Elias realized that the crowd was evenly divided between various shades of sapphire blue, or Ean's ruby-amethyst combination. Fireworks burst overhead, alternately boasting the finalists' avatar symbols in their trailing wake. The MC's announcement recommenced. "Welcome to the SkyRate Grand Championship Race at Shiori Islands!"

Although the skeleman couldn't see his fiancé, he could feel her nervous energy radiating across the tracks. "You can do this, Lightcross," he murmured. "Just stay focused." Despite his calm tone, Elias felt an unconquerable need for a smoke. He deftly removed a cigarette – his third one that day, in reckless defiance of his prior edict – and his fingerbones trembled as he lit it. Piragor chuckled, reaching over to steady his wrist. "Take it easy, Eli. I'd say she's got the best chance of any racer in the whole of TerraWorks."

Elias snorted. "How very astute. I just don't want her to kill herself."

"Right. It would be good if she didn't do that."

The MC's exuberant voice interrupted them. "May I have your attention, beloved citizens? We have a special announcement!"

"Mmm. What's this?" Elias leaned forward on the bleachers, eyes bright with curiosity. Piragor shrugged. "I don't know. They've never done this before."

The MC continued. "The architects of the Shiori Track have a *little* surprise for our finalists."

A low rumble issued from the levitation tracks. Several of them began to shift. New loops, tunnels, and challenging turns morphed into place. Most intimidating of all, the Shiori dive lengthened, its notorious tunnel burrowing underground. The audience's collective gasp flooded the stadium, followed quickly by cheers and applause.

"How about that, folks! Give the SkyRate architects a round of applause!"

Excitement and enthusiasm rippled from the crowd. Piragor's demeanor paled. "Oh, gods. It's basically a whole new track. That's *insane.*"

Elias emitted a low whistle. "By the Terran Pantheon! Consider me impressed."

"Yeah, man, it's cool and all that. But how is Ean going to handle this?"

The artificer mage shrugged, folding his gleaming arms. "I'd imagine that she has a better chance of beating Emodicus now. I saw a few of his run-throughs, and I assure you, he could fly the original track with his eyes closed. This will throw Emodicus off just as much as Lightcross."

Piragor's green eyes lit up. "I see what you mean. They're on more equal footing now."

"Precisely. Elementary, my dear Watson."

Piragor glanced at him blankly. "Who the Hades is Watson?"

Elias laughed. "Nevermind."

A miniature earthquake rippled beneath Ean's skyboard. Her jaw dropped in amazement as the tremors radiated outward, culminating in various sections of the Shiori track raising, lowering, or outright vanishing as new ones took their places. "Almighty Kanthesis!" she breathed. "And every unholy deity of the Pantheon. I did *not* see this coming."

Looking over her shoulder at Emodicus, she felt a little bit better when she saw his expression was just as shocked as her own. *Looks like even the great Gale Emodicus didn't anticipate this. That just might give me the edge I needed.* Ean reached into her vest pocket and withdrew her round red-and-purple glasses. Donning them, a wide smile of joyful anticipation crossed her lips. *No matter what happens next, you're here. You're a Grand Championship finalist. And you get to be the first to race on the Shiori Track 2.0!*

Gale's emotionless tenor fractured her thoughts. "Why are you cackling like a witch? I see nothing funny about this."

Ean could feel her nervous excitement channeling into an all-absorbing vigor. She shifted her weight, unable to stand still. "Focus, darkling elf," she hissed, the ends of her hair lifting and snapping with multicolored static. "This is a night race. It's *my* race. You'll be eating my dust for breakfast."

"Whatever you say, Lightcross." Emodicus resumed his bored, nonaffected tone, but he stole a puzzled glance at the brewing storm beside him. *What's gotten into her?*

The alternating scarlet and violet pulses from her skyboard mimicked lightening beneath her feet. Her hair lifted into a glossy, thickened cloud, alive with electricity. As the countdown began – *In 3... 2... 1. Accelerate* – Ean's ecstatic chuckle grew into loud, maniacal laughter.

Emodicus frowned. *Just what has Elias Mage created?*

Is she... the Anathema?

With an ear-splitting blast, the competitors accelerated into the unknown. Emodicus shook the thought from his bewildered head. His body felt off-balance as it was lurched into unfamiliar turns, curves, and loops. The elf steadied his breathing, crouching slightly, allowing the skyboard's magnetic adherence to take the lead. *Speed is all that matters now. I have to stay ahead of her.*

Night races were dizzying enough on familiar tracks. The dark arches of the tracks were sporadically lit with neon arrows and section indicators. All and sundry passed him in a blur. Aware of Ean's close proximity, Emodicus scowled and tried to intimidate her by banking sharply in her direction. She eased her skyboard out of the way, laughing. "Where's all your smooth confidence gone, 'Modi?"

How can she be joking about this? Emodicus knelt into full aerodynamic position, attempting to maintain control by the subtle lean of his body. Ean remained standing. The two remained nose-to-nose for what seemed to be a lifetime. At length, Ean began to pull ahead, tackling a hellish triple corkscrew with enviable fluidity.

Emodicus stood back up with a growl of impatience, but he saw he was too late. The expanded Shiori dive loomed before them. Lightcross was focused now (and no longer laughing); the half-elf's resolute silence was far more daunting to Emodicus than her laughter.

The finalists plunged over the side, feeling as if the entire universe had been snatched from beneath their feet. There were only a few feeble lights in the tunnel. If it hadn't been for Ean's colorful skyboard, the elf would have seen precious little. As it was, he could see Lightcross falling straight down beneath him. Her lithe figure knelt to absorb the impact as the track's magnetic adherence re-engaged.

So be it. Emodicus closed his eyes.

Five seconds later, the finish line burst into the colors and symbol of Ean Lightcross.

The half-elf skidded to a halt, dismounting before her skyboard powered down. She punched her fists into the air over and over again, "Yes! Yes! By the gods, what a rush! *Yes!*"

Emodicus powered down and approached her to shake hands. "Congratulations."

Lightcross gripped his palm cheerfully. "You're amazing, Emodicus. I'm so honored that I could race against you."

"And win."

She flushed to her ears, laughing. "Yes. And win!"

Emodicus bowed to her. He turned to bow to his disappointed fans, then strode away, his muscular shoulders tense with irritation.

Elias Mage. Be prepared to answer to me.

Ean's eager gaze sought for her fiancé. Puzzled, she ran straight up the bleachers to the section where he'd promised he would be. She found Piragor, but not the skeleton. "Where's Eli?" she yelled, struggling to avoid drowning in the mob.

Piragor held up his hands, indicating helpless ignorance. Lightcross frowned. She turned to descend the stairs. Looking down, she spotted Elias standing just across the finish line, shining brightly beneath the stadium lights.

The audience encouraged her to join him. She proceeded slowly, grinning from ear to ear.

The skeleman waited with commendable patience. His gilt hands were clasped behind his back. The spiked collar of his leather trench coat framed his golden skull, which was just as handsome to Ean as the head of any living prince. Once she stood before him, he descended on one knee.

Her first remark convulsed the crowds with mirth. "You've already proposed, genius."

Elias chuckled. "Ean Lightcross, will you marry me? Right here, right now."

"Oh, gods." Ean trembled. Elias cradled her shaking fingers in his, raising his voice over the stadium's deafening shrieks. "Until death do us part, my dear."

"Until death do us part."

Elias stood and swept his wife into a passionate kiss. The fireworks above them erupted into a new avatar symbol. Eli's skull grasped a rose between its teeth, while Ean's double cross bloomed along the frontal bone. "You never do anything halfway," Ean smiled, tracing his cheekbone with her finger. "That's one of the many things I adore about you."

"Oh, this is just the beginning. The night is still young." So saying, Elias cradled her in his arms and removed a transport gem. "Hold onto me tight, my wife."

A thrill tickled her nerves. "Say that again."

Elias obeyed, with his deliciously low laughter. "*My wife.*"

19

TO FIND THE HOLY GRAIL

The following evening, Ean logged into TerraWorks and glanced around the castle suite. Elias had not arrived yet. Humming contentedly, Ean swiped through her outfit options and chose a black satin dress with high slits. On her way out of the bedroom, she spotted her Holobox sitting on the charging station. Grinning, she tapped the device and greeted Hexadecimal. "Rise and shine! Mommy's home."

Hex bowed. "Good evening, Mrs. Mage." He wore a tiny crown of cherry blossoms in honor of their wedding. The half-elf giggled. "*Mrs. Mage.* Now, *that's* going to take some getting used to." She attached the Holobox to her shoulder strap. "Elias isn't here yet. Want to explore the castle with me?"

"I would be honored."

Ean passed through the opulent silver doors, her footsteps pattering down the long corridor. "This is Vermillion Castle, built right on the edge of Lilla Forest. It's small, but it's private. We have the entire place to ourselves."

"It is just the sort of getaway you'd enjoy, Ean-san. Your husband is very thoughtful."

"I think so, too." Ean's complexion flushed as she smiled. "Look at all these ornate carvings! Oh, this room must be another master suite." Cracking the double doors open, the half-elf peered inside eagerly. "I was right. It's a little smaller than ours, though." She closed the doors and continued down the hall. "That's a library. Elias and I had a midnight snack there yesterday. That's a hallway that connects to the separate bath house; I'm tempted to jump in there and soak right this minute. The tub's rosewater infusions are *divine.* That's an antique billiard room, can you believe it? Vermillion Castle is downright quaint, but I'm in love with it."

"I have just received word from Elias. He says he will be with you in another half-hour."

"Perfect. I'll whip up something to eat."

Approaching the grand staircase, Ean slid down the banister and skipped through the sprawling living room into the kitchen. Checking the ingredients available, she scrolled through her recipe lists until she landed on roast chicken and broth rice. "Wholesome, but not too fancy. Sounds good." She hesitated. "Of course, Elias doesn't usually eat, but his avatar can keep up appearances."

The half-elf prepared the meal, shrugging at the short amount of time her task consumed. "If I had one complaint about TerraWorks, it's that cooking is too easy. It's not much of a challenge." She checked the dining room table, then stole back to the library to fetch a book.

When Elias logged in, he was greeted by a charming scene. The castle was aglow with twilight and warm with the scent of dinner. His wife was engrossed in a novel, firelight playing softly over her satin dress, and highlighting her red hair. His lids crinkled in a smile as he contrasted this peaceful, elegant personage with the volatile, half-maniacal racer from last night. "May I approach the throne, your majesty?"

Color leapt into her face at the sound of his voice. She dropped her book. "Elias!" Laughing, she gracefully extended her hand. "You may approach."

Elias joined her before the fire, reaching down to hold her hand. "You're beautiful."

"Thank you, sir. You're looking very handsome yourself." The skeleman had switched back to his original pearl-white frame, although his cranium remained studded with alternating rubies and diamonds. Elias noticed her gaze lingering on them. "They're infused with various charms, so they're not entirely the result of vanity. They serve a practical purpose."

"I like it. I imagine we'll be seeing more skeleton avatars around TerraWorks, thanks to the fame you've accumulated. Bejeweled skulls will become all the rage."

Elias chuckled. He scooped her up and carried her to the couch. "Do we have some time before dinner, my lady?"

"Of course. We can eat whenever."

Winking at her, Eli unbuttoned his collared shirt. "I've been waiting for this all day."

She crossed her arms, affecting haughtiness. "What, nothing for me? No gifts?"

"As a matter of fact, there might be a little something for you in your inventory." He laughed. "Forgive me – *our* inventory. They're joined now."

"I'll look at it later, if you don't mind." Ean lovingly cradled his skull between her hands, touching their foreheads together. "I could hardly focus at work today. I missed you *so much.*"

"Mmm. Not as much as I missed you."

"Oh, really? I doubt that."

"I'll prove it if I must."

"You must."

In answer, Elias traced his fingers along her arms. He grasped her wrists. Bringing his jaws close to her ear, the skeleman growled, making her laugh. "Is that a challenge?" he whispered.

Much later, the couple relaxed in the castle bedroom. Candles flickered on marble mantles, gentle breezes stirred from the open balcony, and a large vase of gem flowers – one of Eli's gifts – reflected the starlight. Elias was trailing his fingers up and down Ean's bare back. "You asked me once why I had chosen you. Do you remember?"

His wife turned to face him, smiling. "I remember."

Eli lifted a lock of her hair to breathe in its rosy scent. "I want to ask you the same question. Why me?"

"For your deadly good looks, of course."

"Naturally." His midnight eyes blinked in a slow, passive manner, barely repressing a jovial glimmer. "What else?"

"Your determination and your confidence. There's a fine line between being confident and being a self-worshipping jerk, but you've managed to straddle the fence without crossing it."

Eli's boneplate chest rumbled with a despotic chuckle. "Thank you. Proceed."

"And your passion." Ean's ice-blue eyes burned with suppressed energy. "I'll never forget the first time I saw you onstage. I'm aware of how tacky this sounds, but... I swear, I could see the fire of the gods emanating from every part of you. Every look, every gesture, and every bone. You sang like Lucifer himself. Part of me was a little frightened, even, but I couldn't look away."

"Are you still frightened of me now?"

"Sometimes. You *do* have a devilish temper, you know."

Elias laughed. "I see we've progressed to my faults. That didn't take long."

"Sorry." Ean softly kissed his clavicle, causing him to shudder. "You know, I've been meaning to tell you. The last few times we've been this close, I've *wanted* to bite you. It's been giving me a rush, too. Is that normal?"

"Dark charisma is like a drug." Elias caressed her waist. "As you absorb more, you need more at once to experience the same heady effect and inspiration."

"What will happen when we're *both* maxed out?"

"You'll be fine. You're half-elf, so your body is designed to retain or cycle out excess charisma, whichever is needed. At the same time, you'll be able to siphon the energy I can't handle." He snuggled up to her with a tender embrace. "We're factually perfect for each other." Elias stroked Ean's hair as he held her, then withdrew to look her in the eyes. "Ean?"

"Hmm?"

"Let's meet up in person."

Her eyes widened. "You really want to?"

"As long as you can reassure me that you are, in fact, a woman."

Ean laughed. "I swear by the Terran Pantheon that I'm a woman. And you're a man, right?"

"Male, twenty-eight years old, and single. *Very* single."

She poked him in the ribs. "If you weren't logged into TerraWorks so much, flirting with *me,* you'd probably be dating in real life."

"What about you? You're still single, right?"

"No, I'm married. To some skeletal freak named Eli, I believe..."

He poked her in return. "Do you want to meet me?"

She faltered. "To tell you the truth, I'm nervous."

"What about?"

"What if it, you know…" she sighed. "I know it's selfish, but what if meeting in real life detracts from what we're experiencing now?"

"You're afraid the reality will break the dream."

"Exactly."

"You're afraid that I'm nowhere near as handsome as my avatar?"

Ean giggled, scuffing his skull with the palm of her hand. "Oh, I'm *petrified* that you won't actually be a skeleton. The very idea makes me quiver with disgust and rage."

Elias leaned in for a kiss. "Think about it, Ean. I'll honor your decision regardless, but I want you to know that I'll do whatever it takes to meet with you."

"Even if you have to jump on a plane?"

"Yes." His long, ivory forefinger stroked her cheek. "I am truly… deeply… in love with you, Ean Lightcross."

Two weeks later, a young woman with short auburn hair crossed a busy street. It was mid-afternoon, but the coffee shop she entered was still crowded. Ean immediately plugged her holographic assistant into an empty charging port, and sat down to wait.

Her self-conscious gaze darted to her work clogs. *I should have changed before I left.* She bit the end of her thumb to relieve the anxious pressure building in her mind. *This could be one of the best days of my life… or the worst.*

A crisp, determined tread caused her to look up.

The young man walking toward her was pale, but composed, his hazel eyes bright with expectation. A 3-D engineer's division badge shimmered from his lapel. His wire-framed Smart Tech glasses were slipping awry; he deftly pushed them back into place. "Ean Muller?"

She blushed so thoroughly that she felt certain her ears were on fire. "That's me."

He bowed *à la* Elias Mage. "William Klein."

HELIOS
BOOK TWO OF THE TERRAWORKS TRILOGY
RICHELLE MANTEUFEL

Man Devil Press

CONTENTS

1

ALL HAIL THE MAGES

The TerraDome audience summoned the half-elf.

Ean's vermillion lips parted in elated laughter. She stepped forward on the beat, saluting her fans with her guitar's headstock. Her auburn hair sprouted from a black felt hat.

Travis and Desmond flanked her on either side, also wielding electric guitars. The stage lights changed from white to red. As the three began to play, an intimidating skeleton strode onstage, prompting screams from the crowd. His easygoing saunter caught Ean's attention; her smile broadened.

The skeleman stopped next to her. Hand on her hip, he touched his forehead to hers as they both swayed to the rhythm. Their impassioned stares devoured each other. The romantics in the audience cheered them on, projecting the duo's avatar symbol from their Holopals.

Multicolored lights illumined the stadium's cathedral setting. The ceiling flickered with firelight. Various holographic projections announced their album, *Together When We're Dead*. Packed to the brim, the TerraDome quaked with applause.

4-D recorders darted among the spectators, straining to capture the famous couple.

The skeleton broke away from the half-elf, advancing to grasp the microphone. He paced the edge of the platform as he sang. *"Elias!"* the avatars shouted, reaching up to touch him. Amused, Eli noted quite a few fellow skeletons in the crowd. He relished his fans' almighty vigor, his midnight eyes burning.

Ean's solo approached. Elias left the microphone to confront her. His gleeful demeanor waxed treacherous. "Don't stop playing, Mrs. Mage."

The half-elf smirked. Her nimble fingers embraced the strings. "Try me."

As she began, Elias stood behind her and caressed her body. His hands brushed her thighs, then trailed up to slip beneath her shirt. Whistles rippled across the audience while some onlookers flushed. Although Ean's eyes were concealed behind amber lenses, she couldn't mask her grin.

The pyrotechnic effects bathed them in golden light. Ean retained her outward composure, but her heart thrashed in her chest. Thankfully, her hands remembered their dutiful training and continued to apply the correct pressure.

She finished her solo with a flourish, sticking her tongue out at Elias. *So there!*

Her husband chuckled. "Very good." Winking at her, he removed his hands and marched back to the microphone. As his powerful vocals belted out the chorus, Ean steadied her breathing and rejoined Travis and Desmond in the low riffs. The half-elf felt Sindaya's spirited eyes boring into the back of her head. Ean bit her lip. *You'll pay for that later, Elias Mage.*

The song came to an explosive end. Torch fire scorched the atmosphere. Elias punched the air, every gleaming bone reflecting flames. He crouched before the audience, speaking to a few avatars and shaking hands with others. At length he straightened, slipped out of his jacket, and tossed it into the roaring crowd. He returned to his wife. "Come, Aphrodite."

Ean slipped the guitar strap over her head, raising one eyebrow. "I'll drive."

"Like Hades you will." Elias advanced, forcing her to step back. Ean smiled and raised her hands in mild protest. "Down, boy. Let me preserve what little dignity I have left."

"Mmm." Nipping her earlobe, Elias slipped his gilt arm around her shoulders. "If you insist."

The couple headed for the TerraDome studios. Gliding into a vacant room, the half-elf locked the door behind them. She surprised Elias by cornering him first. Ean pushed him back against the wall. "Nice try out there," she breathed, the ends of her hair lifting with miniscule red stars. "But you forget that I'm your equal now. Your charismatic sorcery dwells in *me.*"

Elias slowly removed her glasses. Her ice-blue eyes were wide with electric lure. "The pupil has become the master. Still, I outrank you in combat." He peeled off her hat and tossed it to the floor.

"For now." Ean pressed her lips against his jaws. Her fingertips brushed his ribcage. The skeleman groaned with pleasure, embedding his cold fingers in her hair. She kissed her way down to his clavicle and bit down hard.

Elias staggered against the wall. *"Gods."*

Enigmatic energy infused Ean, flushing her body. The rubies and amethysts on her wedding ring glowed. She exhaled a sigh of sensual relief. Magic coursed through her, seeking purchase. The excess settled into her ring once her form was saturated.

Her eyelids fluttered open as she withdrew. "Hmm. Looks like I might have won this round."

Elias was breathing too hard to reply. He braced his hands against the wall to keep from toppling over. "Gods, Ean. What... was... *that?"*

Giggling, she tilted her head to one side. "Same as usual, wasn't it?"

"No." Still panting, the skeleman shook his skull to clear it. "You just siphoned a *massive* amount of energy. And you're not even phased by it. And…" he eyed her warily, "'Phantom pleasure' doesn't quite cut it anymore. We should invent a new phrase."

"Told you I could drive."

Elias threw back his head to laugh. "I honestly thought you meant Simulacra."

"Oh! That, too." Ean edged closer, smiling, but Elias evaded her. "No, you don't! I couldn't handle another hit. You might kill me."

"As if!" She embraced him and nestled her cheek against his chest. She felt him relax. "I guess we should go back to the house and recuperate."

Elias tugged a lock of her hair. "Will you bring me snacks?"

"Yes." She guided him to the door.

"Will you… pet my skull?"

"Yes."

"Will you… buy me a pony?"

"No."

"I agree. Not my style. How about an undead stallion?"

"Elias!"

He laughed as she chased him outside.

Mid-morning sunlight glistened on the were-cat's glossy coat. The creature yawned and pawed the ground, curved claws digging into the soft earth. The brief chirrup of a furrow pheasant caught the cat's ear. His green eyes shone as he hunched to the ground.

"Travis?"

A feline growl rumbled from the back of his throat. He remained focused on the furrow pheasant.

"Travis, I don't have time to play hide-and-seek. Where are you?"

Startled, the were-cat's prey scurried into Darkling Forest. Travis sat up, hissing with chagrin. "You couldn't have waited a few minutes? You made me lose my dinner."

"What, that tiny snack bird? Come hunt with me, and we'll find something much better."

Travis licked his paws clean. "If you insist, Sinnie. Where's Oleon?"

Sindaya opened her inventory to select her bow and quiver. "Probably in downtown Helios with Kaspar. I overheard them planning to spend the day there until we meet the Mages at Grimoire Tap House."

"Perfect." His teeth flashed in a feline grin. "We'd better get to it, then."

Sindaya nodded. The two entered the outskirts of the Helios training grounds, where the territory was ripe with wild boar and deer. The Darkling Forest rimmed the edge. Soft, curling mist and the whispers of fay creatures echoed from its depths. Even the rambunctious were-cat eyed the forest's edge with a wary expression.

"Wait a minute." Sindaya stopped, fitting an arrow and listening hard. The were-cat's large ebony ears twitched to and fro. "What is it?" he whispered.

After a quiet moment, Travis recognized the sound of distant chanting.

The distinctive cadence – a chaotic, rippling rise followed by an abrupt drop, occurring over and over again – marked the chant as a prayer to Kanthesis the Damned. "Sounds like a meeting of the dark sorcerers," Sindaya whispered. "And not too far from here, either. We should leave."

"Don't you want to take a peek at them?" Travis asked, tense with intrigue. "We don't run into the servants of Kanthesis every day."

"That's an experience I'm perfectly happy to miss."

"Don't be a furrow pheasant, Sinnie." Ignoring her complaints, Travis pattered into the Darkling Forest in pursuit of the voices. Sindaya followed him anxiously, keeping her arrows close at hand.

A thick circle of ancient trees enclosed the shadowed magi. In the center knelt a dark elf, clad in an azure robe that sparkled like a star. He held a long blue thorn in the palm of his hand. Once the chanting drew to a close, the dark elf pricked the center of his palm. A splash of navy blood dropped onto the rock below.

"What do you think they're doing?" Sindaya whispered to the were-cat. Travis shook his shaggy head. "No idea. Does that dark elf look familiar to you?"

Sindaya gave the center sorcerer a long look. "Isn't that Gale Emodicus?"

"Sure is. I had no idea he was a sorcerer."

"Wow. I wonder if Lightcross knows?"

"Why? What does it matter?"

"I think it's cool that she won the SkyRate Grand Championship against a dark elf who's *also* a sorcerer. I know I'd be damn proud of that."

"*Shh.* He's doing something else now."

Emodicus placed something on the bloodied rock. Neither Sindaya nor Travis could make out what it was. Speaking in a low voice, he passed his hands over it several times. Although most of his words were in the tongue of the moon elves, Sindaya and Travis gave a simultaneous start at the name he uttered.

Nodding urgently to Travis, Sindaya motioned that they should leave while the leaving was good. They waited until they'd returned to the training grounds before speaking. "Did you hear what I heard?" Sindaya asked.

Travis morphed into his small, wiry human form. He scratched his ear. "There's no doubt about it. That ritual was definitely for a curse. But why him? And why now?"

"I bet that object on the rocks was one of his belongings."

"Yeah. Should we tell him?"

Sindaya returned her bow and quiver to her inventory. "Duh. Wouldn't *you* want to know if Gale Emodicus had cursed you?"

The were-cat's pointed teeth glinted as he snickered. "Why so serious? TerraWorks is still a game, after all. Might be kind of fun to be cursed. Gale probably just turned all of his clothing inside-out, or something."

Sindaya's manner relaxed. "Yeah, or maybe he stole all his socks. But only the left ones!"

The two friends traded banter for a while. "Anyway, I'm still going to tell him," Sindaya mentioned. "I would want to know."

"Sure. But I think he'll just laugh it off. He's been pretty upbeat since marrying Ean."

Sindaya ruffled Travis' shaggy hair as they started for downtown Helios. "I didn't expect VR marriage to agree with him. It's kind of nice to see that true love still exists... even though they do annoy me sometimes."

The were-cat snuffled and rolled his eyes. "Yeah, sometimes I have to bite my tongue to keep from telling them to *please,* for the love of Nymphoria, *get a room!* But they'll cool off eventually."

"You think so?"

"All couples do. Just a matter of time. And in VR, I'd cut that time in half."

"Hmm. Maybe you're right."

2

GRIMOIRE TAP HOUSE

"Hey, grandpa! Can't you go any faster than that?"

"Who are you calling *grandpa?*"

Ean cupped her hands around her mouth to shout, "Oh, I don't know, the only person in my vicinity who's going twenty on a skyboard. I'm kicking your boney ass! You're not even trying."

Elias shot her a devilish glare, kneeling into A-position. "I was just warming up. You needn't sass your husband."

"Well, hurry up. Everybody's going to be waiting on us." Ean circled Elias, rapidly banking aside as he gunned the engine. "You're buying, *grandma,*" the skeleman yelled, saluting her as he barreled ahead.

"Not fair!" Giggling, the half-elf whipped her skyboard into full pursuit. The couple joked and traded comic gestures as they flew from TerraWorks to Helios. Once they landed, Elias cornered her in the SkyRate lobby. "Looks like I beat the Grand Champion. I expect a reward, Lightcross."

"I know, I know. I'm buying." Ean sighed dramatically. "Skeletons can't get drunk, though, so I don't even get to see you tipsy. What a waste."

Elias trapped her against the wall. "Then you'll have to reward me some other way."

Ean smiled and fluttered her lashes, the picture of innocence. "What other way?"

As Elias moved in for her kiss, a piercing shatter interrupted them. Ean's sharp cry of dismay turned several heads. "My ring!"

"What happened?" Elias stared at the shards of white gold and broken gems scattered across the lobby floor. "What in Hades?"

"My ring. It's... it's broken." Ean stooped to gather the pieces with trembling hands. "It just exploded. I don't know how, Eli."

"By the gods."

Ean glanced up at him, ice-blue eyes melting into tears. "What?"

Eli rested his hand on her head. "The dark charisma."

All the dark charisma that her ring had stored broke loose. Ean's knee-length hair floated and snapped in an electric cloud, and her eyes brimmed with lightning. Overcome by the energy, Ean started to laugh, her warm mirth steadily taking on a maniacal tone. Eli's eyes narrowed with concern. He continued to press his hand against her head, endeavoring to slow the magic's progression and absorb whatever he could. "Just hang in there for a minute, my dear. You'll be all right."

Her face thrust skyward as she continued to laugh, fingers digging into the floorboards. Scarlet and violet pulses consumed her body. Eli closed his eyes. His teeth ground together as he muttered multiple incantations, kneeling beside her to get even closer. "Hold on, Lightcross. Just hold on. Get out of here!" He shouted at the bystanders. The lobby quickly emptied.

The gems in Eli's skull blazed as they struggled to store the energy. Elias grunted from the pain, keeping his hand steady. "It's almost over, Ean."

His wife was slammed back against the wall. Elias clutched his skull in pain. Winded, Ean fell face-down, still fighting the urge to giggle as the excess charisma spent itself. Elias scrambled forward and held her. "Ean? Can you hear me?"

The half-elf blinked, staring at him with a dazed expression. "I'm OK. My head feels so... light. Like something is tickling it. On the inside." She prodded her forehead in confusion.

Elias smoothed his cool hand across her forehead. "You hit that wall pretty hard. I'm taking you straight to the nearest hospital."

"No, I'm all right. Nothing hurts."

"*Nothing* hurts?"

"Nope. And my HP is full. It just kind of... tickled." She giggled again, touching her forehead. "It felt good. Not hitting the wall, of course. But the rest wasn't so bad."

Eli's eyelids crinkled as he winced. "Well, it didn't feel good to me. I had to use my gems as receptacles, and now I have a headache. Just how much charisma have you been hoarding in that ring?"

Ean grimaced. "How should I know? There's no way for me to measure the stuff."

"Well, you should go home and rest. We have no idea what just happened, and I'm feeling uneasy about it. I'll get a transport gem."

"No way! I'm feeling great. Amazing, actually." To prove it, Ean rose to her feet and jogged around the lobby. "See? No broken bones or anything." She grinned. "I'm fine. Let's go meet up with the Spectral Tyrants."

Elias grunted. "Fine. But I'm buying a transport gem anyway, just in case. I'll feel better."

"Sure thing, my love." Ean slipped her arm through his and guided him out of the lobby. "You can all go back in now!" she called to the frightened spectators, who gaped at her as if she was a ghost. Elias watched her keenly… but all he could see was his own joyful, light-stepping, spirited wife. His tense jaws relaxed.

The Grimoire Tap House was packed. An Irish-inspired band played in the corner while avatars chatted over mugs of frothing beer. The tavern's long wooden tables and benches contrasted strongly with the modern booths of the Pulse. Ean glanced around with delight. "I can't believe you've never brought me here before. How fun!"

"By the gods!" Somebody shouted. "That's *Elias Mage!*" Ean felt a tiny stab of envy as a crowd gathered, eager to meet the legendary avatar. Most were happy to acknowledge the SkyRate champion as well, of course, but she was clearly the afterthought.

Eventually, the crowd calmed and dispersed. "There's the gang." Elias nodded toward Desmond, Oleon, Kaspar, and Travis. The were-cat spotted them and scampered through the mob, greeting Ean with enthusiasm. "I think Sindaya is prowling around here somewhere. She got bored of our boyish banter. How's the SkyRate champion?"

"Phantasmic." Ean tussled his disheveled hair with a motherly expression. "And how is my favorite feline?"

"I'm bored, too. Thank the Pantheon you're here! Let's take shots."

"Very cute, my son," Elias declared, patting Travis on the head. "But my love has had an… interesting day." He directed her a sideways glance. "She'd better take it easy."

Ean acquiesced. "Sure." She delved into the crowd in search of Sinnie. Travis and Elias returned to their group. "I've got some news for you," the were-cat informed Eli. "But I figured everybody else should hear about it, too. So we can all watch your back."

A mug appeared in Eli's hand. He drained it dry in a few gulps. "What's up?"

"Gale Emodicus. Did you know he's a sorcerer under the badge of Kanthesis?"

The skeleman shrugged and nodded.

"Well… Sindaya and I were out hunting in Helios along Darkling Forest. We heard some chanting and followed up on it. Emodicus was out there with a few others, and he was brewing some kind of curse. He mentioned your name."

As the were-cat had expected, Elias seemed to relish the idea. He leaned over the table, emitting a dark chuckle. His fingerbones clinked as he touched them together. "How interesting. I wonder when it will take effect?"

"How are you feeling now?" Ollie questioned, lowering his mug.

"Just fine." Elias leaned back again, crossing his arms. "I've burrowed down a few rabbit holes in dark spellcraft, hexing included. For obvious reasons, there's not a whole lot we avatars can do to one another. It'll be no more than a mild inconvenience, at best."

Desmond held up his hand. "Wait a moment, lad. Didn't I overhear you say something about Ean having an 'interesting day?'"

"Mmm." Elias tapped his finger against his mandible. "She did, indeed. Her wedding ring broke, and there's no immediate explanation as to how… or why."

Oleon polished off his beer before inquiring, "What was she doing? Training?"

Eli's golden countenance burned sunset-orange. "No… not exactly."

"By the gods!" The menfolk shoved Elias, drowning his feeble objections in hilarity. "Relax, boys! It was just a kiss, OK?"

"Didn't you craft that ring specifically for her, so she'd have somewhere to store excess charisma?" Travis asked. "What happened when it all came flooding out?"

"We're not sure." Eli's eyes glinted as he re-evaluated the scene. "She seems fine, and she says nothing hurt her. Even claimed it felt good. But I've never heard her laugh like that before. She seemed to be losing her mind for a minute or two."

"Might want to read up some more on dark charisma," Kaspar proposed. "I'd imagine her half-elf attributes could handle the bombardment, but she's still half-human. A sudden exposure to that amount might transform her into a midnight berserker."

Elias leaned in his direction. "What else do you know about it, Kaspar?"

Kaspar propped his elbows on the table. "I know this avatar named Groc the Berserker. He changed his prior class type by exposing himself to concentrated amounts of charisma. He utilizes light charisma, not dark, but both berserker types have a similar combat style. They'll do themselves damage on the battlefield, but their attacks are virtually unstoppable."

"Hmm." Elias ordered and consumed another beer. "Can elves or humans become berserkers?"

"Elves, no. Humans, yes."

Eli nodded. "So, Lightcross has a fifty-fifty chance of becoming a midnight berserker."

"Well, as I recommended, I'd do some more reading before making that assumption. But it's possible. However," Kaspar shook his head, "if Gale's curse is the reason her ring broke, why would he cause that to happen? What would he stand to gain if Ean Mage became a midnight berserker?"

The skeleman considered this. "She'd be volatile on the battlefield. A liability. If we confronted him as a couple, I couldn't rely on her to help me. She might even harm me instead."

"Ah," Travis hissed. "I see what he's doing. He's trying to separate the two of you so he can battle one or the other, but not both at once."

"But in the meantime, he's infused Lightcross with immense charismatic power. She'll probably rival you onstage, Elias." Ollie elbowed him. "How do you feel about that?"

"I'll enjoy it," Eli answered coolly. "Iron sharpens iron. And I do like experiments, after all."

"Don't we know it!" Oleon laughed. "Remember that time when you infused your skull with-"

Elias held up a warning finger. "Shut up, Ollie."

Travis snickered. "Or when he hacked the TerraDome program to-"

The skeleman grabbed Travis in a headlock. "You were saying?"

The were-cat wiggled free and ran for cover. "Ean! Your husband's bullying me again."

Ean was sitting at the bar with Sindaya. She turned to Travis, smiling her sympathy. "Then come sit with me, my son. I'll protect you."

Travis sprang into his feline form, curling into Ean's lap. "You're a little too big for this, Travis," she laughed, stroking his head. He ignored her injunction and purred.

Elias shook his skull. "Show-off." He rose from the bench and extended a fist to the Spectral Tyrants. "Well, boys, my work's cut out for me. Looks like I'll need to do some research, then pay Emodicus a friendly visit."

"Wouldn't want to be him," Desmond chuckled, leaning in for the group fist bump.

"Live while you can!"

"Sleep when you're dead."

Elias approached the bar to collect his wife. "'Scuse me, sir." He dumped Travis out of her lap with one fell swoop. "Next time, ask Ean's permission before you fawn all over her."

"Oh, he's just a harmless little furball." Ean beamed and kissed her skeleman. "Heard my name a few times, by the way. What were you boys discussing over there?"

Eli shrugged and propped an arm over her shoulders. "The usual. Charisma, our mutual rival, and whether or not you might be going insane."

"Hey!"

"Just a theory, my love."

"You seem mighty relaxed about it. You aren't worried about having a crazy wife?"

Elias snorted. "What else is new?"

She menaced his funny bone with a pinch.

3

ELIAS VS. EMODICUS

A stiff wind stirred the heavy mist from the ground. The dark elf wandered through the shadowed arena. His right hand gripped the hilt of an elegant sable blade. He dropped the cerulean hood of his cape as he raised his head, listening intently. "You've arrived at last."

A gilt skeleman strode from the bouldered perimeter. His silver armor glistened in the sun. He unsheathed Sacrimony and gestured 'round the stadium. "Why Stellos?"

"My home base," Emodicus carelessly replied. "We can duel elsewhere if that makes you uncomfortable."

"*Pfft.*" Elias leveled his blade at the dark elf. "I have a bone to pick with you, sir. On behalf of my beloved wife."

The elven sorcerer chuckled, his indigo eyes aflame with the promise of battle. "I do adore your sense of humor, Eli. We ought to duel more often."

"Don't change the subject." The opponents circled one another. "I know you're the villain who broke Ean's ring. What game are you playing, Modi?"

Emodicus sneered, shifting his stance. "You know I hate that nickname."

Eli's jaws snapped together. His eager aspect burned hellishly bright. "If you can defeat me, I promise never to say it again." He lunged with a demonic chuckle. "Can't promise not to *think* it, though!"

Gale parried the blow. Eli's fierce mirth echoed among the rocks as their blades flashed. The rivals were well-matched; Eli's regal brutality was often sidestepped by Gale's imperial grace. The tall, dim trees of Stellos observed the avatars in grave silence. The sharp scent of pine energized their senses.

The dark elf landed a hit, earning a snarl from Elias. Azure energy from Gale's sword drained Eli's HP, bolstering Gale's instead.

"Careful what you wish for, Modi."

Emodicus leapt onto a boulder, grinning. "Let me guess. Your attacks become more powerful as your HP decreases?" He *tsk*'ed, shaking his head. "How unimaginative."

"Not exactly."

A pair of massive gray wings sprouted from the skeleman's shoulder blades. With two powerful sweeps, he landed on the boulder near his foe. *"Esselbyurn!"* he bellowed. The dark elf staggered back with a grimace of pain; a burning sensation weakened his limbs. "Very clever," he panted. *"Crysal aqueous."* Gale's eyes shimmered. The burning sensation diminished. "You'll have to do better than that, Elias Mage."

The skeleman growled. "I'll warrant you won't be stealing my HP again."

Their blades traded further blows. Emodicus targeted Eli's colossal wings. Finding this to be a nuisance, Elias retracted them. Grunting, the skeleman leveled a kick, knocking Gale from the boulder.

The dark elf rallied. He blocked Eli's blow from above, squinting as the skeleman's golden frame caught the light. At the same moment, they both raised a hand to invoke a spell.

"Ricobyurn!"

"Santlyre!"

As a sapphire tsunami devoured Eli's flames, the collision knocked them off their feet. A regenerative healing spell embraced Emodicus. Revitalized, the dark elf regained his footing. "Oh, Eli?" he sang, lifting his hand to display a pearl ring. "Remember your friend?"

Grunting, Elias braced himself up to glare. "All too well."

"Your artificer skills are much appreciated." Chuckling, Emodicus twirled the ring around his finger. "Although, I can't help but laugh when I recall that you actually bought my assistant's 'mermaid imagery' drivel. Did it never occur to you that your craft was serving your rival?"

Elias ground his teeth. "It's always the same with you villains. You talk too damn much." Extending his wings, he swept forward full-force, pummeling Gale into the dirt. "If you lift so much as a *pinky* against my wife again..."

So saying, Elias cupped his skeletal hand around the ring. *"Insanctus dehmohri!"* A dark cloud enveloped it, zeroing in on the pearl. It shattered with a thunderous *clap.* Satisfied, the skeleman nudged the point of his blade against Gale's throat. "Do you understand?"

The elf tilted his head. "So, you *do* know dark magic."

The sword in Eli's hand wavered. "So what?"

"So, nothing. It's just interesting, as you would say yourself."

Just then, the Mage avatar symbol flashed in the corner of Eli's screen. "I'll finish the job if I have to," he threatened, slowly withdrawing his blade. "Just imagine to yourself how fun it would be to spend half a month recuperating your avatar. Because I won't just end you. I'll *decimate* you."

Emodicus stood up and dusted off his cloak. "It would amuse me to see you try."

Snarling, Elias turned his back and stalked away. He stretched his wings to return to Helios. "Until next time," Gale called.

The dark elf waited until Eli was a golden fleck on the horizon. He pulled off his broken ring, regarding it thoughtfully before tossing it away. "I'm growing rather fond of you, Elias Mage." Drawing his hood over his head, he disappeared among the trees.

Meanwhile, Ean was waiting for Elias in Vermillion Castle.

The Mages had purchased it, as they were too fond of their honeymoon memories to part with it. While some aspects remained untouched, the modest castle had been updated with modern furniture and conveniences. Hexadecimal roamed it freely in full-scale mode, serving as a butler, advisor, or friend as occasion arose.

Currently, he leaned over Ean, who was sitting on the floor. She braced her hands against her forehead. "Did you message Elias?"

"Yes, Ean-san. Please drink this potion while your healing tea finishes brewing."

"Thanks, Hexy." Ean took the potion he offered and swallowed it. "I hope he isn't far away. If he wasn't so stubborn, he'd get a Holopal too, and we'd always know where he is!"

"May I carry you to the couch?"

"Please." Ean winced as Hexadecimal lifted her. *"Arigato gozaimasu."*

"Mondai ga nai." After ensuring her comfort, Hex attended to the disheveled living room. "If you had remained in the focus session, Ean-san, this destruction of property would have been avoided."

"I know that!" Ean groaned. "I don't know what happened. One minute I was there, training against Ophidious, and the next... everything went white."

The front door creaked open. Elias retracted his wings and stepped inside. His eyes widened as he absorbed the chaotic scene. "What in Hades happened?" He rushed to Ean's side, kneeling to hold her hand. "Are you hurt?"

"Just a little," his wife admitted. "But it's no big deal." Hex returned with a cup of healing tea. Ean accepted it gratefully. "I was training in a focus session against Ophidious, and I... I just lost control, or something. I must have terminated the session on accident."

Eli's grip on her hand tightened. "You don't remember anything?"

"Not really. Luckily, all my focus sessions are recorded. We can play it back and see what went wrong."

Elias sighed in relief. "Good. Let's do that."

Hex selected the program for them, projecting the HV. Eli stroked Ean's hand as the couple watched. Ean's lithe figure wielded Necrowave, landing lightening-infused hits with practiced assurance. Ophidious became angry. After deflecting a powerful blow, Ean's eyes suddenly changed from ice-blue to dark red. Emanating a reckless laugh, she plunged toward the fay sorcerer with abandon. The head of her hammer pulsed with dark energy.

Focus Session Ophidious exploded in a surge of ruby-amethyst lightening.

The HV ended. A lengthy silence ensued. "By the gods," Elias finally breathed. "I think it's safe to say you're becoming a midnight berserker, Ean."

"My class type changed? How?"

Elias sighed and rubbed his temples. *No wonder they were throbbing on my way home.* "Kaspar told me it might happen. I've been meaning to explain that conversation, but... it slipped my mind."

Ean's pupils lit with an angry spark. "It *slipped your mind* that I've become a berserker against my will? I never chose this!"

"Ean-san is correct," Hex's gentle tenor interjected. "Her class type should not be subject to the whims of any other player. This move was against the TerraWorks code of avatar ethics. Gale Emodicus should be reported."

"You're right. This wasn't fair." Elias tenderly embraced his wife. "I'm deeply sorry, my love. I'll look into this, and I'll make it right."

Ean withdrew. "You should have warned me. I can't *believe* you didn't warn me!" She left the couch and stormed away.

Elias crossed his arms, glaring into the fireplace. "It's not like I did this!"

Hexadecimal floated toward him, hands tucked in his sleeves. "You are responsible for the accumulation of dark charisma, Eli-san."

The skeleman ground his teeth. "But I took precautions. I made her that ring so the energy would be safely stored. No one should have been able to break it."

Hex waited patiently while Eli patrolled the room. "*No one* should have been able to touch that ring. How did he do it? Gods damn the man!" He clenched his deathly fists. "We'll turn his own curse against him. His victory won't last long." A hellish chuckle rumbled from his invisible throat.

"If I may, sir… You may be more responsible than you think."

Elias glowered at the serene Holopal. "Pray tell."

"In your research, have you ever come across the myth of the Skeleton's Anathema?"

The gems in Eli's skull glittered as he shook his head. "No. Tell me about it."

The half-elf paced the balcony in a rage. She hoped the lakeside breeze would cool her heated face, but it didn't seem to be helping. "I can't believe he didn't say anything. Just made jokes about how I might be 'going mad.'" Her hands grasped the ornate railing. "I think he loves me… but sometimes, he can be so… so *cold.*"

Sighing, she flicked her wrist to extract a magenta Whisker. She inhaled its pink wreaths in relief. "I know I can't stay mad at him, though. It's really Gale's fault."

Ean had spoken aloud, expecting Hex's soothing voice to answer. Surprised by the silence, she turned and realized he hadn't followed her. "It figures. He probably likes Elias more than me."

Sulking, she quashed her cigarette and went back inside. She heard the Holopal's level intonation, interrupted every now and then by Eli's handsome baritone. Her rebellious heart yearned for Elias. Skimming down the curved staircase, she entered the living room, still debating whether to yell at Elias or seek the comfort of his arms. "Have you two figured out a plan of action yet?" she asked, eyeing Elias askance.

Her husband's terse demeanor relaxed. "We're working on it." He opened his arms for a hug, but she held back. "Think we could use it to our advantage somehow?" she added. Ean turned away slightly and folded her arms. Her wicked heartbeat sent fresh color into her cheeks; she was desperate to hide it.

"That's just what Hex and I were discussing." She could sense Elias looming behind her. Ean flinched as his cool hands pulled her back against his chest. "We'll figure this out together, my love." He nuzzled her neck, tickling her with his breath.

The telltale blush crawled up her ears. Elias knew he'd won. "No tickling," she warned, shoving him aside – in play this time. A scuffle commenced. The skeleman quickly wrestled her to the floor. "Get lost," he barked at Hex, who swiftly obeyed.

4

EAN'S TAKING RISKS (AGAIN)

L ater that night, Ean patrolled the balcony long after Elias had logged off. She ticked off various points on her fingers. She muttered to herself. She tugged at her hair, sighing, then resolutely bundled her locks over one shoulder. "Hexy."

The Holopal appeared. "Ean-san."

"Contact Emodicus for me."

"By Livewire?"

"Yes."

"Please stand by."

Ean bit her thumbnail as she waited, head bowed. "This is dumb. Oh, brother, is this dumb! But the focus sessions aren't helping anymore, so…"

The pale blue HV of Emodicus flickered before her. "Lightcross. This is an unexpected pleasure." He managed a thin smile. "What can I do for you?"

"I'll get straight to the point." Ean crossed her arms in unconscious imitation of her husband. "While I'm well aware of what you did – and I'm not happy about it – I intend to use it to my own advantage."

"A wise decision."

"Also, since you're the avatar that's primarily responsible, I don't believe asking a favor from you is too far out of left field."

"I'm interested… as long as your proposition is mutually beneficial."

Ean hesitated. "I suppose it'll be helpful to you in a purely informational context. I want to train with you."

"May I ask why?"

"To defeat Ophidious."

"Very ambitious of you," Gale stated, his crafty aspect bright with intrigue. "You'll be alongside Elias when you confront him, I take it?"

"Perhaps. I'd prefer to battle the fay sorcerer alone. That's been one of my goals since before I met Eli, and I intend to see it through."

Gale nodded. "I accept. However, I do have a favor to ask in return."

"I'm willing to pay you for your time, of course."

"No, I don't require GP. I want to race against you at the Metro Cross Track."

Ean's ruddy eyebrows lifted. "That's an exclusive location. But we should be able to get in without any trouble, as long as it's just the two of us."

"Precisely." The dark elf delivered a wicked smile. "And you have to swear not to tell Elias anything about training with me."

The half-elf fiddled with her necklace. "That's not an easy ask, Emodicus. We're not just married in-game, you see. We're also dating in real life. He'll know about our training eventually."

"Well, do the best you can. There will come a time when it will no longer matter."

Ean cocked her head, eyeing the dark elf with suspicion. "This likely goes without saying, but if I have any reason to suspect that you're up to no good, then all agreements are off. No Metro Track, no training, and I'm telling Elias everything. Got it?"

"That's exactly what I would wish," he replied with infuriating coolness. "Now, to business. We will meet in the Stellos training cells starting tomorrow night. When does Elias usually log off?"

"During the weekdays? Around midnight."

"Then training begins at 12:30." He stretched and rubbed his hands together. "I will book our race at the Metro."

"And it's just you and me, right?"

"We'll be the sole competitors, yes. There will be an audience."

Ean stiffened. "Why do we need an audience? I assumed this private race was just a personal vendetta of yours."

"You assumed correctly," Gale confessed, "but what would be the point of defeating the current SkyRate Grand Champion without witnesses?"

Ean prodded the balcony railing. "Oh. Guess that's valid."

Gale nodded. A faint hint of surprise crossed his face. "Despite your madcap energy, you're refreshingly practical. I can see why you get along with Eli so well."

Ean shot him a quizzical smile. "Careful. That *almost* sounded like a compliment."

"What if it was?" The dark elf folded his muscular arms. "If we're not careful to nourish our rivalry, Lightcross, we might end up becoming friends."

"Hmph. I doubt Eli would be amenable to that."

"True. How's he doing, by the way?" Emodicus smirked. "He took a bit of a beating whilst defending your precious honor."

"What? When?" Ean rested her hands on her hips. "You two were in a battle?"

"I assumed you knew. We've got quite a history, Elias and I."

"You hurt him." It was more of a statement than a question; Gale noticed her hands closing into fists. Her irises flashed. "You'd better be prepared for tomorrow night, Emodicus. I don't intend to go easy on you."

The dark elf's grin portrayed airy unconcern. "Cute. Retract your claws, little kitten, and cease your hissing. Elias is fine. I can count off my battle-worthy foes on one hand, but your husband makes the list."

"Then I'll expect the very best from your training."

"And that's what you'll get." Emodicus bowed. *"Namyonet."*

The Livewire projection closed. Unclenching her fists, Ean inhaled deeply and lit a Whisker. "If I can defeat the darkling elf, I can defeat Ophidious."

Then I'll finally be worthy of Elias Mage.

The TerraDome studio buzzed with raw, metallic rhythm. Ean was practicing with the rest of the Spectral Tyrants. Her gold guitar, studded with rubies, glistened in the studio lighting. She nodded to Travis as they leaned back-to-back, savoring the powerful vibrations of their instruments.

Elias kept time against his knee as he listened, eyes closed. Satisfied with their warm-up, the skeleman abandoned his metal chair and signaled them for his first song. He twirled his gilt staff as the song changed to "Benighted."

"TYRANNOUS!

FRANKLY, I CAN SEE BEYOND

BIRAMOUS!
YOUR TWO-FACED WONDER.
GARRULOUS!
LET YOUR MIND BE TACITURN,
QUERULOUS!
I PREFER PHENOMENA."

Elias circled the studio as he sang, stopping to caress Ean's waist. Grinning, she took advantage of the symphonic break to kiss him. Travis and Oleon shook their heads at each other. Kaspar hit a few sour notes on purpose. Even Sindaya – who was more tolerant than the rest of them – rolled her eyes and sighed. "Newlyweds."

The skeleman backed off to administer a glare. "What, I can't kiss my wife?" he shouted over the score. The band laughed and made sardonic remarks.

Elias resumed his patrol, menacing a few of his friends with chilly repartee. Ean's expression sparkled with delight as she played.

After the session ended, the band members funneled out one by one. Ean started to leave with Sindaya. Someone's hand snagged the collar of her shirt. She squealed as she was tugged backward. "Stay a moment," Eli's voice requested.

Ean's throat tightened as she gulped. "Sure."

He waited until the studio door closed. "Just wanted you all to myself," he commented, drawing her close. "You look nervous. Everything OK?"

His wife paused. *It's a matter of when, not if.* "Yeah. I… I talked to Emodicus last night."

A cold glimmer entered his eye. "What did he want?"

"He challenged me to a race at the Metro Cross."

"Alone?"

"Yes. Plus the audience, of course."

"Mmm. He's up to something, that's without question." Elias stroked his mandible. "I'm just not sure what."

Ean tried to look casual. "He admitted that it's a personal crusade. He wants to challenge me for the SkyRate Grand Champion title."

"But it's too early," Eli pointed out, eyes narrowing. "Your title is up for grabs next SkyRate season, not now. What's the point?"

"Personal satisfaction, I guess."

"That doesn't make sense." Eli shifted his weight. "It's also a significant expense to book a private race. Especially at the Metro. Why would he do that?"

"Look, I know it's weird. I can back out if you want me to."

"You said yes?"

"Well, yeah. It's the Metro! I can't turn down an experience like that."

Grunting, Elias shook his skull and walked away. "I don't like this. I don't like it at all. First, he destroys your ring. You're legit OP, to the point where you can't control yourself. Then he wants to set up an exclusive skyboard race and only invites *you*. You know he's up to something, but you said yes anyway. Why are you asking for trouble, Ean?"

Ean tiptoed behind him to rest her head against his back. "I like trouble." She wrapped her arms around him.

"I suppose you do." He emitted a low chuckle. "Well, do as you please. I don't mean to police you. Just… don't go without me, OK?"

Ean kissed the back of his skull. "That was quick. I thought you'd put up more of a fight."

Her husband spun around to encage her in his arms. "I'll keep a close eye on him. We might be able to catch that cerulean spider in his own web."

"Oh, I see. You're using your in-game spouse as bait. Charming."

"You know me." The skeleman winked. "Not a sentimental bone in my body, remember?"

"Didn't need the reminder, but thanks."

Their fingers intertwined as they kissed. Elias weakened as she sucked on his tongue. *"Mmm."*

5

BEWARE THE DARK ELF

"Lightcross!"

The half-elf pulled herself together. "Sorry, Modi. What?" Her brain was on overdrive from her last kiss with Eli. Ean's nerves still tingled, and her skin burned. *By the gods! If this "phantom pleasure" keeps intensifying, I don't know if I'll be able to handle it. Not sure whether to worship the TerraWorks programmers, or hang them…*

"Focus, woman." Gale snapped his fingers. "Is that the only weapon you carry?"

Ean glanced at Necrowave. Her oversized hammer sparkled with intermittent shreds of violet lightening. "Yeah."

"You can't defeat Ophidious with that."

Sighing, Ean gripped the handle and gave her cherished weapon a deft twirl. "And what do you suggest in its place?"

"You need something long-range. Perhaps a rifle enhanced by artificer craft."

Ean groaned. "But I've never used a rifle before."

"All the more reason to switch right away." Emodicus sheathed his blade and beckoned. "Come on. We're going shopping."

"But we're well-known rivals thanks to SkyRate," Ean warned. "Won't it get around on TerraWiki if we're seen shopping together, like a couple of old girl friends?"

"We'll stick to Stellos. As the city of witches and wizards, most of the avatars here keep to themselves. And there won't be many shoppers in the middle of the night."

"Right. Won't a lot of the shops be closed, though?"

"Not the ones that matter. Most of the armories in Stellos are manned by apprentices or Holopals. In the latter case, they're open twenty-four-seven."

Ean flicked her wrist to scroll through her inventory. "Still, I'd rather be safe than sorry." She selected a long purple cloak and lifted the hood. "Whatever makes you happy," said Gale. "Let's go."

He unsheathed his sword again, waving the ebony blade in a circular motion. He spoke a few hurried words. They were instantly transported into the center of downtown Stellos. The marketplace buildings were widespread and mysterious. Their unsociable spaces left plenty of room for the denizens of spellcraft to move unseen. "Cheery," Ean remarked, observing the silent tread of several cloaked figures. "At least I don't stand out."

Gale led the way to the nearest armory. "I'll need you to trust my intuition for this purchase, Lightcross," he said. "If you *really* hate something, then feel free to make your sentiments known; but otherwise, you'll have to assume that I know best."

"Agreed."

They visited a few different stores before finding a rifle that met with Gale's approval. Ean felt more than a little amazed when she found herself enjoying his company. Gale Emodicus was stern, wickedly sarcastic, and often downright rude… not exactly designations for pleasant company.

Nevertheless, his sporadic humor, keen knowledge, and innate acumen sometimes rivaled Eli's. He was also (she admitted to herself) easy on the eyes. The dark elf's sable complexion glistened with a faint indigo sheen. His raven hair boasted a rich, silky texture. He walked with a swift, powerful stride, and his form was graceful in its proportions, muscular in its build. The V-slit in his leather vest betrayed glimpses of softly-glowing cerulean tattoos.

To Ean's embarrassment, he could sense her looking at him. "Fantasizing about my skeletal structure?" he questioned. Ean couldn't help but laugh. "Gods, you caught me. How did you guess?"

"Common practice for all skelephiles, I should think."

"I'm not *that* weird. My love for Elias happens to be an anomaly." Ean paid for her new weapon and embraced it with joy. "You may have converted me, Emodicus. I think I might love it more than Necrowave." She lowered her voice. "But don't tell Necro that, OK? We mustn't hurt my firstborn's feelings."

"What nonsense." The dark elf retrieved his sword. "Let's get back to the Stellos arena. I know it's very late, but I'm guessing you'll want a preliminary introduction to your rifle before you log off."

"Yes, he must be christened. What should I name him?"

Emodicus sighed. "I harbor no opinions of significance."

"Don't be so dull, Modi. Naming a new weapon is extremely important. And fun!" Ean raised the rifle and aimed, resting her finger on the trigger guard. "How about Antivenom? Because he's going to render the serpent king innocuous." She cackled.

The dark elf rolled his eyes. "As I said, I have no opinion." He moved to stand behind Ean, touching her shoulder and elbow to improve her posture. "Don't slouch. And try to aim with both eyes open. It's fine if you end up relying on your dominant eye, but it's best to try with both first."

"OK." An awkward flush stained the points of her ears. "Like this?"

"Much better."

Gale's hand lingered on her shoulder. Ean turned aside to give him a look. "I guess I took this for granted as generally understood, but... I should tell you that I take my marriage to Elias seriously. At least, in the confines of the game."

"Oh?" Emodicus removed his hand. "What a pity."

Her finger tightened on the guard. "Why is it a pity?"

Gale's eyes roamed over her. "Much as three-fourths of me hates to admit this aloud, you're something of a TerraWorks prize. SkyRate Grand Champion, a guitarist for the Spectral Tyrants, and well on your way to improving your combat level, thanks to a certain upgrade to berserker." Ean frowned, inciting further explanations. "You're also quite attractive. Your avatar's details are exceptional. You project an aura of barely-repressed chaos and intense charismatic allure." His dark lips curved into a seductive smile. "I doubt Elias will be able to keep you all to himself."

Ean snorted. "We'll see about that." She shouldered her rifle and strode away, ignoring Gale's firm decree that she return.

In the days that followed, Lightcross trained alone. She avoided both Gale and Elias, practicing diligently with Antivenom and planning her attack strategy with Hex's aid. She commissioned some upgrades from an artificer in the Kingdom of Klad, certain that Eli would question the when's, where's, and how's behind her latest acquisition if she booked his services.

Fortunately, Elias was too busy in his workshop and spying on Emodicus to notice his wife's distance. Ean thanked the Terran stars that she'd reneged on training with the dark elf. Her husband's espionage was irregular, but thorough. She realized he would have found them out very quickly. Instead, she made do with the game's rifle focus sessions, and Hex's research on long-range gun handling.

A week passed before she considered reinstating any contact with Gale. Although she felt her anger with him was justified, she was still irresistibly tempted by the thought of challenging him at the Metro track. As she declared to Hexadecimal, Emodicus "needed to be put back in his place."

Skyboarding was just the way to do it.

As prior, Ean waited until her husband had logged off before pinging Emodicus by Livewire. Her hail went unanswered. Shrugging, she had just opened her logout screen when Emodicus sent her a holotext.

The white font of his message floated at eye level. *You called?*

Yeah. I figured we should clear up a few things, now that we've had time to cool off.

Agreed. I owe you an apology. I spoke inappropriately.

Yes, you did. But I'm willing to forgive you if you promise not to do it again.

I promise. Are you still interested in training with me?

Ean paused, biting her lip. *I've put together a really solid program with my Holopal's help. I'll let you know if I change my mind, but for now, I think I'm good. I still want to race you, though.*

Excellent. I'll let you know when it's booked. Any preference for the date/time?

Nope. Whenever you think you're ready to face me!

Ean could sense his dry mirth. *Right. So confident, as usual. I'm intrigued by the thought of racing against a berserker. Think you can keep it together, Lightcross?*

Can you?

Always.

The half-elf giggled. *We'll see.*

A few minutes lapsed. *Well, it's late. I'll keep you updated on the Metro booking. Say hello to Elias for me. I've felt his menacing spectral eyes boring into the back of my head this past week.*

Well, you did break my wedding ring. You haven't apologized for that, by the way.

Sorry.

And you didn't apologize for getting into that sword fight with Eli, either.

Hey, he's *the one who challenged me. Sorry, though.*

You don't mean it.

You don't believe me?

Of course not. What exactly do you want, Modi?

A second pause succeeded this question. *I want us to be friends.*

Don't you have friends in your little gang of sorcerers, or whatever it is?

The Kanthesis Temple. Yes, I have a few friends there. I don't make friends easily, Lightcross.

Gee, I wonder why.

Ean laughed at her own response. She sat cross-legged on the balcony, enjoying the nighttime breeze. Hex offered to bring her some tea, but she declined. "I'm just about to log off."

Hey, Lightcross. If we're friends, I'll let you call me Modi.

A poor incentive; I do that anyway. So does Elias.

True. Regardless, I want you to know that I'm sincere. I enjoy being your SkyRate rival – I won't deny that – but I'd like to be friends with you. Think about it.

The half-elf tilted her head, grinning. *'K, Modi.*

See you around, Mrs. Mage.

6

TERRAN SECRETS

Alone in his workshop, Elias browsed through his inventory and extracted a thin, sleek volume. He hummed "Illusory" as he skimmed the pages.

Locating the paragraph he wanted, he tapped it twice. The page's font projected at eye level. Eli rested his mandible in his hands as he read.

"The Skeleton's Anathema"

"Although skeletal avatars do harbor some advantages (including immunity to necromancy and zombification), they are notoriously difficult to master. However, the player who perseveres will have a unique avatar on their hands.

"A skeletal avatar's abilities are deceptive, rendering them unknown by most. When the avatar has maxed out, both in his/her performa and combat level, the skeleton will have an exceptional effect on the members of their company.

"For example, it is no secret that excess charisma naturally accumulates around certain races, such as the elves. It can be stored in various objects, such as the jewels of a gem mage, and channeled into magical items. Skeletal avatars take this ability to the next level. Once their performa level has reached one hundred, their excess charisma is absorbed by the company itself. In fact, skeletons will experience certain consequences if they do *not* seek another avatar/avatar group to absorb this pool of energy: light-headedness, restlessness, and inability to concentrate.

"This situation compels the skeleton to join a guild and share that energy company-wide, or seek a companion to absorb it. In the latter case, caution must be taken to utilize precious stones or other receptacles to reduce concentrated exposure. Sudden, intense exposure to a skeleton's dark charisma could change a susceptible avatar type into 'the skeleton's anathema.'

"The exposed avatar maxes out quickly... *too* quickly. As a result, the avatar's class type will change to midnight berserker (a berserker that operates with dark charisma instead of light charisma). They have a highly effective 'rage mode,' or manic state, but they will often harm themselves or a member of their team on the battlefield."

Elias rubbed his skull. "Hmm." His shoulder blades lifted in a shrug. "I assumed she would be able to handle it, since she's half-elf. I hope I wasn't wrong..."

He leaned back in his leather chair, deep in thought. Sunset-tinted flames rippled from his upgraded fireplace. Six glass lamps hung from the workshop's oaken beams. A new stained-glass window, proclaiming the Mage avatar symbol, glimmered in the evening light. Elias sighed and leaned his arms against his massive desk. "Well, it's just a question of damage control now." His eyelids crinkled. "I do *love* experiments."

Yawning, he fiddled with an ornate staff design, adding a few gem-stones. Getting bored with that, he walked into his back room and amused himself with frame renderings. He selected white bones, then black, and finally silver. He transformed the gems in his skull to chrome tourmaline. "Not bad," he remarked, changing his outfit to bronze leather.

A knock sounded at his door. Elias left the room to open it. "Ah. Good to see you, Cyrus."

204 THE TERRAWORKS TRILOGY

"Hey, man." The cyborg fist-bumped him as he entered. "Looking good. I like the chromium plating. Very *Terminator*."

"I see you've been enhancing your aesthetic as well." Eli's gaze grinned at the cyborg's mohawk – made of spikes, not hair – and the new assortment of welding tattoos on his broad arms. "What's that one for?" the skeleman asked, pointing to the ebony traces of a zombie's face.

Cyrus flopped into a plush lounge chair, flexing proudly. "Got that one for besting the Undead Campaign."

Elias sat in the chair beside him. "Congratulations."

"Thanks. Wish you could have joined us, though. Fighting the Zombie King was *thriller*."

"Badass, you mean?"

"What?" Cyrus laughed, kicking off his boots and stretching his part-mechanical feet.

"That's what Ean likes to say," Elias mentioned, chuckling. "Speaking of our female counterparts, how's Mallie these days?"

"Fair to middling. You know, I think she still hasn't forgiven you two for not hosting a big, elaborate wedding."

"We were too tired," the skeleman admitted. "And impatient. We'll leave you and Mallie to fulfill our lost dreams in that regard. You're still dating, right?"

Cyrus grinned. "We're keeping things casual for now, but yes."

"Good for you." Elias winked, flicking open his inventory and distributing a couple of smokes. "I recall receiving some torment for dating in VR. How's the dark side treating you?"

"Better than I deserve," the cyborg laughed. "You know," winking in return, "I had no idea how *realistic* certain sensations would be. I wouldn't have ribbed you so shamelessly if I knew what I was missing."

Eli's tone indicated a smirk. "Well, it's a bit different for us, isn't it? Your sensory reception is inhibited by your implants. (At least, realistically, it would be.) And mine should be nonexistent."

"So, the avatar gods had to compensate for our designs. Boy, did they, though!" Cyrus lit up. A fiendish glee sparked in his yellow eyes. "I'm not even sure what to call it. It's like… a dream that's so intense, you'll literally never forget it. And you want to fucking *live* in it, if you could."

The skeleman nodded. "Ean and I refer to it as phantom pleasure."

"Phantom pleasure! I like it. I'm going to steal that." He exhaled a dark purple cloud. "If you don't mind, that is."

Elias slipped his hands behind his skull, leaning back. "I've trademarked it. You owe me five GP every time you say it."

"Almighty Kanthesis! Aren't you wallowing in lucre as it is, Sir Spectral Tyrants?"

Eli yawned again. "I want to breed an undead stallion, but only from the very finest stock. That isn't cheap."

Cyrus spluttered. "Dude, I don't even want to know."

As they chatted before the fireplace, the training grounds in Helios were darkening. Ean reloaded with a defiant scowl. "This is taking longer than I expected."

Hex's cool tenor floated from the Holobox. "Your enhanced vision will aid you, but I recommend stopping soon. You sound tired."

"I *am* tired. But I need to practice more with Antivenom. I reload too slowly."

The sweet grasses of the training field whispered against Ean's boots as she aimed. *Bang! Bang! Bang!* A slight grin of satisfaction blossomed.

"That wasn't bad. At least my aim has improved today, if nothing else has."

Despite the perfect, airy silence of the countryside, Ean's elvish instincts alerted her to an intruder. Careful to point her rifle barrel-down, she turned to face him. "Evening, Modi."

"Lightcross." He folded his arms. His indigo eyes flashed in the lengthening shadows. "How's Antivenom handling?"

"It's butter-smooth, but I'm not." The half-elf laughed. "I never dreamed I'd be carrying a gun, let alone a fully automatic rifle. It gives me a rush, though. I like it."

"I came to deliver these." Emodicus scrolled through his inventory, selecting two large boxes of magazines. "They're color-coded, so pay attention to that. Reds contain short-range explosives. Use them discreetly; they're expensive. Purples contain poison. Even if your aim isn't great at first, just getting a single shot into your target will cause both initial and gradual damage. Just don't use them to hunt," he added with a chortle. "You'll be poisoning your food."

"Sweet. That's super helpful."

"And charmingly ironic. Antivenom fires venom."

"Dude, venom and poison aren't the same. It depends on how you're exposed-"

"Don't be a smartass." Gale chuckled, knocking her hat off her head. Ean scrambled to retrieve it. "How much do I owe you?"

The dark elf transferred the magazines. He closed his inventory. "Nothing this time around. Consider them a physical representation of my apology."

"Apolo*gies*." Ean corrected, donning her hat. She stored her rifle. "Something tells me you don't have any intention of apologizing to Eli as well."

Emodicus grunted. "I don't."

"I'm astonished!" Ean gasped, her tone dripping with sarcasm.

"He's a big boy. He can resolve his own precious feelings all by himself."

She held up a warning finger. "Now, we're just getting to be friendly here, Modi. Don't ruin a good thing by insulting my husband."

"Hmph." He pushed a few silken threads of hair from his eyes. "As I mentioned before, he and I have a history in TerraWorks. He's not exactly a saint, you know."

Lightcross snorted. "No shit, Sherlock. Saintly types don't aim to be maxed-out skeletons who sing in metal bands."

Gale tucked his hair behind his ears. "Agreed." He surveyed her demeanor and meditated. "You know, you're a lot more relaxed around me than you used to be."

Ean smiled. She held up her fists in a mock boxing pose. "Better watch your back, all the same. What if I'm just winding you 'round my little finger, eh?"

Unimpressed, the dark elf answered in listless monotone. "I'm a significantly tougher nut to crack than Elias, my dear Mrs. Mage."

"Well, I can't fight you on that one." Smacking him on the shoulder, Ean extracted her skyboard and powered up, revving the engine enticingly. "Interested in a quick night race, Modi-san?"

His sharp teeth flashed in a grin. "I thought you'd never ask."

7

AT THE METRO

E an studied the enormous gold-and-silver framework of the Metro Cross Track. It was particularly magnificent in the scalding afternoon sun. The half-elf removed her board and tucked it beneath her arm, smiling. "Well, Modi, in spite of your malfeasance, I owe you a hearty thanks. This is a sight for adrenaline-junkie eyes."

The dark elf nodded and stretched. "The Metro was originally designed and owned by the founder of SkyRate. He layered it with stunning precision and opulence. The Shiori Track would rival it if it were twice as long, but that is not the case."

Ean glanced at him mischievously. "And it's really *ours* for the next two hours?"

Emodicus smirked. "Thought you might need a couple run-throughs."

Ean elbowed him hard. "Since you paid for this booking, I guess I'll have to ingest a modicum of your abuse. But take care you don't push me too far."

"I quiver with fear."

The rivals scaled the long, snaking platforms of the Metro entryway. They passed the landing decks. The half-elf stopped again to admire the elegant archway at the starting line. Blinking out of sleep mode, the Metro's AI system scanned and acknowledged them. *Welcome, Ean Mage.*

Welcome, Gale Emodicus. Please mount your boards, approach the starting line, and assume launch position.

Ean obeyed, tossing Emodicus a quirky grin. "Piragor would *kill* me if he knew where I was right now."

Gale knelt into launch position as well. "Hear from him much?"

Ean just shook her head, but the flush of her pointed ears told Gale more. "Not really. He's set on winning the TerraWorks City Tournament next year, so… he's been training a lot."

"Ah."

The countdown proceeded – *3, 2, 1, Accelerate* – and the rivals were launched into a blinding series of spectacular trackwork. Gale was his unemotional self, coolly tackling the turns, loops, and corkscrews without ado. Ean whooped and hollered throughout the majority, holding her hands above her head for the graceful dive. The Shiori track had felt rough at times, rather like a wooden roller coaster. In comparison, the Metro experience was sleek and smooth. Ean enjoyed herself immensely, and didn't even blink when Emodicus beat her.

"Want to go again?" she instantly asked.

Gale coasted to a full stop. "Yes, if you'll promise to actually pay attention this time."

Ean pouted. "Don't you know how to have fun, Modi? I race because I love it, not just to be the best. Although being the best doesn't hurt," she added, prodding his stern arm.

Just then, Ean's Holobox buzzed against her shoulder. "Ean-san, you've received a message from Elias. Shall I project it?"

"Yeah, go ahead."

Where are you?

Ean frowned. *Sorry. Forgot to mention I'm training with Emodicus at the Metro today. We'll be done in another hour or so.*

He's your competitor, not your training partner. Why aren't you training separately?

Ean sighed and scratched her head. "Actually, that's a good point. Why *are* you doing run-throughs with me, Modi?"

The dark elf smiled (a tad maliciously). "Just tell him the truth. We're friends now."

Ean's eyes widened. "I get the feeling Elias isn't going to like that."

"He'll come around."

She glared. "That would happen much faster if you'd apologize to him."

The slight sneer on Gale's face informed her that he hadn't budged. Ean groaned. "Men." She spoke her response to Hexadecimal. *He's apologized for his former behavior, and we've agreed to complete a couple run-throughs. Piragor is focused on his own skyboarding career with a flight coach, so he doesn't have time to spare. Otherwise, I'd have asked him instead.*

It still doesn't make sense. I'm coming over.

Ean's demeanor tightened. She stalled the engine and dismounted to distance herself from Emodicus. *There's no need to be protective. I can take care of myself.*

You don't know everything I know, Ean. Emodicus is deceptive straight down to his core. He's the one avatar in all of TerraWorks that I would never trust. I'm coming.

You'd just be embarrassing yourself, Eli. I'm fine!

I'll be the judge of that.

Ean swiped the holotext aside and stomped back to her board. "Let's go again, Modi. No point in waiting around here for him to show up."

The dark elf rose an eyebrow. "If you're sure."

Once they crossed the finish line, the skeleman was waiting for them. Gleaming arms crossed, taloned wings folded, Elias strode over to them and nodded to his wife. Despite the tension radiating across the landing deck, Ean's heart still skipped a beat. *Gods, he's hot.*

Emodicus approached Eli stiffly. "Afternoon, Elias."

The skeleman levelled a scathing glare. Turning to Ean, his gaze softened just a bit. "How's the Metro so far?"

"Smooth as chrome. It may be significantly longer than the Shiori track, but Shiori was more of a challenge, to be honest." Ean paused, exasperated as the two men sized each other up. "You're not going to battle again, are you? For the love of the gods, don't do it here!"

"Don't be silly," Gale intoned, firing an equally-inflamed glare right back at Eli. "Your husband wouldn't be quite so *thoughtless*."

Eli's skeletal hand grasped the hilt of his sword. Ean sprang between them, spreading her arms wide. "Oh no, you don't. I was having a perfectly enjoyable day until now. What's up with you two, anyway? Why can't you get along?"

Gale snorted. "Ask *him*." Before Ean could protest, the dark elf mounted his board and shot away. Within seconds, he was a tiny cobalt speck in the sky. "Good riddance," Elias muttered, lowering his hand.

Ean sighed. "Well? Are you finally going to explain why you hate Modi so much?"

The skeleman's glare returned. "'Modi?' You've nicknamed him already?"

She held up her hands. "We've *both* been calling him that, Elias. Mostly as a slight. You're so mad, you're not even thinking straight."

Elias grunted and started to pace. "As you may have guessed, his player was also a beta tester for the combat regions in TerraWorks. We... ran into each other a good deal."

Ean placed her hands on her hips, waiting. "And?"

Elias rubbed his skull. "And, he's just insufferable! He lies, he cheats, he steals. He'll do anything to win, including betray his own guild. Only a fool would trust him." His boney fists clenched. "You're not a fool, Lightcross. You know better than to blindly trust the Fell Sorcerer."

"I don't trust him blindly. Besides, even if I did, didn't I trust *you* blindly? For a time?"

He glanced at her, miffed. "That's different."

"How is it different? I even *married* you!"

Eli's glance narrowed. "And do you regret it?"

"The blind trust? Or our in-game marriage?"

"I mean both, Ean. One clearly led to the other."

The half-elf's face reddened. It would be a lie to claim that she regretted either, and she knew it. But she couldn't bring herself to give him the satisfaction. "I'm saying I wouldn't have a relationship with you today - much less be married to you - if I didn't take the risk of trusting you. My friendship with Emodicus is beginning on the same principle."

Eli's skull shimmered as he laughed. "So, what? Are you going to marry *him* next? Is that the master plan?"

Ean's gaze went cold. She turned around, mounted, and flew away without another word.

She half-expected Elias to follow her, but he didn't.

Ean didn't log into TerraWorks for a few days. She kept herself busy, and privately thanked her common sense that she and William hadn't moved in together yet.

After indulging in some pillow-punching, junk food, and tearful reminiscing while playing the Spectral Tyrant's biggest hits, Ean couldn't take it anymore. She donned her TerraWorks helmet and logged in.

Her avatar rose from the master bed in Vermillion Castle. Hexadecimal was in place, awaiting instructions. Elias was nowhere to be seen. "Any messages?" she asked anxiously.

"One message from Elias, Ean-san."

"Play it back."

The skeleman's recorded face struck her heart. *My dear. I'm sorry I lost my temper. I was angry with Emodicus, and worried about you. I don't want him to hurt you. When you're ready to talk, please come to my workshop. I'll be there. I miss you.*

Ean sighed and texted her response. *I'm on my way. I miss you, too.*

She traveled to Eli's workshop by skyboard, still puzzled. Although Elias did have a temper, his particularly snappish distrust for a fellow avatar didn't make sense to her. Perhaps, if she was just a little more patient with him (and a little more distant with Emodicus), Elias would finally tell her what the trouble was.

As it was nearing the end of the day, Ean hadn't expected the workshop to be busy. She was surprised by the stream of customers popping in and out. Most of his clients immediately opened their brown-paper packages to don their bespelled equipment. She smiled as she passed them. "Eli?" she called softly, poking her head in at the doorway.

"Lightcross."

The skeleman was standing in one corner, chatting to Cyrus. The cyborg interpreted her husband's gentle nod, and politely departed. "Evening, Mrs. Mage," he saluted her as he left. The half-elf nodded her goodnight.

The last few customers dispersed. Elias locked the door. He turned to face her, arms open wide; Ean shamelessly tumbled into them. "I'm sorry," he breathed against her hair, cradling the back of her head.

"I'm sorry, too." Ean kissed his cheekbone. "If you suddenly made friends with... oh, Lurid, for example... I imagine I wouldn't be too happy about that."

He chuckled as he stroked her hair. "No, you would not."

"Still," she teased him by barely touching her lips to his jaws, "I hope you know I don't intend to leave you for another avatar. *Ever.*"

"You mean I'm stuck with you?"

"Damn straight."

He leaned in for a kiss. She ducked, initiating a chase. He cornered her near a bookshelf and braced her against it. His tongue grazed her earlobe. "I still intend to punish you, though," he whispered.

8

THE TRAINING GROUNDS OF HELIOS

The were-cat plunged into the long grass, morphing into his feline form right before he rolled onto the ground. Travis' ebony mane ruffled in the strong wind. Sindaya breathed deeply, shading her eyes from the sunlight. "What a gorgeous day!"

"Mind your head, lad," Desmond called from afar, fitting an arrow as he approached. Kaspar walked behind him, brandishing his naginata. "Hurry up, you two!"

The Mages trapsed behind the others, hand-in-hand. Eli's jaws parted in a yawn. "Coming, coming."

Sindaya and Desmond headed for the archer training section. Kaspar and Travis sparred. Ean and Elias, feeling rather lazy, simply watched for a while. "Well, in the mood for a tussle?" Eli eventually asked, nipping her ear.

"Let's make it interesting," Ean replied with a grin. "Loser has to fix dinner tomorrow."

"Gods, that's horrific. That'll take all of two minutes."

His wife giggled and shook her forefinger. "I mean in *real life,* William."

"Oh. That makes more sense." Elias rolled his shoulders, unsheathing Sacrimony. "I want burgers, by the way. Medium well."

Ean's mischievous smile warmed his heart. "*En garde.*"

The half-elf began her attack with Necrowave. Elias dodged her easily. The two circled one another, attuned to each other's weaknesses. "This feels nostalgic," Eli teased, briefly posing his blade as he'd held his microphone once, in Studio 13.

Ean blushed as she recalled that wild night. "You're trying to distract me, Eli. It's not going to work!"

The skeleman cackled, thrusting Sacrimony forward. Ean darted out of range and flipped back, measuring the distance between them. Toggling her motion shortcut, she switched her hammer for Antivenom. *Surprise, my love!*

Eli's eyes widened. He extended his wings, curving them around himself as a shield. Antivenom's barrage of blanks inflicted minor damage. "Gotcha!" The half-elf bellowed in delight, reloading quickly. Retracting his wings, the skeleman charged her head-on.

A wayward dance began. Elias strove to keep her at close range, and Ean continued to back away to fire Antivenom. Neither of them were making much headway. "Help me out here!" Ean cried, shouldering her rifle to beckon Travis (who had stopped training to observe the dueling couple).

"No way." The were-cat licked his paw. "I'm more scared of Elias than I am of you."

"Kaspar!" Grunting, Ean dodged again as Elias barreled toward her. His stroke deprived her of 15 HP. Tucking and rolling, Ean leapt to her feet and fired Kaspar a desperate look.

Kaspar flourished his weapon. "Count me in." His HP indicator became visible as he joined the battle. Undaunted, the skeleman's diabolical chuckle rang across the training grounds. "*Et tu, Brute?*"

"You may be surprised, Elias. You inspired me to hire an assistant at the forge." Kaspar twirled the naginata with impressive dexterity. "I've had more time to train."

"Excellent."

As Kaspar engaged Eli, Ean was free to regain premium positioning and kneel, aiming with care. *Ready. Aim... and...*

Ean's Holobox vibrated against her shoulder. "What is it?" she barked, keeping her sights glued to Elias. *It's going to take some delicate aiming to hit him without hitting Kaspar. This is good practice for me.*

"A message from Emodicus."

Ean flinched. "What does he want?"

"He asks after your welfare, and wants to know whether you'd be willing to meet him at the Stellos marketplace tomorrow afternoon. There's something he wants to tell you."

Ean lowered her rifle, sighing. "Just what I was afraid he'd say." She considered her options as she watched Elias and Kaspar bantering like a couple of middle school boys. "Tell him I'll only agree to meet if I'm not bound to secrecy. Anything he'd say to me would be fair game to discuss with Elias, if I feel the need to."

"Yes, Ean-san."

While awaiting Gale's reply, Ean fired a few rounds and smiled as some met their mark. "I'm really not half bad, am I, Hexy? Who would have thought?"

"Emodicus has responded."

"Go ahead."

"He says that his information would be of immense interest to you, but he cannot tell you if you will tell Elias."

Ean stowed her rifle and stood up. "Then I can't meet with him. Tell him I'll see him at the Metro."

"Very good, Ean-san."

The half-elf shook her head. "I really don't know what to make of him, Hexy. He's every inch as intelligent, enigmatic, and ambitious as Eli. I suppose that's why Elias dislikes him so much, but... there's got to be something *more.*"

"I quite agree with your assessment."

Ean's deft ears caught the rumble of Eli's victorious laughter. The tingling chime of a consumed healing potion followed. Elias helped Kaspar to his feet. "And another one bites the dust," Ean stated. "Still, I wonder how Elias would fare against me if my manic state was triggered?"

"A fascinating consideration, Ean-san."

"Indeed." Ean's eyes flashed at the thought. She sprinted across the field to Elias, grasping his shirt to pull him into a passionate kiss. "*Mmm,*" Eli breathed, sneaking one hand beneath her shirt to trace her bare skin. "What was that for?"

"No reason."

Kaspar bowed and rejoined Travis. The Mages nuzzled one another affectionately, content to be oblivious.

Ean's Holobox buzzed with another message. She ignored it.

You don't know your husband as well as you think.

Elias breathed deeply. His ribcage expanded as he stretched his hand toward the target. "*Vyrithra Kanthesis.*" A sable smolder lit the exposed roots of the dead tree. The skeleman nodded to himself, pleased. *A little stronger than it was.*

Twitching his wrist, Eli opened his inventory and removed a small spell book. He scanned through a couple pages before resuming his training. A message notification floated from his tablet. He disregarded it, unsheathing Sacrimony. "Vyrithra Kanthesis!"

The blade was engulfed in black flames. A villainous leer crinkled his eyelids. *I'll need to switch forms, of course. But if I can manage so well in this one...*

A bright green flash alerted Elias to someone's approach. He turned quickly, then rolled his eyes in annoyance. "What do *you* want?"

Emodicus emitted a cool smile. "Just a friendly visit."

"Don't waste my time." Elias – very deliberately – stroked his deathly hand along the blade, dispelling the flames without a flinch. "What is it, Modi?"

The dark elf sighed and unfolded his arms. His demeanor was unexpectedly apologetic. "I came to ask for a truce."

Elias gave a bone-dry cackle. "Why should I believe you?"

"Ean would," Gale muttered.

"Ean *what?*" The skeleman advanced, snapping his teeth. "I told you to *stay away from my wife.* Are you deaf?"

The dark elf raised his hands in protest. "I swear, we're just friends, Eli. I wouldn't hurt her."

Sacrimony reappeared, menacing Gale's dusky throat. "You seem to have forgotten that you already have."

Gale sneered. He could see his own reflection in Eli's demonic eyes. "I've done you a favor, Mage. She's a weapon unmatched by any other avatar in TerraWorks. You just don't know how to use her properly."

"*Use* her?" Elias growled.

That did it. Black magic coursed from their blades. Eli's skeleman roar echoed through the training grounds. Multicolored flames emanated from his jaws. Gale kept his head, countering with dark water spells.

Their feud was interrupted by another verdant flash. Ean calmly examined the two, who had frozen in place, grasping each other by the throats. "Evening, gentleman." She removed a Whisker and lit up. "Care for a smoke?"

Gale slapped Eli's hand away. "Really, Ean? Almighty Kanthesis, woman."

Eli laughed. "For once, I agree with Emodicus." He extinguished his sword and sheathed it.

Ean stood between them. She slipped each arm into one of theirs. "I'm hungry. Which of you dashing men is going to feed me?"

The dark elf stiffened. "You'll have to excuse me." He started to leave, but Ean snagged him by the cloak. "I let you sneak off last time, Modi, but you've been basking in the shelter of my grace for too long. What do you have against my husband, sir? I'm not letting you leave until you explain yourself."

Gale flinched. He could feel Eli's gaze burning a hole into the side of his head. "He's been my opponent since TerraWorks launched. That's all."

"Nope. Not buying it." The half-elf shook her head. "Your hatred for each other strikes deeper than a mere tussle between gamers."

Gale and Elias traded helpless glances. Ean huffed, staring from one to the other, then stomped away herself. "Whatever. If you two want to act immature, then have fun. I'll be at the Grimoire."

Gale waited until she left. He confronted Elias. "Are you ever going to tell her?"

"When I'm good and ready. Not that it's any of your business."

"I don't get why it's a secret, anyway."

"I have my reasons."

"It's basically cheating. Every time she trains with you, she thinks that–"

"Watch it. I've taken notes on you, too."

Gale's indigo eyes narrowed. "About what?"

Elias gave him a look. *Stupid questions get stupid answers.*

9

BERSERKER BOARDING

The Spectral Tyrants mounted the bleachers en masse. Travis skipped over them, babbling excitedly, while Oleon trailed him at the pace of a slug. Kaspar, Sindaya, and Elias chatted among themselves. Desmond sat down last, entering notes into his Holopal at lightning speed.

They were early. The open stadium was two-thirds full. Most avatars were killing time by taking elaborate HI's in front of the luminous levitation track. Although Elias engaged in the light dialogue of his friends, his focus remained locked on the pulsing scarlet-and-violet board. Ean was completing her final run-throughs.

She seemed tense. Elias had a bad feeling about this race, and he suspected that he was partially to blame. *I should have shaken hands with Gale, or something. It would have been no better than a farce, but it would have appeased her.*

"Hey, Eli!"

Elias glanced down the stairs and saw Cyrus, Mallie, and Byron waving at him. He nodded, motioning for them to join his group. The Firestone Guild greeted everyone with gusto.

Cyrus sat next to Eli. "How's Lightcross flying this morning?"

"She's tense."

"Why? This is the same dude she won Grand Champion against."

Elias absently twirled his tablet. "Well, it wasn't a crushing defeat by any means. He was only a few board lengths behind her."

A metallic scrape issued from the cyborg's fingers as he scratched his head. "That's true. Still, if she can beat him once, why not twice?"

"That's the spirit." Elias thumped him on the back. "I should have had you pep-talk her before she powered up."

Ean shot across the finish line and reviewed her timing. She was visibly displeased, but that was her final practice run. Powering down, she stowed her board and walked to the side of the launch platform. She leaned against the wall and shut her eyes, still frowning.

Eli ached to jog down and encourage her. But the track was officially closed to everyone except the competitors. He turned back to Cyrus and resumed conversation.

Meanwhile, Emodicus quietly entered the track. He stole up to Ean and leaned against the wall beside her. "One GP for your thoughts?"

Her eyes opened with a smile. They chatted for a few minutes. As the conversation progressed, Gale's demeanor intensified and Ean's frown returned. Her shoulders tensed. Red and purple sparks embellished the ends of her hair, lifting in a static cloud. Gale backed away, a mixture of awe and intimidation in his subtle countenance.

Elias sensed her surge of energy. He held up a hand, stopping Cyrus mid-sentence. "What's going on?" the skeleman hissed, standing up. "What is that bastard up to now?"

"What?" The cyborg followed Eli's gaze. They watched as Ean powered up and mounted her board. She knelt into launch position, signaling to the Metro system that she was ready.

Emodicus readied himself likewise. Elias sat down again, uneasily.

The rest of the spectators had logged into the race. The Metro Cross AI ran through the usual system checks, then began the countdown. *In 3... 2... 1... Accelerate.*

Initially, the two competitors raced very much as they had at the Shiori track. They were a pleasure to watch, Elias admitted: graceful, dominant, and spotlessly synchronized. However, Gale began to pull away. Ean ground her teeth. The irritable energy Elias had sensed before came flooding back. He bowed his head, wincing at the painful throbs coming from the gems on his skull.

Ean's eyes went dark.

Black magic billowed around her skyboard. Ean lifted her hands, embracing and directing it. Her lips murmured an inaudible spell. A deafening hum pulsed from her skyboard, propelling her forward with explosive power.

Elias, along with the audience, leapt to his feet in wonder. His wife didn't practice black magic. Hades, she didn't even know *Elias* knew black magic! *This is Gale's doing. I don't know how, but it's got to be him.* A dire growl escaped Eli's jaws.

Cyrus, cheering for Ean's progress, tossed him a surprised look. "What's up, man? She's winning!"

Eli didn't hear him. His gaze was fixed on Gale. The dark elf didn't even seem upset that Lightcross was beating him (again). In fact, "beating" was an understatement. He was literally eating Ean's dust at this point.

She crossed the finish line as one blurred, ebony-scarlet flash. The stadium cheered. Elias shook his skull. "She'll be disqualified."

"*What?* Why?" Travis screeched. Oleon and Desmond were similarly stunned, but Kaspar's head bowed in affirmation. "The expenditure of charisma to win skyboard races is prohibited. Your board can be enhanced by artificer craft (to a certain extent). But that's the limit."

"That's right." Elias waited for the Metro AI to compute and cite the error. "It was an impressive display. And this race was just for fun, booked on Gale's tab. But why-"

The Metro AI interrupted him. *"Congratulations, Ean Mage. May this additional victory reaffirm your position as SkyRate Grand Champion."*

"What?" Eli spluttered. "I'll be damned." He looked back at Gale. The dark elf was smirking, dismounting his board with the same self-assurance of eld. "It's as if *he* won today," the skeleman muttered, fingering his jaw. "How interesting."

Ean, waving to her fans, ran up to Elias. She embraced him. "He just can't hold us Mages down, can he?"

"No, he can't." As he returned her hug, Eli was rattled by a shock. "Ean! Your eyes."

"What about them?"

"They're…"

Cyrus leaned toward her to study them. "Your eyes are *black.*"

"Are they?" Ean laughed indifferently. "Do you like them this color?"

Ean's Holobox glowed blue as Hexadecimal explained. "Her dark charisma has awoken. She is Ean the Berserker."

Back at Vermillion Castle, Elias growled as message after message to Gale went unanswered. Hexadecimal politely offered him his secreted vial and needle. "Not now," Eli answered, waving them away. "I need to deal with this nuisance of an avatar."

Ean sauntered into the living room. She sat on the rug near Eli's feet. "I told you a thousand times, dearest. I feel just fine. Is it my black eyes?"

"Yes," Elias mumbled. "My wife doesn't have black eyes. She has ice-blue eyes. Angelic eyes. I want them back."

Ean's lyrical laughter steadied him, although it bore a touch of maniacal strain. "That sounded a tad creepy. Anyway, don't I just need to learn how to control the 'rage mode?' I should be right as rain after that."

"Right you are." Elias set his tablet aside and lovingly touched her cheek. "That's far more important than your avatar's eye color."

Ean's hand cradled his. "It's sweet of you to be so protective. But sometimes I think you forget that we're in VR. Emodicus can't *actually* hurt me, you know."

"He'd better not, if he wants to live."

His wife maneuvered to sit in his lap. "Don't worry. I'll kill him myself."

"By the gods! Don't look straight at me when you say things like that."

"You've got ebony eyes yourself, my dear Elias. Don't discriminate against mine."

The skeleman chuckled. His fingers began to stroke her lower back. "I wonder…"

"What is it?"

"I wonder if intimacy is different with a berserker."

"Want to find out?" Ean whispered.

10

HARNESS THE ANATHEMA

G ale approached a regal temple with spindle-shaped towers. His iridescent cloak brushed the ground. He acknowledged the temple guards, slipped inside, and passed into the prayer room.

A handful of temple chanters caused their voices to rise and fall, cycling through litanies in an endless cadence. Gale bowed before the statue of Kanthesis. The deity of the dark sorcerers was portrayed with a gentle yet merciless grin. Emodicus murmured a few prayers of thanks and renewed devotion before rising to his feet. His HP was replenished.

The dark elf left the prayer room, withdrawing a golden key. He unlocked his private sanctuary – careful to secure the door behind him – and sat at his desk with a deep sigh.

Alerted to his presence, his Holopal glowed on the charge port. "Good evening, Emodicus. Might I be of any assistance?"

"No thank you, Zahir. I've accomplished what I meant to do. And yet…"

"Sir?"

"It's odd. She didn't seem to experience any pain. But when I happened to glance at Elias, to see how he was taking the change, he was grinding his teeth in agony. He's too strong to betray himself, of course. But I could tell."

"Their bond is powerful. Ean has been absorbing Eli's dark charisma for quite some time. It is possible she has adapted to the pain."

Gale rubbed his chin. "No, that seems like a defect in the game. My guess is that one of the gems on Eli's skull is infused with a transfer charm, something that absorbs her pain and distributes it to Elias."

"Perhaps. But Ean's new combat abilities and her performa level nearly render her OP. It must be compensated in some way."

"So when she battles as a berserker, she'll damage herself and inflict pain on Elias?"

"That is correct."

"Fascinating." Emodicus broke into a sly grin as he toyed with the scrolls on his desk. "This may be the first serious strain on their relationship."

"How so, sir?"

He braced his chin in his hands. "Well, for one thing, Elias is accustomed to being in the spotlight. Lightcross may hold the title of SkyRate Grand Champion, but the tournaments are transitory events. Her popularity only surged for a season." He held up one finger. "Conversely, the Spectral Tyrants are constantly booked, touring all over TerraWorks City, Helios, Stellos, and Klad Kingdom. Elias Mage is one of the top-ranking avatars in TerraWorks. Now, his wife might start gaining on him. She'll be getting more guild invites than he will, for sure… mostly because he always turns them down."

"Indeed. What else?"

"Hmm." Gale rapped his knuckles against the desk. "This one's a bit more theoretical. But I'm thinking that, as a berserker, she could confront and defeat Ophidious. It'll be a most entertaining battle," he added, the sly grin returning.

"Isn't it more likely that she may confront and defeat *you,* sir?"

The dark elf shook his head. "Not if we're friends."

"Ah. I divine your motivations, sir."

Emodicus snorted. "I'm not that black-hearted, Zahir. I'll admit that my initial motivations were selfish. But she's really quite…" he clipped himself off. "Nevermind. She'll likely shun me after what I told her at the Metro."

"And what was that, sir? If it's not intrusive to ask."

Gale shrugged. "Oh, nothing very momentous, I'm afraid. It worked, though."

"And your long-term goal is to…?"

The dark elf rose from his chair, thrusting the wings of his cloak aside with a powerful swipe. "To harness the Anathema."

Ean shifted her position, squeezing the trigger. *Bang! Bang!* Both bullets hit the moving targets with ease. Cheering inwardly, the half-elf tossed her ginger hair and fired multiple shots. "Take care not to waste ammunition," Hex warned as he materialized on her shoulder.

She squinted at her six-inch companion. "I'm not firing randomly."

"You seem calmer today, Ean-san. That's good."

"I feel bored." Ean sighed and reloaded. "I love training with An-tivenom, of course. I don't mean that. I just… ever since becoming Ean the Berserker, I've got this crazy itch to fight like I've never felt before. Simply training by myself isn't much fun."

Hex managed some dry humor. "You could pick a fight with Modi."

Ean snickered. "I certainly could." Her lips pressed into a thin line as she fired again. "The blue bastard. What was up with that remark?"

Before Hexadecimal could ask *"What remark,"* Ean released a bouquet of bullets that peppered the target with smoking holes. "What's his game, anyway?" she complained between gritted teeth. "One minute he's friendly, and the next, he's the rudest avatar I've ever met."

Ean stood and shouldered Antivenom, relishing its smooth, hefty weight. Slender violet lines cut across its brass body, streamlining its aspect with cyberpunk flair. "Anyway, he's not worth my trouble. Ophidious is."

"You still intend to defeat him?"

"Well, yeah. I might actually have a chance now." She stroked the scope affectionately. "I just need to figure out a consistent way to trigger my manic state." Stowing her rifle away, she extracted her skyboard and prepared to return to Vermillion Castle. "It's getting late, though. About time I logged off. Any messages from Eli?"

"Negative, Ean-san."

"Strange. We haven't seen each other all day."

"Perhaps he is training as well?"

"Maybe. I should have bumped into him, though. Unless he's in Stellos or Klad, for whatever reason." Ean powered up and directed her skyboard to the castle.

A few minutes into her flight, her Holobox buzzed with a message. She recognized the were-cat's avatar symbol. "Travis. Please read it to me, Hex."

"Travis says a few of the band members are meeting at the Pulse, along with Cyrus and Mallie. He wants to invite you as well."

"On my way." Ean changed course.

Below TerraWorks City, there was a low, rapid waterfall that Ean loved to fly over. She'd skim across it swift and steady, enjoying the churning power of the flood against the palm of her hand. The water would flow through her fingers like silk.

As she descended toward the river, the bite of black magic shocked her senses.

Ean's skyboard rebelled. It bucked wildly and careened aside, whipping Ean into several uncontrolled corkscrews as she fought to stay aboard. Realizing it was about to crash, she leapt off, tucking and rolling as it exploded against the crags. She winced as her HP took the hit.

Ean jumped to her feet. An enraged snarl creased her mouth. Seizing Antivenom, she ran headlong into the dark magic's insatiable pull. Spotting a cloaked figure among the boulders, she shouldered her rifle and took aim. "Emodicus!"

The immobile figure slowly raised its bald head.

Ophidious!

Baffled, but still angry, the half-elf felt a surge of vicious energy teasing her nerves. She welcomed it. *Time to see what Ean the Berserker can do.*

A searing exhilaration wracked her mind. The battlefield was striped with red and purple gridlines, alerting Ean to several favorable shooting positions. She darted to the optimal location, kneeling and shouldering Antivenom with practiced confidence. "Four!" she yelled mockingly as she pulled the trigger.

Ophidious launched a simultaneous attack. Ean dodged it, biting back a curse. Since they both fought with dark charisma, the act of gathering and releasing it had a magnetic effect. She wanted to run *toward* it, not away from it; judging from the cursed fay's irritable hiss, he was in the same conundrum.

Ean's new berserker instincts calculated a way to use it to her advantage. Switching to Necrowave, Ean drew her foe into close combat.

Ophidious unsheathed his cursed elven blade. It was grubby and black, stained with the blood of his former kin. *"Kant demilion,"* he muttered.

The half-elf's throat was seized by an acid-green cloud. Panting, Ean hazarded a wry smile as she gathered all the dark charisma she could. Necrowave pulsed with sable and violet lightning. "Eat it," she gasped, launching the orb toward Ophidious.

The fay sorcerer grabbed it and hurled it straight back.

A blinding, white-hot intensity seized her body.

"By the gods, woman."

Groaning, Ean raised her head from the grass. She stared at the measly 1 HP remaining in her gauge. Blinking, she dimly recalled hearing someone speak, and turned her head in his general direction. A blueish blur sat cross-legged beside her. "Emodicus?"

"Yes, it's me." The dark elf snuffed his Whisker smoke. "I was waiting for you to come to. Why did you try to take him on by yourself?"

Ean grunted and sat up. "I didn't. He's the one who started it."

"Really?" A smile bloomed at the corners of his stern mouth. "You must have done *something* to piss him off. That's not his usual MO."

Ean withdrew a healing potion and drank it. "Beats me. Anyway, what are you doing here? You didn't just sit around and watch me fight by myself, did you?"

"That's precisely what I did."

Ean sighed. "You were following me?"

"Correct."

"Why?"

"Curiosity."

"How did you know where I was?"

"Travis didn't send you that message. I did."

The half-elf grimaced. "What? I saw the avatar symbol."

Gale huffed. "You've never heard of avatars faking symbols before? Message shadowing is child's play."

"Seriously, dude. Your penchant for deception is getting on my nerves. What in Hades do you want with me?"

"I've done my homework on berserkers. There's two types: those that draw from light charisma, and those who rely on dark charisma to fuel their manic state. I can tell you what I know, and teach you to control it better."

"In exchange for what?"

Gale stretched and rubbed his shoulder. "I'll be your receptacle. Instead of a ring, etc. I'll draw out your excess charisma and harvest it. That will enable you to maintain control as a berserker, and it will provide me with ample energy for the dark arts."

Ean laughed. She removed her hat and tossed it on the ground. "OK, genius. First of all, I don't trust you any further than I could throw you. Second, I can control myself just fine, thank you."

"Is that so?" Emodicus tapped her once on the forehead. "Then tell me all about the last two minutes of your battle. What happened? And be specific, if you please, Mrs. Mage."

Silence. A cricket or two offered their opinions.

"That's what I thought. Although, I must admit you were performing splendidly until the end. You'll be a first-class berserker once you get your manic state under control."

"And third," Ean resumed, tossing her ruddy head, "Elias doesn't want you anywhere near me. You're risking your avatar's life just by talking to me now."

Ean could tell by the creasing of Gale's forehead that she'd hit home. "I'll… I'll apologize to him," he muttered.

The half-elf's optics widened. "By the Terran Pantheon! Say that again."

Emodicus groaned. "I swear by the Terran Pantheon that I'll talk to Elias."

"This, I simply *must* see."

Ean's broad grin annoyed him. Gale rose to his feet and offered Ean his hand. He pulled her up. The two prepared to fly back to Helios on Gale's skyboard (since Ean's was toast). "One more thing," Ean requested as he powered up. "I get how this would be mutually advantageous and all that. But why me? Couldn't you harvest dark charisma from a million other sources?"

The dark elf hesitated. His azure eyes scanned the horizon. "I think you've got a good chance of defeating Ophidious. I want to be there when it happens."

Ean bundled her hair into a ponytail. "As in… you want to fight him with me? Or you just plan to be a witness?"

Emodicus smiled. "Either. However, I'd be delighted to witness you taking him down on your own."

"But… why?"

He held his finger to his lips. "That's my little secret."

11

ALL THE OLD FAMILIAR FACES

As Elias Mage watched Gale and Ean descend on the same skyboard, Gale relished the deathly curses in the skeleman's eyes. Elias unsheathed Sacrimony, extended his monstrous wings, and marched up to them, countenance ablaze. "*What* is the meaning of this?" rumbled from the deepest fissure of the abyss.

Ean darted in front of Gale, hands clasped. "Now, hold on, my love. I've brought him to make his apology." She took Eli's arm and walked him a few paces away. "Just calm down for a few minutes, and then hear him out."

"Where is your skyboard, Ean? Why were you riding with him?" Eli was fairly quaking with rage. His teeth grated together. Ean tried to stroke his skull to soothe him, but he pushed her hand away. "You know I don't want you to be anywhere near him. Why don't you *listen?*"

"It's not my fault! I was battling Ophidious, and–"

"Alone? Why didn't you call for me?"

The half-elf spluttered. Her gaze dropped to the ground. "I... I didn't..."

"You didn't think of it." Elias sighed. Ean bit her lip, abashed silence penning her confession.

Eli shook his skull. The sight of his beautiful wife standing repentant, her windblown hair framing her rosy cheeks, melted the anger welling inside him. Elias held her face with his cool hands. "You can *always* call for me. Even if I can't come right away... I'll come as soon as I possibly can. You know that, right?"

"I know." Glancing up timidly, she smiled at the love brimming from Eli's expression. She kissed him, sealing their mutual apology, and the two returned to Gale hand-in-hand. "My wife informs me you have something to say," Elias began, sheathing his sword.

"I do." Gale frowned and cleared his throat. "I admit to having selfish – and rather nefarious – designs toward both you and your wife. I apologize. I'd like to start our acquaintanceship over again."

"For what purpose?" Elias sat on the edge of the town square fountain, drawing Ean into his lap. Droplets from the fountain spray glittered on his skull.

"For mutual benefit." Gale cited a brief sketch of his proposal. Eli's countenance remained inscrutable, but his wife could divine the strong suspicion that was far from alleviated. Naturally, he asked the same question Ean had. "You've plentiful sources of dark charisma, Emodicus. Why must it be Ean?"

The dark elf deployed a coy smile. "I'm surprised you have to ask. You should know better than I do what a rarity Ean Mage is. Besides acclimating to dark charisma (thanks to becoming your spouse), now she's a midnight berserker. She's powerful, but volatile; she needs a strong receptacle to stabilize her manic state. She will benefit from this arrangement more than I will."

"And that's why you broke her ring."

Gale paused, then nodded. "Yes. To demonstrate how vulnerable she is."

"Classically devious of you."

"But it worked."

"There's something you've failed to calculate," Elias replied. He placed his hand onto Ean's head, stroking her burnished locks. "*I could be her receptacle.*"

"Yo." Ean nudged Elias. "Why are you both talking about me like I'm not here?"

The dark elf shook his head. "It won't work."

"How do you figure?"

To Ean's bewilderment, Gale's only reply was a long, hard stare. *You know the answer. Must I say it aloud?*

Elias stared back. *I'll kill you.*

"Hey," Ean said, snapping her fingers between their glaring faces. "Would one of you kindly lend your powers of telepathy for a second?"

"Sorry. It's nothing." Eli withdrew his gaze and stood, still holding Ean in his arms. "Well, if Ean intends to proceed with this experiment, I leave it to her choice. What say you, Mrs. Mage?" He extended his wings to fly them home.

"Let's try it." She kissed his cheekbone, lingering close to whisper, "We can always beat him up."

"Damn straight. Consider yourself under supervised probation, Modi."

Gale smiled serenely. "I'm starting to like that nickname."

"Gods, you're such a liar."

"Wait, wait, wait! What are we practicing next?"

Elias sighed. "Pay attention. 'Roaring Twenties.'"

"See, that's what I thought you said." Winking, Ean skimmed through her wardrobe app and grabbed a long tweed coat and hat. Skipping up to Elias, she slipped both onto his boney frame despite his protests. "Almighty Kanthesis!" she whispered, kissing him. "*That's* hot."

Elias glared while the rest of the Tyrants snickered. "Step aside." The skeleman waved her away. He uttered a low growl as he seized the microphone. "I've had about enough of you miscreants today."

Ean made a show of cooling herself off, drawing laughter from Sindaya. Elias pointed to Ean without turning his head. "Calm down." He rose his hand to signal everyone else. As the music slammed against the studio walls, Ean noted (with a smile) that he didn't remove his hat.

The shadows of bomber aircraft cascaded through the room. Ean believed she could almost smell the smoke of detonation. Eli's body shone bronze as he swayed to the beat, raising his hands to welcome the simulated chaos. The half-elf allowed Travis to lead as she slacked off, edging around the holostage to get a better view. *Gods. How did I end up with him, anyway?*

Elias noticed her lurking. He immediately averted his eyes. Ean grinned, knowing he did it to maintain his self-control. She tapped the brim of her hat. *Call an intermission after this, Eli.*

The skeleman touched his brim in return. *Roger that.*

After the song finished, Elias ordered a ten-minute break. The rest of the Tyrants filtered out, shoving each other and joking. Ean leaned against the wall. The couple waited patiently until they were alone.

Elias extended his wings and swept forward, slamming both hands against the wall, trapping her. "I *told* you never to look at me like that during practice, Ean Mage."

"Hmm. I forgot."

"Like Hades you did."

"You know, I think that's what Emodicus meant. When he said you couldn't handle being my receptacle."

"You're saying I'd go mad, too?"

"Hey, I'm not mad!"

"You're a midnight berserker. Basically the same thing."

"How dare you." Ean ducked beneath his arm to walk away. He grabbed her by the waist. "You think you can insult me and still get some action?" She leaned away from him, raising an eyebrow.

"You tell me." Eli licked her earlobe as his hands stole beneath her shirt. Ean felt her knees weaken. "Dammit." She turned, pushing his coat off and kissing him passionately.

12

THE UNHOLY TRINITY

"Finally." Emodicus stood as Ean descended on her skyboard. "Where's your husband?"

"Said he had work to do with Tirion." The half-elf rolled her eyes. "And you needn't look so happy about it."

"Whatever." Gale dusted imaginary lint from his cloak. "Are you ready?"

"As ready as I'll ever be, I guess. Will it hurt?"

"It shouldn't. Might hurt Elias a bit, though."

"What? Why?"

The dark elf tilted his head. "I don't know."

Ean glowered.

"Honest to the gods, Ean. I have no idea why, but your bond with Elias is curiously strong. I think he's found a way to absorb your pain."

"You mean my VR-induced pain? He needn't bother."

"I'm aware. Now, stand here and hold still."

Ean stepped into the chalk circle. "I know Stellos tends to be pretty quiet, but are you sure we're not going to attract any passerby here?"

Emodicus grunted dismissively. "We're fine."

He opened a large silver book and recited the spell he'd written specifically for Ean. She felt a prickle at the tips of her fingers. Intrigued, she held out her hands as dark charisma gathered above them and was absorbed by the dark elf. She experienced a sense of relief and cleansing, like taking a shower after working the fields all day. "That was easy. Too easy." She lowered her hands. "You've been working on that spell for ages, haven't you?"

Gale closed his book. "Why do you think I broke your ring in the first place?"

Ean shook her head. "You've been guiding us straight into your hands all along. Well, I despise you."

"I'm aware of that, too."

"And it doesn't bother you?"

"No. I think you'll change your mind." Cutting off further conversation, Emodicus withdrew his blade and braced himself. "See if you can induce the manic state now."

Ean grabbed her hammer. Dark static scrambled across Necrowave. She paused, gritting her teeth as sable energy snapped from her eyes. "Good!" Emodicus praised her. "Now, control it. Keep your mind on the fight."

As Ean's training advanced, she struggled against the pull of the dark charisma Emodicus wielded. *This would be infinitely easier if I was a daylight berserker,* she complained to herself. Switching Necro for Antivenom, she ran for cover and kneeled. "Smart," Modi called out. He struck the boulder in front of her with several explosive blows. The half-elf jumped on top of it, trusting her new speed as a berserker to blur her movements. Ean's eyes narrowed as she focused and pulled the trigger.

Bang! Bang! Bang!

She smirked as she recognized a few curses among Modi's exclamations. He rushed toward her.

Ean saw real anger in his eyes. A rising thrill began to whiten her vision. *No, no! Keep your mind clear. Resist the temptation to white out-*

A dry, raucous bellow echoed from the crags behind them. Ean glanced up as Elias soared over her, pinning Emodicus to the crags. "Fancy meeting you here," the skeleman laughed. Gale, decidedly *not* amused, sneered as he wacked Elias aside.

The two commenced animated sparring. Ean shouldered her rifle and gaped, aghast. "Hey! I'm the one that's supposed to be getting trained right now." She yelled at them a few more times, but neither of them heard (or cared). Sighing, Ean stowed her weapon and sat on the boulder, chin in her hands.

It was fascinating to watch them. Eli's fire-tinged movements were confident and powerful. Sacrimony glowed with sunset flames. Emodicus moved with sinuous speed, reminding Ean of a were-cat. His azure dark magic was directed with a graceful, aqueous flow. She wondered how long he'd been in TerraWorks to have mastered his craft with such artistic precision.

They talked while they fought. She strained to catch a word here and there, but their spellcraft and the clang of their blades masked them. Elias looked quite happy, though. *It's not often he gets to battle with an equal,* Ean realized, smiling at his boyish enjoyment.

Emodicus was a little stiff, but gradually regaining tranquility. He even chuckled at something Elias said. *He's fighting better now that he's relaxed.* Ean stood up, slipping off her perch to observe them more closely. *Maybe watching the masters work is just as good as training myself.*

The battle ended in a draw. Gale and Eli sheathed their swords and bowed to each other before returning to Ean. "Who won?" she asked, pocketing her hands and grinning.

"Nobody," Elias replied, ribcage heaving. "We got tired. Agreed to a truce."

"*You* got tired," Emodicus retorted. "Anyway, we're supposed to be training Ean. Why did you attack me like that?"

"Cause it was fun," the skeleman answered. "You look like an avatar that takes TerraWorks way too seriously."

Ean poked her husband. "We could say the same thing about you. Just look at yourself, you big ham!"

Gale Emodicus astonished them by laughing... a full, warm laugh that neither of them had heard before. He pointed to the sparkling gems along Eli's skull. "Amen to that. You never spoke a truer word, Lightcross."

Ean smiled, tossing an arm around each of their shoulders. "You know, I've got a good feeling about the three of us. We're going to take TerraWorks by storm."

"No three stooges jokes, please."

"Dammit, Modi. Must you always murder the warm fuzzies?"

The skeleman and the dark elf traded sarcastic looks. *She's cute, but she's nuts.*

Klad's marketplace was abuzz with customers. The warm afternoon sun slanted above the kingdom's stone walls. Vendors eagerly demonstrated their wares. Several bards and dancers practiced. Amid the bustle, a blond human male with bright green eyes moseyed through the bazaar.

Piragor whistled as he stopped to examine a pair of skyboarding boots. "Best in all of Klad Kingdom!" The shop owner chirped, handing the boots to Piragor. He looked them over and nodded, pleased. "I'm sure they are. How much?

"175 GP, sir. A wise investment. They'll last you for the rest of your skycrafting career in TerraWorks."

Piragor winced. "I don't know, man. That's a steep price."

The shop owner flashed him a knowing glance. "Not for a finalist from the TerraWorks City Tournament, I'd imagine." He smiled sweetly.

Piragor sighed. "Very well." His Holopal released the currency. "Thanks," Piragor murmured, stowing the boots in his inventory. *If these don't last me for the rest of my career, I'm reporting you to the mediators.*

"Pleasure doing business with you!"

The SkyRate finalist resumed his wandering. Some familiar faces sped by, and he nodded to them in friendly recognition. A half-elf walked past him on the opposite side… attended by the strong, warm scent of Shiori Islands. Her brilliant curtain of knee-length hair seared his memory.

He waved. "Lightcross!"

The half-elf turned, zeroing in on her old friend. "Hey, Piragor! Long time no see. How've you been?"

"Tolerable." They both laughed. His impressive clothing, more muscular build, and well-trimmed goatee implied that he was much better than "tolerable."

"And how's the grand champion?" he asked, glancing her over.

Ean Mage looked different. Intimidating. Her shoulders and arms – though still feminine – were broader. Her black-and-scarlet outfit portrayed steampunk influence. The new Mage avatar symbol swung from a thick chain around her slender neck. Most shocking of all, her coral lips curved beneath raven eyes. "What happened to your eyes?" He couldn't help asking right away.

"Emodicus happened to them." Ean giggled at the confusion on Piragor's face. "It's a long story. The simple answer is that I'm a midnight berserker."

"Ean the Berserker." He had to admit, it fit her. Ean Lightcross had always carried herself with a certain brace of masculine vigor. Now, it was tailored to her image like a well-altered suit. "So, you're focusing on your combat level now?"

"Yeah. Ophidious better look out," she stated, tossing her hair. "Gale's helping me train, believe it or not."

"I *don't* believe it. How did that happen?"

"Again, long story." Ean pointed to the kingdom's noteworthy taphouse, The Wailing Banshee. "We could grab a few drinks while I explain everything, if you want."

"Sure. I've got some time." Grinning, Piragor knocked her a fist bump for old time's sake. "Gods, it's good to see you. Even if you're a little scarier than you used to be."

"Well, 'you are what you eat.' Blame the dark charisma."

As they chatted over their beers, Piragor kept getting distracted by the subtler differences in his old SkyRate rival. He remembered her movements and manner of speaking as cat-like, irregular and sudden, crackling with static liveliness. While she sometimes fell into her old habits, she seemed more balanced. She wore her confidence like a tangible garment. Piragor wondered if he could reach out and touch it. "No offense, but this is so weird," Piragor admitted once she'd finished her tale. "You're saying Gale Emodicus cheated the system to change your avatar type... without your consent... but now you're friends with him?"

"I wouldn't say we're friends. Just friendly accomplices. Mutual benefit, etc. etc. But he can be charming (when he wants to be). Reminds me of Elias."

"Still sounds to me like he played you two. Personally, I wouldn't have anything more to do with him." Piragor finished his ale with a scowl.

Ean shrugged. "Half of me agrees with you. The human half. My serene elven half says we're all just playing a game, so why take it too seriously? Besides, I like being a midnight berserker. I don't really want to change back."

Piragor shot her an irresistible smile. "You've always been the one to take risks."

"Right. Cheers, man." Ean raised her mug. "To the unholy trinity!"

13

SQUARE HAMMER CIRCUS

*"E*liaaaaaas!"

The skeleman thumped his Compendium shut. "What?" he grumbled. "You know I don't like being bothered in the workshop."

"Sorry." Ean skimmed across the room. She embraced him from behind, arms around his neck. "I just grabbed last-minute tickets for the sky circus. You're not going to make me go alone, are you?"

"Circuses are stupid."

"No, they're fun! You're just in a bad mood, Eli-san. You'll like it once we get there."

"I don't have any transport gems. I'll have to fly there, and I'm tired."

"Ride my skyboard with me. The big one. I've got three of them now, you know… insurance against a certain fay sorcerer… whose name I dare not utter within our stainless sanctum."

Elias grunted. "You'll make me fly you back home anyway. Do I look like an idiot?"

"Hey, I just do that because it's romantic."

Eli returned to his Compendium. "Too tired. Go by yourself."

"How grumpy we are!" she said to the skeletal inkstand on his desk. "Maybe I'll invite Modi instead. He's *always* grumpy, so I won't resent him for it."

Slam. Compendium abandoned, Elias detached his wife and donned his jacket. "Let's go."

Ean took his hand. "We haven't been on a date in a while. It'll be nice."

"You're right."

As he stalked out the door, skull gems afire with evening light, Ean stared at him with laser intensity. "Now what?" he demanded. She just smiled. "OK, OK. I'm sorry. Tirion wasn't getting pearl infusions, and I got irritated with him. It's not that hard."

Ean softly kissed his jaw. "You had trouble with them before. Patience is the key, remember?"

"Yeah." Elias nuzzled her. "I've just been cooped up in there too long. Thanks for dragging me out."

"What else are wives for?" Ean selected her broad black skyboard and powered up. "You've got boarding boots, right?"

"Yep."

Elias mounted behind her. He kept one hand on her shoulder, and the other on her waist. "An interesting design," he called over the hum of the skyboard engine. "This one's more like a glider."

"Strictly for transportation. Not racing."

"Makes sense."

Ean flew at a leisurely pace. As the countryside beauty of Helios drifted below, she felt Elias pull her a little closer. "How was your day?"

"Good. Shopped on Shiori Islands. Spent some time in Klad Kingdom, just wandering around. Ran into Piragor."

"And how's he doing these days?"

"He looks great. Says he's been working with a flight coach. He's coming after the grand championship title next season."

"Not surprising. Do you think he could win?"

A flush of embarrassment raced up her ears. "Yeah, I think I'd probably be in trouble. It's not easy to keep up with my skycraft when I'm attending to my combat level. How in Terra did you and Modi manage to max out both gauges?"

"By the virtue of beta testing. You didn't have that advantage."

"It still sucks."

"That must be the circus." Elias nodded to the massive, slowly-shifting squares on the skyline. Ean accelerated toward them. "That's it."

She lowered into the landing deck, powered down, and dismounted. She stowed her board once Elias stood beside her. "This is weird," Elias commented, eyes crinkling sardonically as he looked around.

"Then we'll fit right in."

The Square Hammer Circus platform consisted of three enormous cubes. They were in constant, steady motion as performers of various races put on magical displays. Many avatars paraded about with rare exotic animals. Some ancient classics – a carousel, a haunted house, and sideline games for prizes – bolstered nostalgia. But the rest of the circus was thoroughly modern. Ean squealed, clapping her hands together and dancing like a child. "Where should we go first?"

"I feel like shooting something. Or smashing something."

"Perfect!" Ean grabbed his hand and guided him to the high striker. "Sign says if you win, you get tickets for free food."

Eli's eyes glinted with perceptive humor. "For you, then, my dear." Seizing the hammer, the skeleman tested its weight. Inhaling slowly, Eli lifted it and brought it down with a crash. "Close, sir!" cried the rented Holopal who observed the game's players. "Try it one more time."

Ean touched the hammer's handle. "Let me try!"

"Very well." Elias stood aside, arms folded. Ean swung a few practice strokes first, as her husband had. She walked up to the striker, careful to keep her dominant hand near the head of the mallet. Elias fingered his jaw. "You know the trick to this one, don't you?"

"Maybe." Eliciting an angelic smile, Ean grunted as she brought the hammer down, sliding her right hand down to meet her left. *Clang!*

The couple departed victorious, food tickets in hand.

"You're stronger," Elias observed. His gaze fluttered down her muscular forearms. "If I'm not careful, you're going to best me in combat, as well."

Ean lit a magenta Whisker. "I'll settle for beating Modi and Ophidious."

"Will you?" Eli darted an impish look. "Well, there's one thing you'll never beat me at, Mrs. Mage."

Ean responded with a knowing smile. *Not here, you freak.* "Two things, actually. I'll never sing as well as you do. And no matter how good I look," she added, flexing, "there's no other avatar that's as devilishly attractive as you."

Eli's animated mirth caused several avatars to smile. "I assure you, my lady, you're my equal in that regard. You may not have noticed the various criminals lusting after you," Eli's forefinger generally indicated the passerby, "but you definitely turn heads."

"I didn't notice." *I only see you, Eli.*

Her skeleman's demeanor intensified with the look Ean knew too well. "Not here!" she stated, hands up in defense.

"Too late." Elias picked her up. He started in quest for shaded solitude. Ean objected with all the force she could muster. To her profound relief, he agreed to fly them home. "VR public is still public," laughed Ean, arms around his neck. "What's gotten into you?"

His dark eyes flashed. "I need my wife."

Gale Emodicus prowled from tent to tent, eyes glazed over with boredom. *What a childish pastime. No wonder circuses went out of style decades ago.* The dark elf stifled a yawn. An overeager Holopal tried to tempt him to play shootout, but Gale waved it aside with contempt.

He caught the scent of something far more tempting: roasting turkey legs. Gale made an about-face and cornered the food stalls. He sat to consume his treat in quiet enjoyment. Standing back up, he trudged past a few other games.

The glint of bronze crowned with gems caught his attention. *Elias.*

Having just failed at the high striker, Elias Mage was in the act of passing the hammer to his wife. Gale smirked, lifting the hood of his iridescent cloak. *Looks like Ean thinks she can get a better score than Eli can. Adorable.*

Clang!

The dark elf's slanted brows rose. *She's getting stronger.* Subtly impressed, Gale followed the couple as they claimed their tickets and meandered through the fair. Their chitchat was light and comical… it waxed flirtatious. Elias gazed at Ean with the unmistakable passion of a man thoroughly and hopelessly enamored. He picked her up, and – in reckless disregard of place and person – melted into the shadows.

Gale turned aside. Sitting on the edge of a bench, he contemplated a few notions that were entirely new to his cynical mind. Shaking his head, he wrapped his cloak around him against the chilly atmosphere.

14

PASSING THE TEST

Mist rose above the lake as Ean paced, grasping Antivenom. Her lashes fluttered as she glanced to and fro. The atmosphere in Stellos was cloudy and shadow-bound, keeping the half-elf on high alert as she investigated everything that moved.

Gale and Elias were prowling somewhere, waiting for her.

Ean lingered on purpose. As she'd hoped would happen, the two had finally begun to relax around each other. Although they remained a far cry from being friends, she suspected it wouldn't take much more effort, or time.

Still, smiling to herself, *it won't hurt if I dawdle a bit.*

Suddenly, a were-cat's stinging howl split her ears. Whipping around to face it, she braced herself and took aim. Travis landed on all fours, baring his teeth. *Bang!* Antivenom punished him with a solid blank. The were-cat yelped, ducking behind a boulder for cover. "Nice one!" he cried from his sanctuary.

Ean shouldered her rifle, finger gripping the trigger guard. "I see my darling husband has a surprise or two planned for me."

"Sorry!" Travis called out.

"No, you're not."

"Yeah, your reaction was kinda worth it, honestly."

"Traitor." Ean the Berserker's optics flashed white. "All right, you ice-blooded scoundrels," she yelled, stomping into the middle of the Stellos training cell. She held her arms open wide. "Why not everybody at once, eh?"

A breathless silence whispered from Darkling Forest.

Gale's voice answered her… "Granted."

The dark elf moved in first. His unrivaled grace continued to impress Ean, even as he called upon the lake waters and turned them against her. His dark charisma tasted like sweet plum wine. It rippled across her tongue and warmed her, feeding her energy. She wanted to run to him – to drink it all in – but she controlled the urge. Ean kept her distance, changing positions frequently and kneeling to steady her aim.

Kaspar attacked next. He twirled his naginata with poise, staring her down. Ean switched to Necrowave. Thanks to the hammer's electric infusions, it could launch mid-range lightening attacks. Kaspar's speed gave her some trouble, though; she had to battle the temptation to full-on rage as she failed, again and again, to pin him down. *Not yet. You can't rage yet. Get everyone closer.*

Kaspar dodged aside, allowing Sindaya to take over. Her wicked smile as she fitted the arrow to her bow tempted Ean to smile in return. The half-elf exchanged weapons again, utilizing some of her berserker velocity to toggle back.

Sindaya didn't last long against Antivenom. Wincing from the sting of the blanks, Sinnie also ducked behind a boulder and stayed put. Chuckling, Ean reloaded and kneeled, aiming at the next attacker soaring low over the ground. *There he is.*

The mighty sweep of Eli's silver-gray wings battered the air. His right hand clutched Sacrimony. Ean's dominant eye narrowed against the scope. Inhaling, she smelled the spiced tinge of an ebony Whisker. Combined with the distinctive, smokey saffron of Eli's dark charisma, it was nearly too much for her. Her vision went white for a moment. She struggled to keep the manic state at bay.

Sorry, handsome. Hate the game, not the player. She fired.

Elias dodged the blanks. Exasperated, Ean stood and tossed her hair. *Eff it. Here goes nothing.* Provoking Gale and Kaspar with a hand-picked bouquet of Terran curses, Ean lunged toward Elias, brandishing Necro.

The three of them descended on her at once. Ean swung her hammer low, allowing the pale cloud in the corners of her mind to override her senses. A searing white flash... the thunder of collision... and piercing laughter... then... nothing.

Ean flinched, sitting up with a start. A light rain drizzled over the training cell. Confused, the half-elf fumbled to her feet, scowling at the clammy feeling of wet clothes. "What happened?" she asked, tapping the Holobox on her shoulder.

Hexadecimal appeared. "Ean-san. It appears your manic state was utilized successfully."

"Oh. Good... I guess." Glancing around, she felt a strange mixture of pride and distress when she realized most of her friends were still out. "I'm glad I ransacked the castle storage earlier for healing potions. I just thought I'd be having to use them myself." She flew to her friends, administering each dose with care. "Gods. It must have been quite the blow."

"It was, indeed. I recorded the battle, should you care to review it."

Once she'd healed Kaspar, Gale, and Sindaya, Ean looked for her husband. "Where's Elias? Did he get knocked out, too?"

"Temporarily," Hex answered.

"Where did he go? And why did he leave everyone else here?"

"I believe he is retrieving more healing potions, Ean-san."

"Our inventory is linked, though. He should have noticed that I had enough." Dismissing the oversight, Ean clapped Gale on the shoulder. "Hey, man. Sorry I knocked you out."

Gale's indigo eyes beamed with amusement. "No need to apologize. You did extremely well. I'm sure Elias is proud of you."

"I'd say I was the smart one of you lot," Travis piped up, jogging up to them in human form. He grinned. "Once I saw that look on her face, I knew to stay as far away as possible."

"What look?" Ean asked.

The were-cat's reply was halted by the growl of a motorcycle engine. Elias performed an impressive stunt leap over the crags. He glided into the cell on Simulacra. "Brought more healing supplies," he reported, reproaching his wife with a spirited glare. "I always knew she'd snap one day."

The group laughed and targeted Ean with further banter. She ignored them with an airy toss of her head, addressing Eli. "So, how'd I do?"

"Words fail me." The skeleman's aspect shone with pride. "I truly don't know what to say. You're really something, Ean Mage."

"Thank you." Ean's hand cradled the back of his skull as she kissed him. "I wanted to live up to my new last name. For you to be proud of me. That's what I wanted… more than anything else."

Eli's expression brimmed with sentiment. He embraced her playfully. "More than being SkyRate Grand Champion, even?"

She giggled, trapping his wandering hands against her waist. "OK, you got me. I wanted both those things equally."

"I've always been proud of you, Lightcross. Didn't you know?"

"Maybe a little." She winked. "But the way you're looking at me right now… I covet that look all the time."

"Don't be greedy."

The couple locked into a passionate embrace. A few dramatic groans and "Get a room!" comments embarrassed Ean, inspiring Elias to extend his wings and shield them both. Safe among the feathers, they kissed for quite some time. They didn't emerge until Ean's hair had been thoroughly tussled.

"Ought to get some wings myself," Kaspar joked. Elias bumped him with his shoulder blade.

"I think we should celebrate Ean passing her test," Travis proposed. "To the Pulse!"

15

PIPE TALK

G ale took a few mincing steps across the threshold. Gaze fraught with misgivings, he scanned the workshop entry for traps before proceeding further. Elias chuckled. "I wouldn't take the risk of harming a potential customer, even to snare *you*." He beckoned the dark elf inside. "Have a seat right here. I've just expanded the fireplace."

As he spoke, Eli grabbed a handful of pyro crystals and threw them into the grate. The flames burst and crackled, turning green, purple, and blue by turns. The soothing scent of crushed lavender filled the room. "Just a few minor artificer tweaks." Elias sighed with contentment and stretched his boney feet toward the fire.

Gale sat down. "Thanks for inviting me."

"You know," the effects of the Pulse rendering Elias convivial, "you're not half so bad, Modi. At least, once you've got a couple beers in you." Browsing his inventory, he removed a black pipe and lit it.

Gale withdrew a violet Whisker. "If I may?"

"'Course." Scented smoke billowed from his jaws. "Since we're here (and it's just us), I'm sure there's a few questions we'd both love to ask each other. Who wants to go first?"

"I'll go first." Emodicus propped his ankle on his knee. "Does Ean know about the Skeleton's Anathema?"

Elias snorted. "Aren't we the most direct, mow-over-the-bush pack of avatars ever to be sworn! No, she doesn't know about it. Unless someone else told her," He added, eyelids crinkling in a scowl.

"Wouldn't have been me." Gale winced and rubbed his shoulder, still a mite sore from Ean's test. "I admit to being a blackguard, but even I have my limits."

"Glad to hear it." Eli's gaze softened. "What made you hold back?"

"Same toxic trait you suffer from. Curiosity."

"How interesting." Elias leaned his skull against the seat. "My turn. Why did you flirt with Ean a few weeks ago? What was your motive?"

Gale tried to laugh. "She told you about that? And that was two questions, not one."

"The latter is implied by the former."

"Fine. I'll be brief, then." The dark elf's lips exhaled violet smoke. "Three reasons. One, she's highly attractive (as I needn't explain to *you*). Two: At this point, she's well on her way to becoming just as unique and talented as you are. And three, she's a walking magnet for dark charisma. Her companions will never be at a deficit."

Elias clacked his jaws together. "Well, I may despise your words themselves, but I admire their honesty. You're entirely self-absorbed."

"So is everyone else since the dawn of mankind."

"Fair point." Elias paused to refill his pipe. "I'm guessing you think I saw her potential right away, and wanted to romance her for my own advantage. Yes?"

The elf's slanted eyes lowered. An uncommon softness stole over his expression. "I used to think so. I'm still tempted to. You get this certain infernal look whenever her skills advance. Like a puppet master pulling the strings. Although…"

Elias clenched the pipe stem between his gleaming teeth. "Although?"

Gods. I'm going to regret this tomorrow. "I think… I believe you really do love Ean." He gestured to the vivid ruby on Eli's head, the foremost gem of the bunch. "The charm you infused there didn't escape me. Ean feels almost no pain as a midnight berserker, because you made sure she wouldn't. You've taken it upon yourself."

Eli nodded and glanced away. Gale could tell that he was silently touched. "Don't tell her."

"Sure."

The ex-enemies shared a companionable silence. Emodicus snuck his feet onto the coffee table. "Still, you should reign in your fiendish obsession with experimentation. Sooner or later, you'll offend your friends. Ask me how I know."

Eli's eyes twinkled. "You used to have friends?"

"Don't be an ass. I'm a loner by choice."

"I see." The skeleman swallowed his laughter. "At any rate, perhaps you could assist me with my little 'fiendish obsession.' If you're feeling brave, that is." He snapped his teeth together again, this time with a small, excited tap.

Gale sighed. "We've just started talking on friendly terms, and you think I'm going to submit as your guinea pig? Bull shitake."

"Trust me, I know what I'm doing. This experiment is a year in the works." Elias pushed off his chair and strode to his desk. He unlocked it and withdrew a vial and a green needle. "I've calculated the dosage for the various races. It should work beautifully."

Emodicus stood and folded his arms. "What in Hades is that?"

Eli's hellish chortle rose from his chest. "Modified zombie venom."

"By the gods! You're crazy if you think I'm going to take *that*."

"Now, don't be a 'fraidy-cat, Modi," Elias sang, filling the syringe and tapping out the air bubbles. "Like I said, I've been toying with this for a year now. It's harmless."

"To you, maybe. Skeletal avatars can't be zombified."

"I've taken the proper precautions." Elias jerked open the drawer again, showing Gale some pouches containing antivenom. "I keep a stock of the cure at all times."

Gale took a step back, arms still crossed. "No way. Come near me with that thing, and I'll crack your jaws apart."

"Tut-tut, Modi. Such violent language." Elias inserted the needle at his bite mark. "Then just watch this time, OK?"

"Whatever."

The dark elf watched as Elias slipped into a trance-like state. His resulting prattle and banter was coherent enough, though childlike. Emodicus rose an eyebrow. "How long does this usually last?"

"Hmm?" The skeleman's glazed eyes wavered. "About ten minutes."

"That's not very long."

"No, but it's enough to take the edge off a hard day. It's phantasmic stuff!"

As the venom wore off, their conversation turned to lighter subjects. The dark elf made his excuses. "It's late, Eli. I'm going to log off."

"I expect I won't be far behind you." Elias saw him to the door. He extended his hand. "Thanks for coming."

"It was... enjoyable." Gale stared down at their clasped hands in mild astonishment. "To think we'd ever see the day," he muttered.

Elias released his hand. "There's just one thing, Modi." He tucked his hands into his leather pockets.

"What's that?"

"Don't flirt with my wife. If I ever hear of it happening again, you're getting the green needle. *The whole thing.* Got it?"

"Duly noted." Chuckling, Gale made a mock salute and melted into the night.

"Let's take on some witches in Stellos."

Elias glanced up from an artificer volume. "As in, right now?"

Ean scurried up to her husband and knelt, snuggling up to his ribcage. "I've trained enough. I'm ready to fight some real baddies!"

The skeleman sighed, playfully burrowing into his chair. "But I'm so comfortable."

The half-elf rolled her eyes. "Your precious recliner isn't going anywhere. Come on, Eli! I'm restless. Oh, and let's invite Modi to come along. They won't stand a chance against all three of us."

Eli gave her a look. "You've been training with him too much. You're overly reliant on his assistance. Let's go alone."

"Hey, aren't you worried I'm more reliant on *you?*" Ean poked him.

"You're my in-game spouse. You're supposed to rely on me."

"How true." Ean smiled up at him. He cupped her chin affectionately. "Ean?"

"Mmmhmm?"

"Do you think Emodicus is handsome?"

"Of course. I have eyes, don't I?"

"Mmm." Elias tugged a lock of her hair. "Is he more handsome than your husband?"

"Not by a long shot."

"What does that mean? I'm still acclimating to your archaic expressions."

Ean giggled and kissed his glinting forehead. "All dark elves are strikingly handsome. Emodicus may be a prince of the darkness, but he's one among many. You're the titan of Helios… and there's no one else like you."

"Ah." Elias leaned back in his seat, flexing. "Elias Mage, the Titan of Helios! I'll adopt that title very nicely, thank you ever so much."

"You're full of it!" Ean laughed as he pulled her into his lap. "To the witches of Stellos, then," he consented. "But I require a little charisma alleviation first."

"Is that what we're calling it now?" Ean trailed her fingers down the center of his chest. "Also, you don't need me for that anymore. As a midnight berserker, I absorb dark charisma as naturally as breathing."

Elias tapped his lower jaw. "I suppose it doesn't sound very romantic, does it?"

"You can't help it; you're strictly practical."

"What? I can be romantic!"

"About once every three months or so."

"You're joking." Elias stared. "Right?"

"Not by a long shot."

Holding her gaze, Elias leaned his forehead against hers. "I'll make you eat your words, Ean Mage."

"Please do."

He carried her to the castle bedroom.

16

ONE SECRET TOO MANY

Three weeks later, Ean traveled through Darkling Forest on high alert.

According to TerraWiki, Ophidious had been seen in the area. The half-elf knelt to examine tracks in the ground. "Ogre," she mumbled. Holding Antivenom carefully, she continued her soundless trek through the brush.

Her mind drifted back to earlier that afternoon. Ean frowned. No amount of begging, pleading, or bribery had sufficed to get Elias to hunt Ophidious with her. Not a single ounce of interest sparked from his visage. *Come to think of it, he always shuts down when I mention taking him with me against Ophidious.*

His reluctance didn't make any sense. Unless…

Is Elias secretly intimidated by Ophidious? Does he not think he would win against him?

It was beyond Ean's capability to imagine that Elias Mage was afraid of anyone. However, Modi had hinted more than once that Ean didn't know her husband as well as she supposed. Maybe there was a weakness or two he kept hidden.

Stretching, Ean dismissed her ponderings. *It's nice to have a "just me" hobby, at least. No need for us to be attached at the hip 24/7.* Shifting her rifle's weight, she stopped to pick a few mushrooms and store them before marching on.

The forest was pleasantly quiet and cool. A mite too quiet for Ean's current tastes. Toggling her home screen, she turned on one of her favorite songs and bopped to the beat as she walked. She got caught up in it, belting out the lyrics full-volume.

She froze.

Ophidious was standing beneath an oak tree, watching. Something suspiciously close to amusement lurked in his expression. He held an elaborate dark staff in his left hand, dotted with various gemstones.

Hmm. Where have I seen that staff before?

Ean jerked into action. She knelt and aimed in one fluid motion. *Bang! Bang! Bang!* The bullets hit home. Ean cheered as she saw his HP decrease by thirty percent. "You're screwed now, buddy!"

Ophidious pounded his staff against the ground, triggering a magical shield. Reloading with her precious explosive bullets, Ean picked up speed and tore backward to maintain a safer distance.

The cursed sorcerer seemed to sense her plans. Dark charisma gathered at his fingertips as he flew toward her, closing the distance. *Shit.* Ean tried to confuse him by utilizing her berserker speed.

Her charisma gauge emptied by half. *Didn't want to use that so early on.*

As the battle intensified, Ean's frustration increased. Her opponent seemed downright psychic. He interpreted every intent, and adjusted to her combat style and weapon use with ease. Her aim was on point, but his shield remained impenetrable. Pure fury overcame her as she switched back to Necrowave. *Screw this!*

Her manic state activated.

As Ophidious knocked her hammer aside, pressing her throat with the end of his staff, she felt its gemstone's facets digging into her skin. The priceless cut of the diamond choked her with a sudden realization.

Four weeks ago, she'd seen this staff model on Eli's desk. An HI rendering.

Her rage mode fizzled out as her concentration broke. *Ophidious and Elias are...*

The sorcerer noticed the flash of recognition in her stare. He switched weapons (though it was too late). Ean backed away, brows raised. "You get your weapons serviced by Elias Mage, don't you?"

He didn't answer. The half-elf's brows creased as she scowled. *Those two are in cahoots! How else can Ophidious be so intimately aware of my combat style? My weapons? It's the only thing that makes sense! But, Elias...*

Why would he betray her like that?

Back at Vermillion Castle, Hexadecimal attended to Ean's low HP. Thanks to her shattered concentration, her manic state hadn't come full circle. She'd lost again. Nevertheless, she cared far less about that than she cared about the fact that her messages to Elias were unanswered. Apparently, he hadn't logged in yet.

Grumbling, Ean waved Hex aside. She stalked around the living room. "It certainly explains a couple of things that haven't added up. His reluctance to come fight Ophidious with me. His earlier remarks that I wasn't likely to win against him. The times he's vanished in TerraWorks for hours, with no real explanation. Gods, I've been blind! And Emodicus tried to warn me that something was off. That there were things I didn't know."

Ean's Holopal prepared to mediate. "Perhaps you should simply ask Elias for an explanation first."

"I'm *trying.*" Ean tapped her message screen and pointed to the evidence. "He's not answering me."

"Be patient, Ean. I can assure you with full confidence (and significant evidence) that come what may, Elias Mage sincerely cares for you. He would never harm you intentionally."

Ean stopped pacing. Her expression relaxed. "I'm sure you're right. Still… it feels like a betrayal to me, you know? Since our first date at the Pulse, Elias knew that I intend to defeat Ophidious. Come to find out, he's had insider information about him and his weapons all along, and never said a word about it."

"Elias dislikes cheating, Ean-san. He may have felt that such a disclosure would be akin to cheating."

"That does sound like him," Ean admitted. "Well, I thank the gods for *you*, Hexy, and no mistake. But waiting around here is driving me nuts. Should I ask Emodicus to tell me what he knows?"

"The choice is yours to make, Ean-san."

The half-elf paced a few more times before stopping again. "I can't take the waiting. I'm going to try messaging Emodicus."

"Very well. Livewire?"

"Not this time. Holotext will do."

Evening, Modi. This may seem sudden, but remember when you tried to tell me something I needed to know? About Elias? Something's come up. I'd like to hear what you have to say. Ean bit her lip as she hit *Send.*

The dark elf replied in a few minutes. *Not sure I want to tell you anymore. May not be in your best interest. I think I understand what Elias is trying to do.*

Ean sighed. *I really want to know. Elias isn't answering me, and I need to talk to somebody about what happened today. I need some answers.*

I'll meet you at the Fountain of Nymphoria in Helios.

Gale recognized Ean's skyboard as she descended. He rose from the edge of the fountain, wrapped in his lustrous blue cloak. "What happened?" he asked before she'd dismounted.

Ean leapt off her board and stowed it. She fiddled with her necklace. "I think Elias and Ophidious know each other."

Gale motioned for her to walk with him. They began to circle the fountain slowly. "About a month ago, I saw an HI Elias had drawn of a new sorcerer's staff. Today, when I hunted Ophidious down in Darkling Forest, he fought with that exact same staff. He's one of Eli's clients, but I suspect he may be more than that. They may be friends."

Emodicus blinked. "What makes you think they're friends?"

"Oh, little things that add up. Elias refuses to fight Ophidious with me... even though he's usually insistent that we battle together. And he's hinted that I'm never going to be able to beat Ophidious. Also, if they *are* friends, that would explain why Elias never betrayed his intimate knowledge of the sorcerer's weapons. That wouldn't be fair."

Gale clasped his hands behind his back, giving her a knowing look. "It wouldn't be fair to you, either."

"Right." Ean nodded. "I want to slay Ophidious via cunning and skill, not by knowing things I shouldn't be privy to. If *you* understand that – short as our friendship has been – then Elias certainly does."

Gale's stern mouth broke into a soft smile. "You remind me of a locked magical tome, Lightcross. Precious few are granted the key. But once they have it, every page can be examined with ease."

She laughed. Her polished tresses floated in the nighttime breeze. "Meaning I'm not as dark and mysterious as Piragor seems to believe?"

Gale snorted with an air that said *pfft, that commoner?* "To the light class avatars, you'll always remain a mystery. Not to the wielders of dark charisma."

"Can't argue with you there."

As they strolled in tandem with their identical elvish tread, Gale relaxed to an extent Ean hadn't witnessed before. His irises burned violet with a nocturnal spark. The lilting tune he hummed was barely audible, yet her pointed ears distinguished it from the wind. "So, Modi. What did you want to tell me about Elias?"

The dark elf hesitated. He surprised Ean by gently leaning his hand on her shoulder. "Before I answer that, you should know that Elias and I are officially friends. He invited me to his workshop after you logged off, and I accepted."

"And no blood was shed?" Ean jested.

Gale smiled. "No blood was shed. After all, I've often admired him even as my rival. Admiration is one step away from friendship, so it is said."

"Yes. I wondered for ages why you two didn't get along, when it seemed so blatantly obvious to me that you *should.*"

He shrugged. His hand lingered, but in a brotherly fashion. "Elias and I are acquainted in real life. We've never met in person, but we've both posted to TerraWiki frequently, and we started talking that way. Through online debates, to be precise."

"*Ooooh!*" Ean breathed, eyes wide. "So, you've both been faking your rivalry all this time?"

"No. It was very real. We found out that we're both beta testers, so when TerraWorks was officially released, we were naturally competitive against each other. I first fought against him while he was perfecting his preliminary avatar, not the one he uses now."

Ean smiled her comprehension. "You knew him back in the good old days. I bet you know lots of embarrassing details," she teased. "Did he experiment a lot back then, too?"

"Oh, yes." Gale rolled his eyes. "But somewhere among the chaos, the accidental hexing, and the artificer buffoonery, he managed to perfect *both* his avatars. He switches between them effortlessly." The dark elf ceased walking, cementing Ean to her place with a pointed stare.

Ean Mage caught her breath. "You're saying that William is Elias *and* Ophidious."

"Right you are." Grinning at her reaction, he recommenced his playful tune.

The pleasant *plish-plash* of the fountain spray was interrupted by a giggle. Looking back at her, Gale was astounded to see a wide smirk splitting Ean's face. "What's so funny?"

Ean started to laugh. She doubled over, bracing her stomach. Gale began to feel somewhat concerned. "Lightcross?"

"We didn't meet at the concert," she panted, still giggling between phrases. "The first time… he saw me… he was Ophidious."

The dark elf fiddled with his sword hilt. "And that's hilarious somehow?"

"The way I stared at him… and was all like *hey!*… Oh my gods, I was a moron." She fairly shrieked at the memory. Ean Lightcross, standing before a rare Terran monster, and grinning like the clueless idiot that she was.

Emodicus got the joke. "And he pursued you anyway."

"And he pursued me anyway." Her dark eyes sparkled as she continued to laugh. "Gods, but I love him!"

Later, the Mages strolled hand-in-hand through Helios. Most of the shops were closed, but the couple didn't mind; nighttime walks were their favorite. Ean glanced up at Elias, again admiring his self-assured stride, and the way the passing lamplight flickered across his reflective visage.

Elias noted her infatuated face. "Haven't I warned you not to look at me like that in public?"

"Hmm?"

Her dazed response ensnared him further. Stopping, he pulled her in for a kiss. "What's on your mind, Mrs. Mage?" he queried once they parted.

"I'm not sure whether to tell you or not," the half-elf answered roguishly. "I rather like the fact that I know something you don't know. It happens so rarely."

"You know I have to bother you now until you tell me," he threatened. He curled his skeletal fingers into tickling position. Ean shrieked and started to run – then froze dead in her tracks. "Almighty Kanthesis!"

"What?" The skeleman traced her stare. His eyes widened in disbelief.

Another couple was also strolling by, absorbing the nocturnal sights. One was a tall, white skeleton who – minus the lack of gemstones on his skull – could easily be mistaken for Elias himself. Holding onto his arm was a stunning woodland elf. Her black hair framed her petite face in velvet-smooth curls. A floral pentagram hung from her neck, marking her class type as an elven witch.

The elf noticed them first. She jerked her companion to a halt and pointed to Elias and Ean.

The skeleton's jaw dropped. "By Nymphoria! It's the Mages!"

Ean was too stunned to reply.

Elias folded his arms. "And who in Hades are *you?*"

—

Anathema
Book Three of the Terraworks Trilogy
Trilogy
Richelle Manteufel

Man Devil Press

CONTENTS

1

SHENANIGANS

"Would you keep it *down,* Ean?"

"Me? You're the one with the big mouth." Ean Mage coughed. "He's coming! Everybody shut up."

Axel dashed into the workshop. It was empty. Specter firelight crackled from the open hearth – the only sound to be heard. Having confirmed that Tirion was absent, Axel sailed to Eli's chair and hid something under the cushion. He patted it with a devious snicker.

Willow supervised with a face of calm detachment. "It is times like these when I recall why I don't want children. I'm already raising one."

Axel ran back out, motioning for silence. "Everybody act natural."

The three wandered from the workshop, affecting to examine the flowers around the fountain of Nymphoria. Ean hooked Willow's arm and chatted with sisterly zeal. Axel, brimming with mischief, jumped into the fountain and basked in the spray. "Come cool off with me, Willow," he cried.

The elf-witch shook her head, raven curls waving. "You know I don't like to be cold, Axie."

"It's not cold! It's cool and refreshing."

The sweep of colossal wings battered the air. A gilt skeleman alighted with grace, his skull coruscant with rubies. Ean's cheeks flushed. Her quickening breath betrayed her desire, potent as ever despite the passing years.

Elias Mage opened his golden arms. His wings retracted. "Aphrodite."

"Mephisto." Grinning, Ean skipped into his embrace. "How'd the session go?"

"Very well." Eli nipped her earlobe. "Travis showed up. Not that I would have minded calling you in, if you weren't otherwise engaged."

"Good boy, Travis. Praise the Terran Pantheon!"

"Indeed." Elias held her hand as they walked to his workshop. "Evening, Axel. Willow. Any plans for tonight?"

"Let's hang out here," Axel proposed, stealing a peep at Ean. She seconded the motion. Willow nodded her assent.

The two couples filed indoors. Axel's silver-gray eyes were snapping with preemptive glee. Ean fired him a warning glare. *Steady, boy.*

"By the gods, I'm tired," Elias mumbled, kicking off his shoes. He flexed his boney feet. "I must be getting old. Our practice sessions never wore me out before."

Ean's Holobox glowed. "You'll never be old, Eli-san."

"Kind of you to say, Hexy-san," the skeleman rebuffed. He tweaked Ean's nose. "I hate to burst your lovely bubbles, you two, but we're all getting older by the minute."

"Ever the charming fatalist." Ean, overflowing with housewifely graces, pulled out his chair for him. "Have a seat, my love."

"Don't mind if I do."

Squeee! POP!

Pink glitter entombed Elias in a sparkling shroud. He sat stock-still while his *friends* screamed with mirth. Even Willow was laughing.

He waited in grim silence until the last glitter fell. He brushed himself off. "And whose delicate sense of taste must I thank for this?"

Ean, still giggling, managed to point out the fellow skeleton rolling in the corner.

Axel gasped, "It was Ean's idea to pull a prank!"

"But *you* suggested the glitter box," Ean objected.

Axel rolled to his feet, eyelids crinkling. "Of course! It's so very… birthday-ish."

Elias stalked over to the culprit (trailing sparkles). He thanked Axel with a resounding smack to the skull. He turned to his wife. Ean's eyes widened. She tried to duck behind Willow, but her husband grabbed her, pinning her back against his chest. "Surely that's not your only present for me, is it?" he murmured against her hair, arms locking her in place.

"Oh, Eli. I'm insulted." Ean kissed him. "Your *real* surprise is else-where."

At first, Elias wasn't thrilled.

He was coaxed into the TerraDome, packed into the crowd like a sardine, then abandoned. Even Axel and Willow were nowhere to be seen. The skeleman pocketed his hands and sighed.

A rippling anticipation stirred the audience. Looking up, he saw Ean Mage front and center, flourishing a red guitar. His deft glance at the drums revealed Axel Prendergast. Elias stifled a laugh at the skeleton's twinkling sunglasses. *He never does take my concerts seriously.*

The empowering tone of the rhythm set Eli's mind ablaze. The song was fun-loving and fiendish. Elias imagined himself leading the way into the jaws of Armageddon, unsheathing Sacrimony for a final battle to the death. His eyelids crinkled in a grin. *This is Ean's doing, without a doubt.* He flashed the sign of Draco's Son, earning a nod from his wife.

Although Elias was well acquainted with Ean's lyrical improvement, the newfound authority in her voice amazed him.

> "THE DEATH-DEFYING SOUND,
> ARISING FROM THE GROUND!
> OUR MIRACLE, ONCE MADE,
> WILL SAVE THEM FROM THE GRAVE!"
> "ONE LAST TERRIFIC FLIGHT
> INTO THE STARLESS NIGHT.
> COME WITH ME BRAVE, MY DEAR;
> THE SIREN'S CALL WE HEAR!"

From beatific heights to cavernous depths, Ean's masterful octaves invited Elias to leave his mortal frame behind. The skeleman raised his fists in ecstasy. He closed his eyes to drink in the wine of her voice.

He remembered the trembling Ean Lightcross who had sung onstage four years ago. She was shy, hesitant, and dressed in shadowy clothing that melted into the background. Now, Ean Mage commanded attention in a sweeping scarlet ensemble. Her blood-red locks flowed with her movements. The iridescent tattoo of the Mage symbol glistened on her right shoulder. Elias wondered if an entourage of cartoonish heart bubbles was blooming above his head. He distracted himself by wedging closer to fist-bump Travis.

The score ended. The ambitious title *Ean of Apocalypse* fired across the TerraDome ceiling. Elias laughed, helping his wife off the stage. "Your stage name, I presume?" he shouted above the applause.

"I am a woman of many names," she declared. Her bold grin destroyed what little fortitude Eli had left. "Come here," he murmured, drawing her into his arms.

Their kiss was interrupted by a tap on Eli's shoulder. His glare lightened. "Oh, it's Modi. How've you been, man?"

"Heard birthday offerings were in order." The dark elf bowed and offered a long, rumpled parcel. Elias accepted it gingerly. "It's not something that could kill me, I trust?"

Gale snapped his fingers. "Gods damn it. Foiled again."

Ean giggled. She opened the gift for Eli while he held the box. "Sweet!" She lifted a long, tapered silver blade. The sword gleamed with dark purple energy. "I call it *Spina Lucifer*," Emodicus explained. "It's important to have a solid backup blade, if anything ever happened to Sacrimony."

"You're right. I've been putting that off. This is great!" Elias clapped him on the back. "Thanks, Modi-san."

"Excellent craftsmanship," Ean commented. "Did Kaspar help with this?"

"Sure did," Kaspar himself replied. The rest of the Spectral Tyrants trailed behind him. "It wasn't easy, practicing that new song *and* forging this blade, but nothing's too good for Elias Mage."

"Seriously, gang. This is nice." Elias filtered from one friend to the next, extending gratitude and banter.

Ean leaned her arm against Gale's broad shoulder. "I'd say this was a success. I'm glad you infused the sword yourself. I thought about hiring somebody in Klad, but gifts are better when they're personal."

The dark elf nodded. "It took longer than I anticipated. But it turned out well. And now, I've had a taste of artificer craft."

"Did you have fun?"

"I did."

Ean and Gale continued to exchange friendly remarks. Elias made his way back to them, acknowledging several more avatars in the interim. "You'd better not be flirting with my wife again."

Gale pointed out Ean's chummy posture. "*She's* coming onto *me*, man."

"No way!" Ean choked, smacking Gale's arm. Elias laughed. "No radical measures necessary, Mrs. Mage. I know you're helplessly charmed by my good looks."

Ean slipped her arm around Eli's waist. "Got one more present for you."

"Oh?"

Elias inhaled the ocean wind. His gilt toes burrowed into smooth, silky sand. He'd never seen the Shiori beaches at night, and the Terran sky of multicolored stars and moon rings was impressive. "Best birthday ever," he remarked.

Ean's fingers traced his ribcage. "Even better than last year?"

"Well, that party *was* epic," he answered. "Vermillion Castle barely held all our friends. But being here alone with you…" He finished his thought by bringing her hand to his face, cradling it with a heart-stalling expression.

She surprised him with a playful tackle, holding him down and straddling his waist. "You don't mind getting a bit sandy, do you?" she inquired.

"Nope."

Ean flushed at the yearning in his eyes. "You know, I think this is the first time I've ever been able to hold you down. How interesting."

"True." Eli's seductive chuckle made her smile. "But what if I'm faking it?"

"You don't think I'm strong enough?" Ean's grip on his hands tightened. Eli eyed her toned shoulders and arms. "You're strong. However," he flipped her on her back, nipping her ear, "you can still be caught off guard, my dear."

Her eyebrow rose. "What if I *wanted* you to drive, though?"

"It would be my pleasure."

It took a long, long time for Ean to get all the sand out of her clothes.

2

ACCESS DENIED

William logged in the next day.

First, Elias stopped by the castle library to shelve the spell books he'd finished. Grabbing some new volumes, he added them to his inventory and prepared to fly to his workshop.

The castle's main doors locked behind him with a satisfying *ker-chack*. Elias stretched, observing the crisp morning weather with enjoyment. "Nothing like TerraWorks on a Saturday morning." He extended his wings. *Wait. I haven't handled Spina yet. Let's see how Modi's handiwork holds up.*

Flicking his wrist, Eli opened his inventory and tried to select his new sword. The containment box blinked red. *Weapon access denied. Higher combat level required.*

Eyes narrowing, Elias tapped it again. *Access denied.*

"Hmm." Shrugging his shoulder blades, he took off for downtown Helios. "I'll send a holotext to Modi after I land. He must have made a mistake."

Elias tried a few more times after he landed. No dice. Sighing, he scanned his wrist at the shop doorway and entered. He snatched his tablet off the desk. *Hey, Modi. If you locked my sword access on purpose, you're a jerk. What's the password? EliasHasNoBalls?*

Emodicus responded. *By the gods, you're hilarious. I didn't do anything to your sword other than infuse it with dark charisma, which you're beyond capable of wielding. Did you try rebooting?*

Was hoping to avoid that. I'll be back in five minutes.

Eli toggled his screen motion for the home menu. He selected *Reboot*. William Klein waited patiently while the inside of his helmet displayed the loading icon. Logging back in, he resumed the game as Elias Mage.

He reopened his inventory, browsed it, and tapped Spina Lucifer. *Access denied.*

Elias growled. "OK, now I'm getting pissed." Gale's avatar symbol flashed at the corner of his screen. Eli read the new holotext. *Hey, you may not believe this, but I can't equip several of my weapons, either. Maybe it's a game glitch.*

Maybe. Rebooting didn't do anything. Let me try Sacrimony.

The skeleman unsheathed his beloved firstborn. Its lustrous blade was meant to burst into golden flames, but not one spark whispered from its length. He ground his teeth. "Ricobyurn!"

Spellcraft attempt denied. Higher charisma level required.

"Almighty Kanthesis!" he spat. Switching to his avatar progression page, he stared in horror at the meager gauges, formerly full to bursting.

Combat, level one. Charisma, level one. Performa, beginner.

Sheathing his sword, Elias pounded his desk with a solid punch. "*How can this happen?*" Fighting to contain his rage, he resumed his conversation with Emodicus by Livewire.

Thankfully, the dark elf answered. His pale-blue image projected above the tablet. Not bothering with any greetings, he bellowed "My gauges are *empty*, Elias. I'm back to level one." His indigo optics flashed fire.

Eli folded his arms. "So am I. Is it just us, though? Has anyone else messaged you about this?"

"I've been searching TerraWiki with Zahir. Apparently, the top ten avatars in TerraWorks were the only ones affected. Which means Ophidious is also null and void, I'm afraid."

The skeleman punched his desk again. "Gods damn it!"

"It's too targeted to assume this was a system glitch. We've been hacked. Nobody knows the source."

Elias groaned, fingerbones rubbing his temples. "So, we need to try to find the source... But in the meantime, we've got to train hard and fast so we're not stuck at level one. Our avatars won't be able to fall from an apple tree without dying."

"Right. We should train together. Less risk of expiring as often if we have each other's backs."

"Sounds good to me." Elias took a deep breath. His dead face brightened as he tried to think like Ean. "Let's look at the bright side (if there is one). We can fool around a bit and get to know each other better. Also, Tirion's doing well, so he can take care of my workshop. Will the Kanthesis Temple get along without you?"

"I don't see why not... though I have reason to believe my position as Fell Sorcerer is at risk." Emodicus frowned and rubbed his chin. "What about the Spectral Tyrants?"

"Oh, gods." Eli's voice strained. "My performa."

"Performa is linked to charisma accumulation, right?"

"Yes. I'll still sound like myself, but the effect on the audience won't be half as strong. The clarity, the intonation, the sensations... they'll all be negatively affected. *Damn* it all!" Elias punished his desk with a third assault.

"Relax. You're going to bust your knuckles. Could you cheat?"

Elias winced at the word. "How?"

"By harvesting dark charisma from Ean. Isn't she with the Firestone Guild often because her berserker's instincts drive her to fight?"

"Yes, that's true."

Gale tilted his head. "That means she's constantly cycling through dark charisma. On top of that, she's the Skeleton's Anathema. If anyone could handle a few setbacks in charisma accumulation, it's her."

The dark elf's heightened spirits didn't escape Elias. "You're wanting to try this yourself, I suppose?"

Gale hesitated. "If it's all right with you."

The skeleman rolled his dark eyes. "I've tried and tried to keep you away from her. There's just no helping it. Make it quick, will you?"

Gale cracked a wry grin. "I could have crushed on *you* instead. Count your blessings, Mage."

Ean leapt into the saddle. Simulacra grumbled as she torqued the accelerator. Eli's bike seemed to like her; her body settled into its lean curves as if they were custom-measured. Giggling, the half-elf shot ahead, silken hair twisting in the wind. *They'll never catch up now.*

Behind her, the Firestone Guild was reduced to specks. She could sense Axel and Willow making sinister remarks while Cyrus and Mallie laughed.

Ean spared a millisecond to admire her ring. Its chaotic cluster of infused amethysts and rubies made her smile. *Eli's handiwork is so distinctive. A controlled chaos. Just like me...*

Dodging a few boulders, Ean jolted Hexadecimal out of sleep mode. "Yo, wake up, Hexy! Tell Elias I'm on my way home."

Her Holobox blinked. "Ean-san. I must warn you that Eli will want a report of your current velocity."

"Very funny."

"Oh, you could tell I was in jest?"

"He knows I'm not reckless. Correction… not *that* reckless. Not with Simulacra." Ean the Berserker smirked, sweeping the ground in a low turn. "At any rate, he gave me the ignition password. He wouldn't have done that if he thought I couldn't handle it."

"That is correct."

Laughing, Ean whipped around bushes and tore through icy puddles. Spotting the gates of Helios, she increased her speed until the scenery was a blur. One part of her… the midnight berserker part, she figured… *wanted* to crash. To experience the rushing, crushing adrenaline of her body enacting its little soap opera of VR death.

Elias wouldn't be happy, though. He'd probably change the password.

Ean braked. Simulacra smoked to a stop just in front of the gates. To her shock, the Firestone Guild was waiting for her. Byron shook his head, chestnut hair tumbling over his eyes. "Haven't you heard of transport gems, Mrs. Mage?"

The half-elf dismounted with a shameful grin. "Maybe. But they're expensive, and they aren't much fun." She fist-bumped Cyrus and saluted Axel, then threw her arm around Willow's slender shoulders. "You should ride with me sometime, girl. You'd love it!"

"I have no desire to die."

Ean dissolved into mirth. "But you're a witch, Madame Prendergast. You regenerate without the pesky hospital visits the rest of us are beholden to."

"It's still a drain on my charisma." Despite her cool words, Willow leaned her head against Ean's with sisterly warmth. "I'd consider it if you let *me* drive."

"Well, I wouldn't mind. But the husband might. Speak of the devil," Ean detached herself, "I'd better go see what he's up to. If I leave him alone too long, he starts experimenting on our pets. Things get ugly." She smiled to herself as she stowed the motorbike.

"Thanks for your help today, Lightcross," Cyrus added. "You're rocking Antivenom."

"Thanks for inviting me. Later, guys!"

As Ean strode through Helios, multiple avatars called her name. She smiled and nodded to them. Scanning the horizon, she quickened her pace, running the forest's edge on the dirt road to Vermillion Castle. Birds sang from the lush vegetation. The burble of brooks and waterfalls freshened the air. Sighing with happiness, Ean slowed down and withdrew a Whisker smoke. "This is the life, eh, Hex?"

The Mage avatar symbol flashed near her hand. Ean tapped the symbol. *Are you almost home, Ean? Something's come up. I need to talk to you.*

Ean spoke her holotext reply. *Two minutes away.*

The half-elf crossed the drawbridge over the sparkling moat. She scanned her wrist at the castle doors. They creaked open to reveal Elias and Gale, arms crossed, faces stern.

Ean flinched. "I didn't drive *that* fast," slipped from her lips before she could stop herself.

Elias didn't laugh. Ean flushed to the points of her ears. "OK, so I got it a little muddy. I'll clean it, I promise."

Gale stepped forward, guiding her inside. "This isn't about the motorcycle. We've got a hacker situation."

"A hacker?" Ean perched on the scarlet couch, stunned. "There hasn't been a successful hack in the history of TerraWorks. It's too well-protected. What happened?"

"We're not sure," Gale replied. Ean stole at glance at Elias, who was abnormally silent. "But only the top ten avatars were affected. We've all been brought back to level one."

"Level *one?*" Ean's mouth fell open. "In combat or charisma?"

Elias sat down next to her. "Both."

"Gods." Ean's lips closed. She blinked hard, trying to absorb the concept of the famous Elias Mage at level *one.* Her hand instinctively sought his. "What are you going to do?"

"Train like Hades," Gale sighed. He sat in one of the armchairs across from them. "With the assistance of your dark charisma, if you'll allow it. In the meantime, we'll be doing what we can to find the source of the hack."

"You'll have to take my place in the Spectral Tyrants," Elias added, withdrawing his hand. He braced his skull in his hands. "I know it's a lot to ask of you. But otherwise, we'd be canceling everything until further notice. I can't afford to let that happen."

"But you can still sing, Elias. There's no need to back out."

Eli's voice dropped low. "You'll understand once you hear me. It just doesn't sound right. But you've learned a lot. If you stick to symphonic metal scores, you'll be in alignment with the band's image and true to your natural vocal style."

"I'll do my best. For you." Ean tried to take his hand again, but Elias shifted away. "I know you will," he murmured. He stood and mounted the winding staircase to the library, each step heavy with dejection.

Ean's raven eyes brimmed with sympathy. "I've never seen him like that before."

"Neither have I." Emodicus leaned forward in his chair. "He's taking it even harder than I am, and I'm fit to bite an orc's head off right now."

"That wouldn't taste very nice, would it, precious?" Ean quipped, trying to lighten the atmosphere.

Gale's self-control was impermeable. "No. Not very nice at all."

"Isn't there something else I could do?"

The dark elf rose and jerked a thumb to the front door. "Just kindly step outside and stand still, like a good girl. I'll chalk up a sorcerer's ring and borrow some charisma."

Ean sighed and pushed off the couch. "If you think it's necessary."

"Don't be greedy, Mrs. Mage."

"Now, where have I heard *that* before?" Ean questioned as Gale prodded her out the door.

3

ADJUSTING ROLES

E an clapped her hands. "Hey! Ollie, put the beer down. Where's the
song list Elias was working on? And where in Hades is Travis?"

"Late!" Sindaya, Desmond, and Kaspar answered.

"Almighty Kanthesis! All right. I'll message Axel and Willow. Axel can
play guitar or drums, and Willow can be my backup singer."

"What about me?" Desmond protested.

"You're still a backup singer, Des. I need another woman in case I
choke up, or something." *Which is more probable than I'll be admitting out
loud,* she privately complained. Practicing a single song for Eli's birthday
was one thing. Leading the concert tours themselves? Entirely another. *I
think I might faint.* "Where's that list?" Ean demanded.

"You'll have to message Elias for it. He has this thing about keeping all
his TerraDome plans under lock and key. Thinks somebody might steal
them and copy them," Sindaya explained, posing with her drumsticks.
"Where is he, anyway?"

Ean shrugged. "Hacker situation. He'll be fine, but for now, you'll have
to put up with me." She tapped her Holobox out of sleep mode. "Ask Eli
for the song list, Hex."

Her Holobox buzzed against her shoulder. "Right away, Ean-san."

Whenever Elias sent her anything, he usually attached a loving or quirky message with it. This time, the song sheets were shared without any message at all. Ean's face fell. *He's taking this so hard. I don't blame him, but I'm getting more and more worried.*

Ean shook her head and recommenced her duties. "OK, we'll be changing a few of these songs. There's no way in Hades I can sing the heavy metal hits."

"I thank Nymphoria for your wisdom," Axel's cheerful tenor remarked. "Because there's no way in Hades we'd let you try."

Ean turned to shake the skeleton's pearly hand, smiling. "Good to see you, Axie. I'm in desperate need of your optimistic company. Is your wife with you?"

"In the flesh," Willow's lilting voice answered. She floated across the flooring, draped in a diaphanous cloud of ebony. The gown's velvet folds hugged her immaculate figure. Ollie and Desmond stared after the pale curve of her bare back and the sable curls that graced it. "You can sing, right?" Ean asked her, glaring at the boys.

"I can." Willow kissed Axel's cheekbone with quiet affection. "I sometimes sing for Axie's psychedelic rock band."

"By the gods! That slipped my mind. I'm not taking you away from a band tour or anything, am I?" Ean said, biting her lip.

Axel waved her concern aside. "No, I'm afraid we're nowhere near the level of popularity to justify a tour. I was inspired by the great Elias Mage, but I don't labor under any delusions. We're not worthy to kiss the feet of the almighty Tyrants."

"Aren't you?" Oleon chuckled. He extended one sweaty, booted foot. "Go ahead, then!"

He chased Axel around while the skeleton screeched "Unworthy! Unworthy!" His pale hands rattled in the air. Ean groaned, dropping her face into her hands. "Don't tell me that every practice session is going to be like this," she lamented.

Travis kicked the door open, beer case in hand. "Pretty much!" he cried.

"It's a little like herding cats," Sindaya confessed.

"More beer!" cheered Ollie.

Ean massaged her forehead. "May the gods preserve me through this night."

The alarm of a high-intensity focus session blared through the arena. Elias and Gale regrouped and stood back-to-back. "Did you engineer this?" Gale barked, shifting his stance. "We're aren't ready for high-intensity sessions!"

"We can't afford to progress slowly, Modi." Elias twirled his standard blade, snarling with dissatisfaction. *I miss Sacrimony.* "You and I are being replaced even as we speak." *And Ean is leading the Tyrants. With her looks, her vibrancy, and her chaotic intrigue, it's only a matter of time before…*

Multiple enemies generated, surrounding them. Gale huffed. "This is going to hurt."

Eli's short laugh was dry. "It's supposed to."

The skeleman and the dark elf fought ferociously. They had to withdraw several times, paying careful attention to their HP. *Gods, this sucks.* Elias absorbed another chunk of energy from his healing gem. *I still can't believe this happened.*

By the time the session ended, they were panting from exertion. The red gridlines vanished. Gale doubled over, hands braced against his knees. "That hacker deserves to be hung from his toenails."

"Agreed." Elias sheathed his sword. "My healing gem is almost out of juice. Do you have any potions left?"

Emodicus winced. "A few. I'll let you have one if we can go break at the castle."

"Can't afford to."

The dark elf softly punched Eli's shoulder. "Look, Eli. I'm just as mad as you are. I can't stand being at level three, either! But we need to rest. We're going to get massacred if we keep pushing ourselves this hard."

The skeleman's grip on his hilt tightened. "With every minute, the other top-ranking avatars are taking advantage of this. We may never catch up."

"I know."

A short silence. Elias fiddled with his hilt. A cold wind stirred the grass that rimmed the training arena. "You're worried about Ean, aren't you?" Gale asked in a low voice.

"… Yes."

"No need to be. She handles herself well."

Elias grunted.

"And she won't need to practice for the SkyRate challenge for a few months. By then–"

"By the gods!" Incensed, Elias drove the point of his sword into the ground. "I forgot all about the challenge race. She's got that on her plate, too."

Gale was surprised by Eli's vehemence. "As I said, she handles herself very well. I'm certain she'll take it in stride."

Eli ignored him. He brushed dirt off his blade and returned it. "Let's go to the castle. I should check on her."

The skeleman extended his wings while Gale mounted his skyboard. They traveled in silence. As they descended on the drawbridge, Ean's slight figure darted outside to meet them. "Elias! Are you guys OK? You didn't answer my messages." Nodding to Emodicus, she embraced her husband affectionately. "I was worried about you."

"I'm fine. Not my first rodeo, you know." Eli's hug was rather cold. "What have you been doing?"

"Reading, mostly. I'm trying to figure out how I can help you regain your charisma level." She withdrew a small volume and held it up, excited. "It looks like if we sing together, you might be able to absorb my charisma. Like I used to do with you."

Elias shook his skull. "I don't need to do that. I can practice on my own."

"Elias." Ean glanced at Gale: *Give us a minute.*

The dark elf nodded and wandered away, treading the paths of the castle gardens. Ean sighed. She looked at Elias with a tender smile. "I know you started out as a loner, so accepting help is the opposite of what you want. But I'm your spouse here *and* in real life. You're not a loner anymore. And the Spectral Tyrants are eager to help you, too."

Her husband stiffened, averting his gaze. "You told them what happened?"

"Well, yeah. I kind of had to. It doesn't make sense for you to suddenly withdraw from the TerraDome's leading band."

The skeleman uttered a faint growl. "You should have asked me first."

Ean sighed again, splaying her arms. "What was I supposed to say? That you got sick? Illnesses don't last long in this game; there's always a cure. Besides, you're a skeleton, and undead avatars are immune nine times out of ten."

"I would have preferred that to letting all my friends know I'm-" He stopped short, indicating the low-level weapons and equipment he now wielded.

Ean stepped closer. Her hand cupped his face. "You haven't changed, Mephisto. You're just as incredible and unique as ever. You have the same strength, the same potential. We don't think less of you."

Elias finally looked her in the eyes. He sighed. His hand brushed hers, then lowered it from his face. "You don't know what this is like, Ean. I feel... lost. Like half of me has been erased. And I don't know if it'll ever come back."

"You're right. I *don't* know what that feels like. But you have a friend who does." Ean's head tilted toward Gale. "I'm sure he's feeling the same way. Keep training together, and you'll both level up in leaps and bounds."

Elias watched as Gale leaned over a rosebush. The dark elf's gentle smile was calming to witness. "I'm sorry," the skeleman whispered, gathering his wife into his arms. "I'm so angry. All those years of training... the perfection of my dark performa with the Tyrants... my renown as an artificer. It's all gone."

"Not for long." Ean pulled him into a kiss. The bite of her dark charisma shocked Elias. Shaking, the skeleman stumbled backward. "Almighty Kanthesis! I can't even kiss my wife right now."

"That's not your fault," Ean laughed. "I just led my first session. You didn't prepare me for the delinquency of certain members, by the way... but the rush of performa more than made up for it."

His lids crinkled in a skeleton's smile. "Wish I'd been there to see it."

"You'll have to spare some time for the next one." Ean winked. "I guarantee you'll feel inspired, or your money back."

They held hands as they entered the garden. "Hey, Modi! You hungry?" Ean called, skipping next to her husband. "I could whip up some grub."

The dark elf turned, smiling at Eli's invigorated look. "As long as there's meat involved. A lot of meat."

"Oh, I don't think you need to ask," Elias chuckled. "She's a carnivore."

4

PRENDERGAST COTTAGE

Axel muttered a curse as he dug through the crate. Books and papers flew in all directions. "Isis! Do you have my concept designs?"

His Holobox blinked to life. "Yes, Axel. I believe you asked me to store them yesterday."

"Gods damn it. I can never keep track of what you do or don't have." The skeleton pushed the crate away. "And where's my wife? Out foraging?"

The Holobox glowed orange as it scanned for Willow's location. "Yes. In Darkling Forest."

"Typical." Axel sat at his cluttered desk and pulled up some designs. "I was hoping she'd give me some input. Her advice is the difference between me being an artist, or being a *starving* artist."

"You are very gifted, Axel."

"Sure. Thanks anyway, Isis." Still, his Holopal's soothing tone did something for his nerves. He hummed as he cleared his desk. "Don't know why I'm feeling jumpy today. There's something in the air, it seems."

Axel and Willow Prendergast lived in a humble cobblestone-lined house. The western windows opened to the honey winds from Helios. Thin trees embraced their home with windblown branches, an endless shower of leaves whispering against the roof. Tight corners, secret staircases, and curtained window seats melted into the shadows. Axel's artistic endeavors and drum sets reposed in haphazard state. By contrast, Willow's elements of witchcraft were perfectly aligned on their altars and shelves. Prendergast Cottage was both comforting and spooky, in a charming way.

The wooden door scraped open. Willow stepped in. The elf-witch's presence was announced by the smell of incense, tea, and lavender. She swept to a candle on a corner table and lit it. "Something stirs amiss," she murmured, watching the flame. She tried to read the shapes of the rising smoke. *I need more practice.*

"Willow!" her husband called. Rushing into the room, he greeted her with a quick tug of her glossy hair. "Will you come look at some art for me? I need your opinion."

"In a minute, darling." Willow's soft kiss placated him. "I'm going to do some scrying. Something's happened… but I don't know what."

Axel's silver eyes glittered. "Good omens? Or bad ones?"

Her gaze fell on the nearest window. "It's hard to say. There was an influx of dark charisma from some of the avatars in town. More so than usual."

"That's great!" Axel avowed. "The residents of Helios are really making a name for themselves. Well, I won't distract you anymore." He stroked her raven curls. "Although that's no easy task, my queen."

Smiling in a cool, preoccupied way, Willow's hand brushed his skeletal fingers as she left. "I have the most beautiful wife in all of TerraWorks," her husband declared as he resumed his art.

Willow ascended the stairs to her room. Closing the door, she cleaned her scrying bowl and lit a few more candles. Chanting her handwritten spell, she breathed slowly and concentrated on the bottom of the bowl. *Please, Lady of the Moon, elder goddess Selene. I want to make sure he's OK.*

A breathtaking array of flowers engulfed her senses. Willow recognized the Vermillion Castle gardens. Elias and Ean stood outside of the gate, seemingly arguing. Ean spread her arms wide in a helpless gesture. Eli's body language was cold and stiff. The elf-witch frowned. *I knew he'd be taking this hard. Poor Elias.* But where was the dark elf?

Ean came closer, touching Eli's face. The skeleman relaxed as their conversation leveled. Joining hands, the Mages entered their garden and found Gale Emodicus. *Good. As long as they work together, they're going to be all right.*

Satisfied, Willow ended the spell. Her crystal-clean fingernails tapped the armrests of her chair. As an elf-witch, Willow was a mistress of dark charisma. She could aid Elias and Gale from afar… gently, subtly. She knew they wouldn't accept direct assistance. "It'll be delicate work. But I think I can manage."

Toggling the avatar progression screen, Willow examined her charisma gauge. Her pale face flushed with surprise. *When did I reach that level? How strange.*

Her inbox flashed with an unknown avatar's symbol. Frowning, Willow's finger tapped it reluctantly. She read the cryptic message aloud; "Be so good as to accept this benevolent gesture. From Robin Hood."

There was no gift attached. Perplexed, Willow toggled back to the progression screen. Her charisma gauge was almost full. *Is "Robin Hood" doing this?*

And if so, why?

Back at Vermillion Castle, the scent of roasting venison lifted Gale's spirits. He sped to the dining hall. "Ah," he breathed, removing his shimmering cloak before the blazing hearth. "There's no fragrance in the world to equal that." His indigo eyes twinkled.

Ean's mirth rippled from the open kitchen. "And there's no love in the world to equal a man's unrequited passion for his food. Did you find all the herbs?"

The dark elf nodded. "And some mushrooms. We're having a regular feast!" Gale opened his inventory and transferred the ingredients. "Just make sure to cook the broadcaps longer than the other specimens. And when you add the herbs, make sure the spices you added prior are–"

Ean's tone fell flat. "I know how to cook, Modi-san."

Eli's dark chuckle intervened. "My dear, you'll have to acknowledge that Emodicus is the superior chef. Why don't you take a break? Let him finish dinner."

Ean hesitated. "Hey, Modi, did your fall from grace include your cooking level?"

"No," he growled.

"Gods! Just asking!" Ean entered the dining hall from the kitchen. Her rosy locks were tussled – certain testimony that she and Elias had more than made up. "You can finish up in here, if you want to."

Gale shrugged. "Thanks. It'll take my mind off my troubles." He walked into the kitchen and confronted Elias at the stove. "I'll take over from here."

Elias moved aside. "Mind if I watch the master work?"

"I don't care."

Gale opened the culinary sub-screen. He paused to gather his hair into a ponytail. His sable complexion shone in the firelight as he handled the pots and pans with an expert's assurance, adding a generous pat of butter to the steaming mushrooms. Elias folded his arms and whistled. "Impressive. You know, I might have lost my heart to you if I hadn't fallen for Ean first."

Raising one brow, Emodicus indulged a rare, lighthearted grin. "You still might."

"There'll be hell to pay," Ean's voice threatened from afar. Gale and Elias chuckled. Ean rested her chin in her hands, smiling. *It's so good to hear them laugh.*

"No one can seduce me away from your charms," her husband assured her, carrying in a platter of piping hot potatoes. "And if Gale wants access to your cache of dark charisma, he'd better think twice before inciting your wrath." He placed the dish on the table. Standing behind Ean, he stroked her collarbone and nuzzled her ear.

"I knew you guys were joking," Ean smirked. "You don't have to reassure me." She graced his cheekbone with a few quick kisses. "I'm just glad to see that glimmer of diabolical humor again. I was afraid I'd die of boredom before you cheered up."

Elias laughed. "Turned out all we needed was food. Coming, Modi?" He called, striding back into the kitchen. The two re-emerged with several more plates. Ean clapped and cheered, jumping up to fill the beer pitcher. "Live while you can!" she cried, setting it on the table with a *thunk.*

"Sleep when you're dead!" Elias and Gale finished, raising their mugs.

Light prattle and wit punctuated hearty bites of food. Ean reached for another roll. "So, since we kind of brushed on the subject earlier..." She smiled deviously. "Why *don't* you have an in-game spouse yet, Modi?"

Emodicus shrugged as he savored the venison. Swallowing, he produced another rare grin. "I'm waiting to meet someone like you, Lady Mage."

Elias chuckled as Ean blushed. "You'd better find someone less stubborn, my brother. Stubbornness seems *so* adorable during the dating phase, but I assure you, it's a trying thing to be married to."

"Yeah, 'cause *you're* such an angel," Ean retorted, scuffing his skull. Elias pretended to bite her finger. "As you can see, we make do," the skeleman professed. "But every now and then I have to remind Mrs. Mage who's the boss."

Ean's fork stopped halfway to her mouth. Her glare shot daggers. *You'll pay for that later, Elias Mage.*

Eli's hellish demeanor sparkled. *Looking forward to it.*

The dark elf rolled his eyes. "Don't put me off my appetite, you two. Save it for the bedroom."

"I will," Ean retorted, devouring her forkful. Elias returned his attention to his plate. "So, you haven't met the right avatar?" he asked Gale. The skeleman glued his burning gaze to the venison as he cut it into meticulous slices.

Gale cleared his throat. "I've been on a few VR dates. None of them took."

"You *do* go on dates? Figured you were too busy training for SkyRate," Ean teased. She grabbed a slice of pie. "Why haven't you challenged me since the Metro Cross, by the way?"

Emodicus finished his mushrooms before he answered. "Been keeping a close eye on Piragor's training. He'll probably surpass me due to... recent events." The dark elf frowned. He attacked a roll with more violence than necessary. "I like skycraft, but I've been focusing on my lead in the Kanthesis Temple."

Ean nodded, washing down her pie with a swig of beer. "Piragor rode my heels the entire time. I'll most likely lose the challenge race..." She lowered her mug with a smack. "Gods! That's only a few months away."

"I forgot about it, too," Elias admitted. He laid a gilt hand on her shoulder. "Don't worry, Ean. I've decided to let my combat level slide for now. I'll focus on rebuilding my performa, so I can sing with the Tyrants again. Then you can practice."

Ean sighed. "I appreciate it, Eli, but that's going to take too long."

"It may not take as long as you think." Elias projected his progression screen. He pointed out the charisma gauge. "Look at this."

Gale and Ean leaned forward. Ean's lips parted in surprise. "Level eight? You were level three this morning. What did you do?"

The skeleman's infernal sparkle returned. "You mean what did *we* do?"

Gale groaned. Ean lifted the bread basket to hide her face.

5

MEERSCHAUM CASTLE

E lias grunted as he was jostled by the passerby. Lifting the hood of his cape, he moved to the shadows, hoping not to be recognized. *To think I'd ever see the day.* Sighing inwardly, he nestled into a friendly corner and perused his surroundings.

Meerschaum Castle was an immense, rambling estate bordering Klad Kingdom. Its oversized courtyard was the perfect space for entertainment. The Spectral Tyrants were performing tonight. As multicolored torches were lit, Elias struggled against the envy welling within him. *This must be how Ean feels sometimes.*

He raised his head. Nodding to the empty stage, he muttered "You've got this, Lightcross."

Although Elias Mage's temporary absence had been publicized, the Tyrants still packed a full house. The skeleman felt relieved *and* anxious. He chatted his teeth together, shifting from one foot to the other.

The band members arrived onstage. Axel appeared first, sitting at the drums with a joyful wave. Elias snorted at the skeleton's glittering lapel.

Kid's got style like a diamond vampire. When I return, that's the first thing that's going to go.

Next came Oleon, Travis, Kaspar, and Desmond. They settled into their usual places, testing their instruments while the eager were-cat revved up the crowd. Willow Prendergast drifted into view. Her sinuous tread and floating attire attracted many pairs of eyes, including Eli's. *Well, Axie's a lucky bastard and no mistake. Still, there's no woman in Terra like my Ean.*

Speaking of which, where was she?

Elias scanned the stage for his wife. Puzzled, he moved closer, careful to hold his hood near his face. A sudden poke to his shoulder blade caused him to jump.

"Hey, Eli! Thought that was you." Sindaya giggled at his glare. "Why are you lurking about like a robber?"

"Why aren't you playing tonight?" Elias countered, folding his arms. Sinnie shrugged. "Gave Axel a chance, since his wife is singing backup anyway. Turns out he's damn good. I don't mind getting a break."

Eli's stern eyes softened. "Oh. I thought you quit."

She scoffed. "Not a chance in Hades."

"Glad to hear it. Where's Ean?"

Sindaya started to point, but Ean herself answered his question.

Simulacra's familiar roar swelled across the courtyard. The half-elf vaulted onstage, hair rippling behind her in a scarlet cascade. The audience cheered as she screeched to a halt, smoke rising from the tires.

Her roguish smile lit Eli's heart as she revved the engine. "We are?" she yelled, raising her arms.

The crowd responded: *"The Spectral Tyrants!"*

"We are?"

"Spectral Tyrants!"

"WE ARE?"

"SPECTRAL TYRANTS!"

Black metal chords slammed from the stage. Ean laughed. She dismounted, the folds of her steampunk coat billowing around her boots. Twirling the microphone in her hand, she sang, echoed by Desmond and Willow.

Eli's ribcage froze with bated breath.

Ean moved with the confidence of a seasoned performer. Striding across the stage, she interacted with the audience. She made good use of her impressive range. Willow's angelic soprano doubled the effect. The skeleman's unseen heart beat fast.

Aphrodite.

Her words and movements were rife with dark charisma. Elias trembled, craving it with every breath he took. Craving *her.* The bite of her performa was painful, but he didn't care. Her poison was worth the sting.

His need increased as the concert progressed. Once Ean abandoned her coat, headbanging, knees to the floor, Elias stopped resisting. He marched straight up to the front.

The finale extended as Axel wailed on the drums. "Thank you!" Ean cried, rising to her feet and saluting their fans. "You've made this a beautiful night!"

Elias caught Ean's eye. She smiled, dropping her microphone and holding her arms open wide. "Mephisto," she murmured as he reached for her.

His reply was deep with intimate longing. "Aphrodite."

He helped her off the stage. Ean kissed him passionately as the 4-D recorders darted around them. "See? Just like old times," she chuckled. Her Mage tattoo burned with new charisma.

Eli's fingers traced the tattoo's perimeter. "You're going to share, right?"

Ean glanced at her shoulder. "Is the rose glowing?"

"Yep."

She smirked, draping her arms around his neck. "Then, yes. I'll share."

Elias rummaged for a transport gem. "Wait!" Ean complained. She was too late. Meerschaum Castle courtyard vanished in a verdant flash.

Ean kissed Elias to the edge of the bed. He sat down, drawing Ean into his lap. His bare ribcage shimmered in the candlelight. *"Mmm,"* he breathed, fingers embedded in her hair as she swayed against him.

Ean stroked his ribs. Eli's gilt frame burned sunset orange. He stared deep into her eyes, hypnotized by the sheer power of her gaze.

She traced the ruby on his skull. Embracing Elias, she whispered a spell to encourage the release of dark charisma. Eli closed his eyes as the rush of shadow magic flooded his senses. This time, his ecstasy culminated in a sharp bite of pain; Ean's charisma was insanely strong. The skeleman fell back against the bed, breathing hard.

Ean's soft giggle seemed to float over his head. "I'm rather enjoying this role reversal."

"Shut up." Elias grabbed her wrists and pulled her down with him. His hand trailed up her smooth body to circle her breast. "It's my turn."

The half-elf shuddered as he leaned close to lick her ear. "I love that," she sighed, closing her eyes in turn. Elias teased her with his tongue as he moved down her body. Ean clutched the pillow behind her head, moaning with pleasure.

Her heartbeat pummeled through her limbs. Ean gasped, relishing the perfect relaxation that settled over her. Elias laid down next to her. "My wife," he murmured, stroking her hair with a loving expression.

"My husband." Ean cuddled close.

Starlight slanted from their bedroom window. "This was an incredible night," Ean sighed with a look of pure bliss.

"I'm *so* proud of you." Eli linked their hands together. "You weren't nervous at all."

"No, I wasn't." Disbelief seeped from her words. "I've tried to draw inspiration from your image before, but this time… It was different. I didn't have to think about it."

"That's because you don't need to pretend to be me. You're Lady Mage, the *Anathema*. You don't need to be anyone else."

His wife thanked him with a kiss. "That's the nicest compliment I've ever gotten."

Meanwhile, Gale and his Holopal Zahir were hard at work. The dark elf slouched over his desk in the Kanthesis Temple. Zahir fed him a steady stream of info on the current top hackers. Together, they abandoned one theory after the next. Gale bit his lip in frustration. "The answer *must* be here."

A knock at his door made him scowl. Mumbling, Gale vacated his chair and stomped to the door. "Willow Prendergast?" he queried, mystified by the witch's lovely but unexpected presence. "Can I do something for you?"

Willow glided in with ghostlike silence. The door closed. "I hope I'm not interrupting anything crucial," she began, "but something happened that may concern you." As she moved past him, the flawless curves of her light skin shone in the moonlight. Gale's throat constricted as he swallowed hard; there weren't many avatars that could rival her beauty. "I'm listening," he murmured. He offered her his chair.

The elf-witch declined. "I prefer to stand. Have you ever received a holotext from someone calling himself Robin Hood?"

"Robin Hood?" Emodicus shook his head. "Can't say I have."

"I noticed an unexplained spike in my charisma gauge. It was followed by a message from this 'Robin Hood.' My attempts to trace it were unsuccessful, but I believe it's safe to assume that this is the hacker who nullified the top ten avatars."

"Wait." Gale's brows creased. "Someone orchestrated some kind of cheesy Robin Hood maneuver? 'Steal from the rich and give to the poor'?"

Willow's smooth lips twitched with microscopic disdain. "I wouldn't call myself *poor.*" Her rippling laughter bore a touch of menace. "Few avatars, my in-game spouse included, have a proper appreciation of my powers." The witch's contempt vanished as quickly as it had manifested. "No. It appears Robin Hood has other ambitions, but is masking them by trying to win favor. You don't get far in TerraWorks without friends."

"Hmm." Emodicus touched his jawline. "Have you told the Mages?"

"I intended to, but they were… occupied."

Gale held up his hands. "I do *not* want to know."

"My scrying attempt was blocked," the elf-witch smiled.

"Oh, the game's rigged to do that? Thank the Pantheon."

"Your asperity would thaw with haste if you tried intimacy yourself, darkling elf."

He sniffed and crossed his arms. "Well, that will never transpire unless you happen to know someone who'd like a brusque, sarcastic dark elf who's never been romantic a day in his life."

"You mean the aloof, dark, and handsome type? You can have your pick."

"It's not that easy, but thanks."

Willow shook her finger at him. "Reserve always attracts at the start. It speaks confidence. However, it is an obstacle to long-term relationships."

He smiled. "Do you speak from experience, my lady?"

"I do indeed." Willow curtsied and headed for the door. "I'm afraid that's all the wisdom I have time to impart. I'll let you know if I find out more about the hacker."

"Appreciate it." After a pause, Gale couldn't resist calling out "You don't have a single twin, do you? A cousin? A best friend?"

The witch's answering mirth made him smile. "No. I am quite alone."

Gale turned to Zahir with a sigh. "There goes the precise pattern I'd desire in a wife, right down to the way she laughs. Figures."

"I thought your type was more like Ean Mage, sir."

"Back when I first knew her, maybe. Now? Too chaotic. I don't want a berserker."

"I see." The Holopal's light spun around as it made a search. "I shall gather all available information on Willow Prendergast for you."

"No! Knock it off, Zahir! I didn't mean that." Gale smashed the power button on the Holobox. "Great gods above and below. Have respect for the lady."

6

THE SEA WYVERN

The bell tower struck noon. Ean shifted her leather messenger bag, breathing in the ocean air and stretching her limbs. "Gods, I love Shiori. I'm so relaxed here. Even when I should have shaking knees," she added with a grin, extracting her campaign invitation. "The Cthulhu Campaign. I *never* thought I'd fight in one of the toughest crusades in Terra!"

Hexadecimal hovered over her shoulder. "Perhaps you're reminded of your grand champion win, Ean-san."

"That's more likely," the half-elf admitted. "Now that you mention it, I'd better savor that feeling. There's a ninety-eight percent chance I won't associate Shiori with victory much longer."

"Why is that?" Hex inquired. He projected to full-scale size, falling into soundless step with Ean as she entered the docks. "I've been streaming Piragor's public training sessions," she replied. The half-elf grimaced. "He was always good, but I'm not exaggerating when I call his skycraft *masterful*. Reminds me of Gale's flight pattern. I've fallen behind, so… yeah. He's going to beat me at the challenger race this year."

"You don't seem as upset as I would have predicted, Ean-san."

Ean shrugged. Her auburn ponytail tumbled over her shoulder. "I think it's time somebody else held the title. I've got new goals in mind."

As she spoke, Ean spotted the radiant outline of a burgundy frigate. Its name was boasted in bright gold lettering. "The *Sea Wyvern*. That's my ride." She tapped the Holobox to stow Hex. Grinning, the half-elf sprinted up the gangway, tearing straight into the arms of a colossal cyborg.

"Avast, ye elfling!" Cyrus Agillus chuckled. His chrome hands grabbed her by the forearms, lifted her, and set her aside. "You mustn't begin by running over my crew." Cyrus' golden eyes flickered over her travel coat, waterproof leggings, and sturdy seaboots. "You look prepared to endure five hurricanes. Taking your commission seriously?"

"Why wouldn't I?" Posing like a prize fighter, Ean dealt her old friend a resonant punch (that he barely felt). "My combat level is finally high enough to do the Firestone Guild some good."

Smirking, the cyborg flexed his bulky silver arms. He pretended to punch her back. "Sure. Although I can't promise not to tie you up when the sirens come. How do midnight berserkers handle the siren's call?"

"TerraWiki says I'll be in trouble," Ean confessed. Her tone implied that she was more fascinated than worried. "Just make sure you use good, strong rope, and you shan't have a worry in the world."

He blessed her ponytail with a fraternal pull. "Then welcome aboard, Lady Mage."

Ean snapped a salute. "Captain."

"Look alive, gang!" Cyrus called out. "Come meet our sharpshooter. This is Ean Mage."

Mallie and Byron vacated their stations to greet her. Several new avatars – two elves, three dwarves, one shapeshifter, one half-draconian, a human, and a magus droid – introduced themselves. "It's especially nice to meet *you*," Ean mentioned as the magus droid advanced.

Ean's eyes sparkled curiously. She admired the rare droid's complexion of dark blue steel. Its lengthy stream of purple hair was gathered in two thick pigtails. Teardrop jewels shivered from the droid's ears, neck, wrists, and ankles, twinkling like tiny stars whenever it moved. A suncharge shield covered its eyes. "Likewise," the droid replied. Its voice was cold. "I am Aura Scythe. Pronoun preference, female."

"And this is my first mate," Cyrus resumed, directing Ean to the half-draco. "Lore Pendragon. Hails from the House of Behemoth. Mid and long-range fire attacks, broadsword, and Dragon's Breath in a pinch."

Ean shook Lore's scaled hand, careful to avoid his talons. The hybrid's muscular human build morphed into draconian arms, legs, and a spiked tail. Two curved horns sprouted from his head above pointed ears and high cheekbones. Coal-black lines slanted around reflective yellow eyes. Most impressive of all (thought Ean), Lore's blood-gold scales were shadowed by the tinge of *natural* dark charisma.

Dracos had no need to harvest charisma. They *grew* it. Ean's eager smile was quite flattering. "I haven't met many half-draconians. Remind me to ask all about the pros and cons later."

"I can tell you this instant," Lore replied with a good-natured smile. His voice was surprisingly deft and cool, more baritone than bass. A lingering smoke wisped from his nostrils. His breath smelled of saffron and ginger. "The pros: stamina, armor, and instant charisma. The cons... well, my voracious appetite... but the worst thing is the shedding. Nasty seasonal business. I'm more vulnerable then."

"That doesn't sound fun," Ean admitted. "But I'm thrilled you're here. It'll be an honor to see you in action."

Lore's serrated teeth flashed in his answering grin. "It will be an honor to fight with *you*, Anathema."

Ean's eyes widened. "How did you know about-"

Lore chuckled. "What refreshing humility. You're just as famous as your husband, you know." Excusing himself with a slight bow, Pendragon returned to Byron's side to study the maps.

Shrugging, Ean hunched belowdecks. *Better claim where I want to sleep.* On her way back up, she was stopped and nailed to the planks by Aura's icy stare.

"Why did he call you that?" the magus droid demanded.

Ean shifted her bag, sighing. "Ever heard of the Skeleton's Anathema?"

"No."

"Most players haven't. Even I had no idea until Hex *finally* thought to mention it." She gave her Holobox a derisive flick. "Apparently, intense exposure to a skeletal avatar's charisma can change your class type. I'm a midnight berserker thanks to Eli's performa." *And Gale's tomfoolery,* she privately added. "Phantom charisma is a wee bit different from typical dark charisma, though. It's a subtype. There are aspects to it that I still can't explain."

"So… you cheated."

"Eh?" Ean squinted at Aura.

The droid's emotionless mien was unsettling. "I'm not fond of avatars who obtain celebrity status by *mistake*. The draco's admiration is flattering, no doubt, but you'll have to prove your mettle to impress *me*." And with that, the magus droid stomped away, as if shaking the dust of Ean Mage from her feet.

The half-elf gave a low whistle. "Got quite a chip on her shoulder, that one. But I like her."

Glancing up from the maps, Lore shot Ean a serpentine smile. "It won't take her long to adjust."

Ean studied him a long minute, then grinned. "You remind me of someone. I think we're going to be friends, Lore Pendragon."

A shrill whistle summoned everyone to the main deck. "All hands report!" Lore shouted.

Ean finished her holotext to Elias. Hitting *Send,* she left her hammock and darted abovedeck. She waited next to Mallie, draping her arm across the petite pixie's shoulders; but her gaze sought the half-draconian.

He was standing by Cyrus. Lore's massive hands were clasped behind his back as he sized up each crew member. His irids glittered, piercing yellow gold purified in a deadly blaze. Miniscule threads of lava knit each scale together.

Ean's eyes glowed. *Almighty Kanthesis! I wish Elias could see him in person.* Holotexts weren't doing his devilish grandeur any justice. *And it would be kind of weird to ask him to pose for an HI when I just met him.*

Ean peeled her gaze away as Cyrus outlined their crusade. "Welcome to the Cthulhu Campaign," he began with a wide grin. "Where we will be testing our limits with stormy weather, wicked sirens, hungry sea serpents, and a hundred other *inconveniences.* If we're strong enough, we may get to battle Cthulhu himself."

Excited affirmations scattered 'round. Mallie grasped Ean's hand.

"You should all know your roles by your campaign invitations," the cyborg continued. "But I'm reviewing them with everyone present. As you all know, I'm the captain. Lore Pendragon is my first mate."

The half-draconian bowed his head.

"Solomon Pierce, second mate. Byron Thatch, gem mage and lookout. Maximus Terrigon, chief engineer." Cyrus rattled off the names of a few more positions. "And Ean Mage, sharpshooter. She'll be manning the fighting top." Ean snapped a quick two-finger salute.

"Aura Scythe, soldier's command. She'll be my right hand when the pirates and monsters arise." Aura tilted her head. Her expression was hidden behind the blue steel visor. "Saved the best for last," the captain resumed, smiling at his in-game spouse. "Mallie Agillus, company healer. She'll also be planning our meals with the cook, so make sure you pay her your respects, lads."

Mallie blushed as the crew thanked her in advance.

"Now, as you've likely noticed, there's no scrubbers. That means you're all responsible for cleanliness aboard ship. No shirking, and no bribing others to do your work for you. Mallie's drawn up a chore schedule in the mess hall. Go check it out when you're dismissed."

As Cyrus wrapped up his speech, Ean sensed a pair of scorching eyes on her. She looked up. Lore withdrew his stare.

It's just the pull of phantom charisma. I'm fraught with it. Still, the way he'd looked at her reminded her of Elias. Ean spun her cluster ring and sighed. *I wish he had agreed to come. He said he'd be a burden. Well, at least he isn't training alone.* Emodicus had promised to look after him. Specifically, he'd promised not to let him perform risky experiments on himself to try to regain his power faster, which Ean was ninety-five percent sure he'd do.

At dismissal, Captain Cyrus initiated a rousing cheer. Ean started heading to the mess hall with the others, but Cyrus waved her aside. "I've got a special request for you, Lady Mage."

"Anything, Cy. What's up?"

"Would you be open to performing here on the ship? Just for one night." He held up a fistful of transport gems. "I'll even call in your tyrannous reinforcements for you."

Ean nodded, tossing her sleek hair. "Sure! That would be fun. Kind of like a witcher's pep rally, yeah?"

Cyrus winked. "Great minds think like me."

"Oh, please." Ean laughed.

7

THE FIRST BATTLE

Elias Mage and Gale Emodicus stretched on the living room floor, eyes closed. The windows were open. A late afternoon breeze floated in, joyously ruining their sorted manuscripts.

One sheet landed on Gale's face. Grunting, the dark elf slapped it aside and tried to get up. "No use," he slurred, melting back into the carpet. "Damn, this is powerful stuff, Mage."

Eli's eyes squinted open. "Thank ye."

Silence resumed. They listened to the fountain in the castle gardens. Eli yawned, staring at the azure skyline. "Wonder if the Sea Wyvern has set sail?" he murmured.

"The what now?"

"Sea Wyvern. Ean's ship."

Gale's pupils twinkled beneath a slow, lazy blink. "What campaign did she join again?"

"The Cathulu… no… Catuluh… By Kanthesis, that's hard to say." Elias sat up and mimicked the winding wave of octopus arms. "Legendary sea monster thing."

Gale chuckled. "Oh, yeah."

"Say it, Modi."

"Uhm… no."

Eli hummed to himself. "I'd be pretty good at charades."

"While high on MZV."

"High on what?" Elias collapsed again and stared.

"Modified… zombie… venom. Takes too long to say."

"Guess it does."

Gale twiddled his thumbs. "Level ten now. We're not bad."

Elias groaned. "Don't remind me. It's *horrific*. Do you realize how long it's going to take us to max out again?"

The dark elf grinned. "At least I'm having more fun this time around. You're a good friend, Eli-san."

The skeleman snapped his jaws. "Right back at 'cha, Modi-san."

Eli's tablet chimed with a new message. Grunting, he planted his palms on the floor and heaved himself up. "Still stranded, man," Gale called from the carpet. "Help."

Elias stumbled over. He yanked Gale to his feet and prodded him over to the couch. "Better stay there 'till it wears off," the skeleman advised. Wandering to his tablet, he picked it up and tapped the Mage symbol.

Mephisto! Am messaging you from my hammock belowdecks. We're to sail at sunset. (Didn't know it would take that long to prep, but it really does.) As you warned me, Cyrus is putting on airs already and trying to sailor-speak. I might walk the plank voluntarily… Oh, I wanted to tell you there's a half-draconian on board! He's first mate. I thought their avatar design sounded impressive, but trust me, they're 100 times more so in person. He's friendly and he seems to like me. The battalion commander doesn't, though. I'll need to keep my wits about me when she's around.

We're being summoned to review the crusade. Text me when you get this. I may be busy, but I'll answer when I can. Please visit us sometime (remember to get clearance from Cyrus first, or your transport gem will be blocked). Love you.

By default, holotexts were projected at eye level; Gale read her message too. He snorted. "*Mephisto*. You two are still at it, I see."

"At what?" Eli's boney fingers flew as he wrote back.

"How long have you been married? Three years?"

"Four. And?"

"That's got to be a TerraWorks record, or something. How do you make it work?"

"Mmm." Elias hit *Send,* then fingered his gilt jaw. "How do we make it work? Well, as tacky as this sounds, we're naturally well-suited for each other. At least we *were,*" he muttered aside. "She's out of my league now."

"Temporarily." Gale threw one of the pillows. It smacked Eli in the face. "Though it *is* amusing. The great Elias Mage reduced to wolf hunts, while his midnight berserker wife is off to battle Cthulhu."

Elias flicked a piece of trash at him. "You're not helping, jerk face."

"Hey, we're in the same boat. A teeny tiny fishing boat, while we glare longingly up the planks of the mighty Sea Wyvern."

Eli punished Gale with a headlock. "Whoops, you just capsized our boat, Eli," Gale sang. "Hope you know how to swim."

"Better than you, idiot. We're decreasing your dose next time," Eli said, throwing him off the couch with a *ker-thunk*. "You're insufferable."

"You're too kind." Gale's dark head dropped against Eli's foot. The dark elf fell fast asleep. Elias shook his skull. "Definitely decreasing the dose."

He amused himself by constructing a pillow fort around Gale. Afterward, Elias returned to the desk. He projected a favorite HI of Ean and sighed. *I miss you, Aphrodite.*

TWO DAYS AT SEA

"Enemy ahoy!"

Nobody heard her. Ean cupped her hands around her mouth. "I said, *enemy ahoy!*" she shouted. She withdrew her hands and flicked her wrist, scrolling for Antivenom. "Main deck, pronto, you feckless pack of ingrates!" She shouldered her rifle with a demonic laugh. "By the gods! I've always wanted to say that."

Cyrus shook his head at her from below. "I call the shots, Ean." Motioning for Lore to initiate the battle call, the captain positioned at the helm. "Are you in range, Lightcross?" he asked Ean, calm as fate. Aside, he gave rapid instructions to the helmsman.

Ean braced herself and glared through the scope. The low, seductive music of sirens tickled her ears. *Don't white out. Don't white out.*

Cyrus glanced at her when she didn't answer. "Be strong, Ean. You've got this."

Suddenly, Ean felt hot breath on the back of her neck. She squealed, whirling around to face Lore. "Holy Cernunnos! Why are you in the fighting top? You're supposed to be with the captain."

"He told me to bring these." Lore held up several braids of thick rope. His sardonic smirk annoyed her. "In case you start to white out."

Ean turned her back to him. "I can control my manic state, thanks."

She resumed her stance, aiming with care. The fighting top was none too roomy. Ean still felt the draconian's hot breath on her skin. Her hands trembled. *Those gods-forbidden sirens. I need to shut them up!* "You can go back now. I'll be fine."

He stood beside her and took a long look at her face. "I think I'd better stay here." Lore dumped the ropes into a pile. "Just in case."

"You're needed below."

"Not really. I can target the sirens quite well from here."

"Can you?" Her voice quaked. She scowled and gripped the finger guard. *Well, that's just great. The dark bloom of his charisma is hard enough to resist…*

"This is perfect." Lore lifted his hands. He focused on the sirens, inhaling deeply. Sparks lit at his talons until a glowing, dripping ball of lava-like fire accumulated between his palms. Chunks of flame broke away from it, hissing as they plunged into the waves below. Ean's eyes widened. *Whoa. Draconian fire really* is *different from other fire magic.*

Lore drew his arms back and thrust them forward. The fire launched toward the pod of sirens perching on some rocks. It exploded, scattering like fireworks. For a moment their enemies' alluring song changed into angry screams. Then they redoubled their attack, circling the ship. Their carnivorous teeth flashed in the cannon fire, glinting behind full, seductive lips.

"I think you just made them mad," Ean commented, trying to laugh. The prickle of heat across her neck now encompassed her entire body. She inhaled a shaky breath. "And you may have cooked me a little in the process." The half-elf wiped away beading sweat.

Lore smiled serenely. "My apologies, Anathema. Let's see what your rifle can do."

Ean drew another steadying breath. *Focus, woman!* She could almost hear Modi yelling at her. *Funny that he gives me courage even when he's not around.* Again, she planted her feet in stance, balancing her rifle and aiming through the scope. She targeted the siren closest to the hull.

The sirens' song reached its crescendo. A powerful vibration seized Ean, embracing her in wave after wave of temptation. *Come with us. Come with us. Bring him with you, the prince of flames. Come with us. Be one of us, Ean Mage.*

Antivenom slipped from her grasp. Ean panted, falling back against Lore. He caught her and held onto her shoulders. "No, you don't. Stay here."

A white cloud grew at the corners of her vision. *No. Don't white out!* Ean closed her eyes tight and swallowed hard. *Concentrate on the wind. Feel the spray cooling your skin. Then focus, and aim, and shoot. You can do this.*

The heat seeping from Lore's form was strangely comforting. A low chuckle rumbled through the half-draco's chest. "Do I get to tie you up now?"

Blushing at his suggestive tone, Ean's eyes snapped open. "When Hades freezes over." In one fluid motion she broke free of Lore's hands, snatched her rifle, and shot.

Her target clutched its bleeding chest. Wailing with rage, it slipped beneath the waves and sang no more. Ean the Berserker cheered. "That's the stuff. Now, let the games begin!"

It was like she had flipped a switch. Lore Pendragon watched her with awe. The midnight berserker leapt from the fighting top, sliding from the ropes to shoot from various angles. Siren after siren met her death, screaming as she fell. The half-elf's eyes shone deep red, mirroring everything they took in from the spars to the sea foam. *The myth appears to be true. If she* isn't *the Anathema, then it doesn't exist.* Smiling, Lore prepared another fire attack.

Cyrus continued to shout orders. The helmsman strained against the rush of a rising storm, no doubt conjured by the sirens. Aura stood in the crow's nest with Byron as they both launched mid-range magical attacks. The rest of the battalion manned the cannons. One by one the sirens fell.

And yet, the high-pitched tune of a single siren kept buzzing in Lore's ear. He shook his head hard. His vision swam in golden dust. *Give in. Come to us. Come to us, wielder of flames. Cool yourself in the sweetest fathoms. Come to us. Bring Ean Mage.*

He knew why they wanted Ean. They wouldn't consume her, they'd change her. A midnight berserker as a siren? He could imagine the havoc she would wreak.

Then, the siren crooned something far more sinister.

Bring with thee Anathema, the Phantom Lord.

Lore's eyes narrowed. *The Phantom Lord?*

In TerraWorks, the Phantom Lord reigned over the undead in Hades. It certainly wasn't Ean. It was a massive skeleton king that kept himself hidden from the overworld. Hardly anyone had ever seen him.

BANG!

The last siren was gone.

Ean scampered back into the fighting top, breathless. "That was a historical moment for the *Sea Wyvern*." Her maniacal smile was the final blow to Lore's senses. "Are you OK? You look kinda wobbly."

Lore's lips pulled back from his teeth. Hands cupping Ean's back, the draconian yanked her forward and held her against him. She resisted and pushed him away, but not before he'd extracted a solid, delicious morsel of phantom charisma.

His head instantly cleared. Lore withdrew, leaning against the foremast. His face twisted in confusion. "Ean... I'm sorry."

The half-elf winced, probing the bite mark. "No major harm done. Damn those pesky sirens. Should have tied *you* up, I think," she chuckled.

Lore's chest tightened as he struggled for breath. Without another word, he left Ean alone in the fighting top. Ean just shrugged and whistled a jolly tune. *Good old berserker's high.* "Who's next? Summon the sea serpent, lads!" She snickered as a few crew members flipped her off.

As Lore ignored the cross ropes and jumped straight down to the deck, the decadent tang of phantom charisma danced on his forked tongue. He'd seldom tasted anything as satisfying. *Almighty Kanthesis. What is that woman?*

8

A MARITIME CONCERT

"Hey, Ean!"

The half-elf looked up from arranging her hair. "What's up, Mallie?"

"Surprise for you in the mess hall."

"Be there in a minute."

As Mallie left, Ean stifled a yawn. "Didn't anticipate so many days of… nothing. I'm tempted to log out until Cyrus sends word. But that wouldn't be fair to the other gamers."

"A wise reflection, Ean-san."

"At least you're here, Hexy." Ean smiled and pantomimed a fist-bump with her holographic pal. "Let's go see what Mallie cooked up."

Humming, Ean skipped to the mess hall, saluting her friends as she passed them. A tall bronze shimmer caught her eye. Leaning against the mini bar, joking with Cyrus, was none other than Elias Mage.

"Eli! You black-hearted jackanapes. Why didn't you warn me?" Laughing, she rushed into his arms and pulled him in for a kiss. "If I knew you were coming, I would have waged war for the showers."

"Not to worry." Elias nuzzled her. "Just picking up on sea spray. Or is it sweat? Traces of gunpowder. And…" His eyes narrowed. "Brimstone? Saffron? The hell am I smelling right now?"

As he spoke, his fingers traced Ean's bitemark. The skeleman's snarl of fury made her flinch: *"Who did this?"*

"At ease, Mage," Cyrus reassured him. "The sirens worked him up."

"Who?" Eli's hand wandered to his hilt. Ean grabbed it and linked her fingers with his. "The half-draconian, Lore. Don't blame him for it. As Cyrus said, we were fighting the sirens. Whole place was plastered with dark charisma. Could barely keep it together myself."

"That's no excuse." Eli's blade announced itself with a *shing!* He marched to the door; Ean snagged him by the elbow. "Please calm down, my love! He apologized as soon as it happened, and he's been keeping his distance ever since. You're just going to embarrass him even more."

"Good."

"It won't happen again, OK?" His wife pouted. "Come on. Don't go scaring off my fledgling friendships."

With another growl, Elias returned his sword to its sheath. "I want to meet him all the same. Just to remind him that you're married, and who exactly you're married *to*."

Ean grinned. *Well, he could use an ego boost.* "I'd be honored to introduce you, sir. But first…" Taking hold of his lapel, she tugged him into the narrow corridor and indulged her pent-up cravings.

"Ah," Elias sighed, hands buried in her hair.

The ocean mimicked twilight in an exquisite painting of orange, yellow, and pink ombre. Churning sea foam embraced the ship. Mallie skipped from one lantern to the next, lighting them with a flick of her nimble fingers.

Ean rehearsed with the Tyrants in the captain's quarters. Even though they tried to keep it down, the walls still shook. Elias, several rooms down, could feel the beat rattling the ceiling. He chuckled to himself and went above-deck.

A warm southern breeze welcomed him. Eli's ribs expanded in a deep, satisfied breath. *There's something about sea air. It's just what I needed.*

"Mage."

Eli rested his hands on the railing. "Pendragon."

Lore leaned against the bulwark. A trace of saffron flavored the air. "Couldn't help but notice our introduction was a mite stiff. I apologize for the accident with your wife."

The skeleman's grip relaxed. "As Ean said herself, no real harm done."

"None at all. She's very strong."

"Hmph." Eli's sidelong gaze implied *As if you know anything about it.*

The half-draco grinned. Unlike Gale Emodicus, Lore's countenance bore an unexpected frankness. Friendliness, even. "Ean picked the waters clean of those sirens, using their own spell as fuel against them. She's quite something. The sheer power she inspires… the smolder of the undead lingers." He nodded. "No doubt that's thanks to you."

"I suppose. I never transferred it intentionally."

Lore lit a sunset Whisker. "So, there's something behind the Skeleton's Anathema myth?"

Eli looked suspicious. Lore's visage remained calm, emulating serene curiosity. "There seems to be some truth to it," Eli admitted. "There's no denying the results. She may not be the first midnight berserker (nor the last), but her capacity for dark charisma is unmatched."

The skeleman's tone warmed with pride. His hands slipped into his pockets as he admired the appearing stars. "She can absorb and manipulate the charisma of others, even light charisma, and fit it to her ideal image. Ean Mage will go down in Terran history as one of its most unique avatars."

Lore lifted a sleek, sable brow. *He's speaking like an avatar designer.* Red-brown wreaths of smoke attended his query, "Are you as naïve about the Anathema as you pretend to be?"

"Maybe. Or maybe not." Elias tilted his golden-bronze skull, eyes bright with amusement. "Don't imagine I'll waste my time trying to convince any five-minute acquaintance."

Lore offered his pack of Whiskers. "To five-minute acquaintances, then."

They smoked in silence as the horizon darkened. A sudden clamor of voices and laughter announced the Tyrants' approach. Lore pitched his Whisker overboard, but Elias kept his gripped between his teeth, eyeing Ean with a mischievous expression.

Ean had just gained the stairs. She marched back down to poke Elias in the ribcage. "Interrupt my concert at your peril, sir."

"My severe and untimely peril, I doubt not." His voice was grave, but his eyes laughed.

"Be good. There's a nice undead lad." Smirking, Ean patted his skull and sauntered up to Lore. "Hey, if you ever want to play with us Tyrants, let me know." She distributed a smack on the shoulder that nearly knocked him down.

"Sorry," Elias chuckled as she regained the upper deck, taking three stairs at a time. "When she's worked up with performa, she doesn't know her own strength."

"Apparently." Lore rubbed his shoulder. "That actually hurt."

Ean's cape billowed in the wind. She waited as the Tyrants arranged themselves behind her. Skipping the intro, they tore right into the first song. Desmond stepped forward on the bagpipes while Sindaya played a *bodhrán.* Travis and Ollie added their hard-rock enhancements. The crew cheered and stomped their heels to the beat, enthralled with the Tyrants' seaworthy style.

Lore stole a glance at Eli. The former band leader seemed impressed, but even Lore could tell he was a touch saddened as well. He was working hard to regain his former strength, but in doing so, he was missing out on the band's progress. The skeleman leaned against the bulwark, smoking with a contemplative air.

Ean Mage took full advantage of their nautical inspiration. Each song was imbued with seafaring lore, adventurous spirit, and a longing to pursue the unknown. Elias brightened as the concert advanced, but near the end, his gaze dropped to the floorboards.

Ean ended "Ghost Love Score" on a powerful note. Without warning, the roar of displaced ocean water finished the concert for her.

She ducked, astonished as a sea serpent breached to starboard. Its piercing cry rattled their ears. Purple and green scales flecked its snakish hide. The creature's reptilian mouth gaped to reveal rows of serrated teeth.

"Our grand finale, ladies and gentleman!" Still hyped up on performa, Ean laughed and posed in front of the serpent. Aura, stiff and exasperated, grabbed Ean's arm and threw her out of the way.

"Battle stations!" Cyrus cried. He grabbed a nearby spear and attempted to pierce the beast's scales. "Tyrants to the captain's quarters unless you can fight well!"

Aura flexed her blade-wielding arm with a thin smile. She'd seemed bored with the concert, but her tedium melted away in the face of battle. *Typical,* Ean chuckled to herself as she swung into the fighting top and withdrew Antivenom.

Painfully reminded of his low combat level, Elias followed her closely. "What can I do?" he panted, damning his hacker to the depths.

"Keep me steady." Ean was bracing herself as well as she could, but the serpent's perpetual diving and swerving amid cannon fire pitched the ship to and fro. She struggled to aim. "Don't let me fall."

"You got it." Elias anchored himself against the top beam, bracing Ean with his free arm. A smile lit her face as she peppered the beast with poisoned bullets. "I'm glad you're here, Eli," she yelled over the chaos.

"Even though I'm useless?"

"You're never useless!"

She spared a few seconds to turn and kiss him. "Ean!" Aura barked from below. "Not now, idiot."

"Sorry!"

Ean's bullets didn't accomplish much. The serpent bellowed and charged underwater, its sinuous body writing beneath the waves. It reappeared on the port side, lunging toward Cyrus.

Eyes flashing, Ean seized the halyard and flew to his aid. Elias grabbed another rope to jump after her. A burst of glowing lava and smoldering brimstone seared his vision. Once he blinked the black spots away, he looked down again and saw Lore preparing another mass of draconian fire.

Ean was next to him. She launched mid-range electric attacks with Necrowave, cackling with delight as the hammer's charges proved more effective. The serpent cringed and shuddered, plagued by Lore's lava and Ean's lightening. At last, their foe plunged below and did not return. *It's not dead,* Eli thought, *but it won't be bothering us again, methinks.*

Elias slid down the ropes. Ean fist-bumped Lore, still laughing. "Best finale *ever,*" she exclaimed, raising her arms to the starlit sky.

"Couldn't have done it without you, Anathema," Lore conceded.

The rest of the crew surrounded the half-elf and the half-draconian, administering praise. Elias kept his distance. He watched Ean for a few subtle minutes. Her bronze, muscular forearm flexed beneath the Mage tattoo. It had absorbed so much dark charisma that it glittered like

Summerland's coves. Sighing, he searched his inventory for a transport gem and slipped away.

9

MAGE ISLE

The next day, Ean was logged in for all of ten minutes before the warning bell sounded.

The attack was over in the blink of an eye. Ean recalled the screech of the *Sea Wyvern* splitting apart, miles of tentacles writhing among the wreckage. She remembered the fathomless maw of Cthulhu as it lapped up seawater and hapless prey. She knew it was huge – the Lovecraftian inspiration was the uncontested king of the TerraWorks ocean – but mere knowledge was nothing next to experience.

Clinging to a cabin door, Ean spluttered mouthfuls of glass-green brine. The half-elf was irritated but unharmed. She jostled her Holobox. "Hex! Rise and shine. Where to, buddy?"

Hexadecimal floated above her shoulder, tranquil as ever. "Due east. There's an island nearby, yet unexplored but teeming with fresh water sources and edible vegetation." The Holopal pulled up the shared inventory screen, demonstrating Eli's meager stash of transport gems. "You could skip the monotonous swim if you like."

"Nah. Eli hates it when I use up his gems. There's an unspoken agreement that I'll only use them when necessary." Sighing, she kicked off her boots, barely managing to catch them before they sank. "Stow these."

"Yes, Ean-san. I will coach you around the currents."

"Thanks, Hexy." She grimaced, starting to swim at a relaxed pace. "Slow and steady wins the race. Especially if there's sharks."

"As a matter of fact, Megalodons were recently installed in this area."

"I did *not* need to know that right now."

"My apologies, Ean-san."

Ean dragged herself on shore, soaked and winded. She spared a moment to admire the crystal-bright blueness of the sky and waves. "This is nice. Almost *too* nice." The half-elf squeezed seawater out of her hair.

"There's fresh water from an underground source," Hex supplied, "and various fruit trees further inland. I suggest we set up camp there."

"Roger that." Ean hauled to her feet, scowling at her dripping clothes. "Here's hoping for a spring big enough to bathe in. I feel disgusting."

She followed Hex's map. Not far away, a large cavern yawned above a stream of blue water. Ean's fingers traced the surface as she filled her canteen. The pool's refreshing temperature was tempting. "Gorgeous," the half-elf murmured, straightening to examine the grotto.

She couldn't resist laughing. The crags above her head looked very much like teeth; the slanted triangle above it could easily pass for an empty nasal socket; and a rippling stream of island "tears" cascaded from one of two identical gaps for eyes. "Skull Rock. How very apropos. You know, Hexy, some things about this game seem downright staged." She shrugged. "Well, we know what to name the island." Ean and Hex spoke in tandem: "Mage Isle."

Ean spent the rest of the day poking about Mage Isle, gathering fruit and vegetables to her heart's content and adding landmarks to the map. It was an enchanting place, but something about that fact in and of itself set Ean's teeth on edge. "This is too good to be true," she asserted to Hex (for the tenth time). She dropped another golden-red grapefruit into her inventory.

"Is this island overrun with monsters every night? Or maybe all the water is poisoned? Or are the wild hogs carrying a loathsome disease? I've never been so thrilled to be shipwrecked before."

"You've never *been* shipwrecked before, Ean-san."

"And this." She nodded to Skull Rock, ignoring him. "That's altogether too much. Methinks it's no accident that I'm here. Should we see what's inside?"

"That is up to you, Ean-san."

"It would make sense to camp there. If it's safe."

"Agreed."

Peeling off her coat, Ean traipsed into the cavern and scanned the rock face for footholds. Aided by Hexadecimal, the half-elf climbed up to a shelf-like structure jutting out just behind the eye sockets. A transparent stream rippled past her feet, tumbling out of the right eye socket in a flush waterfall. "A bit chilly, but otherwise ideal," Ean remarked. "We'll build a fire pit. What's *that?*"

"Ean-san?"

Something glimmered in the depths. She stared into the dark. "Further back. I see something."

"Take care, Ean-san. There may be snakes."

"Ten-four, Hexy."

It took a few minutes of steady climbing, but eventually Ean's hand brushed against another shelf. This one was much smaller. Her fingers wandered over the cold, clammy surface, at length touching a glassy object that clinked against the wall. It was roughly the size of her hand. "It doesn't bite, does it?" she called to Hex, half-jokingly.

"It appears to be a gemstone."

"No way! Mage Isle has *treasure*, too? OK, I've died and ascended to Summerland." Ean grasped the gem with care, only allowing a cursory glance or two before stowing it. "It's freaking huge. I can't tell what color it is. Let's go back and light that fire."

Twilight had fallen. As the half-elf descended and arranged the fire pit, the star-smocked heavens gleamed dark purple. Sunset orange yet clung to the skyline's graceful skirts. Floral gusts drifted through the cavern. The music of rippling, tumbling water echoed through its mysterious depths. "This is awesome," Ean giggled, daring to strip down to her long shirt and luxuriate before the fire. "I'll have to text Eli and try to get him out here. But first..."

She extracted the gemstone.

The dark red stone was neither cut nor polished. However, a bright shine in its center bore the promise of flawless beauty. Ean sat cross-legged and turned it in her hands. "A ruby, maybe? But what is it doing here? Did someone leave it behind?"

The stone began to vibrate.

Ean gasped, dropping it and leaping to her feet. The gemstone's musical *clang* rang from the rocks, hurting her ears. Its inner sparkle grew brighter, casting dark shadows into Ean's widened eyes. She took a step backward, then another...

More shadows generated from the stone, dodging the light and mocking it. They tumbled into Ean's eyes. She cried out, turning away and slipping on the damp cavern floor. "Make it stop!" she shouted to Hex.

He answered, but she couldn't hear him.

The shadows flew into her ears, her mouth, and every crevice or crack of the cave - anywhere they could gain entrance. Holding her breath,

Ean slowly reached out with one foot and kicked the gem into the water. Caught in the stream, it tumbled from rock to rock until it lurched over the lip of the socket, soared down the waterfall, and splashed into the pool below.

Ean stayed on the cave floor, eyes closed and ears covered. "Hex? Is it… is it over? Almighty Kanthesis! What was that?"

"I believe you're safe, Ean-san."

The half-elf stood and rubbed her eyes. "Well, I feel OK. But that was the scariest thing I've experienced in quite a while."

"Notwithstanding the Cthulhu, I suppose?"

Ean smirked. "Yeah, that was pretty damn scary. Anyway… Before we log off for the night, could you scan the island for survivors? I highly doubt we're the only ones who made it here."

"I sense multiple life forms, Ean-san. It will take time to distinguish-" He stopped.

"Distinguish what?"

"Someone is approaching the cavern."

She heard the distinct *clink-clack* of taloned feet. "It's Lore. I can tell. Lo, Draconian!" she called, bracing against the rock wall. "What took you so long?"

A pair of horns and slanted yellow eyes menaced her from below. "I was hunting, halfling elf. You weren't lounging the entire day, I trust?"

His sharp stare reminded Ean that she was barely dressed. Her face colored crimson. "Uh, no… I've got a lovely fruit salad all ready to compliment your *pièce de resistance*." She hissed at Hex to clothe her in the first dress he found. "And I can make a banana pudding for dessert," she added, smoothing the folds of her skirt and mentally rehearsing some choice words for Hex. *I shouldn't have had to ask!*

"Cyrus and Aura aren't far behind." Lore scaled the wall with ease and brushed past Ean, ignoring her heated face. "Mallie and a few others were devoured by the Cthulhu, unfortunately."

"Oh, damn. Wouldn't want to experience *that.*" As usual, the deceased avatars would revive at the nearest hospital; but in this case it would be far away. Only an expensive transport gem could bring them back to the campaign. "It's a shame. I bet Cyrus is pissed."

"Well, having no battle consequences in TerraWorks would render the game dull."

"True."

An awkward silence descended as they rummaged around the cavern. Ean set up a late supper while Lore reconstructed her fire pit with superior expertise. He rekindled it with his breath. Ean longed to tell Lore all about the strange ruby, but shyness closed her lips. *He's probably sulking because we lost… but whatever the reason, he looks kind of irritable.* Irritable draconians weren't creatures you wanted to cross.

"Hallo the house!" Cyrus' voice bellowed from the cavern's mouth. "A fitting palace for doomed souls. What a crushing defeat!" His tone implied that he'd rather enjoyed almost being eaten. Ean hollered her greetings, relieved to have additional company.

"A shame about Mallie," Lore said as the cyborg hoisted himself up. Aura scrambled up after him, determined to be sour and ignoring everybody.

"'Tis, but she wasn't too keen on coming in the first place. She'll be happier back in Shiori." The captain nodded to Ean and clomped to the fireside. "I'm starving."

Roasted wild boar, a colorful fruit and berry salad, coconut water, and banana pudding made from dried milk packets satisfied everyone. Even Aura mellowed a little. Cyrus kicked up his heels on an obliging stone. "Now," he began, lighting his pipe, "The question is whether we use the last of our transport gems, signal for passing ships, or enjoy ourselves for a week or two. This island is bursting with resources. What say you three?"

"I vote for staying and exploring," Lore replied. "It's unmarked. There might be side quests and, who knows? Even treasure."

"Speaking of which," Ean piped up. She enlightened her comrades regarding the red stone. "It didn't do any harm," she finished. "But it might not be a bad idea for us to pair up when we search the island. It seemed to be calling something. Or *someone*."

"The instant you're alone you run headlong into trouble, Lightcross. I mean *Lady Mage."* Cyrus chuckled at his blunder. "Sorry. You'd think I'd remember by now."

"It doesn't bother me. I've got a pile of names. Elias calls me Aphrodite," she added (instantly wishing she didn't).

"What divine worship!" Cyrus quaked the cavern with his laughter while Ean blushed. "Shut it," Ean growled, punching him.

The cyborg pushed her aside. She yelped as she fell over. "Anyway, that's a good idea. We should stick together. You and Lore make a good team, so you two should back each other up. I'll scavenge with Aura." Cyrus removed his sleeping bag and rolled into it. "Let's get a good night's rest, everyone. And don't feel too discouraged about today. Precious few ships have made it past the Cthulhu. We'll get him next time!"

Ean composed a quick message for Elias before logging off. Lore was tucked among the rocks with nary a speck of bedding, perfectly content, broad arms cushioning his scale-flecked head. Ean thought of a baby dragon and snorted.

10

THE PHANTOM LORD

Tinted water flowed against the rock walls.

Ean whipped her head back and forth, confusion plastered on her face. "This isn't Skull Rock. What in Hades–"

She was standing in an utter *beast* of a cavern: austere, morose, and unwelcoming. An enormous set of double doors wore massive chains that drooped in a forbidding frown. There wasn't a crumb of sunlight anywhere. She thanked her lucky stars for elf vision. *Am I underground?* "Maybe I'm under Mage Isle. But how did I get here?"

Silence. "Mmk, it seems I'm alone." She hesitated, then spied what appeared to be writing over the stone doors. "What's that say?" Leaping from rock to rock, she landed gracefully and read the inscription.

ALL HAIL ANATHEMA THE PHANTOM LORD, SHE OF THE IRON THORN CIRCLET, THE HAND OF DARK CHARISMA, MIDNIGHT SOVEREIGN OF THE UNDEAD.

AS FORETOLD, SO MOTE IT BE

"OK. I'm officially weirded out now." Ean cast a nervous glance 'round the cave. "This was set up for *me*. But whether for good or evil, I can't tell." After another pause, she shrugged and tore down the old chains. "Nothing ventured, nothing gained!"

Ean peeped behind the doors. She began to smile.

She saw a dim underground passageway studded with polychrome gems. "Sweet. If this is the entrance to Hades, I think I'm going to like it here." Chuckling, she skipped down the vast, snaking halls, stopping from time to time to touch a particularly bright gem. "Curiouser and curiouser! I'm feeling quite at home," she said to the sapphires. "Eli should see this." She tapped the Holobox. "Eh, Hexy? My man? Care to shoot Elias a summons?"

No response. The Holobox didn't even blink.

"Odd." Ean poked it again. Nothing. "I guess it makes sense that it wouldn't work down here. But it's a *game*, so… what's that meant to do? Promote a sense of realism?"

Neither the Holobox nor the gemstone brigade offered their opinions.

"I'd better stop talking to myself," she muttered. "Well, further in and deeper down we go. I hope there's some wicked bosses. I could use a treasure haul."

The passageways widened as she descended. Soon Ean spotted two guards, one on each side, standing at grim attention and holding bright, thornlike spears. "Gentlemen," she nodded to them, noting that they were skelemen. "How interesting. I *really* wish Elias was here."

More gemstones. More guards. A stern pillar or two. At the end, another massive set of double doors and another inscription. *Hades Reigns Below*

"Hmm. A throne room, judging from the opulence of this entryway." Ean glanced at the rubies, obsidian, sapphires, and bronze that curled around the doors in the shape of flames. "Best to gear up for a fight."

As she scrolled through her weapons, her finger paused over Necro. Some instinct caused her to select *Spina Lucifer* first, securing it to her waist. *I don't think Elias will mind. It'll be like having him with me.*

Stretching to relax her muscles, Ean tossed her hair and motioned for the skeletal guards to let her in. They opened the doors without a word.

The Phantom Lord inspected his challenger.

The half-elf advanced with admirable grace, each step rife with confidence. Blood-red hair swayed past her waist. Her hands clenched – more with excitement and anticipation than fear – and her dark eyes shone with the suppressed power of a midnight berserker. The Mage symbol glowed imposingly from her bare shoulder.

Impressive. Not that he'd ever say so aloud, of course. An aura of command and adventure surrounded her, as well as the softer, feminine hint of a floral island breeze. "So, this is what we've come to," he drawled, yawning. His immense skeletal jaws snapped shut with a *clack!* "The aspiring Phantom Lord is a *woman.*"

Ean deployed a charming smile. "Does that surprise you? We've taken the world by storm." She coolly examined her fingernails, implying that bowing, scraping, or cowering just wasn't in her repertoire.

The skeleton king rose from his throne, his crown of silver and gold thorns glinting in the dark. "Prepare thyself, little half-blood."

Ean assumed her position, then straightened with a shriek: "Wait!"

She poked through game options until the wild intro of "Ride the Lightening" blasted through the throne room. "I'm ready now," she laughed, shifting back and forth to the beat and twirling Necro.

She rushed forward, hair streaming.

Her cluster ring glowed as it harvested charisma from the frenzied music. As the king's crown glowed as well, Ean realized that she was unintentionally feeding her enemy dark charisma. *Oh, well. I'm having way too much fun!*

They traded a flurry of blows. Necro was swiftly exchanged for Spina Lucifer, but as Ean had never practiced with it, she found it awkward to wield. *By Hades! I could have been more prepared for this. Nothing I can do about it now.*

The wicked white cloud teemed at the edge of her senses, tempting her to succumb and embrace her full power. Ean welcomed it with a joyous cheer.

Much later, Gale and Ean stared each other down.

It was a hot day on Mage Isle. Ean was still panting, ruddy hair a tangled mess, sweat on her forehead, hands shaking. Yet an undeterred aura of triumph embraced her like a garment, and a new cape of scarlet silk fluttered from her shoulders. Her black Holobox sported a leering skull. And last (but far from least), a circlet of gleaming skyward thorns rested above her brows.

"Why – don't you tell me – anything, you jerk?" she managed between ragged breaths.

Amused, the dark elf spied Spina Lucifer on her hip. "I see Spina has been christened. Baptized in blood of the undead, eh? That's the stuff."

"Don't you dare – ignore – me!" Ean marched forth and jabbed him in the chest. "You just admitted that you *knew!* You knew the whole time that Anathema was prophesied to become the Phantom Lord."

"Yes. I knew."

"And Eli?"

"Yes. He knew."

Inhaling deeply, "The second he arrives, I'm going to murder both of you by *wholesale.*"

Gale could tell by the glint in her eye that she was joking… mostly. But the heightened level of darkness flooding from her was imposing nonetheless. Her eyes were bright with charismatic chaos.

He gave a sarcastic bow. "Looking forward, my Lord."

She laughed. "That's going to take some getting used to."

From behind her, Eli's voice murmured "You're telling *me.*"

He embraced her before she could turn. "I felt the pull of your phantom charisma clear across the sea." His glossy teeth grazed her ear. "I've arranged a victory dinner with all our friends, but we'll have to go somewhere… *private* first."

Ean smiled and leaned back against him. "Ten-four, Mr. Mage."

Gale sighed. "Don't the two of you ever stop?"

"What's the trouble, Modi? Jealous?" Elias shamelessly caressed his wife's waist. "You could get married yourself. I highly recommend it." His fingers brushed the hilt of Spina Lucifer. "You fought with this?" he queried, unsheathing it. "You should have practiced with it first, absurd woman!"

"I had no time!" Taking the sword from Eli, the half-elf held Gale at bladepoint. "I *would* have had more time if either of you bothered to prepare me."

"We're not spoil-sports, Ean. You had a lot more fun discovering Hades on your own, didn't you?" Gale protested, holding up his hands. She glared at him for a long moment, then sheathed her weapon. "I suppose."

"You *know* you did." Elias continued to stroke her. "You're making my knees weak," Ean whispered, kissing his jaw. "Get us out of here, you crazy man."

"Ten-four, Anathema."

As the couple vanished in a glittering green wave, Gale turned and walked to the skull cavern to meet with the Firestone Guild. Unbidden, Willow Prendergast entered his thoughts. *You could get married yourself.*

"Sure. Except the one avatar I'd want to marry is spoken for."

He kicked at every rock in his way.

11

ANATHEMA ENTHRONED

Ignoring the skeletal guards, Elias threw open the doors himself.

The cavernous room flickered with dewdrop gems, tiny speckles of undead starlight. He chuckled as he recognized the hardcore rhythm of "Here to Stay" echoing from the abyss. *That's my girl.*

A throne of ebony glass – looking like it had been shattered into a million pieces and put back together again – towered from a matching ascension of glass stairs. They glowed red and purple. Ean lounged, quite at her ease with one leg propped over the arm rest, laughing at something one of her guards just said.

Elias cleared his throat and bowed. "Anathema."

Her head snapped 'round at his voice, her smile deepening. Eli blinked in surprise; her eyes were dilated, fully flexed with an ecstasy of adrenaline and charisma. "I believe *my Lord* is appropriate," she huffed, faking displeasure as she stood.

Ean descended slowly, one spiked, thick-soled boot at a time. She stared at Eli in a way that made his cheekbones burn. "Sorry. Can't manage it, my dear. Far too masculine."

"Manage it this once, and you'll get a present," she sang. She stopped in front of him and crossed her arms, grinning.

"What present is that, O Phantom Lord of peerless beauty and enigmatic chaos?"

She threw back her head to laugh. "Excellent. Take your present, then, Mephisto."

With a single passionate kiss, Eli's charisma gauge reached maximum. Elias yelped as if a yellow jacket had stung him. "Ean! How'd you do that?"

"Don't you know, O Wielder of Sacred Knowledge?" she teased. "I thought you knew all about Anathema and the Phantom Lord."

"I'm not the expert, much as I'd like to be. I'll have to pick Modi's brain." He nuzzled her, the rubies in his skull sparkling with all their former glory. "He's finally confessed that he broke your ring then befriended you in order to bask in your wealth as Phantom Lord. 'Can't beat her, then join her,' in his own words. A scoundrel to the end, hmm?"

"What a surprise." Her dry tone portrayed the opposite.

"Yes. And yet, he's proven himself time and again as a valuable ally." Eli executed a flourishing bow. "On his behalf, I beg our Lord for a lightened punishment."

Ean sucked on her lower lip, tapping one foot. "What's the fun in that?"

Elias chuckled. "Cthulhu it is. Alone. Sans surplus phantom charisma."

"Done."

Locked in their embrace, they both looked annoyed when an intruder was announced. "Lore Pendragon, my Lord."

She sighed. "Let him in." Her hand wrapped around her skeleman's waist as his arm rested on her shoulders. "I won't let him take too long," she whispered against Eli's cheekbone.

Ean felt Elias stiffen at the sight of the handsome half-draconian. The corner of Lore's mouth twitched with a subdued smile. "Hail, Phantom Lord." He bowed. "Might I ask a boon of thee?"

The half-elf cocked her head. "And what boon would you ask?"

"Pray allow me to train with you."

"May I ask why?"

"It's the quickest way to level up so we might face Cthulhu victorious."

"Speak of the sea devil!" Ean smiled at Elias. "Sounds like a plan. I'd better let Modi train with me, too."

"Sure. Just remember that I get to go first." Eli stepped back a few paces and unsheathed Sacrimony, flushing with delight as golden flames rippled down its length. "Finally. By the gods, that's a sight for sore eyes!"

Ean withdrew Spina Lucifer. "It's high time we crossed blades, Mephisto. Rather exciting, isn't it?"

"You dare cross *this* sword?" Eli's hellish eyes glinted with mischief. "How brave of you, my dear."

"May I watch?" Lore asked.

"If you want."

The couple circled one another. "Somehow you're not so intimidating anymore," Ean teased him. "I think I might be scarier than you."

"In your dreams, maybe." Her lithe yet powerful stride thrilled him, as it always did. "Just wait 'till I'm maxed out in combat again, too."

"Say what you will," she laughed, "but I'm heart-glad to see you devilish again, my love. I missed you!"

"I missed me, too."

Distracted by her answering mirth, Ean mistimed her parry as Eli lunged. "Look alive, my Lord!" he bellowed. The gilded flames from Sacrimony merged with the dark clouds of Spina Lucifer. "I think you're really in trouble this time," Lore called out to Ean. "I've never seen Elias like this."

"It'll become an old sight pretty soon," smiled Ean as she sidestepped his next attack. Her snake-like rapidity startled Elias, but he was adjusting quickly. "Maybe I'll let him win for old time's sake."

Eli's dark chuckle resonated in her eager heart. "Oh no, you *are* in trouble, my dear."

The two were well-matched. Elias wasn't at full combat level, but Ean didn't have the experience with the blade that Elias had. Lore's yellow eyes glinted with increasing interest as the Mages danced around each other, gold and silver, red and purple, black and white. *A handsome pair. Brimming with power, bright with affection, subtle mischief in their eyes.* He could feel the sexual tension between them pulling like magnets.

Lore noticed his gauge gradually filling with dark charisma. Even at a distance, the Mages' magic was strong enough to reach him. He marveled at the sensation.

The couple's sparring ended with the new Phantom Lord on the ground, breathless, smiling at the point of Sacrimony's glinting blade. "Beaten, beaten!" Elias sang, laughing and extending his boney hand. "And I don't think you faked it, either."

Ean shrugged. "Maybe. Or maybe not." Elias pulled his wife to her feet. She slipped her fingers into his ribcage and yanked him close. "You'll never know for sure, will you, Mr. Mage?"

His thumb traced her chin. "My lady of mystery."

She kissed him. Lore looked away, embarrassed. "I suggest we meet at Skull Rock later. If we're going to beat Cthulhu, we need a massive training session. And a whole new plan of attack. And to strengthen our defense, we'll have to-"

He rambled on. It took a minute for the couple to separate. Ean smiled, still engrossed in her husband's demonic eyes. "Right. Let's call Gale in, too."

Gale sat apart from the Firestone Guild. He scrolled through old messages, making short answers to his Holopal's chitchat, his fingers tapping aimlessly through his inbox. Cyrus made one final attempt at motioning the dark elf over, but Gale declined again with the slight shake of his ebony head. "Got some messages to answer."

The cyborg shrugged his chrome shoulders and talked to Aura. As the guild debated strategy against Cthulhu, Gale heaved an inaudible sigh.

"We're going to need more people on our team. More ships," Aura was insisting. "If we try to go against Cthulhu alone, we'll get ripped apart just like before."

Cyrus' confident voice answered. "I can try to recruit a fleet. But most of my friends are committed to other campaigns right now…"

The soft green flash of a transport gem startled Gale. "You called for me?"

Gale stood and cleared his throat. "I… I did. I wondered if you had any more news on the hacker."

Willow Prendergast took in her surroundings with that soft, deft look particular to herself. Her draping gown, stitched with the symbol of the moon goddess, trailed the sea cave floor. "I believe I'm getting close," she answered. "That's why I haven't been logging in as often."

Her velvet smile had a touch of darkling mischief to it. It sent a quiver down Gale's stern spine. "You're a hacker, too?"

"Takes one to find one." Willow swept past him and eyed the Firestone Guild. "Friends of yours?"

"I'm sure you recognize most of them. The Sea Wyvern crew, from the concert night on board?"

"Oh, yes. I spy the half-draconian." Staring, she drew in a deep yet silent breath. "I taste rich phantom charisma from his aspect. I'll have a chat with him presently. Before that," turning her easygoing gaze back to Emodicus, "have you any other business with me, dark elf?"

"You said you're getting close. What have you learned so far? Whom do you suspect?"

"I cannot share that with you until I have proof."

Gale frowned. "I wouldn't tell anyone else."

"I doubt it not. However, I wouldn't cast blame and suspicion unless my words were founded in truth. Innocent until proven guilty, you know."

The fluid smoothness of her voice lured Gale closer. Ean's ferocious, feline chaos had drawn him in, too... But something about the tranquil chasm of Willow's presence was even more alluring. Soothing. "At least give me a hint?" he asked, wanting to take her hand but restraining himself.

She started to shake her head, but stopped. "Very well." Giving him a mysterious look, she uttered the words *"First as one, then as two; Single flames now twin anew. Find ye where allegiance lacks; Dual fetters hold him back. He who solves this riddle; A new flame shall whittle."*

The elf-witch smiled at his befuddled expression. "Good luck, Gale Emodicus."

She vanished.

12

THE METRO AGAIN

"E an!"

A blond pixie burst into the throne room. She looked entirely out of place among the undead, causing one or two of the guards to snicker.

The Phantom Lord glanced up from a scroll. "I'm busy, Mallie. Can't this wait?" Sighing, the half-elf muttered under her breath, "Turns out this is an actual job in some respects. Hades must run smoothly, just like a real kingdom."

Mallie shook off a guard who tried to dissuade her. "It took me forever to get access here, Ean! Get your royal ass to the Metro! Your SkyRate challenge race against Piragor is *today*."

"Today?" Ean uttered a shriek and dropped the manuscript. "Almighty Kanthesis! Where's my board?" Flicking her wrist, she delved into her inventory and scrolled at the speed of light. "Eli was supposed to remind me!"

Hands on her hips, Mallie shook her head. "You've been all over each other. It's no surprise he's distracted. Hurry up! You have just enough time for one run-through before the track is set."

Ean snatched her skyboard and powered up. "On my way." She spoke aside to Hex, "Tell Elias to meet me at the track."

"*Wakarimasu,* Ean-san."

Mounting the board, Ean wobbled unsteadily. "Woah, girl!" Beating her butterfly wings, Mallie flew to her side and steadied her balance. "Easy does it. Maybe you're more out of practice than we thought," she murmured anxiously.

"It's not that. Skycraft is just like riding a bike; it's intuitive once you've learned how." The half-elf sighed and rubbed her head. "I've had a raging headache ever since logging in."

"Oh? That's a shame."

"And I'm sleepy. Which is weird, because I was totally alert before turning on my helmet."

"Hmm. I don't suppose…" The pixie shrugged. "No, probably not."

"What is it?" Ean asked with a yawn.

"Um… you can't… your avatar isn't *pregnant,* is it?"

An extremely long silence.

Ean coughed. "What?!?"

"The game is rigged to make pregnancies brief, but realistic. Headaches and drowsiness are the first signs."

Ean forced a laugh. "Elias is undead, Mallie. They can't breed."

Mallie looked uneasy. "Actually, if they're married long enough, undead avatars can unlock that ability. It's called *gravidamancy.*"

"Don't you think Elias would have, you know, *mentioned* that?"

Mallie paled. "Maybe he didn't know, either?"

"Holy Cernunnos." Ean groaned and rubbed her temples again. "I'll kill him."

"It's kind of exciting though, right?"

"A half-skeleton baby wobbling around? I think the word you're searching for is creepy."

"Anyway, you need to hurry. You'd better talk to Elias after the race."

"Not sure there's a point in showing up," Ean grunted. "I won't be able to concentrate at all. Screw you, gravidamancy!"

"Just do your best, dear. And have fun!" Mallie's color returned and she sparkled, clapping her hands. "It looks like I'll be able to use my midwife training after all! I'm so excited!"

"Oh, *do* shut up, Mallie."

The gleam of the Metro track dazzled Ean's eyes. She winced, selecting her sun visor from inventory. *Well, as Mallie said, I should try to have fun at least.*

The throb of her skyboard gradually revived her. Ignoring the pangs in her temples, she shot her rival a wicked grin. "Long time no race, Piragor."

Her old friend gave a cheery salute. "Haven't seen you on the practice runs. Too good to hang out with us skycraft junkies, eh?"

Ean huffed. "You may not have noticed this subtle tribute to my station," pointing to the crown of thorns, "but you may address me as *your majesty* from now on."

Piragor mirrored her savage grin. "Doesn't look very aerodynamic, *your majesty.*"

"Screw you!"

The two laughed as the system counted down. *3- 2- 1- Accelerate.*

The roar of the audience bolstered Ean's courage. As she tore through the track, the corner of her eye caught the telltale glint of her husband's frame nestled in the crowd. *Aww, how sweet of him to get all gussied up just for me!* She had grown accustomed to his polished, bright gold physique.

Seated next to him was the Firestone Guild, including Mallie dressed in mayflowers. She waved to Ean and cheered. Ean didn't have time to wave back before she'd already sped past her, but she felt more like frowning at Mallie anyway. *You'd better not tell Elias before I do!* She cursed herself for not swearing Mallie to secrecy.

One of the Metro's sharpest turns was coming up. Ean knelt, shifting her weight, and nearly prayed to Hades before remembering she *was* Hades. "As I wish, so mote it be!" she declared instead. She leaned into the turn–

Her stomach roiled.

Gasping, Ean turned too sharply and crashed into the siderail.

She heard the collective cry of the audience before the screen blacked out.

She logged back in to the sensation of being choked. At first, she thought her ebullient skeleman had a penchant for spousal murder. Then, she realized he was merely hugging her so tightly that her avatar couldn't breathe.

"Have... mercy... husband!" she gasped, prying at his cold arms. "Can't... breathe!"

"Sorry!" He released his hold and straightened above the hospital bed. "The android healer just informed me that we're going to have a child! I can't *believe* it, Ean!"

She sat up cautiously. "Neither can I. Did you know it was possible?"

"I came across gravidamancy quite a while back, but I didn't think much of it. There's not a lot of undead avatars that stay married long enough. Or get married in the first place."

Ean scuffed his skull with an affectionate smile. "We're breaking records again, I see. Ware the Mighty Mages!"

"We should print that on a t-shirt."

"What'll we name the baby?"

He touched his fingerbones to his jaw. "Been thinking about that. I think we should wait until we see what our child looks like, then name him/her. Let inspiration guide us."

"Sound logic, Mage." Ean swung her feet to the floor and stood. "Hey, Hex. Did they schedule the rematch yet?"

Her Holopal materialized and bowed. "They've sent a few options for your approval, Ean-san."

"Hmm." Ean opened the message and perused the suggested dates. Her finger was about to select one when she paused. "Elias?"

"Yes, my dear?"

"Would you be disappointed in me if I just bowed out? Let them declare Piragor the new champion?"

Elias wrapped her in his arms. "Still not feeling well?"

"Yeah. I'm better, but a little woozy. And VR pregnancies proceed rapidly. Soon, I won't be able to race at all."

"We could postpone it until after you have our child."

"True. But then I'll be busy raising it. No, I think it wouldn't be fair to poor Piragor to make him wait that long. He's been hankering after the title for a solid year, training tooth and nail. He deserves to be SkyRate Grand Champion."

"Hmm." Elias nuzzled Ean's neck. "It's a kind gesture, but we both know he'll resent the idea of taking the title without finishing the race. What if you had someone take your place? Who is the highest in rank after you?"

"Guess," Ean said with a laugh, nuzzling him back.

"Oh, no."

"Oh, yes. Our darling, dark, cantankerous Modi."

"Well, it'll be a good race and no mistake."

"It'll be fun to cheer Gale on," Ean grinned. "We could throw him a little afterparty, too. I *love* SkyRate parties."

"I know." Eli's voice deepened to a throaty, seductive purr. "Remember when we got stuck in the SkyRate elevator, and–"

"Not here!" Blushing, Ean extracted his naughty hand from her clothes. "A hospital droid could walk in any second."

"So what?"

Rather questionable sounds floated into the hallway.

13

DARK ELF RISING

Lilac aspens glittered in the wind, clustered around the Metro track in artistic patterns. Gale Emodicus squared his shoulders. He mounted his cerulean board and flew to the starting line. "Go, Modi!" he heard Ean scream. He glanced aside and had to chuckle. Her burgundy gown scarcely masked the swell of her belly, and she was stuffing her face with an entire box of spiced popcorn (to Eli's bereft dismay).

Willow Prendergast sat on the other side of her.

Her husband was nowhere to be seen. Puzzled, Gale shrugged and focused on the pulsing starting line. *I've met my former goal; Ean is now Anathema, the Phantom Lord. My access to rare phantom charisma is secure. Now…*

Now for SkyRate Grand Champion.

He stole one last glimpse of Willow. *3- 2- 1- Accelerate.*

"*Yeeaahh!*" Ean yelled, jumping up and spilling popcorn everywhere. Elias plucked a piece from her hair and ate it. "Who do you want to win?" he asked, helping her sit back down. "Tell me honestly."

"Honestly, I don't know. They both deserve it."

"That's how I feel about it. I think Gale stands one *tiny* inch higher in my estimation, though."

"That's because he's a dark elf, dear. Piragor sports light charisma. He's your natural opposite."

"Yes. Well, it suits him."

"Yeah, it does." Ean leaned against him as they watched Piragor and Gale clear a corkscrew loop. "He looks great," Ean enthused. "I mean, they both do. But Piragor has grown up something fierce. He never had arms like *that* before."

Elias gave her a look.

"OK, so I have a weakness for strong man arms. So what?"

"I'll make sure to buff up later." He "flexed" his humerus, making her laugh.

Back on the Metro, Gale was having trouble keeping up. Piragor's training in the past year was guiding him straight and true. Naturally, Gale had been focusing on regaining his status after the hack, and one month of playing catchup may not be enough.

Still, when Ean asked him to please take her place, he couldn't refuse. If there was a chance to show Willow what he could really do –

He pushed a lock of hair out of his eyes, grimacing. Why did it matter what she thought of him? She was Axel's wife. *Why do I keep forgetting?*

Maybe because he hadn't seen Axel around lately. *Why isn't he here?* Gale found it difficult to imagine *not* spending as much time at Willow's side as possible.

Her form, such pure elegance… The way she walked, as agile as a dancer… Her voice, ever soft and steady, her gaze so calming…

Pay attention!

Throwing such thoughts away, Gale laser-focused on the race. He started to catch up again. Piragor sensed his presence and accelerated.

Their boards were nose-to-nose. As they knelt into aerodynamic position, Gale couldn't guess who was going to win.

What if they tied? The consideration disgusted him. *I think I'd rather lose.*

He opened his eyes just in time to see a flash of cerulean blue.

"It's Gale Emodicus!"

The spectators erupted into cheers. Elias was on his feet, shouting, and holding his gilt fists in the air. Ean would have spilled the rest of her popcorn, but she'd eaten it all. The empty box sailed through the air and landed on an unfortunate dwarf's head, baptizing him with a smear of buttered spices.

After he'd accepted his trophy and GP, new skyboard, and official SkyRate Sponsorship medallion, Gale elbowed through a sea of fans to get to his friends. "I love winning by accident," he joked, darting a smile at Willow.

She stood and approached him, footsteps as silent as ever, even on the bleachers. "Have you solved the riddle?" she asked.

"You don't beat around bushes, do you? Not yet," he admitted.

"I never beat around the bush. What a dreadful waste of time."

Gale smiled slowly. "Then we'll be very good friends." After an embarrassed pause he added "Where is Axel?"

Willow's cheeks colored. *I've never seen her blush before.* "Toying about at home, I expect," she replied. "He's been… busy."

"He must be," Gale began, but he was stopped by a certain half-elf practically smothering him with a victory hug. "I'm SO PROUD OF YOU," she yelled, eyes brimming with happy tears. "I feel like I just watched my son become famous." She withdrew and punched him in the shoulder. "You're the best, Modi!"

The dark elf touched his stomach with an astonished expression. "I think I just felt your kid kick me in the gut."

"Really?" Ean eagerly pressed her hand to her womb. "I was so excited I didn't notice. Here now," she addressed her child, "pick on somebody your own size, why don't you?"

"He's strong," Elias proudly supplied. "We just found out it's a boy. What say you to that, Uncle Modi?"

"Congratulations. And please don't hug me again."

The Mages, the Firestone Guild, and Willow laughed.

"Mephisto."

"Mmm?"

"Did you know we can have our baby blessed with certain talents or traits?"

Elias chuckled and closed the scroll he was reading. "You mean like a fairy godmother?"

Ean threw her own scroll at him. "No! Well... actually, pretty much."

The couple was enjoying a much-needed rest in Vermillion Castle. Ean crossed the living room to sit in Eli's lap. "Anyone trained in magic and midwifery can do it. I was thinking we could ask Mallie."

"I assume GP is required?"

"Yes. It'll be costly, but we can afford it."

Elias traced her cheek. "What were you thinking of asking for, Aphrodite? Glass slippers and a pumpkin coach?"

She tweaked his cheekbone. "We're limited to three. I was thinking intelligence, wisdom, and charisma. That can get him into any trades and hobbies he likes."

"Agreed. Can we ask for certain physical traits?"

Ean sighed and rubbed his skull. "You're worried he'll be half-skeletal, too? I don't know what to expect."

"Neither do I. We're not the first undead conception, but it's never happened with a skeletal avatar before."

Ean hesitated. "We can change how he looks, but that's the costliest order of all. Also… it seems wrong somehow. Shouldn't we accept him the way he is?"

"One can make that same argument about commissioning any gifts at all."

"I know. But over time he can gain intelligence, wisdom, and charisma on his own. This just gives him a boost. He can decide for himself whether to change his looks."

Elias mulled it over for a few minutes. Ean played with the hood on his black cape, covering and uncovering his skull. "I think you're right," he concluded. "We'll let him make that choice later."

"Oh…" she winced, pressing her hands against her stomach. "It's a good thing we decided that… right now."

"It's time?" Eli's dark eyes flew wide open.

"It's time. Hex? Call Mallie."

14

THE PHANTOM LORD'S SON

L ore Pendragon checked the map. *I'm almost there.* Adjusting his tunic, he appreciated the sights of Verdant Valley as his rented skyboard coasted along the levitation tracks.

The half-draconian had been surprised to receive an invitation. He knew Ean quite well, having sailed, fought, and trained alongside her, but Elias remained rather aloof. Yet they'd both remembered him. It warmed his heart, he admitted to himself.

He saw Vermillion Castle. The warm brown stone of the ancient building was complemented by the deep green of climbing vines. The pristine gardens were well tended; Lore could see Ean's Holopal watering the gold roses. And the shining lake hugging the castle's eastern corner was the finishing touch to a charming (if antique) scene that anyone would be thrilled to call home.

As he crossed the drawbridge, Hex floated before him. "Sir Pendragon, welcome. I shall announce your arrival."

"No need," Lore commented. He glanced down at the moat. "I had no idea Ean's tastes were so antiquated. She doesn't *look* it."

"Lady Mage is the summation of many noble tastes, past, present, and future."

"I see."

The door lifted to reveal a courtyard. Hex led him through. Another set of doors opened into the castle itself. Lore's scales brightened in the light of flaming chandeliers. His bare, taloned feet sank into the blissful softness of thick carpets. *I hope my claws don't tear them.* Proceeding with care, he followed the Holopal into the living room where the christening would take place.

The Firestone Guild and the Spectral Tyrants were already there. Travis was swinging from a chandelier, much to Eli's displeasure (Ean was too busy laughing to scold him). The Prendergasts were there, though they both seemed stiff and uncomfortable; and the new SkyRate Grand Champion was there, clumsily holding a tiny bundle that squirmed and kicked.

"Lore! I'm glad you made it." The Phantom Lord greeted him with a hearty handshake. "I know this isn't your sort of thing."

"Nonsense. I'm happy to celebrate the birth of your son." Ean Mage was already restored to phantomic glory, strong and keen and lithe, hair alight with red and purple stars. "Now that you're restored to health, will you be joining us for Cthulhu training?"

"Yep." Ean snapped a salute. "And I'll be bringing a host or two from Hades. We'll need a few more ships. Cyrus agreed."

"Praise the Pantheon." Lore's demeanor cheered. "I think our odds will at last be evened. But did my eyes deceive me? Was *Emodicus* holding your son just now?"

"Dear Uncle Modi," Ean laughed. "Yes, I finally talked him into it. He had to be bribed, though. Modi! Get your ass over here. You've met Lore Pendragon, yes?"

"Not officially." The sable elf ambled over. His indigo eyes looked mildly distressed. "Here," he said, dumping the baby into his mother's arms sans ceremony. "I don't think he likes me very much."

"Don't be silly, Modi-san. He never cried one bit." Ean cradled her son with a loving word or two. "This is Gale Emodicus, Fell Sorcerer to Kanthesis, recently the SkyRate Grand Champion. And this is Lore Pendragon, first mate on the Sea Wyvern, and the latest member of the Firestone Guild."

They acknowledged each other with slight nods. The half-draconian's ruddy, smoking aspect contrasted with Gale's raven and indigo features. "A pleasure," they said simultaneously.

"Talk about two sides of the same coin," Willow interposed. "A twin flame stands before me. I feel a shifting of fate."

Gale's brows rose as he looked at her. She gave a slow, mysterious nod, then slipped back into the chattering crowd before he could speak.

"Gather 'round, all!" Elias shouted, standing on a chair and raising a mug of ale. "Thank you for coming to the naming and christening of my son. Special thanks to Mallie," gesturing to the beaming pixie, "for agreeing to bestow the Fairy's Gifts."

Ean stood next to her husband and folded back the blanket covering their son. Lore advanced to get his first good look.

A small human skull with narrow ice-blue eyes blinked from the blanket folds. His tiny hands, however, wore smooth infant flesh. The rest of him followed suit. In every other feature, he was a normal human baby.

Elias placed his skeletal hand on the baby's pearlescent cranium. "Your mother and I name thee Cernun Emodicus Mage. May you reap honor and glory, through life or through death, in the name of the god Cernunnos. Hail!"

"Hail!" Everyone echoed, raising their mugs. Mallie approached the child bashfully. "And may wisdom, intelligence, and charisma lighten your burdens," she trilled, waving a birch wand. "Be blessed, Cernun Emodicus Mage!"

Lore looked at the dark elf. Gale kept his eyes fastened to the carpet, but his veiled expression was delighted and deeply touched.

An evening of merrymaking followed. Ean and Elias traveled through the crowd, chatting and shaking hands. Smack in the middle of a rousing song, little Cernun suddenly glowed white and sprouted from an infant to a lisping, climbing toddler. "Guess we should have held his christening sooner," Ean laughed. "Who wants some cake?"

Cernun continued to grow rapidly, which pleased his parents to no end. Elias taught him fencing, jousting, and the basics of wizardry, while Ean gave him lessons in skycraft and had him shadow her as the Phantom Lord's assistant. Once he was sixteen(ish), he was permitted to train with the Mages and the Firestone Guild as they prepared to confront Cthulhu one more time.

The three Mages and Gale met outside of Stellos. "The Spectral Tyrants will be joining us," Elias announced, scanning his tablet. "Adding their numbers to Ean's Hades crew, it's safe to say that Cthulhu is as good as dead."

"Sweet. Which album should we play while we bust his ass?" Ean asked for the millionth time.

"We agreed on *Ghost*, Mom," Cernun (who would stop to headbang in the middle of a fight) reminded her. Elias laughed, trapping his son in a headlock and menacing his skull. "You're the Phantom Lord's son, all right."

"Uncle Modi!" Cernun pleaded, scrambling with his father. "Oh no, you don't," Elias snorted. "You're old enough to look out for yourself."

Gale came anyway, raising a cool brow at Elias. "Cerry," he addressed Cernun, raising his hand to push Eli aside.

Elias turned and caught Gale's arm. Lore – who was never far from Gale – ran to join the ranks. Soon the four were in an all-out fracas, dust flying, a creative assortment of curses staining the ears of bystanders. Ean cast her eyes heavenward and turned to Cyrus. "Well, you and I might as well get to sparring."

"Looks like it," the cyborg chuckled. "Let's back away a smidgen more."

The brawl ended when Lore swept his tail under Elias and Cernun's feet, tripping them both. "Hey Dad," Cernun commented, standing and dusting himself off. "Remind me to talk to you about something important later."

"How much later? You know I'm going to forget."

"After we defeat Cthulhu."

"You do realize that might never happen?" Gale warned, wiping dirt off his face.

"Have faith, Uncle! We've trained so many times. We know all its tricks. And we'll have the Tyrants fighting with us."

"Just don't get distracted," Ean sang teasingly, elbowing the dark elf. "A certain lovely, recently-single elf-witch will be helping us, too."

"Shut it," Gale growled. Lore tried not to smirk.

"Why'd she and Axel break up?" Cernun asked.

"Nobody knows. Neither of them will say."

"Haven't even seen Axel in ages. It's like he vanished from the face of Terra."

Gale and Lore shared a knowing look, but said nothing.

15

A NIGHT IN THE LIFE OF HADES

Hexadecimal appeared at full scale. Tucking his hands in his wide scarlet sleeves, he bowed. Ruby hairpins held his long black mane in place. "My Lord. It seems another ghoul has escaped and is haunting a tavern in Stellos. We must recapture him."

Ean waved her hand. "Send Zaine. He's got more patience for that."

He bowed again. Searching in his sleeve, he withdrew a sealed scroll. "And this just arrived for you from the Kanthesis Temple."

"You may read it."

"The Fell Sorcerer greets you and asks if you'd be interested in completing a quest with him. If successful, you will win the *Grimoire of Nymphoria.*"

Ean snorted. "Let me guess. He wants to copy it, let me have the original, and in exchange for his kind-heartedness, he wants to harvest phantom charisma?"

Hex closed the scroll. "You have hit the nail on the head, my Lord."

The Phantom Lord cackled. "That's our Modi for you. Predictable as the tides."

Ean's favorite guard, Mauldrin, confronted her with a bow. "My Lord Hades. Your blade has returned from Klad fully restored." Kneeling, he presented Spina Lucifer, shining from hilt to tip. "The smith has been compensated. I added the tip you specified."

"Thanks, Mauldrin. At ease."

The bronze skeleton guard stood, bowed again, and took his place by the Hades Throne. Ean stretched and sighed with contentment. "Not as busy tonight. I wonder if Emodicus is logged in? Check for me, Hexy, *onegai.*"

The search indicator light spun around his head. "Not at the moment, my Lord."

She slapped her knee. "Damn. Would have been a perfect night for that quest. Funny," she chuckled at herself, "I don't hate quests anymore, now that I've got some power." She flexed her arms. "I could go capture that ghoul myself! Want to come along, Mauldrin?"

"I'd be honored, my Lord."

She fired him a wide smile. "You can call me Ean when it's just us."

Mauldrin hesitated, fumbling with his spear. "Could we compromise, my Lord? Perhaps I could call you Lady Mage. It doesn't sit well with me to use your first name."

"If you insist." Like most AI-generated players (that weren't cast as foes), Mauldrin was stainlessly polite. "I have a question, Hexy," she said. "What's the moral guidelines of being the Phantom Lord?"

Hexadecimal paused. "What do you mean, Ean-san?"

She shrugged, crossing her leg over her knee. "For example, does anything in the Terra regulations state I *have* to collect wayward ghouls?" Her smile looked a touch malevolent. "Seems to me if I don't clean up *every* mess, the players will have more fun."

"Fun?"

Ean held up her hands. "Who doesn't love a haunted tavern?"

"Apparently, Stellos residents don't."

"Good point." She tapped her fingernails on the arm rests. "Stellos does take itself too seriously. Bet the Kingdom of Klad would think it's a hoot." Ean howled at the mental image. "In fact, why don't we go bottle up that ghost and let it loose in the Wailing Banshee?"

"Respectfully, I wouldn't recommend letting it loose anywhere but here in Hades, where it belongs. My Lord."

"Oh, Hexy. You're no fun at all. What do you think, Mauldrin?"

"The decision is yours, Lady Mage."

"You're both repulsively first-class." She beamed at her Holopal and scuffed Mauldrin's skull. "Don't forget the ghost catcher, Mauldie. Let's go!"

Onidus Cauldron was a dim, shady-looking place. Witches, wizards, hunters, and mages hunched over shadowed round tables, sipping their drinks, and avoiding conversation whenever possible. The barkeeper swept the marble countertops and snatched away spiderwebs with ominous care. Potted plants and creeping vines, bleak with sober gray stardust, draped from the tavern walls. An enchanted piano, equally sober, tapped out melancholy tunes.

Every patron masked themselves in heavy cloaks of black, navy, or mystic purple. Various symbols for the God and Goddess hailed from their garment lining. An elf-witch, similarly garbed, swept into the establishment and ordered the Specter Special via an elite form of Terran sign language. She chose an empty table to drink in solitude.

With a warbled hesitation, the enchanted piano stopped dead.

The elf-witch rose her head. The other customers briefly regarded the instrument. They returned to their drinks. A couple of them conversed quietly with their Holopals in various languages.

Curious, the elf-witch left her table and tapped the bone-white keys. *Dong. Ding. Dong.*

The perverse instrument burst into a wild tune.

Customers jolted to their feet. The barkeeper cursed, fumbling beneath his counter for a ghost catcher. With a mighty, specterous moan, the ghoul flew from the piano and menaced the elf-witch with a sneer. She smiled, faint delight swimming in her soft eyes.

The ghost soared around the tavern. He overturned plants, shattered a stained-glass window, flipped all the holy imagery upside-down, and spilled the drinks. Most of the customers just left, muttering antipathies. The elf-witch slipped one delicate hand into her cloak and removed a willow wand. *"Echogastium,* heed what I say. To Hades bound, now find thy way!"

Just then, a half-elf dressed in scarlet silk bounded inside. "Gangway!" she cried, holding aloft a skull athame. "Now, Mauldrin!"

An armored skeleton guard entered. His right hand dangled a ghost catcher. Much like a dream-catcher, its delicate webbing shone with tiny beads and stones. He held it in front of the ghoul, gently swinging it back and forth.

Ean carved mystic symbols into the air with the athame. "Holy Cernunnos, this guy's got fight," she exclaimed. The ghoul shrieked, motionless but resisting the spirit bottle Mauldrin presented.

The elf-witch stepped closer. She waved her wand again. "Echogastium!"

Their combined suppression worked. With an angry howl, the ghost was swept into the spirit bottle. Mauldrin jammed the cork in the bottleneck. "Almighty Kanthesis. He made me break a sweat!" Ean laughed, wiping her forehead. She turned to the elf-witch. "Hey, thanks. What's your name?"

The witch lowered the hood that shaded her face. "Evening, Lady Mage."

"Oh, it's Willow." Ean gestured to her willow wand, smiling. "I should have known."

"I didn't know the Phantom Lord was reduced to spirit catching," Willow said, raising one amused brow. "Hades must not be as exciting as I supposed."

"It usually is. I'm having a slow night."

Willow glanced behind Ean. "Is Cernun with you?"

"Not tonight. I told him not to bother. He's hunting instead."

"A pity." The elf-witch returned her wand. "Catching spirits can be quite entertaining. You should bring him next time."

Mauldrin and Ean exchanged shamed glances. *Not when we're going to do something naughty, though.* "Well, I'll see you around!" Ean chirruped, snatching the spirit bottle and darting out. Willow swept after her and clutched her arm. "Ean Lightcross Mage. What exactly are you planning to do with that ghost?"

"Nothing."

"Your ears are bright red. You're up to something."

"Who, me? I'm a responsible, married, mothering adult."

"You're going to plant it somewhere."

"I would never."

Willow marched over to Ean's guard. "AI players never fib. Mauldrin, what is she up to?"

His jaws pried open. Ean dragged him away by the humerus. "Bye, Willow! Good to see you." She snapped her fingers and pointed. "Looking gorgeous, by the way."

Within a fortnight, the Wailing Banshee gained quite the reputation as a ghouling haunt.

16

DEATH BY WITCH LIBRETTOS

The Sea Wyvern, clean from stem to stern, glowed in sunrise glory. Ean pulled her sleepy son on board. "Wakey, wakey, Cernun! Get ready for the battle of your life!"

Elias staggered after them. Stretching and yawning, he rubbed his eyes and took a deep breath of sea air. "You know, I think I could live on board a ship. There's something about the ocean."

"You'd get tired of it, believe me," Cyrus laughed, motioning for Lore to give the order to raise sails and hoist anchor. Mallie fluttered up to Cyrus to bestow a good-morning kiss. "Well, I'm terrified. But I'll give this beast one more go."

"We're here!" Travis cried, bounding onboard in werecat form. Kaspar, Oleon, Sindaya, and Desmond followed him. "Ollie had to be bribed, but we all made it."

"Do I *have* to fight?" Ollie groaned. "Can't I just offer my moral support? Or play something? I'll be the fight song DJ."

"Nice try, but I think Cerry has that covered," Gale chuckled. Cernun glanced up from cleaning his sword and gave a salute *à la* Ean.

"Sure he can handle it? He's not… you know, particularly adept at multitasking."

"I'm not the scatterbrain I used to be," Cernun protested.

"It's true." Ean kissed her son's cheekbone. "He's a man now, and I'm so proud of him I could cry."

"Please don't, Mom."

Ean headlocked him instead and rubbed his emerald-studded skull. Cernun Mage, true to his name, was a gifted hunter and famous with the blade. At nineteen, he knew more about astronomy, herbology, and tracking prey than his father. "Mind sparring with me a bit?" he asked, calmly submitting to his parent's affectionate menaces.

"Thought you'd never ask, my son."

Ean took a few steps back. Holding out her arms, a reddish-purple glow enveloped her body. Piece by piece, her common sailor's garb changed into the ebony vest, pants, and spiked boots of the Phantom Lord. A scarlet silk cape tumbled from her shoulders, partially affixed by the skull-head covering her Holobox. The crown of thorns settled above her red brows. Spina Lucifer secured to her waist.

Once her dramatic transformation had finished, Ean looked around the deck, arms akimbo. "Eh? What's everyone gawking at?"

Gale smirked. "Good gods. Somebody's been watching too much *Sailor Moon*."

"What's that?" Ean queried, fluttering her lashes.

"If you don't know what that is, you'll have to trade in your *Nerd Archives* card."

"You wish!"

Ean, Gale, and Cernun took turns sparring. Elias and Lore leaned against the bulwark to watch. Lore struck a match, offering an extra Whisker smoke to Eli. "You know, I'm not sure the Phantom Lord is supposed to be that… *happy*."

"I know what you mean," Elias laughed. His midnight eyes glistened with pride as he watched his wife execute a playful pirouette, dancing around Gale and tapping him in the armpit. Gale yelped at the sensation of the cold blade. Cernun cracked up, causing Gale to target him with extra determination. "It didn't make sense at first. But... somehow, her chaotic energy has changed Hades for the better. You should see how much fun she has running the underworld. Even the AI-generated players adore her. Our son included," his gaze resting warmly on Cernun.

"She's something, all right. You're a lucky man."

"And I'm a lucky woman," Ean cried, tossing her hair. "You do realize I can hear you two?" She pointed to her elven ears. "Really! How long has it been, Eli? Five years?"

"And *you* constantly forget about my talent in ocumancy," Elias reminded her. "Don't act like you're perfect, Mrs. Mage. It makes my bones itch."

"Phantom Lord to *you*, sir!"

"Oh? Is that so?" Elias drew Sacrimony and plowed into the fray. "On guard, woman!"

Ean shrieked and tried to escape. Her husband cornered her in the navigation room. "Maxed out again, remember?" he whispered, grazing his teeth along her sensitive ear. "You won't get away from *me*."

"Monster ahoy!"

The call they'd been waiting for.

Cyrus, Lore, Aura and Cernun sprang into action first. Lore called upon his draconian fire and prepared leaping, sizzling masses of lava. Aura and Cernun climbed to the fighting top, magically-enhanced arrows readied on bowstrings. "Where's your parents?" Cyrus called to Cernun. He shrugged. Cyrus growled and rushed to the helm.

The minute he was gone, Cernun turned on his favorite album and maxed the volume.

The vessel shook with the almighty summons of black metal. Ean tumbled out of the navigation room with Necro, Eli at her heels. Both looked guilty as sin. "Gods," Gale muttered, then blushed; Willow manifested at his side, wand in one hand, athame in the other. Her floral pentagram glowed in the slender hollow of her neck. "Evening, Gale."

"… Evening, Willow."

She gave him a soft smile and hurried to the bow, making mystic symbols with the iron athame. The dark elf ripped his gaze from her and ran below to help the Tyrants load the guns.

The beast recognized their ship. Its gigantic head rose from the depths, shoulders and arms breaking the surface. Writhing tentacles masked its enormous maw. Cthulhu emitted a growl so deep and low that the ship and surrounding ocean trembled.

"Fire!" Cyrus shouted from the helm.

The other ships around them obeyed, crewed by the Phantom Lord's army. Cannons boomed. Arrows sliced the air. Lore's fire and Ean's lightening bewildered the monster. Elias snatched Spina Lucifer from Ean's waist and used to it summon dark clouds of poison, muttering darkly, a menacing smile in his eyes. "Give it all we've got, lads!" Desmond cried, fitting another magic arrow to his string.

Willow stood motionless. Her hands lifted high, she grasped her athame tightly and called over the chaos of battle, voice enhanced by her spellwork, "Lore! Gale! To me!"

They flew to her side, exchanging puzzled glimpses.

Willow held her iron blade to the sky. "Draconian fire and poisoned water. Now!"

Gale nodded. Moving with flawless synchronization, the dark elf and the half-draconian merged their magical attacks and melded them to her athame. The instant their spellwork took, the elf-witch called *"Ryth-sithamene!"*

The witch blade soared toward Cthulhu.

It gathered speed. Soon they couldn't track it. Judging from the powerful explosion and the monster's cry, it must have hit its mark. "Excellent!" Gale cried. "But your blade?"

"I can make another."

"You're a blacksmith, too?"

Willow smothered a gentle laugh and darted back to regather her magic. "Ask me questions *later,* sir."

The angered beast began to stir the waters into a spout, sucking their ships closer. "Right," the dark elf grinned.

In the fighting top, Cernun and Aura traded significant looks. "He didn't like that at all," Cernun mentioned. "Aura. Do you think you can-"

"Way ahead of you." The magus droid detached the blade from her arm. Cernun's emeralds glowed in his skull. Once the blade shone green, he extended his projective hand. "Rythsithamene."

Aura could barely hear him among the shouts and cannon fire, but she smiled her approval. *We make a good team.*

Cernun's ice-blue eyes smiled in response. *Yes, we do.*

The green burst of energy flooding Cthulhu's chest inspired a fleet-wide cheer. The Hades ships continued to distract the beast with cannon fire. "I think we've almost got him!" Travis shouted from below. "Do that again!"

"With what?" Cernun yelled, leaning over the fighting top rails.

Ean stopped casting lightning from Necro. She held her beloved weapon with a sad expression. "It's time, Necro. I hope you know how much I love thee."

"Hurry up!" barked Elias, raising his hands and gathering magic.

"All right." Ean sacrificed her weapon with a reluctant sigh.

"Rythsithamene!" Elias Mage shouted.

The hammer lurched forward.

An explosion of red and purple. Shards of sparking electricity. An ocean-rending bellow. And with a final deep, pained cry, the mightiest beast of the TerraWorks seas breathed no more.

Fireworks ruptured over the *Sea Wyvern.*

Cheers arose as Gale and Willow Emodicus descended from the quarterdeck. The elf-witch's train of ebony lace fluttered in her wake. Gale clasped the hand of his fair bride. "I solved your riddle," he murmured amid applause.

Willow's furtive smile warmed his dark-elf heart. "I know."

"Do you think he'll ever come back?"

"After the thrashing you and Lore gave him? I doubt it." She slipped her arm through his with a soft laugh. "And the TerraWorks mediators wouldn't allow it. Not after he hacked their system."

"Good." Gale's hand brushed her waist. The couple began their first dance.

"This is *so* cool," Ean gushed. She smoothed her dark navy gown, its regal length ablaze with tiny diamonds. "We should have gotten married at sea."

Elias adjusted his scarlet trench coat with a snort. "I didn't have the patience, dear. And neither did you."

She stuck out her tongue. "You *used* to be romantic."

"*Used* to?"

Elias Mage twirled his wife and lowered her into a dip. "You'll be eating your words tonight, Aphrodite." His teeth grazed her neck. He breathed in Ean's elusive island scent and closed his eyes, relishing it.

"Mephisto," whispered his half-elf beauty.

AFTERWORD

I'D LIKE TO THANK THE FOLLOWING BANDS FOR INSPIRING ALMOST EVERY
SCENE IN THIS QUIRKY, HARDCORE, NONSENSICAL TRILOGY **THAT AB-
SOLUTELY NEEDS TO BE AN ANIME:**

Avatar

Blackbriar

Dragonforce

Eluveitie

Ghost

Guns N' Roses

Kamelot

Korn

Metallica

Nightwish

Soilwork

I also graciously acknowledge the sacrifice of the hard lemonades I consumed.

And last, but not least, I thank all my reviewers in advance. I hope you enjoyed hanging out with the Mages as much as I did. Everyone needs a touch of escapism sometimes. If you enjoyed this series, please leave a review on Amazon and let the world know!

Blessed be!

FOLLOW THE AUTHOR

FACEBOOK: Richelle Manteufel Books

INSTAGRAM: Richelle Manteufel Author

Follow the Author on Amazon.com for new release notifications

MANTEUFEL BOOKS

LIFE HURTS. BOOKS HEAL. READ MORE.

Made in United States
Troutdale, OR
08/04/2024

21757024R00228